LAST
THINGS

LAST THINGS

C. P. SNOW

NEW YORK

CHARLES SCRIBNER'S SONS

CONTENTS

LAST
THINGS

I
RESOLUTIONS

ONE

RETURNING HOME

As the car passed the first houses away from London Airport (the September night had closed down, lights shone from windows, in the back seat one heard the grinding of the windscreen wiper), Margaret said:

"Is there anything waiting for us?"

"I hope not."

She meant, bad news. It was the end of a journey, the end of a holiday, coming home. We had each of us felt that edge of anxiety all our lives: not only when there was something to fear in a homecoming, but when, as now, there was no cause at all. As a child of eight, I had rushed from the day's outing full of dread, back to my mother's house, expecting what fatality I couldn't name. I had known that happen often enough since, and so had Margaret. It used to get hold of me, coming home across the Channel, just about the time that I could see the cliffs. But that was a long time ago, before the war: travel had changed by now: and, if it was going to happen—often it didn't, but that night Margaret and I were trapped by the old habit—it was along the motorway, the airport left behind.

Yes, people had learned to call it *angst,* appropriating a stronger word. In fact, this state, except that it hadn't a cause, was much more like what gamesplayers called the needle, or what others felt when they went into an examination

3

room or knew they were due to make a speech. Curiously enough, the top performers never lost it. You had to be a little nervous, so they said, to be at your best. It wasn't all that dreadful. One learned to live with it. And perhaps, as one grew older, it was a positive reassurance to find the nerves at one's elbows tightening and to be reminded that it was possible to be as keyed up as one used to be.

Still, Margaret was unusually silent, not leaving much interval between cigarettes, willing the car into London. It wouldn't have soothed her, or me either, to tick off the worries and reason them away. The neon names of factories high above the road: the standard airport journey, it might have been anywhere in the world: point A to point B, the topology of our time. It was familiar to us, but it seemed long. The east-bound traffic in the Cromwell Road was thick for eight o'clock at night.

In Queens Gate, bars of gold on the streaming pavements. A wait at the park gates. The glint of the Serpentine, the dark trees. At last, our block of flats.

Margaret said, the driver will help you in, I'll go ahead. While I was bringing the bags out of the lift, I saw our door open and heard her voice and the housekeeper's. All was well, came loud Italian repetitions. Margaret's father—no, no bad news. All was well. A letter from Mr. Maurice waiting for her. A postcard from Mr. Charles. All was well. The housekeeper embraced the whole of Margaret's family sense and obligations.

In the drawing-room, lamps reflected in the black sky over the park, Margaret and I exchanged sheepish smiles. Pouring out drinks, she said: "Well, there doesn't seem anything disastrous for the moment, does there?" She was touching wood, but she was happy. We sat on the sofa, the bright pictures welcoming us, letters on the coffee table close beside our glasses; as the last reflex of the journey home, she riffled through them, but left them still unopened. If there had been anything wrong with her father, there would have been a message from Helen. He was too much an invalid to leave alone, and her sister had come to London to be on call, so that we could take our holiday. It had been our first holiday by ourselves for months or years. It was peaceful, but also strange, to sit there in the empty flat.

Any earlier summer, one of the boys or both would have been returning with us. Margaret leaned back, her colour quite returned. Neither of us wanted to stir. At last she picked out an envelope from the pile, the letter from Maurice, her son by her first marriage.

She read, eyes acute but without expression. Then she broke out: "He seems very well and cheerful." She looked at me with delight: she knew that I, like everyone in the family, was fond of Maurice. As for her, her face was softened, love shining through, and a curious kind of pride, or even admiration.

The letter, which was several pages long, came from nowhere more remote than Manchester. Maurice was working as an assistant in a mental hospital. Without complaint. Without self-concern—though, as he had done it before in vacations, he knew there weren't many more menial jobs. It was that lack of self-concern which Margaret admired, and might have wished for in herself and hers. Yet there was a twist here. For the truth was, she didn't really like it. All her family were clever, people who might denounce life's obstacle race and yet, as it were absentmindedly, contrived to do distinctly well at it. Maurice, her first child, whom she loved with passion, happened to be a sport. As a child, he had looked as though his temperament was going to be stormy: and then in adolescence (the only boy I had ever seen change that way round) he became more tranquil than any of us.

He was not in the least clever. He had that summer failed his examinations, for the second year running, at Cambridge. She had hoped that he might become a doctor, but that was out. Maurice himself accepted it with his usual gentle amusement. He thought he ought to try to be as useful as he could. "I don't know much," he had said, talking of the hospital, "but I suppose I can look after them a bit."

In secret, Margaret was distracted. She knew that his friends, as mystified as she was, were beginning to believe that he was one of nature's innocents or saints. But could you bear your favourite child to be one of nature's saints?

Meanwhile, I had been reading the postcard from Charles, her son and mine. He was not at all innocent, and he was extremely able. He looked older than his half-brother, though he was still not seventeen. He had had a brilliant career at school, and had decided, independent, on his own, to spend a year abroad before he went to Cambridge. He was writing from Bucharest. "Rumanian is interesting, but I'd better economise on languages if I'm going to have one or two good enough. People won't talk Russian here; and when they do aren't usually very competent. Plum brandy is the curse of Eastern Europe. On the other hand, standards of primness —behind closed doors—markedly and pleasingly low." It reminded me of the postcards I used to receive from another bright young scholar, Roy Calvert, a generation before.

"Well," I said, after Margaret had passed over Maurice's letter, "you pay your money and you take your choice."

I was pretending that I was more detached than she was. She knew better.

For herself, Margaret couldn't help remembering Charles as an affectionate small boy. Now he was as self-willed as we had been. In the past she had imagined the time when her sons were grown-up, and nothing but a comfort. She said, realism deserting her: "If only each of them could give the other a little of what he doesn't have."

She was harking back to them, reading Maurice's letter again (would he look after his health?), as we picked our way through the rest of the mail. Five or six days of it. The ordinary professional letters. An invitation from the Lester Inces for the following weekend. A note from the wife of my nephew Pat, married that summer, child expected in January, hoping to see Margaret. Invitations to give lectures. Letter from a paranoid, asking for help against persons persecuting her by means of wireless messages. Two lines on a postcard from old George Passant, sent from Holland. Agenda of a meeting.

That was all. Nothing exciting, I said. That was the last thing we wanted, said Margaret, as we went in to eat at leisure, by ourselves.

We had arrived back on Tuesday. The next Monday morning we were again returning home, this time in a train, autumn fields bland in the sunshine, no shadow over us: in fact, in contented, mocking spirits, amused by the weekend. For we hadn't been able to resist the Inces' invitation. Margaret's sister had been willing to stand in for another week, I was glad of a little grace before I started a new book.

More than that, we had been inquisitive. The young took up our attention now, and it was a relaxation to have a look at middle-aged acquaintances.

In fact, it turned out fun to see Lester Ince installed in his second avatar, in his recently established state. It was, as it had unrolled before our eyes those last two days, a remarkable state. He had run off—or she had done the running off —with an American woman who was not merely rich, but as her friends said, rich-rich. They had raced through their divorces in minimum time, and they had simultaneously been looking for a stately home. They had found it: one of the most famous and stateliest of homes: nothing less than Basset. Basset, where Diana Skidmore used to perform as a great hostess, and where Margaret and I, though nowhere near the smart life, had sometimes been among the guests. But that had been in the Fifties, getting on for a decade ago (this was 1964), and Diana had got tired of it. No one seemed to be certain why, but, just as decisively as she once talked to ministers, she announced that she had had enough, and closed the house within a month. She was reported to be living, quite simply, in a London flat, seeing only her oldest friends. Basset had stayed empty for several years.

Then came the Inces. They had heard of it: they inspected it: they bought it. Together with associated farms, tenantry, trout streams, pheasant shooting, and outspread acres. Basset had become more opulent, so the knowing ones said, than ever in its history; Margaret and I had regarded it all, that weekend, with yokel-like incredulity, or perhaps more like American Indians confronted with the twin miracles of Scotch whisky and fire-arms. In my less stupefied moments, I had been trying to work out how many hundred thousands of pounds they had spent.

Lester Ince as landowner. Lester Ince in a puce smoking jacket, at the head of his table in the great eighteenth century dining-room, ceiling by Thornhill: Lester pushing the decanter-runners round, after the women had left us. Well, one had to admit, there were considerable bonuses. The food in Diana's time had always been skimpy, and usually dim. Not now. There used not to be enough to drink. Lester Ince, who remained a hearty and a kindly man, had taken care of that.

Still, it seemed a slight difference of emphasis away from the Lester Ince who was a junior fellow of my old college only ten years before. He had written a highly regarded work on the moral complexities in Joseph Conrad: but his utterances, almost as soon as he was elected, had been somewhat unexpected. He had surveyed his colleagues, and decided that he didn't think much of them. Francis Getliffe was a stuffed shirt. So was my brother Martin. The best college hock Lester firmly described as cat's pee. The comfortable worldliness of Arthur Brown was even less to his taste. "I should like to spill the crap about this joint," someone reported him saying in the combination-room: at that stage, he had a knack of speaking what he thought of as American demotic.

As a result of this kind of trenchancy, he became identified as one of the academic spokesmen of a new wave. This was protest. This was one of the voices of progressive opinion. Well, there seemed a slight difference of emphasis now.

To a good many, particularly to those who couldn't help finding leaders and then promptly losing them, the conversation at Basset that weekend might have been disconcerting. This used to be one of the major political houses. A number of ministerial careers had been helped, or alternatively hindered, in Diana Skidmore's drawing-room. It was possible that policies—though did any of us know how policies were really made, in particular the persons who believed they made them?—had at least been deviated. Basset was not a political house any longer. But, in spite or because of that, it had become far more ideological than it had ever been. Diana's Tory ministers hadn't indulged much in ideology: the Inces and their friends were devoted to it. The old incumbents didn't talk about the cold war: now, there were meals when the Basset parties talked of nothing else.

That was election autumn, both in America and England. Ince's wife thought that we were not sufficiently knowledgeable about the merits of Senator Goldwater. He mightn't have everything, but at least he wasn't soft on communism. As for our general election, if the conservatives didn't come back, there was a prospect of 'confiscatory taxation,' a subject on which Lester Ince spoke with poignant feeling.

Once or twice we had a serious argument. Then I grew bored and said that we had better regard some topics as forbidden. Lester Ince was sad; he believed what he said, he believed that, if they listened, people of good will would have to agree with him. However, he was not only strong on hostly etiquette, he was good-natured; if the results of his political thinking put us out, then we ought to be excused from hearing them. "In that case, Lew," he said, with a cheerful full-eyed glint from his older incarnation, "you come to my study before you change, and we'll have a couple of snifters and you can talk about the dear old place."

He meant the college, for which, though it had treated him well, he still felt a singular dislike. In actual truth, he had altered much less than others thought, less even than he thought himself. Protest? Others had been sitting in the places he wanted. Now he had settled his ample backside in just those places, and it was for others to protest. When young men seemed to be rebelling against social manners, I used to think, it meant that they would, in the end, not rebel against anything else.

In the train, Margaret and I agreed that we each had a soft spot for him. Anyway, it wasn't every day that one saw an old acquaintance living like a millionaire. As the taxi took us home from Waterloo, we were thinking of persons, acquaintances of his roughneck years, who might profitably be presented with the spectacle of the new-style Basset. The game was still diverting us as we entered the flat.

Beside the telephone, immediately inside the hall, there stood a message on the telephone pad. It read, with the neutrality and unsurprisingness of words on paper:

Mr. Davidson (Margaret's father) *is seriously ill. Sir Lewis is asked for specially, by himself. Before he goes to the clinic, please call at 22 Addison Road.*

As with other announcements that had come without warning, this seemed like something one had known for a long time.

TWO

GOD'S FOOL

In Addison Road, Margaret's sister was staying with some friends. As she kissed me, her expression was grave with the authority of bad news. Silently she led me through the house, down a few steps, into a paved garden. It was not yet half-past eleven—I had not been inside my flat for more than minutes—and the sky was pearly with the morning haze. She said:

"I'm glad you came."

For a long time, we had not been easy with each other. She had been stern against Margaret's broken marriage, and put most of the blame on to me. All that was nearly twenty years before, but Helen, who was benign and tender, was also unforgiving: or perhaps, like some who live on the outside uneventful lives, she made dramas which the rest of us wanted to coarsen ourselves against. She was in her early fifties, five years older than her sister: she had had no children, and her face not only kept its youth, like all the others in her family, but did so to a preternatural extent. It was like seeing a girl or very young woman—with, round her eyes, as though traced in wax, the lines of middle age. She dressed very smartly, which that morning, as often, seemed somehow both pathetic and putting-off: but then it didn't take much to make me more uneasy with her, perhaps because, when I had been to blame, I hadn't liked being judged.

She was looking at me with eyes, like Margaret's, acute and beautiful. She hadn't spoken again: then suddenly, as it were brusquely, said:

"Father tried to kill himself last night."

As soon as we read the message, Margaret—distressed that he didn't want her—had tried to find an explanation: and so had I, on the way here. But, obtusely so it seemed later, neither of us had thought of that.

"He asked me to tell you. He said it would save unnecessary preambles."

That sounded like Austin Davidson first-hand. I hadn't met many men as uncushioned or as naked to life. He despised the pretences that most of us found comforting. He despised them for himself, but also for others, quite regardless of what anyone who loved him might feel. That morning Helen said (she had lavished less care on him than had Margaret), almost in his own tone: "He's never thought highly of other people's opinion, you know."

She told me how it had happened. As we all knew, he had been in despair about his illness. Until his sixties, he had lived a young man's life: then he had a thrombosis, and he had been left with an existence that he wouldn't come to terms with. A less clear-sighted man might have been more stoical. Austin Davidson, alone in Regent's Park except for Margaret's visits, had sunk into what they used to call accidie. A tunnel with no end. There had been remissions—but his heart had weakened more, he could scarcely walk, and at last, at seventy-six, he wouldn't bear it. Somehow—Helen didn't know how—he had accumulated a store of barbiturates. On the previous evening, Sunday, about the time that I was drinking pre-dinner 'snifters' with Lester Ince, he had sat alone in his house, writing notes to his daughters. Then he had swallowed his drugs, washed them down with one whisky, and stood himself another.

But he had done it wrong. He had taken too much. A few hours later, stupefied by the drug, he had staggered about, violently sick. While vomiting, he had fallen forward, gashing his forehead against the handle of the W.C. Near by, he had been discovered at breakfast-time, covered with blood but still alive. They had driven him to the —————clinic.

"Fortunately," said Helen, "he seems to be surprisingly well. I don't know whether I ought to say fortunately. He wouldn't."

She had destroyed the two notes unopened. He had been at least half-lucid when she talked to him in his hospital room. He had asked, several times, to see me, without Margaret. So Helen had been obliged to give the message.

"I wish," I said, "that he had asked for her. She minds a great deal."

"That's why he'd rather have you, maybe," said Helen.

The midday roads were dense with cars, and it took forty minutes before the taxi reached the clinic. On the way, I had been wondering what I should find, or even more what I should manage, to say. I was fond of Austin Davidson, and I respected that bright, uncluttered mind. But it wasn't the respect that one might feel for an eminent old man. It was an effort to think of him as my father-in-law. Except when the sheer impact of his illness weighed one down, he seemed much more like a younger friend.

It was the clinic in which, during the war, I had first met Margaret. I thought I remembered, I might be imagining it, the number of my room. At any rate, it was on the same ground floor, at the same side, as the one I was entering now.

In his high bed, flanked by flowers on the tables close by —the ceiling shimmered with sub-aqueous green reflected from the garden—Austin Davidson looked grotesque. His head, borne up by three pillows, was wrapped in a bandage which covered his right eye and most of his forehead: even at that, there was a bruise under the right cheekbone, and the corner of his mouth was swollen. More than anything, he gave the appearance of having just been patched up after a fight. Among the bandages, one sepia eye stared at me. I heard his voice, dulled but the words quite clear.

"You see God's own fool."

I felt certain that he had prepared that opening, determined to get it out.

"Never mind."

"If one's got to the point—" he was speaking very slowly, with pauses for breath and also to hold his train of thought —"of doing oneself in—the least one can do—is to make a go of it."

"Lots of people don't make a go of it, you know." To my own astonishment, at least in retrospect, for it was quite spontaneous, I found myself teasing him: dropping into a kind of irony, as he did so often, putting himself at a distance from the present moment. The visible side of Davidson's face showed something like the vestige of a grin, as I reminded him of German officers during the war. Beck took two shots at himself, and then had to get someone to finish him off. Poor old Stülpnagel had blinded himself, but without the desired result. "You would expect them to be better at it than you, wouldn't you? But they weren't."

"Too much fuss. Not enough to show for it."

He was drowsy, but he did not seem miserable. To an extent, he had always liked an audience. And also, was there, even now a stirring of, yes, relief? Had he wanted to persist —it didn't matter how much he denied it?

"Tell them. No more visitors today. Margaret can come tomorrow. If she wants."

"Of course she will." Margaret was his favourite daughter; but he had never appeared to realise that his detachment could cause her pain.

"She's prudish about suicide." His voice became louder and much more clear. "I simply can't understand her."

After a moment:

"Extraordinary thing to be prudish about."

Then he began to ramble, or the words thickened so that it was hard to follow him. *Sources of supply*. That might mean the way he got hold of his drugs. Some people wouldn't act as sources of supply. Prudish. Glad to say, others weren't like Margaret—

It might have been strange to hear him, even in confusion, engaged in a kind of argument, scoring a dialectical triumph over Margaret. But it didn't seem so. I was easier with him than she was: easier with him than with my own father, at least on the plane where Davidson and I were able to talk. Not that Davidson managed to be any cooler than my father. In fact, in his simple fashion, without trying, he had been as self-sufficient and as stoical as Davidson would have liked to be.

There had been nothing histrionic about my father's death, which had happened a few months before. None of us had been present. He was in his late eighties, but he hadn't thought to inform us that he was failing. On the last evening, in his own small room, he had asked his lodger, who was almost a stranger, to sit with him. "I think I am going to die tonight," so the lodger had reported him saying. He was right. It wasn't given to Austin Davidson to die as quietly as that.

Even in stupor Davidson kept making gallant attempts to carry on the argument. Then I thought he had fallen asleep.

Out of semi-consciousness he made another effort.

"I'm always glad to see you, Eliot."

It sounded like a regression to the time when he first met me, before I married Margaret, when he was going about in his vigorous off-hand prime. But, as I went away, I wondered if it hadn't been a further regression, back to the pride, arrogance, and brightness of his youth, when he and his friends felt themselves the lucky of this world, but, with manners different from ours, did not think of calling one another by their Christian names.

THREE

A THEME RE-STATED

The next time I saw him was on the Wednesday, since Margaret and I decided to share the visits, each going on alternate days. It was a tauntingly mellow September afternoon, like those on which one looked out of classroom windows at the start of a new school year.

Half-sitting in his bed, pillows propping him (that was to be his standard condition, to reduce the strain on his heart), Austin Davidson had been spruced up, though underneath the neat diagonal bandage across his eye there loomed another deep purple bruise which on Monday had been obscured. His hair, thick and silver grey, had been trimmed, the quiff respectfully preserved. Someone had shaved him, and he smelt fresh. He was wide awake, greeting me with a monocular, sharp, almost impatient gaze.

"I should like some intelligent conversation," he said.

To understand that, one needed to have learned his private language. Since he first became ill, he seemed to have lost interest in, or at least be unwilling to talk about, the connoisseurship which had been the passion of his life. He wouldn't read his own art criticism or anyone else's. He chose not to look at pictures, not even his own collection, as though, now the physical springs of his existence had failed him, so his senses, including the sense that meant most to him, were no use any more.

18

Instead, he fell back on his last resource, which was some-thing like a game. But it was a peculiar sort of game, to some of his acquaintances unsuitable, or even fatuous, for a 'pure soul' like Davidson. For it consisted of taking an obsessive day-by-day interest in the stock exchange. In fact, it was an interest that had given him pleasure all his life. Like all his circle, he had heard Keynes, with his usual impregnable confidence, telling them that, given half an hour's concen-trated attention to the market each morning, no man of modest intelligence could avoid making money. Unlike others of his circle, Davidson believed what he was told. Certainly he was a pure soul, but he enjoyed using his wits, and playing any kind of mental game. This also turned out to be a singularly lucrative one. He had been left a few thousand pounds before the First World War. No one knew how much he was worth in his old age; on that he was ret-icent, quite uncharacteristically so, as about nothing else in his life. He had made over sizable blocks of investments to his daughters, but he had never given me the most oblique indication of how much he kept for himself.

So 'intelligent conversation' meant, in that bedroom at the clinic, an exchange about the day's quotations. He became almost high-spirited, no, something more like playful. It was a reminder of his best years, when he seemed so much less burdened than the rest of us.

Listening to him, I had to discipline myself to take my part. In any circumstances, let alone these, I didn't serve as an adequate foil. I could act as a kind of secretary, telephon-ing his stockbroker from the bedroom, so that Davidson could overhear. He wasn't satisfied with academic discus-sions: that would have been like playing bridge for counters. But I discovered that his gambles were modest, not more than £500 at a time.

Apart from my secretarial duties, I wasn't a good partner.

I didn't know enough. I assumed that, until he died, I should have to try to memorise the financial papers more devotedly than I had ever thought of doing.

Though he spun it out, and I followed as well as I could, that day's effort dwindled away. Pauses. Then a long silence. His eye had ceased to look at me, as though he were turning inward.

After the silence, his voice came back:

"I shan't get out of here. Of course."

He wasn't asking for false hope. He made it impossible to give.

I asked: "Are you sure?"

"Of course."

Another pause.

"They won't let me. People always interfere with you." He was speaking without inflection or expression.

"The one thing they can't interfere with is your death. Not in the long run. You have to die on your own. That's all there is to it, you know."

He added:

"I told Margaret that."

Yes, he had told her. But he wasn't aware of—and wouldn't have been concerned with—her response, to which I had listened as we lay awake in the middle of the night. It wasn't the cool, such as Davidson, who felt most passionately about death. Margaret, whose appetite for living was so strong, had to pay a corresponding price. She wouldn't have talked, as more protected people might, of any of those figures which, by pretending to face the truth, in fact make it easier to bear. The swallow coming out of darkness into the lighted hall, and then out into the darkness again. That was too pretty for her. So were all the phrases about silence and the dark. Whatever they tried to say, was too near to say like that.

She struggled against it, even while she was searching for the C Major of this life. The C Major? In sexual love? In the love of children? She knew, as a cool and innocent man like Davidson never could have done, that you could hear the sound and still not have dismissed the final intimation. And, by a curious irony, having a father like Davidson had made that intimation sharper: made it sharper now.

That was why, lying awake in the night repeating to me his acerb remarks about his fiasco, she wasn't reconciled. She was torn with tenderness, painful tenderness, mixed up with what was nothing else but anger. It was a combination which she sometimes showed towards her own children, when they might be doing themselves harm. Now she couldn't prevent it breaking out, after her father tried to commit suicide, and then talked to her as though it had been an interesting event.

In the dark, she kept asking what she could do for him, knowing that there was nothing. At moments she was furious. With all the grip of her imagination, she was re-enacting and re-witnessing the scene of Sunday evening. The capsules marshalled on Davidson's desk (he was a pernicketily tidy man): the swallows of whisky: the last drink, as though it was a modest celebration or perhaps one for the road. It might have been a harmless domestic spectacle. Capsules such as we saw every day. An old man taking a drink. But, just as in the trial I had had to attend earlier that year, objects could lose their innocence. For Margaret the capsules and the whisky glass weren't neutral bits of matter any more.

They were reminders, they were more than that, they were emblems. Emblems of what? Perhaps, I thought, as I tried to soothe her, of what the non-religious never understand in the religious. Margaret, though she didn't believe, was by temperament religious. Which meant, not as a paradox but as a condition, that she clung—more strongly than her father could have conceived possible—to the senses' life, the species' life. So when that was thrown away or disregarded, she felt horror: it might be superstitious, she couldn't justify it, but that was what those emblems stood for.

Her father, however, settled her in his own mind by saying again, as though that were the perfect formulation, that she was prudish about suicide. After a time during which neither he nor I spoke, and he was looking inward, he said, quite brightly:

"Most of you are prudish about death. You're prudish about death."

He meant Margaret's friends and mine, the people whom, before his illness, he used to meet at our house. They were a different generation from his, most of them younger than I was (within a month I should be fifty-nine).

"You're much more prudish than we were on that fairly relevant subject. Of course you're much less prudish about sex. It's a curious thought, but I suspect that when people give up being prudish about sex they become remarkably so about everything else." (I had heard this before: in his lively days, he used to say that our friends dared not talk about money, ambition, aspiration, or even ordinary emotion.) "Certainly about death. You people try to pretend it doesn't exist. I've never been able to bear the nineteenth century" —the old Bloomsbury hatred darted punctually out—"but at least they weren't afraid to talk about death."

"It's the only thing in one's whole life that is a hundred percent certain."

"It's the only thing one is bound to do by oneself."

Later, after he had died—which didn't happen for over a year—I was not sure whether he had really produced those two sayings that afternoon. The difficulty was, I had so many conversations with him in the clinic bedroom; they were repetitive by their nature, and because Davidson was such a concentrated man. Talk about the stock exchange: then his thoughts about dying and death. That was the pattern which did not vary for weeks to come, and so the days might have become conflated in my memory.

It often seemed to me that the other themes of his life had been dismissed by now, and there was only one, the last one, which he wanted to restate. *You have to die on your own.* And yet, he had never said that. I was inventing words for him. Perhaps I was inventing a theme that was, not his, but mine.

I hadn't felt intimations of my death as deeply as Margaret. But, like all of us, intermittently since I was a young man, as often as a young man as when I was ageing, I had imagined it. What would it be like? There were the words we had all read or uttered. You die alone. *On mourra seul.* The solitude. I thought I could imagine it and know it, as one does being frightened, appalled, or desirous.

There it was. It wasn't to be evaded. Perhaps that was why I invented words for Davidson which he didn't utter. And read into him feelings which I couldn't be certain that he knew.

But certainly he said one thing, and did another, which I was able to fix precisely on to that afternoon.

"Nearly all my friends are dead by now," he said. "Most of them had moderately unpleasant deaths."

I was thinking, of those who had mattered to me, Sheila and Roy Calvert had died, though not naturally. Many of my acquaintances were reaching the age-band where the statistics began to raise their voice. Looking at us all, one couldn't prophesy about any single casualty, but that some of us would die one way or the other—within ten, fifteen years —one could predict with the certainty of a statistician. Only a fortnight before, while Margaret and I were still abroad, I had heard that Denis Geary, that robust schoolfellow of mine who had been a support to us a few months before, had gone out for a walk and been found dead.

"Of course," said Davidson, "there's only been one myth that's ever really counted. I mean, the afterlife.

"It's a pity one can't believe in it," he said.

"Yes." (Not then, but afterwards, I remembered kneeling by Sheila's bed after her funeral, half crazed for some sign of her, not even a word, just the shadow of a ghost.)

"It's a pity it's meaningless. I don't know why, but one doesn't exactly approve of being annihilated. Though when it's happened, nothing could matter less."

One wouldn't ask for much, Davidson was saying, just the chance to linger round, unobserved, and watch what was going on. It was a pity to miss all that was going to happen.

That was one of the few signs of sentimentality I had seen him show. Soon he was remarking sternly, as though reproving me for a relapse into weakness, that it was not respectable to talk about an afterlife. There wasn't any meaning in it: there couldn't be. It was the supreme wish-fulfillment. "Which, by the way," he said, brightening up, "has done the wretched human race a great deal more harm than good." He went on, still half-reproving me, telling me to think of the horrors that had been perpetrated in the name of the afterlife. Torturing bodies to save souls. Slaughter to get one's place in heaven. "If people would only accept that this is the only life there is, they might be a shade more civilised."

No, I didn't want to argue: he was getting some sort of comfort from his old certainties. It seemed a perverse comfort. Yet he still believed in the enlightenment he grew up in, the lucky oasis, the civilised voices, the privileged Edwardian hopes.

Then he did something which also might have seemed perverse, if he had preserved the consistency of which he was so proud. It was a warm afternoon, and he was covered only by a single sheet. Suddenly, but not jerkily, he pulled it aside, and with eyes glossy-brown as a bird's, oblivious of me, gazed down towards his feet. Against blue pyjama-trousers, his skin shone pale, clear, not hairy: the feet were large, after the thin legs, with elongated, heavy-jointed toes. For some time I could not tell what he was studying so observantly. Then I noticed, over the left ankle, a small roll of swelling, so that the concavity between ankle-bone and talus had been filled in. On the right foot, the swelling might have been grosser; from where I sat, it was difficult to make out.

Davidson went on gazing, as intently, as professionally, as he used to look at pictures.

"The oedema's a shade less than this morning. Quite a bit less than yesterday," he said. He said it with a satisfaction that he couldn't conceal, or didn't think of concealing. Throughout his illness, for years past, he must have been studying his ankles, observing one of the clinical signs. Even now, night and morning (perhaps more often when he was alone), he went through the same routine. But it wasn't routine to him. Sunday night—he had swallowed the capsules. All he said to me since, he meant. Nevertheless, when he inspected his ankles and decided the swelling was a fraction reduced, he felt a surge of pleasure, not at all ironic. No more ironic than if he had been in middle age and robust health, and had noticed a symptom which worried him but which, as he tested it, began to clear away.

FOUR

DOMESTIC EVENING, WITHOUT INCIDENT

Visiting her father every other day, Margaret's behaviour, like his, began to show a contradiction which really wasn't one. She couldn't help becoming preoccupied with a future birth, with the child my nephew's wife was expecting in four months' time. Margaret had not previously given any sign of special interest in Muriel, and so far as she had a special interest in Pat, it was negative, or at least ambivalent. Sometimes she found him good company, but when he had gone away she thought him worthless. And yet Margaret took to visiting them in their flat, and then invited them to dinner at our own, together with Muriel's mother and stepfather.

That was a surprise in itself, a surprise, that is, that Azik Schiff should come. He was himself inordinately hospitable and in his own expansive fashion seemed to like us all. But he was also very rich: and, like other rich men, did not welcome hospitality unless he was providing it himself. However, he had accepted, and as we waited for them all, I was saying to Margaret that one of the advantages of being rich was that everyone tended to entertain you according to your own standards. Just as all gourmets were treated as though the rest of us were gourmets. It seemed like a natural law, a curiously unjust one. Certainly the food and drink which had been set up for that night we shouldn't have produced for anyone less sumptuous than Azik.

The young couple arrived a few minutes before the other two, but as soon as Azik entered the drawing-room he took charge. None of us had dressed, but he was wearing, as though in competition with Lester Ince, a cherry-coloured smoking jacket. He gave Margaret not a peck but a whacking kiss, and then stood on massive legs evaluating the room, in which he had never been before. In fact, he was more culti-vated than any of us: the pictures he understood and ap-proved of: but he was puzzled that, apart from the pictures, the furniture was so ramshackle. He had guessed our finan-cial position—that was one of his gifts—and knew it as well as I did. Why did we live so modestly? He didn't ask that question, but he did enquire about the flat. Yes, we had a lot of rooms, having joined two flats together. How much did we pay? I told him. He whistled. It was cheaper than he could have reckoned. He couldn't help admiring a bargain: and yet, as he proceeded to explain, living like that was good tactics, but bad strategy.

"You should buy a house, my friends," he said paternally (he was several years younger than I was) as at last he settled down on the sofa, his chest expanded, looking like a benevo-lent, ugly, and highly intelligent frog.

Rosalind, his wife, braceletted, necklaced, bejewelled with each anniversary's present, was looking at me with some-thing like an apprehensive wink. She had known me when she was Roy Calvert's mistress and later his wife: that was years before Margaret and I first met: Rosalind had known me when I was cagey and secretive, and it was a continual surprise to her that I didn't mind, or even encouraged, Azik to interfere in my affairs. She was always ready to help me evade his questions, even after all the times when she had seen him and me get on so easily.

No, I said to Azik, if one has been born without a penny, one never learned to spend money. Azik shook his great

head. "No, Lewis," he said, "there I must take issue with
you. That excuse is not satisfactory. It doesn't do credit to
your intellect. First, I have to remind you that your lady
bride" (he beamed at Margaret: Azik spoke a good many languages imperfectly, and one of those was American Business
English) "was not born without a penny. So there should be
a corrective influence in this family. Second, I have to remind you that I also was born without a penny. I have to
say that I have never found it difficult to spend money."
With which Azik expounded on a "certain little difference"
between the tailor's shop near the old Alexanderplatz where
he was born, and his present home in Eaton Square.

Someone said (when Azik was projecting himself, he filled
the room, and it wasn't easy to notice who else was trying to
edge in) was it true, the old story, that if one had been born
rich and then had everything taken away, one never minded
much?

Azik pronounced that he had known some who suffered.
People were almost infinitely resilient, I was beginning, but
Azik went on with a shout: "You and I, Lewis, say we've lost
everything tomorrow morning. You aren't allowed to pub-
lish a word. These children don't believe it, but we should
make do. You'd pretend that nothing had happened and go
and get a job as a clerk. As for me"—he put a finger to the
side of his nose—"I should make a few shillings on the
side."

He was benevolent and happy, parodying himself, showing off to Rosalind, whom he adored. None of us had such a
flow of spirits, nor was so harmoniously himself. There
might have been one single discontinuity, only one, and
even that I could have exaggerated or imagined.

It happened when Margaret asked about the second
drinks. On the first round she and I had had our usual long
whiskies, and so had Pat: Azik had had a small one. He re-

fused another, and watched our glasses being filled again.

Suddenly, quite unprovoked, he said:

"No Jew drinks as you people do."

"Oh, come off it, Azik," I said. I mentioned something about parties in New York—

"They are not real Jews. They are losing themselves."

Real Jews, Azik went on, took sex easy, took wine easy: they didn't go wild, as 'you people' do. I had never heard anything like that from him before. He might be overpowering, but he didn't attack. We all knew that he kept up his Judaism; he went, not to a reformed synagogue, but to a conservative one, even though he said that he had no theology. All of a sudden, just for that instant (or was I reading back to my first Jewish friends?) Judaism seemed the least natural, or the least comfortable thing about him—as though it were a proud hurt, an affront to others.

He relaxed into paternal, prepotent supervision.

"Ah well," he said, "enjoy yourselves."

He was the only one to enquire about young Charles. Last heard of in Persia, I said, on his way to Pakistan. We had heard nothing for a fortnight.

"You must be worried, Lewis," he said, with a rush of fellow-feeling.

I said, "a little": the dinner party had distracted me, until then.

"Oh, he'll be all right. He lands on his feet," said Pat.

"That you should not say." Azik turned sternly on to Pat, who for once looked outfaced, sulky, quite aware that he had shown jealousy of his cousin, glancing at his young wife, whose face was reposeful, as though she had not noticed anything at all nor heard of Charles.

As we sat at the dinner table, I was paying attention to Rosalind. Beautifully accoutred as she was, she had nevertheless let her hair go grey: that must have been a deliberate choice: she knew what was required of the elegant wife, no longer young, of a great tycoon. Her thin, freckled hands displayed her rings. As before, she sometimes gave me a look—sidelong from her cameo face—as though we shared an esoteric private joke. But all she talked about was Azik's business, and how next week she would have to entertain the Prime Minister of Brazil. "It's all in the game, you know," she said, with a dying fall which sounded sad and which was nothing of the kind. I sometimes wondered whether she ever thought that, if it had not been for fatality, she would still be married to a distinguished, perhaps an unbalanced, scholar (it was hard to imagine what Roy Calvert would have become in his fifties). Probably she didn't. Rosalind lived on this earth. She might sigh over memories, but she would sigh contentedly and get on with the day's work, which was to keep Azik cheerful and well.

On my left, her daughter Muriel was quiet, cheekbones and jawline softened by pregnancy. Then I caught a flash of her eyes, as though she were surreptitiously making fun of Rosalind or me or both. It was the kind of green-eyed disrespectful flash I had seen often enough in her father, whom she had never known. She was polite to me as she was to everyone, maddeningly polite, but I didn't begin to understand her. She had not once asked me a question about her father, though she must have known that I had been his closest friend. One day, out of curiosity or provocation, I had tried to talk about him. "Did you think that?" she had said decorously. "Oh, I must ask Aunt Meg" (as she called Margaret, of whom she seemed to be fond). Again, she must have known that Margaret and Roy had never met.

When, for an instant, Pat engaged his mother-in-law in conversation, Muriel asked a few soft-voiced questions about the autumn theatres. She knew that I wasn't much interested, and rarely went. Was she being obtuse, or amusing herself? She was abnormally self-possessed and strong-willed, that was all I knew about her. Like a good many other men, I found her—in some inexplicable and irritating fashion— very attractive.

Just then—we had finished the fish, Azik was smelling his first glass of claret, for which, in spite of his earlier strictures, he had considerable enthusiasm—I heard Pat utter the name of Margaret's father. Startled, turning away from Muriel, I looked down the table. Pat was smiling at Margaret with something between protectiveness and triumph. His brown eyes were shining: he had his air of doggy confidence, of one who managed to please but wasn't easily put down.

"Yes," he was telling her, "he was in better spirits, I'm sure he was."

"You mean, you've seen him?"

"Of course I have, Aunt Meg."

It became clear that Pat was telling the truth, which could not invariably be assumed. It also became clear that Austin Davidson had talked with his innocent candour, and that Pat knew everything we knew, and had—certainly to his wife and her mother—passed most of it on. Pat had paid, not one visit, but several: for an instant Margaret looked stupefied, astonished that her father had told us nothing of this. But why should he? He had other visitors besides ourselves, but he didn't think it relevant to mention them.

The greater mystery was, how Pat had learned that Davidson was in the clinic at all, and how he had got inside the place himself. As for the first, he was one of those natural detectives or intelligence agents, whom I had come across, and been disconcerted by, more than once in my life: and further, he had always been specially inquisitive about Davidson, and anxious to know him. Not from motives which were entirely pure: Pat was an aspiring painter, and he believed that an eminent art critic, even though retired, must have retained some useful acquaintances. Anyway, insatiably curious and also on the make, Pat had somehow obtained the entree to Davidson's bedroom, quite possibly using my name without undue fastidiousness.

Once there, it was no mystery at all that Davidson had encouraged him to come again. Pat was on the make, he was a busybody, a gossip, often a mischief-maker, and several kinds of a liar: but he was also kind. In the presence of the isolated old man, Pat would try to enliven him, using all his resources, which were considerable: for he was more than kind, to many people he was a life-giver. The unfairness was, he had that talent far more highly developed than persons of better character: when I came to think of it, life-givers of Pat's species had, so far as I had met them, usually been people who wouldn't pass much of an examination into their moral nature. That had been true of my boyhood friend Jack Cotery, whom in a good many ways Pat resembled. It was probable, I thought, that Pat's visits were more of a help to Austin Davidson than either Margaret's or mine.

"You must believe me," Pat said to Margaret, "he's looking forward to things now, he's picking up, you'll see."

"I've known him longer than you have, haven't I?" said Margaret.

"That's why you don't see everything about him now," Pat replied, with his mixture of tenderness and cheek. No, he insisted, you have to notice that Davidson was eager for his little pleasures: he was allowed five cigarettes a day, and each one was an occasion: so were his cups of tea. He had made his own timetable to live by. He would go on living for a long time yet.

He had put that 'other business' behind him, Pat was persuading her. It had been an incident, that was all. Margaret did not believe him, and yet wanted to. In spite of herself, she was feeling grateful. Pat had heard all about Davidson's plan to kill himself. And yet he could forget it, from one minute to the next: it wasn't that he was too young to understand, for often the young understood suicide better than the rest of us. Perhaps he was just too surgent. Anyway, his optimism came from every cell of his body. He was positive that Austin Davidson would survive and that his life was worth living.

Azik, left out of this conversation, was giving his wife uncomfortable glances. Not that he hadn't listened to it all before: not that he was embarrassed for Margaret, or found his son-in-law unduly brash: more, I thought, because Azik had the delicacy of the very healthy, who did not much relish the echoes of mortality. Finally he said to Margaret that he would send her father more flowers, and addressed me down the table on the subject of next week's general election. Yes, it would be a near thing. The American election wouldn't be. Things looked a bit more promising all round, said Azik: for about that time, a year or two before and after, he, like other detached and unillusioned men, was letting himself indulge in a patch of hope. That was the case with Francis Getliffe and with me: with Eastern European and American friends, including even David Rubin, the least optimistic of men. In world outlook, there was more hope about than at any time since the Twenties. We did not enjoy being reminded of that afterwards, but it was so.

About our local affairs, Azik was repeating what he often told us, it didn't much matter who got in. He proceeded to lecture us, with the relish of a born pedagogue, on the limits of political free-will. Margaret was grinning surreptitiously in my direction: she enjoyed hearing me being treated as an innocent. Like me, she was fond of Azik, and his ingrained conviction that we were ignorant, though not entirely unteachable, was one of the endearing things about him. But she couldn't resist asking him if he wasn't being disingenuous. After all, it was common knowledge that he had made lavish contributions to Labour Party funds.

Azik was imperturbable. "That doesn't affect the issue, my friends," he said. "That is a little piece of insurance, you understand?"

Did we? Azik liked playing the game all ways. He was a shrewd operator. If a Labour government came to power, there were advantages in having friends at court. Yet that, I thought, was altogether too simple. Azik wished to pretend to us, and to himself, that he calculated all the time: but he didn't, any more than less ingenious men. He was an outsider, and he was, in some residual fashion, of which he was half-ashamed, on the side of other outsiders. For all his expansiveness, the luxury in which he revelled, he was never ultimately at ease with his fellow-tycoons. He had once told me that, coming to England as an exile, he had felt one irremovable strain: you had to think consciously about actions which, in your own country, you performed as instinctively as breathing. He was also another kind of exile: rich as he had become, he had to think consciously about his actions when he was in the company of other rich men.

It sometimes occurred to me—not specially at that dinner table—how differently he behaved from the Marches, who had been the first rich family to befriend me when I was young. They too were Jewish: they were not, and never had been, anything like so plutocratic as Azik had become. And yet, though they were slightly more sceptical about politics than their gentile counterparts, their instincts were the same. After generations in England, they thought and spoke like members of the English *haute bourgeoisie,* like distinctly grander and better connected Forsytes. If, when I first knew them, anyone had made contributions such as Azik's to the wrong party, some of the older members might have been capable of saying (though I didn't remember hearing the phrase in the March houses) that he was a traitor to his class.

Nevertheless, after dinner, Azik did recall to me one of those patriarchs, my favourite one. We were sitting in the drawing room, brandy going round. It was quite early, not long after ten, but Pat had begun to fuss ostentatiously over his wife. Twice he asked her, wasn't it time for him to take her home? Coolly, demurely, she said that she was perfectly well.

"Of course she is," said Margaret. "This isn't an illness, don't you realise that?"

"If it is," said Rosalind, "it's a very pleasant one."

There was an unexpected freemasonry. Margaret and Rosalind agreed that, when they were carrying their children, they had never felt better in their lives. They also agreed that they wished they could have had more. Azik gave them a condescending hyper-masculine smile, as though women were women, as though (he must have known when he listened to his wife's confidences, that she and Margaret had less in common even than he and I, and liked each other a great deal less) he wasn't above remarking that they were sisters under the skin.

"That's all very well," he projected himself again. "But I say young Pat's right. He's got to be careful." He gave his wife a beaming glance. "You don't have your first grandchild every day. He's got to be careful. As far as that goes, I must say, I'm not happy that they're being careful enough. I don't like the sound of that doctor of theirs. They ought to have the best man in London—"

Azik had been studying the Medical Directory, in search of their doctor's qualifications, and was deeply suspicious as a result. It was then that I had a memory of old Mr. March, Charles March's father, the patriarch whom we used to know as Mr. L., going through the same drill. When his daughter was expecting a baby, or his relatives were ill, or even their friends, Mr. March would carry out sombre researches into doctors' careers, and emerge, with indignation, prophecies of disaster and fugues of total recall, expessing his disapprobation and contempt for what he called *practitioners,* and above all for the particular practitioner in charge of the case.

Even Azik couldn't let himself go in his freedom so totally as Mr. L. Yet for an instant the images got superposed, the two of them, abundant, paternal, unrestrained, acting as they felt disposed to act.

With a good grace, Muriel got ready to go. Her step was still elegant and upright: as she said goodbye, she gave Margaret a smile which was secretive, lively, amused. Gallantly, like someone who would be glad to execute an imitation of Sir Walter Raleigh but hadn't the excuse, Pat draped a cape over her shoulders.

When they had left and we heard Pat drive the car off down below, Ariz had a word to say about their living arrangements, the Chelsea flat, paid for out of Muriel's money, for she kept them both. For once Azik had no immediate suggestions for improvement. Then, having disposed of the topic of his stepdaughter, he introduced another one, like a child saving the jam to the last, that of his own son. This was the only child Azik and Rosalind had between them, born when she was over forty. One never met Azik without, in the end, the conversation coming round to David, who had already been the subterranean cause of Azik's sympathy about Charles. And, in fact, the conversation, at least with Margaret and me, tended to repeat itself, as it did that night. David was high-spirited and very clever. He was at a private day-school in London: Azik wanted him to go later to a smart boarding-school. If so, we kept telling him, he ought to be at a boarding school now. It would be harder for him,

much harder, to leave home at thirteen or fourteen. "No,"
said Azik, as he had done before, "that I could not do. I
could not lose him now."

It was the old argument, but Azik enjoyed any argument
about his son. It even kept him up later than he intended.
David. The possibilities with David. David's education. Azik
went over it all again, before his gaze at his wife began to become more intense, more uxorious, and he felt impelled towards his power-base, his home.

FIVE

RED CARPETS

The chamber of the House of Lords glowed and shone under the chandeliers, the throne-screens picked out in gold, the benches gleaming red, nothing bare nor economical wherever one turned the eye, as though the Victorian Gothic decorators had been told not to be inhibited or as though someone with the temperament of Azik Schiff had been given a free hand to renovate the high altar of St. Mark's.

It was a Wednesday afternoon, about half-past five, the benches not half-full, but, as peers drifted in from tea, not so startlingly empty now as they had been an hour before. I had come to hear Francis Getliffe make a speech, and he had found me a seat just behind the Bar, at ground level. I had heard him speak there several times, but that afternoon there was a difference. This time, as he got up from the back benches, he was on the right hand of the throne, not the left. The election, as we had guessed at the dinner party with the Schiffs, a month before, had been as tight as an election could be: but it had been decided, and a Labour government had come to power. So, for the first time, Francis was speaking from the government side.

He had never been a good speaker, and he was using what looked like a written text. He wasn't a good reader. But he was being listened to. The debate was on defence policy, and it was well known that he was a grey eminence: no, not so grey, for his views had been published, in his time he had gained negative popularity because of them. Ever since he was a young man, in fact, he had been an advisor to Labour politicians. As he grew older, no one had more private influence with them on scientific-military affairs. That was when they were in opposition, but now he was being attended to as though this were an official statement.

As a matter of fact, it was as guarded as though it might have been. Francis was both loyal and punctilious, and though he had to speak that afternoon, he wasn't going to embarrass his old colleagues. One had to know the language, the technical detail, and much back history, to interpret what he was, under the courtesies, pressing on them. Under the courtesies—for Francis, whose politeness had always been stylised, had taken with gusto to the singular stylisation of that chamber. In his speech he was passing stately compliments across the floor to "the noble Lord, Lord Ampleforth." One needed a little inside information to realise that Lord Ampleforth, who was something like Francis's opposite number on the Tory side, was a man with whom Francis had not agreed on a single issue since the beginning of the war: or that Francis was now telling his own government that, in three separate fields, the exact opposite of Lord Ampleforth's policies ought to be their first priority.

Polite hear-hears from both sides as Francis sat down. Lord Lufkin, sprawling on the cross-benches, looked indifferent, as though certain he could have done better himself. In the back tier of the opposition benches, I saw the face of Sammikins, hot-eyed, excited, but (since I last met him, twelve months before) startlingly thin.

The courtesies continued. Lord Ampleforth, who spoke next, paid compliments to the noble Lord, Lord Getliffe, "who brings to your Lordships' House his great scientific authority and the many years of effort he had devoted to our thinking on defence." Lord Ampleforth, who despite his grand title had started his career as a radio manufacturer called Jones, was a rougher customer than Francis and more of a natural politician: he drew some applause from his own side when he expressed "a measure of concern" about Francis's "well-known" views upon the nuclear deterrent. Even so, one again needed a little inside information to grasp what he really felt about Francis. It helped perhaps to know that he had, during the time of the previous government, rigorously removed Francis from his last official committee. More courtesies. The noble Lord's international reputation. The wisdom he brought to our counsels. Assurances of support in everything that contributed to the country's security.

As soon as Lord Ampleforth finished, Francis got up from his place and nodded to me as he went out, so that I joined him in the lobby. He gave me a creased saturnine smile. As we walked over the red carpet down the warm corridor—so red, so warm that I felt rather like Jonah in one of his more claustrophobic experiences or alternatively as I had done after an optical operation, with pads over both eyes—Francis remarked:

"That chap reminds me of a monkey. A very persistent monkey trying to climb a monkey puzzle tree. That is, if they do."

All I knew of monkey puzzles was the sight of them in front of houses more prosperous than ours, in the streets where I was born. However, Francis was not occupied with scientific accuracy. Lord Ampleforth had climbed, he was saying, over all kinds of resistance: on the shoulders of, and in spite of their efforts to throw him off, better men than himself. Including a number of the scientists we knew.

"He'll go on climbing," said Francis with cheerful acerbity. "Nothing will ever stop him. Not for long."

Affable greetings along the corridors. Congratulations to

Francis on his speech. Lord Ampleforth had an astonishing gift, Francis was saying, for ingratiating himself with his superiors: and an equally astonishing gift for doing the reverse with those below.

We entered the guest room. More matiness, from men round the bar, more congratulations on the speech. I couldn't help thinking that they might have found Francis's present line of thought more stimulating. But he was popular there. As we sat in a window seat looking over the river, lights on the south bank aureoled in the November mist, people greeted him with the kind of euphoria that one met in other kinds of enclave, such as a college or a club.

One of the new ministers, from a table close by, was engaging Francis in earnest, low-voiced conversation. So, getting on with my first drink, I gazed from our corner into the room. It wasn't altogether novel to me: when Francis was in London, I sometimes met him there: but my first visit had been much further back, in the Thirties, when I had been invited by an acquaintance called Lord Boscastle. So far as I could trust my memory, it had been different then. Surely there had been less people, both in the chamber and around this room? Somewhat to his surprise, Lord Boscastle's first speech for twenty years had not been much of a draw.

Had the place really been socially grander, or was that a young man's impression? I remember noticing, even in the Thirties, that there were not many historic titles knocking about. Lord Boscastle, who bore one and was a superlative snob, had once remarked, with obscure and lugubrious satisfaction, that the House was quintessentially middle-class. Well, that night, there were still three or four historic titles on view. One of them was sitting at the bar, with a depressed stare imbibing gin. There was another, at a table surrounded by his daughters: my maternal grandfather had been a gamekeeper on his grandfather's estate. A number, though, had come up from the Commons, or their nineteenth century ancestors had; some had been successes in politics, some had missed the high places, and some had never hoped for much. There were several life peers, as Francis was, and some women. Round the room one could hear a variety of accents: about as many as in the Athenaeum, which was a meritocratic club, and a good deal more than in the other club I sometimes used.

Most of these people might have seemed strange to their predecessors in the Lords a hundred years before. No doubt the professional politicians (and there had been plenty of professional politicians there in the nineteenth century, even if, like Palliser, they were landed magnates too) would have found plenty to talk about to the modern front-benchers: there was no tighter trade union in England, then or now. But still, it was like our college, Francis's and mine. The fabric of the building hadn't altered: the survival of politeness in which Francis had been indulging in the Chamber, that hadn't altered either, not by a word: the forms remained the same, while the contents changed. It had perhaps been a strength sometimes, this national passion for clinging on to forms, nostalgic, pious, wart-hog obstinate. Alternatively, it could have released our energies if we had cut them away. And yet, for this country that had never been on, there had never been a realistic chance. Bend the forms, make them stretch, use them for purposes quite different from those in which they had grown up: that had been the way we found it natural (the pressures were so mild we didn't feel them, as mild as the soft English weather) to work. Sometimes I wondered whether my son and his contemporaries would find it natural too.

I mentioned as much to Francis that night. I had recently heard from Charles, and so could think about him at ease.

His was a generation that to Francis, whose children were older, seemed like strangers.

The loudspeaker boomed out— 'Defence debate. Speaking, the Lord ————.' Within two minutes of this news, the population flowing into the guest room had markedly increased. Among the deserters was Lord Ampleforth, pushing his way towards the bar, heavy shoulders hunched. Glancing across to our corner, he nodded to Francis, a flashing-eyed, recognitory nod, as from one power to another. Francis called out:

"Interesting speech, Josh."

We watched Josh acquire his whisky, and glance round the room.

"Looking for someone useful," Francis quietly commented. Apparently, whatever Josh was in search of, he didn't find it. He swallowed his drink at speed, gave another flashing-eyed nod to Francis, patted two men on their shoulders, and went out, presumably back to the Chamber, even though Lord ———— was still up.

Francis, settling back in his chair by the window, did not feel obliged to follow. He was comfortable, ready to sit out the next few speeches, until out of courtesy he returned for the end of the debate. If it hadn't been for his own choice, he wouldn't have been as free as that; he would have been on the front bench, waiting to wind up for the government. For, the weekend after the election, he had had an offer. Would he become a minister of state? To take charge of the nuclear negotiations? He had told me before he replied, but he wasn't asking for advice. He had said no.

There was one objective reason. He knew, just as I knew, without the aid of Azik's benevolent instruction, how little a minister could do. The limits of free action were cripplingly tight, tighter than seemed real to anyone who had not been inside this game. We had both watched, been associated with, and gone down alongside a Tory minister, Roger Quaife, who had tried to do what Francis would have had to try. And Quaife had been far more powerful than Francis could conceivably be. The limits of freedom for this government would be much less than for the last. Francis would fail, anyone would fail. He had done a good deal in the line of duty—but this, he said bleakly, was a hiding to nothing. If he had asked my opinion, I should have agreed.

But that wasn't all. He had been an influence for so long. He had been criticised, at times in disfavour, privately defamed—but always, like other eminent scientists called in to give advice, covered by a kind of mantle of respect. That closed and secret politics was different from politics in the open. Francis hadn't been brought up in open politics. At sixty-one (he was two years older than I was), his imagination and thin skin told him what it would be like. Francis had plenty of courage, but it was courage of the will.

But that was not all either, or even most of it. His major reason for saying no, almost without a thought, was much simpler. It was just that he had become very happy. This hadn't always been so. His marriage—that had been good from the beginning. If he hadn't been lucky there, if he hadn't had the refuge of his wife and children, I had sometimes thought, he would have broken down. Even now, though his face looked younger than his age, his hair still dark, carefully trimmed on the forehead, by a streak of vanity, to conceal that he hadn't much dome on the top of his fine El Greco features, he bore lines of strain and effort, bruiselike pouches left by old anxiety under his eyes. For many years his creative work hadn't gone well enough, according to the standards he set himself. Then at last that had come right. In his fifties he became more serene than most men. To those who first met him at that time, it might have seemed that he was happy by nature. To me, who had known him since we were very young, it seemed like a gift of grace. His home in Cambridge, his laboratory, where, since he was a born father, the research students loved him as his children did, his own work—what could anyone want more? He just wished to continue in the flow of life. Yes, in the flow there were the concerns of anyone who felt at all: his friends' troubles, illnesses, deaths, his children's lives. His eldest son, more gifted than Francis himself, was eating his heart out for a woman who couldn't love him; his favourite daughter, in America, was threatening a divorce. He took those concerns more deeply just because he felt so lucky and thus had energy to spare. That was the flow, all he wanted was for it to stretch ahead: he wasn't going to break out of it now.

So he had refused. Some blamed him, thinking him over-proud or even lacking in duty. The job had gone to an old wheel-horse of the Party, who was given it for services rendered. "He won't last long," said Francis that night, ruminating on politics after the departure of Josh. "There's talk that they may want to rope you in. Well, you've always had to do the dirty work, haven't you?"

He grinned. He had spoken quite lightly, and I didn't pay much attention. I should have asked a question, but we were interrupted by acquaintances of Francis inquiring if they might join us, and bringing up their chairs. Two of them were new members on his own side, the other a bright youngish Tory. They were all eager to listen to him, I noticed. He was relaxed and willing to oblige. But what they listened to would have puzzled those who had known him only in his stiffer form, fair-minded and reticent in the college combination-room.

For Francis was giving his opinions about the people who had worked on the atomic bomb. His opinions weren't at all muffled: he wasn't bending over backwards to be just: he had an eye for human frailty and it was sparkling now. "Anyone who thinks that Robert Oppenheimer was a liberal hero might as well think that I'm a pillar of the Christian faith."

"X" [an Englishman] "never had an idea in his head. That's why he gave everyone so much confidence."

"Y" [an American] "is an anti-Semitic Jew who only tolerates other Jews because the Russians don't."

Some of Francis's stories were new to me. Several of his characters I had met. I had thought before, and did so again that evening, that since he became content he had shown it differently from most other men. A good many, when they had been lucky, felt considerable warmth and approval for others who had been lucky too. Somehow it added to their own deserts. Well, Francis was not entirely above this feeling: but more and more he felt a kind of irreverence, or rather gave his natural irreverence, carefully concealed during his years of strain, its head. Buttoned-up, stuffed, deliberately fair—so he had seemed to most people when he thought that he mightn't justify himself. His wife Katherine knew him otherwise: so did his children: so did I, and one or two others. But with everyone else he was determined not to show envy, not even to let his tongue rip, at the expense of those who were enjoying what he so much longed for. Those who did better creative work than his had to be spoken about with exaggerated charity. It made him seem maddeningly judicious, or too good to be true. He wasn't. As he became happy, he became at the same time more benign and more sardonic. I didn't remember seeing that particular change in anyone else before.

He was talking about David Rubin. Yes, he was one of the best physicists alive, he was a better man than most of them. It wasn't decent for anyone to be so clever. But the trouble with Rubin, Francis said, was that he enjoyed being proved right more than doing anything useful. He had never believed that any of us could do anything useful. If he knew that we were all going to blow ourselves up in three hours' time, David would say that that had always been predictable and remind us that he had in fact predicted it.

I was enjoying myself, but I had to leave. As I retraced my way over the red carpets, I was hoping for a glimpse of Sammikins, just to ask how he was. I had an affection for him: he was a wild animal, brave but lost. He hadn't come into the guest-room for a drink, which was strange enough. I wanted to glance into the Chamber, to see if he was still sitting there, but an attendant reminded me that that wasn't allowed, guests had to pass without lingering on to the red carpet on the other side.

SIX

MARRIAGE, ELDERLY AND YOUTHFUL

Margaret had had her suspicions for some time, but they were not confirmed until the evening of Hector Rose's dinner party. She and I had arranged to meet in a Pimlico pub, because she was coming on from Muriel Eliot's flat and Rose (among the other unexpected features of his letter) had given an address in St. George's Drive. As soon as Margaret arrived, I didn't need telling that she was distressed—no, not brooding, but active and angry. Her colour was high, her eyes brilliant, and when I said "Something the matter," it was not a question.

"Yes."

"What is it?"

She looked at me, seemed about to break out, then suddenly smiled.

"No. Not yet. Not here."

Her tone was intimate. We both understood, she didn't want to spoil the next few minutes. It wasn't just an accident that we were meeting in this pub. The place had memories for each of us, but not particularly pleasant ones, certainly not unshadowed ones. We used to drink there, early in the war, when I was living in Dolphin Square, close by: right at the beginning of our relation, long before we married, when we were already in love but in doubt whether we should come through. Sitting there now, more than twenty years later, or walking round the corner to the square, we felt as we had done before, the Dantesque emotion in reverse: no greater misery, he said, than to recall a happy time in sadness: turn that the other way round. At some points our sentimentalities were different, but here they were the same. The scenes of the choked and knotted past—if we had any reasonable pretext, as on that night, we went and looked at them with our present eyes.

Margaret had asked for bitter, which she rarely drank nowadays. The pub was humming with background music, in the corner lights on a pin-table flashed in and out, all new since our time. But then we had not noticed much, except ourselves.

She gazed round, and smiled again. She said:

"Well, what's it going to be like tonight?"

We hadn't the vestige of an idea. The week before I had received a letter in a beautiful italic hand that once had been so familiar, when I used to read those minutes of Rose's, lucid as the holograph itself. The letter read:

My dear Lewis,

It is a long time since I said goodbye to you as a colleague, but I have kept in touch with your activities from a distance. When I read your work, I feel that I know you better than during our period together in the service: that gives me much regret. It is unlikely that you could have heard, but I have recently re-married. It would give us both much pleasure if you and your wife could spare us an evening to come to dinner. [There followed some dates to choose from.] I have retired from all public activities, and so you will be doing a kindness if you can manage to come. Yours very sincerely,

Hector Rose

In the years when I had worked under Rose in Whitehall, and they were getting on for twenty, I had never met his wife. It was known that he lived right at the fringe of Highgate: when he entertained, which wasn't often, he did so at the Athenaeum: there was no mention of children: he kept his private life locked up, as though it were a state secret. Underneath his polite, his blindingly polite manners, he was a forbidding man, in the sense that no one could come close. He was as tough-minded as any of the civil service bosses, and I came to admire his sheer ability more, the longer I knew him. But that façade, those elaborate manners—they were so untiring, so self-invented, often so ridiculous, that one felt as though one were stripping off each onionskin and being confronted by a precisely similar onionskin underneath. There were those who thought he must be homosexual. I couldn't have guessed. By this time he was sixty-six, and reading his letter Margaret and I decided that he must have married a second time for company (I remembered reading a bare notice of the death of the first wife, with the single piece of information that she, like Rose himself, had been the child of a clergyman). Otherwise, the only inference we could draw came from his last sentence. Rose used words carefully, as a master of impersonal draftsmanship, and that sounded remarkably like a plea. If so, it was the only plea I had ever known him make. He was the least comfortable of companions, but no one was freer from self-pity.

So, as Margaret and I walked, with our own perverse nostalgia, across the end of the square, past the church and the white-scarred planes, along the street for a few hundred yards, we couldn't imagine what we were going to. When we came outside the house itself, it was like the one that I had lived in towards the end of the war, under the eye and land-ladyship of the ineffable Mrs. Beauchamp: a narrow four-storey building, period latish nineteenth century, ramshackle, five bells flanking the door with five name-cards beside them. Rose's was the ground-floor flat: it couldn't be more than three or four rooms, I was reckoning as I rang the bell. It was another oddity that Rose should live in this fashion. He had no private means, he might not have earned much since he retired from the Department, but his pension would be over £3,000 a year. That didn't spread far by this date, but it spread farther than this.

But, when he opened the door, all was momentarily unchanged. Strong, thick through the shoulders, upright: his preternatural youthfulness had vanished in his fifties, but he looked no older than when I saw him last.

"My dear Lewis, this is extraordinarily good of you! How very kind of you to come! How very, very kind!"

He used to greet me like that when, as his second-in-command, I had been summoned to his office and had performed the remarkable athletic feat of walking the ten yards down the corridor.

He was bowing to Margaret, who had met him only two or three times before.

"Lady Eliot! It's far far too long since I had the pleasure of seeing you—"

His salutations, which now seemed likely to describe arabesques hitherto unheard of, had the knack of putting their recipient at a disadvantage, and Margaret was almost stuttering as she tried to reply.

Bowing, arms spread out, he showed us—the old word *ushered* would have suited the performance better—into the sitting-room, which led straight out of the communal hall. As I had calculated when we stood outside, they had only one main room, and the sitting-room was set for dinner, napery and glass upon the table, what looked like Waterford glass out of place in the dingy house. Round the walls were

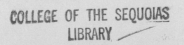

glass-fronted bookshelves, stacked with volumes a good many of which, I discovered later, were prizes from Marlborough and Oxford. A young lecturer or research student at one of the London colleges, just married, might have been living there. However, neither Margaret nor I could attend to the interior decoration, when we had the prospect of Rose's wife herself.

"Lady Eliot," said Rose, like a master of ceremonies, "may I present ————. Darling, may I introduce Sir Lewis Eliot, my former colleague, my distinguished colleague."

As I muttered "Lady Rose" and took her hand, I was ready for a lot of titular incantations, wishing that we had Russian patronymics or alternatively that Rose had taken to American manners, which seemed unlikely. It was going to be tiresome to call this woman Lady Rose all night. She was alluring. No, that wasn't right, there was nothing contrived about her, she was simply, at first sight, attractive. Not beautiful: she had a wide mouth, full brown eyes, a cheerful up-tilted nose. Her cheeks seemed to wear a faint but permanent flush. She must have been about forty, but she wouldn't change much, at twenty she wouldn't have looked very different, a big and sensuous girl. She was as tall as Rose, only two or three inches shorter than I was, not specially ethereal, no more so than a Renoir model.

Margaret gave me the slightest of marital grins, jeering at both of us. Our reconstructions of the situation . . . elderly people 'joining forces,' marriage for company. If that was marrying for company, then most young people needed more of it. As for Rose's putative plea, the only reason for reviving our acquaintance seemed to be that he wanted to show her off, which was simple and convincing enough.

In actual fact, as company in the conversational sense, she wasn't a striking performer, as I discovered when we set out to talk. She was superficially shy, not at all shy deeper down.

She was quite content to leave the talk to us, beaming placidly at Rose, as though signalling that she was pleased with
him. I picked up one or two facts, such as that there had been
another husband, though what had happened to him was
not revealed. If there had been a divorce, it had been kept
quiet. I couldn't gather how she and Rose had ever met:
she didn't belong to any sort of professional world, she came
perhaps—there was a residual accent—from origins like
mine. I knew that when Rose left the service he had taken
a couple of directorships: my guess was that he had come
across her in one of those offices, she might have been his
secretary.

Well, there they were, eyes meeting down the table. "Jane
darling, would it be troubling you if you reached behind
you—" The one aspect which baffled me completely was
why they should be living like students. It might have been
one of the games of marriage, in which they were pretending
to be young people starting out. If so, that must have been
his game, for she would have been satisfied wherever they
had lived.

She was an excellent cook. On nights when we had worked
late together, Rose and I used to split a bottle of wine, and
he had recollected that.

He was talking with elaborate animation to Margaret
about the differences between Greats in his time at Oxford,
and the philosophy in hers at Cambridge. Jane listened and
basked. As for me, I was engaged in a simple reflection. A
woman had once told me that she didn't know, no one could
possibly know, what a man was like until she had gone to
bed with him. It was the kind of comment that sounded wise
when one was young, and probably wasn't. And yet, looking
at that pair, remembering how so many people had pigeon-
holed Rose, myself among them, I felt that this once there
might be something to it.

Table pushed back after the meal, for the room was small though high-ceilinged, we sat round the grate, in front of an electric fire. Rose and his wife had finished drinking for the evening, but hospitably he had put a decanter of port on the floor. Some more fine glass, from the archdiaconal or even the Highgate home. I mentioned former colleagues, I tried to get him to say something about his career.

"Oh, my dear Lewis, that's really water under the bridge, water distinctly under the bridge, shouldn't you agree? I don't know whether Lady Eliot has ever had the misfortune to be exposed to the reminiscences of retired athletes," he was gazing, bleached-eyed, at Margaret, "but I assure you that mine would be, if anything, slightly duller."

"I don't believe that," said Margaret, who still found him disconcerting.

"But then, my dear Lady Eliot, if you'll permit me, you haven't spent getting on for forty years in government departments."

"Do you regret it?" I said. I had learned long since that one had to tackle him head on.

"Regret in what particular manner? I'm afraid I'm being obtuse, of course."

"Spending your life that way."

Rose gave his practised, edged, committee smile. "I follow. I should be inclined to think that, with my attainments such as they are, I shouldn't have been markedly more useful anywhere else. Or perhaps markedly less."

"That's a bit much, Hector," I broke out. I said that, when I first reported to him and for years afterwards, he had been tipped to become head of the civil service. That hadn't happened. He had finished as a senior Permanent Secretary, one of the half-dozen most powerful men in Whitehall, but not at the absolute top. Most of us thought he had been unlucky, and in fact badly dealt with. (I noticed that this

seemed to be news to his wife, who had blushed with something like gratification.) Did he mind?

"I doubt if it would have affected the fate of the nation,
my dear Lewis. I think you will agree that the general level
of our former colleagues was, judged by the low standard of
the human race, distinctly high. That is, granted their terms
of reference, which may, I need hardly say, be completely
wrong, a good many of them were singularly competent. Far
more competent than our political masters I learned that
when I was a very lowly assistant principal, just down from
Oxford. And I'm afraid I never unlearned it. Incidentally,
out of proportion more competent than the businessmen
that it was my misfortune to have to do official business
with. Of course my experience has been narrow, I haven't
had Lewis's advantages, and my opinion is *parti pris*." He
was speaking to Margaret. "So you must forgive me if I
sound parochial. But for what it is worth, that is my opinion. That is, the competition among my colleagues was rela-
tively severe. So a man who by hook or by crook became a
permanent secretary ought to feel that he hadn't any right to
grumble. He's probably been more fortunate than he deserved. There was an old Treasury saying, Lewis will remember, that in the midst of a crowd of decent clever men
anyone who became a permanent secretary had of necessity
to be something of a shit."

Rose delivered that apothegm as blandly as his normal
courtesies. His wife chortled, and Margaret grinned.

"Well," said Rose, "I qualified to that extent."

"Hector," I said, "you haven't answered my question."

"Haven't I, my dear Lewis? I really do apologise. I am so
very, very sorry."

We gazed at each other. We were less constrained that
night than we had been during the years in the office. And
yet he was just as immovable, it was like arguing with him

over a point on which I was, after all the paraphernalia, going inevitably to be over-ruled.

Rose was continuing, in his most unargumentative tone.

"Recently I had the pleasure of introducing my wife to the Italian lakes. Actually we chose that for our honeymoon —"

"Lovely," said Jane.

"Yes, we thought it was a good choice. And, as a very minor bonus, I happened to come across an inscription which might interest you, Lewis. Perhaps, for those whose Latin has become rusty, I may take the liberty of translating. It is pleasantly simple. GAIUS AUFIDIUS RUFUS. HE WAS A GOOD CIVIL SERVANT.

"Don't you think that is remarkably adequate? Who could possibly want a more perfect epitaph than that?"

I knew, and he knew that I knew, that he was parodying himself. I nodded my head, in acquiescent defeat. Impassively he let show a smile, but, unlike his committee smile, it contained a degree of both malice and warmth. Then he gave us, his wife for the first time assisting in the conversation, a travelogue about Como and Garda, the hotels they had stayed in, the restaurants they would re-visit when, the following spring, they proposed to make the same trip again. This honeymoon travelogue went on for some time.

Then, when we got up and began our goodbyes, Rose encircled us with thanks for coming. At last we got out into the road, waiting for a taxi: the two of them, while they waved to us, stood on the doorstep close together, as though they were ready to be photographed.

As we drove past Victoria through the Belgravia streets, Margaret, in the dark and sheltering cab, was saying:

"How old is she?"

"Late thirties?"

"Older. Perhaps she's too old."

"To old for what?"

"A child, you goat." Her voice was full of cheerful sensual nature. "Anyway, we'd better watch the births column next year—"

She went on:

"Good luck to them!"

I said yes.

She said:

"I hope it goes on like that." She added: "And I hope something else doesn't."

We had both enjoyed the bizarre but comforting evening, and I had remembered only intermittently (and that perhaps had been true for her) that she had news to break. Now she was angry again—at me, at herself, at the original cause —for having to fracture the peace of the moment.

"What is the matter?"

"Your nephew."

Muriel had told her the story that afternoon. Pat was having other women, certainly a couple since the marriage, with the baby due in the New Year. It was as matter-of-fact as that.

"He's a little rat," said Margaret.

With the lights of Park Lane sweeping across us, I remarked:

"You can't do anything."

"You mustn't defend him."

"I wasn't—"

"You want to, don't you?"

I had never been illusioned about Pat. And yet Margaret was reading something, as though through the feel of my arm: an obscure male freemasonry, or perhaps another kind of resistance she expected, whenever her judgments were more immediate and positive than mine.

We didn't say much until we were inside our bedroom.

"It's squalid," said Margaret. "But that makes it worse for her."

"I'm sorry for her."

"I'm desperately sorry for her."

Her indignation had gone by now, but her empathy was left.

"I know," I said. I asked how Muriel was taking it.

"That's a curious thing," Margaret gave a sharp-eyed, puzzled smile. "She seems pretty cool about it. Cooler than I should have been, I tell you, if you'd left me having Charles and done the same."

A good many women would have been cooler than that, I told her.

She burst out laughing. But when I repeated, how had Muriel reacted, her face became thoughtful, not only protective but mystified and sad. In her composed, demure fashion, Muriel had been evasive about her husband during previous visits; this time she had come out with it, still composed but clinical. Not a tear. Not even a show of temper.

"What do they think they're playing at?" said Margaret. "He wasn't in love with her, we never believed he was. He was after the main chance, blast him. But what about her? It doesn't make sense. She must love him, mustn't she?"

"After all," she went on, "she's only twenty-two."

A silence.

Margaret said: "I don't understand them, do you?"

She was upset, and I tried to comfort her: and yet for her it was no use being reflective or resigned. For, though this mess was quite far away from her—it wasn't all that dramatic or novel, and Muriel was no more than a young women she knew by chance—it had touched, or become tangled with, some of her own expectations. None of us had expected more from all the kinds of love than Margaret. With her father, those afternoons as she sat by him in his loneliness, she had felt one of them finally denied: and with her sons also, as she grew older, there was another kind of isolation. Maurice passive, gentle, but with no flash of her own spirit coming back: Charles, who had spirit which matched hers, but who responded on his own terms. She had invested so much hope in what they would give her: and now, despite her sense, her irony, she sometimes felt cut off from the young. That was why Pat and his deserted wife became tokens for her: they made romantic love appear meaningless: all her expectations were dismissed, as though she belonged to another species. It wasn't like that, I tried to tell her, but I did no good. Unlike herself, so strong in trouble close to hand, that night—on the pretext or trigger of an acquaintance's ill-treatment—she felt lonely and unavailing.

"Never mind," I said, "you'll feel different when Carlo (our name for Charles) is back."

"What will he be like then?" she said.

She asked, would he understand the situation of Pat and Muriel better than we did. Neither of us could guess. It was hard to believe that he had much in common with either.

SEVEN

FAIR-MINDEDNESS

On the aternoon of Christmas Day, Margaret and I were
sitting in our drawing-room, along with Maurice, who had
the day off from his hospital. Over the park outside, the sky
was low, unbroken: no rain, not cold, a kind of limbo of a
December day. We had put off the Christmas meal until the
evening, since my brother Martin and his wife and daughter
were driving down from Cambridge. No newspapers, no letters, a timeless day. I suggested that we should go for a walk:
Margaret looked at the cloud-cover, and decided that it
wasn't inviting. Maurice, as usual glad to oblige, said that he
would come with me.

We didn't go into Hyde Park, but instead turned into the
maze of streets between our flat and Paddington. Or rather I
turned that way, for Maurice didn't assert himself, and happily took what came. It wasn't that he was a weak character:
in his own fashion, he was a strong one; but it was a fashion
so different from mine, or my own son's, that I was no
nearer knowing what he wanted, or where his life would go.
Since he came to me, at the age of three, when I married
Margaret, he and I had always got on well: there hadn't
been the subliminal conflict of egos that had occasionally
broken out in my relation, on the surface ironic and amiable, with young Charles. Sometimes it seemed that Maurice
didn't have an ego. I had been concerned, because it made

Margaret anxious, about his examination failures. I had also been concerned, because I was enough of a bourgeois born, about whether he would ever earn a living. Which had a certain practical interest, since otherwise I should have to go on supporting him.

He walked at my side, face innocent, good-looking, not feminine, but unhardened for twenty-one. As usual, he was unprickly, free from self: yet, I had often wondered, was that really true? It was the puzzle that one sometimes met in people who asked very little for themselves. They cared for others: they did good works and got nothing and claimed nothing: they had no rapacity or cruelty: so far as human beings could be, they were kind. Nevertheless, occasionally one felt —at least I did—that underneath, they had a core more impregnable than most of ours. Somehow they were protected. Protected as some men are by shields of vanity or self-regard. Certainly Maurice made one feel that he was in less danger than any of us. Maybe it was that, more than his kindness, which made him so comfortable to be with.

Under the monotone sky, the high houses, also monotone, similar in period to the one where the Roses were living, more run-down. In the square, neon signs of lodging houses. Church built when the square was opulent (a million domestic servants in London then, and the slum-poor nowhere near these parts), Christmas trees lit up outside. Sleazy cafés on the road to Paddington station. A few people walking about, slowly, in the mild gloom. A scrum of West Indians arguing on the pavement. Christmas decorations in closed shops. Here and there on the high house fronts, lighted windows.

Once or twice Maurice reminded me of stories which he had told about those streets, for he knew them well. In his holidays he used to join a friend of his, the vicar of a local parish, on pastoral visits, making a curious unsolemn and faintly comic pair, the vicar stout, becassocked and birettaed, Maurice as thin as a combination of the idiot prince and a first class high-jumper. It was their way of enjoying themselves, and they had been inside many more rooms in the Paddington hinterland than the vicar's duty called for. Yes, some of the sights weren't pretty, Maurice had reported, unshockable: you could find most kinds of vice without going far. Also most kinds of suffering. Not the mass poverty of the Thirties, that had been wiped out. But alcoholic's poverty, drug addict's poverty, pensioner's poverty. Being poor when you're old, though, that's not the worst of it, Maurice had said. It's being alone, day after day, with nothing to look forward to until you die. For once (it had happened one night when he returned home, a couple of years before), Maurice had spoken with something like violence. Genteel poverty behind lace curtains. A lucky person had a television set. If anyone feels like being superior about television, when they're old they ought to live alone without one. You know, Maurice had gone on, they look forward to seeing Godfrey (the vicar) and me. I suppose one would if one were alone. Of course we can't do much. We can just stay talking for half an hour. Anyway, Godfrey isn't much good at conversation. But I suppose it's better than nothing.

As we walked along, solitary figures passing us in the empty streets, lighted windows in the houses, I was thinking, he had been behind some of those windows. They weren't as taunting when one got inside, as when one gazed at them from the street as a young man. For an instant, I was, not precisely remembering, but touched by a residual longing from, other Christmas Days long past, when I had also gone out for walks on deserted pavements, just to kill time, just to get through the day. That had been so in the provincial town, after my mother died: slipping out after Christmas dinner, necessarily teetotal, at Aunt Milly's, I used to tramp the streets as the afternoon darkened, gazing up garden paths at bright and curtained sitting-rooms, feeling a kind of arrogant envy. That had been so again, my first year in London: my friends all at home, no George Passant to pass the evening with, and I with nothing to do. The streets must have looked much as they did that day with Maurice, but that I had forgotten or repressed, and where I finished up the night.

"Not exactly cheerful," I said, as though commenting on the present situation, indicating a young man who was dawdling past us.

"Poor old thing," said Maurice, who really was commenting on the present situation. "He doesn't look as if he's got anywhere to go—"

For any connoisseur of townscapes, that afternoon's had its own merit. The unvaried sky lay a thousand feet above the houses: the great city stretched all round one, but there was no sense of space: sky, houses, fairy lights on Christmas trees all pressed upon the lost pedestrians in the streets. Yes, the townscape had its own singular merit, but it was good to be back (did Maurice feel this too?) among the lights of our own drawing-room, able to find our own enclave.

To be realistic, it was not quite such a well-constructed enclave as it might have been. At least, not when we sat down to dinner. Physically all was well. The food was good, there was plenty to drink. But in Margaret, and in me watching her, the nerves were pricking beneath the skin. One reason everyone round the table knew. That was the first Christmas Charles had not been at home. Shortly he would be celebrating his seventeenth birthday in Karachi; for the time being he was static and safe. Then he would start his journey home, all overland, travelling alone, picking up rides.

The whole Eliot family was there, eating the Christmas dinner, except the youngest—

The whole Eliot family, though, that was a second reason for constraint, which perhaps, I couldn't be certain, Martin and his wife didn't realise. They had duly arrived, with their daughter Nina, while Maurice and I were out on our afternoon walk. We hadn't seen any of them since the summer, at Pat's wedding, but this family party had been planned long since. So, as a matter of course, Pat and Muriel had been invited. After Muriel's disclosures, Margaret had asked her if she still wanted the pair of them to come. Yes, Muriel replied, without expression. There they were at dinner, Muriel on my left, by this time heavily pregnant, hazel eyes sharp, face tranquil, Pat on Margaret's left, working hard to be a social stimulant.

It was difficult to know whether anything was being given away. Once Pat tried his brand of deferential cheek on Margaret: she was polite, but didn't play. Pat, whose antennae, always active, were specially so that night, must have known what that meant. But his father and mother did not seem to notice. Maurice tried, like a quiet impresario, to make the best of Pat's gambits. Margaret didn't like dissimulating, but when she was keeping a secret she was as disciplined as I was. From the other end of the table, all I could have told —if she hadn't warned me—was that she laughed very little, and that her laughter didn't sound free. While Pat, whose brashness was subdued, kept exerting himself to make the party bubble, Martin was attending to him, with a faint amused incredulous smile which I had seen creep on him before in his son's company—as though astonished that anyone so unguarded could be a son of his.

By my side, Irene didn't often meet Pat's quick frenetic brown-eyed glance, so like her own, but instead kept me engaged with Cambridge gossip. As she did so, I heard Muriel, voice clear and precise, taking part in repartee with Pat: no sign of strain, no disquiet that I could pick up. Later, I observed her talking to Nina, her sister-in-law, inconspicuous in her parents' presence, more so in Pat's. She might be inconspicuous, but she was a very pretty girl, so far as one could see her face, for she had hair, in the fashion of her contemporaries, which trailed over one eye. Also in the fashion, her voice was something like a whisper, and I couldn't hear any of her replies to Muriel. Of the two, I was judging, most men would think her the prettier: but perhaps most men would think that Muriel provoked them more.

In the drawing-room after dinner, Muriel announced that, as this was a family Christmas party, she proposed to put off her bedtime. Very dutifully, Pat argued with her—"Darling, you know what ————" (her doctor) "said?"

"He's not here, is he?" said Muriel, and got her way. They didn't leave until half-past eleven: it was midnight before Martin and I sat by ourselves in my study, having a final drink.

Now at last it seemed to me like an ordinary family evening, peace descending upon the room. We hadn't talked, except with others present, all that night: nor in fact since the summer, the day of our father's funeral. Martin proceeded to interrogate me, in the way that had become common form since we grew older. Nowadays his workaday existence didn't change from one term to another, while mine was still open to luck, either good or bad. So that our roles had switched, and he talked to me like a concerned older brother. How was the new book going? I was well into it, I said, but it would take another year. Was there anything in this rumour about my being called into the government? He was referring to a piece of kite-flying by one of the parliamentary correspondents—*New Recruits?*

I knew no more about it than he did, I told him, and mentioned the conversation with Francis Getliffe in the Lords' bar. This correspondent wrote as though he had been listening, or alternatively as though the House of Lords was bugged. As had happened often during my time in Whitehall, I had the paranoid feeling that about half the population of Parliament were in newspaper pay.

I had heard nothing more, I repeated to Martin. I supposed it was possible. They knew me pretty well. But it would be a damned silly thing for me to do. "Oh, if they do ask you, don't turn it down out of hand," said Martin, watchful, tutorial, as cautious as old Arthur Brown. He went on, he could see certain advantages, and I said with fraternal sarcasm, that it was a pity he ever withdrew from the great world. Great World, I rubbed it in. We both knew enough about it, partly by experience, partly by nature. Martin gave his pulled-down grin.

He would like just one more drink, he said, and went over to the sideboard. Then, as he settled back in his chair, glance turned towards his glass, he said, in a casual tone:

"I don't think Irene knows anything about these goings-on."

"What do you mean?" It was a mechanical question. I had understood.

"That young man of ours playing round." Pat's Christian name was actually Lewis, after me, and Martin seldom referred to him by his self-given name. Suddenly Martin looked full at me with hard blue eyes.

"I gathered you had heard," he said.

"Yes."

"I'm sure she doesn't know."

That seemed to give him an obscure satisfaction. Irene had never liked the marriage, although it had taken Pat off their hands, providing him with the money he had never earned.

"Did you realise," I asked, "that we knew—before tonight?"

"Never mind that." He wouldn't answer, and left me curious. He might have picked it up in the air, for he was a perceptive man. But I thought it sounded as though he had been told. By whom? He was not intimate with his daughter-in-law. Bizarre as it seemed, it was more likely to be his son. Martin felt for his son the most tenacious kind of parental love. It was, Martin knew it all by heart, so did Margaret, so did Azik Schiff, so did Mr. March and old Winslow long before we did, the most one-sided of human affections, the one which lasts longest and for long periods gives more pain than joy. And yet, one-sided though such a relation as Martin's and his son's had to be, it took two to make a possessive love. With some sons it couldn't endure; if it did endure, there had to be a signal—sometimes the call for help—the other way. Pat had cost his father disappointment and suffering: there had been quarrels, lies, deceits: but in the midst of it all there was, and still remained, a kind of communication, so that in trouble he went back, shameless and confiding, and gave Martin a new lease of hope.

The result was that Martin, who was usually as quick as any man to see the lie in life, who had an acute nose for danger, was talking that night as though I were the one to be reassured. He did it—I had heard him speak of his son in this tone before—with an air of apparent realism. Yes, there must be plenty of young men, mustn't there, who think of amusing themselves elsewhere in the first year of marriage. No one was ever really honest about the sexual life. How many of us made fantasies year after year? There weren't many who would confess their fantasies, or admit or face what their sexual life had been.

I didn't interrupt him, but he could have guessed what I was thinking. Did he remember, earlier that year in our native town, how we had talked during the murder trial? Talked without cover or excuses, unlike tonight. There was a gap between fantasy and action, the psychiatric witnesses had been comfortably saying. It was a gap that only the psychopaths or those in clinical terms not responsible managed to cross. That made life more acceptable, pushed away the horrors into a corner of their own. Martin wouldn't accept the consolation. It was too complacent for him, he had said, as we sat in the hotel bar, talking more intimately than we had ever done.

Now, Martin, swirling the whisky in his glass, looked across the study from his armchair to mine.

"I agree," he said, as though with fair-mindedness, "not so many people act out their fantasies. But still, this business of his must be fairly common, mustn't it? You know, I'm pretty sure that I could have done the same."

Shortly afterwards, he made an effort to sound more fair-minded still.

"Of course," he said, "we've got to face the fact that he might turn into a layabout."

He used the objective word, his voice was sternly objective. Yet he was about as much so as Francis Getliffe complaining (with a glow of happiness concealed) that people said his son Leonard was a class better as a scientist than himself. Both of them liked to appear detached. It made Martin feel clear-minded, once he had suggested that the future might be bad. But he didn't believe it. He was still thinking of his son as the child who had been winning, popular, anxious to make people happy—and capable of all brilliant things.

"I thought they were getting on all right tonight, didn't you?" said Martin. "He'll shake down when the baby is born, you know. It will make all the difference, you'll see."

He gave a smile which was open and quite unironic. Anyone who saw it wouldn't have believed that he was a pessimistic man.

EIGHT

SIGHT OF A NEW LIFE

The New Year opened more serenely for Margaret and me than many in the past. True, each morning as the breakfast tray came in, she looked for letters from Maurice or Charles, just as one used to in a love affair, when letters counted more. And, as in a love affair, the fact that Charles was thousands of miles away sometimes seemed to slacken his hold on her. Distance, as much as time, did its own work. Reading one of Charles's dispatches, she was relieved that he was well: but she was joyful when she heard from Maurice. Sometimes I wondered, if she and I could have had other children, whom she would have loved the most.

The flat was quiet, so many rooms empty, with us and the housekeeper living there alone. Mornings working in the study, afternoons in the drawing-room, the winter trees in the park below. Visits to Margaret's father, back to the evening drink. Once out of the hospital, it was all serene, and there was nothing to disturb us. As for our acquaintances, we heard that Muriel was moving into Azik Schiff's house to have her baby—Eaton Square, Azik laying on doctors and nurses, that suited him appropriately enough. Margaret kept up her visits to her, as soon as she was installed, which was towards the end of January, with the baby due in a couple of weeks.

About six o'clock one evening, the birth expected any day

now, there was a ring at our hall door. As I opened it, Pat was standing on the threshold. There wasn't likely to be a more uninvited guest. I knew there couldn't be any news, for Margaret had not long returned from Eaton Square. He entered with his shameless smile, ingratiating and also defiant.

"As a matter of fact, Uncle Lewis," he said, explaining himself, "I would rather like a word with Aunt Meg."

He followed me into the drawing-room, where Margaret was sitting. She said good evening in a tone that he couldn't have thought indulgent (it was the first time she had seen him since the Christmas dinner), but he went and kissed her cheek.

"Do you mind," he said, bright-faced, "if I help myself to a drink?"

He poured himself a whisky and soda, and then sat on a chair near to her.

"Aunt Meg," he said, "I've come to ask you a favour."

"What do you mean?"

"I want you to let us call this child after you."

For once Margaret was utterly astonished, her face wide-open with surprise, and yes, for an instant, with pleasure.

Her first response was uncollected. "Why, you don't know whether it's going to be a girl."

"I'm sure it will be."

"You can't be sure—"

"I want a girl. I want to call it after you."

His tone was masterful and wooing. Watching with a certain amusement from the other side of the room (I had not often seen anyone try this kind of blandishment on her), I saw her eyes sharpen.

"Whose idea was this?"

"Mine, of course, what do you think?"

Margaret's voice was firm.

"What does Muriel say?"

"Oh, she's in favour. You'd expect her to be in favour, wouldn't you?"

"I don't know, she might be." Margaret hadn't altered her expression. "But she hasn't quite your reasons, after all."

"Oh come, Aunt Meg, I just want to show how much I feel for you—" For the first time he was protesting—as though he had just recognised that he was no longer in control.

"When did you think this up?"

"A long time ago, months ago, you know how you think about names."

"How long ago did you hear that Muriel had told me?"

"Oh that—"

"You don't like being unpopular, do you?"

"Come on, Aunt Meg, you're making too much of it."

"Am I?"

He threw his head back, spread his arms, gave a wide penitential grimace, and said:

"You know what I'm like!"

She looked at him with a frown, some sort of affection there:

"Is that genuine?"

"You know what I'm like, I've never pretended much."

"But when you say that, it means you're really satisfied with yourself, don't you see? Of course, you want to make promises, you want us all to be fond of you again, that's why you're here, isn't it? But really you don't feel there's anything gone wrong—"

"Now you're being unfair."

Even then, he wasn't ready to be totally put down. Apologetic, yes—but still, people did things, didn't they? People did things that hurt her and perhaps they couldn't help themselves. Like her father. There were others who didn't feel as she did. Somehow Pat had discovered, it must have been from Davidson himself, that once he had applied to us for drugs. Still, he found someone else, didn't he, said Pat, not brashly but with meaning. "It's no use expecting us to be all the same."

Margaret told him that he was making things too comfortable for himself. For a time they were talking with a curious intimacy, the intimacy of a quarrel, more than that, something like understanding. It was easy to imagine him, I thought, behaving like this to his wife when she had found him out, penitent, flattering, inventive, tender, and in the end unmoved.

But Margaret didn't give him much. Soon, she cut off the argument. She wasn't responsible for his soul or his actions, she said: but she was responsible for any words of hers that got through to Muriel. It sounded as though she wanted to issue a communiqué after a bout of diplomatic negotiations, but Margaret knew very well what she was doing. Pat, as a source of information, particularly as a source of information about his own interests, was not, in the good old Dostoevskian phrase, a specially reliable authority. He was not, Margaret repeated, to give any version of this conversation. He was not to report that Margaret would like a girl to be called after her. Margaret herself would mention the proposal to Muriel the next time she saw her.

Pat knew the last word when he heard it. With a good grace, with a beaming doggy smile, he said, Taken as read, and helped himself to another drink. Soon afterwards, he knew also that it was time for him to go.

Did he expect to get away with it, I was speculating, not intervening, although Pat had tried to involve me once or twice. Like most bamboozlers or con men, he assumed that no one could see through him. More often than not, bamboozlers took in no one but themselves. In fact, Margaret had seen through him from the start. Of course, the manoeuvre was a transparent one, even by his standards. He had studied how to slide back into favour; he may have thought of other peace-offerings, before he decided what would please her most. Incidentally, he had chosen right. But a woman didn't need to be as clear-sighted as Margaret to see him coming, gift in hand.

So he had, with his usual cheek, put his money down and lost it. Lost most of it, but perhaps not all. Margaret thought him as worthless as before, perhaps more so: she knew more of his tricks, he had even ceased to be interesting: and yet, despite herself, sarcastic at her own expense, she was, after that failure of his, left feeling a shade more kindly towards him.

Muriel, as usual polite and friendly, did not give away her thoughts about the baby's name, so Margaret told me. "I've got an idea she's made her own decision," said Margaret. If that were so, we never knew what it was. For the child, born a few days later, turned out to be a boy. He was to be called, Margaret heard the first time she saw him, Roy Joseph. And those names were certainly Muriel's own decision, Margaret was sure of that. In fact, Muriel had said that she would have liked to call the boy after her stepfather, but you couldn't use *Azik* if you weren't a Jew. So she fell back on Roy, after her own father, and threw in Joseph, which was one of Azik's other names.

Anyway, whatever the marriage was like, this was a fine little boy, said Margaret, and took me to see him on her next visit, when he was not yet a week old.

The first time I went inside a prosperous house in London, nearly forty years earlier, I had been greeted by a butler. In Azik Schiff's house in Eaton Square, one was also greeted by a butler. That didn't often happen, in the London of the Sixties. But even Azik, many times richer than old Mr. March, couldn't recruit the footmen and the army of maids I used to meet in the March household. Still, the Eaton Square house was grander, different in kind from those most of our friends lived in—the comfortable flats, the Kensington, Chelsea, Hampstead houses of professional London. So far as that went, Azik wouldn't have considered adequate for his purposes the politicians' houses in Westminster, a good deal richer, that I used to know.

Azik, as he liked to announce, was fond of spending money. In the hall at Eaton Square, the carpets were deep: round the walls there were pictures which might have belonged to the antechamber of a good, though somewhat conventional, municipal gallery. That was true of Azik's pictures throughout the house. His taste wasn't adventurous, as Austin Davidson's had been. Azik had bought nothing later than the impressionists, except for one Cézanne. He had been cautious, out of character for him, perhaps not trusting either his judgment or his eye. But he had a couple of Sisleys, a Boudin, a Renoir, a Ruysdael—he might have been cautious, but we coveted them each time we went inside his house.

Getting out of the lift, which was one of Azik's innovations, Margaret led me to the master bedroom on the third floor, the whole of which Azik had made over to his stepdaughter. Inside the high light bedroom (through the window one could see the tops of trees in the private garden), Muriel was sitting up in bed, a great four-poster bed, a wrap round her shoulders, looking childish, prim, undecorated. She said, good afternoon, Uncle Lewis, with that old-fashioned correctness of hers, which often seemed as though she were smiling to herself or pretending to drop a curtsey.

"It's very good of you to come," she said.

I said no.

"Aunt Margaret likes babies. It can't be much fun for you."

Margaret put in that I had been good, when Charles was a baby.

"That was duty, though," said Muriel, looking straight at me.

I was, as often, disconcerted by her, not sure whether she had a double meaning, or whether she meant anything at all.

She made some conversation about Charles, the first time I had heard her mention him. Then there was a hard raucous cry from a room close by, from what must have been the dressing-room.

"Yes, that's him," she said, with composure.

"Oh, come on, let's have him in," said Margaret.

"That will be boring for Uncle Lewis, though."

With other young women, that might have seemed coy. Not so with her. I told her that I hadn't expected to wait so long. She gave a grin which made her look less decorous, and pressed the bell by her bedside.

As a nurse carried in the baby, Margaret said:

"Let me have him, just for a minute."

She pressed the bundle, arms slowly waving, to her, and looked down at him, with her expression softened by delight.

"I do envy you," she said to Muriel, and from the tone I was sure that remark had been made before. Yet Margaret's pleasure was as simple as it could be, all the life in her just joyful at the feel of life.

She passed the child to his mother, who settled him against her and said, in a clear voice:

"Hallo, old man."

It might have happened, it almost certainly must have happened, that my mother showed me Martin soon after he was born. But if so I had totally forgotten it, and everything to do with his birth, except that I had been sent to my aunt's for a couple of days. No, the only days-old baby I remembered seeing was my son. The aimless, rolling eyes: the hands drifting round like an anemone's fibrils. As a spectacle, this was the same. Perhaps the difference, to a photographic eye, was that this child, under the thin flaxen hair, had a high crown to his head, the kind of steeple crown Muriel's father had once possessed.

But when I first saw my son, it hadn't been with a photographic eye. It hadn't even been with emotion, but something fiercer and more animal, so strong that, though it was seventeen years ago, it didn't need bringing back to memory, it was there. That afternoon in Muriel's bedroom, perversely, I did watch the pair of them, mother and baby, with something like emotion, the sort of emotion which is more or less tender, more or less self-indulgent, which doesn't trouble one. My brother's grandson. Roy Calvert's grandson. Would this child ever know anything about Roy Calvert, who had passed into a private mythology by now? How much did I recollect of what he had been truly like?

This child would live a different life from ours, and, of course, with any luck, live on when our concerns, and everything about us, had been long since swept away. Did one envy a life that was just beginning? Pity for what might happen, that was there. Pity was deeper than the thought he would live after one. But yes, the impulse for life was organic, in time it would overmaster all the questions, it would prevail over pity, all one would feel was the strength of a new life.

NINE

PIECES OF NEWS

Several afternoons that April, Margaret and I walked through the empty flat to an empty bedroom, making quite unnecessary inspections in time for Charles's return. It was the room he had occupied since he was three years old: not the one where we had watched him in his one grave illness, because after that, out of what was sheer superstition, we had made a change. This was the room, though, to which he had come back on holidays from school.

From the window, there was the view over Tyburn gardens which I had seen so often, waking him in the morning, that now I didn't see at all. The shelves round the room were stacked with books, which, with a streak of possessive conservatism, he refused to have touched: the geological strata of his books since he began to read, children's stories, C.S. Lewis, Henry Treece, other historical novels, Shakespeare, Latin texts, Greek texts, Russian texts, political treatises, modern histories, school prizes, Dostoevsky. Under the shelves were piles of games, those also not to be touched. Once or twice Margaret glanced at them as the wife of Pastor Brand might have done. We didn't know where he was, nor precisely when to expect him. There had been a cable from Constantinople, asking for money. He had had to stop for days in an Anatolian village, that was all the hard news.

"Well," said Margaret, looking at the childhood room, "I think it's how he likes it, isn't it? I hope he will."

On the bright chilly April days we were listening for the telephone. But, while we were waiting for news of him, we received other news which we weren't waiting for: two other pieces of news for which we were utterly unprepared, arriving in the same twenty-four hours.

The first came in the morning post, among a batch of press cuttings. It was an article from a paper, which, though it was well known, I didn't usually read. The title was simply *Secret Society,* and at the first glance was an attack on the new government's "back-room pundits". There was nothing specially new in that. The government was already unpopular with the press: this paper was thought of as an organ of the centre, but a lot of abuse was coming from the centre. Like most people who had lived or written in public, I was used to the sight of my own name, I was at the same time reading and not-reading. Lord Getliffe. Mounteney. Constantine and Arthur Miles. Sir Walter Luke. Sir Lewis Eliot—

The writer didn't like us at all, not any of us. That didn't matter much. What did matter was that he had done some research. Some of his facts were wrong or twisted, but quite a number true. He had done some neat detective work on the meetings ("grey eminence" meetings) which we used to hold, through the years when the present government was in opposition, in Brown's Hotel. He reported in detail how Francis had been offered a post in October; he knew the time of Francis's visit to Downing Street, not only the day but the hour. But what made me angry was the simple statement that the same offer might soon be made to me.

Whatever I said, I shouldn't be believed, I told Margaret. No correction made any difference. That was an invariable rule of public life.

"It's a nuisance," she said.

"It's worse than that. If they were thinking of asking me, they wouldn't now."

"That doesn't matter, you know it doesn't."

"Even things I don't specially want, I don't like these people sabotaging. Which, of course, is the whole idea."

Margaret said—and it was true—that I was upset out of all proportion.

That afternoon, Margaret went out, and it was after tea-time before she joined me in the drawing-room. She looked at me: she knew, better than anyone, that my moods, once set, were hard for me to break, and that I had been regressing to the morning's news.

"I've got something else for you," she said.

I replied, without interest. "Have you?"

"I've been to see Muriel."

That didn't stir me. I said again: "Oh, have you?"

"She's got rid of Pat."

At last I was listening.

"She's got rid of him."

"Does she mean it?"

"Oh yes, she means it. It's for good and all."

Margaret said, she hadn't begun to guess. Nor had I. Nor, so far as we knew, had Azik or Rosalind. Possibly not the young man himself. It was true, Muriel had remained at Eaton Square, a couple of months now since the baby was born: but that seemed to us like a spoiled young woman who enjoyed being looked after. Not a bit of it. During that time she had, with complete coolness, telling no one except her solicitor, been organising the break. Her solicitor was to dispose of the Chelsea flat: he was to buy a house where she would take the baby. She had sent for Pat the evening before, just to tell him that she didn't wish to see him again and that an action for divorce would, of course, go through. So far as Margaret could gather, Muriel had been entirely calm during this interview, much less touched by Pat's entreaties, wiles, sorrows, and even threats than Margaret herself on a less critical occasion. It seemed to me strangely like Muriel's father disposing of a college servant. In a methodical, businesslike fashion she had, immediately he left, written him a letter confirming what she had just said.

"I've never seen anything like it," said Margaret.

We felt, for the moment, nothing but surprise. It was clear that Muriel had made her decision months ago, kept it to herself, not altered it by a tremor, and worked out her plans. She didn't seem heartbroken: she didn't even seem outraged: she just behaved as though she had had enough of him. As we talked, Margaret and I were lost, neither of us could give any kind of insight, or even rationalisation. Why had she married him? Had she been determined to escape from a possessive mother? Her life, until she was twenty, had been shielded, by the standards of the day. Rosalind was both worldly and as watchful as a detective, and it had been difficult for Muriel not to stay a virgin. Perhaps Pat had been the most enterprising young man round her. Certainly he had contrived to seduce her: but there might have been some contrivance on her part too, so that she became pregnant and stopped any argument against the marriage. Yet all that seemed too mechanical to sound true. Was she one of those who were sexually avid and otherwise cold? Somehow that didn't sound true either. Was it simply his running after women that made her tired of him? Or was that an excuse? She might have plans for the future, but if so those too she was keeping to herself. She might be looking for another husband. Alternatively, it seemed as likely that she had no use for men. Neither Margaret nor I would trust our judgment either way. She had her child, and that she must have wanted; Margaret said that in a singular manner, on the surface undisturbed, she was a devoted mother.

While we were still talking, still mystified—it must have

been getting on for seven—there were Italian cries, our housekeeper's, penetrating to us from rooms away, cries that soon we made out as excited greetings, which must have come from the front door. "Here he is! Here he is!" she was shouting, and Charles entered the room.

As Margaret embraced him, she broke out:

"Why didn't you let us know?"

"Anyway, I'm here."

He needed a shave, he was wearing a jacket, roll-top sweater, and dirty jeans. It was the first time I had seen him sunburnt, and he wasn't over-clean after the travel. He looked healthy but thin, his face, high cheekboned, masculine, already set in the pattern that would stay until he was old. He stretched out on the sofa, long feet protruding over the end.

I asked him to have a drink. After Islamic countries, he was out of practice, he said: yes, he would like a gin. He began to describe his route home: he wanted to hear, we were glad to have him there, we were trying to throw off the beginning of the day. He was in high spirits, like one who has made a good voyage. Suddenly he threw his legs off the sofa, sat up straight, gazed at me with alert eyes.

"You're looking sombre," he said.

Of Margaret and me, I was the one whose face he could read the quicker.

I said something evasive and putting off.

"You've got something on your mind."

I hesitated, said no again, and then reached out for the press-cutting.

"I suppose you'll have to see this sooner or later," I said as I handed it over.

With a scrutinising frown, Charles read, and gave a short deep curse.

"They're not specially fond of you, are they?"

"One thing I'm worried about," I said "is that all this may rebound on you."

"I shall have worse than that to cope with."

"It may be a drag—"

"Never mind that."

"Easier said than done," I told him.

"You're not to worry about me." Then he said, in an even tone:

"I told you years ago, didn't I, I won't be worried about." He said it as though it were a good-natured domestic jibe: that was ninety percent of the truth, but not quite all.

Then, he tapped the cutting, and said he hadn't read English newspapers for months until that day. He had got hold of the morning's editions on the way over. There was one impression that hit him in the eye: how parochial, how inward-looking, this country had become. Parish-pump politics. Politics looked quite different from where he had been living. "This isn't politics," he said, looking contemptuously at the cutting. "But it's how this country is behaving. If we're becoming as provincial as this, how do we get out of it?"

He was saying that vigorously, with impatience, not with gloom. In the same energetic fashion, he said:

"Well then, is that all the bad news for the present?"

That was an old family joke, derived from the time when he began to read Greek plays.

"The rest isn't quite so near home," I answered. "But still, it's bad news for someone. You tell him," I said to Margaret.

As he heard about Muriel, he was nothing like so impatient. He was concerned and even moved, more than we had been, to an extent which took us by surprise. So far as I knew, he had had little to do with his cousin, and both Pat and Muriel were five years older than he was. Yet he spoke about them as though they were his own kind. Certainly he did not wish to hear us blaming either of them. He didn't say one word of criticism himself. This was a pity—that was as far as he would go. Still with stored-up energy, poised on the balls of his feet, he declared that he would visit them.

"They might tell me more than they've told you," he said.

"Yes, they might," said Margaret. "But Carlo, I'm sure it's gone too far—"

"You can't be sure."

Margaret said that it was Muriel who had to be persuaded, and there weren't many people with a stronger will. Charles wasn't being argumentative, but he wouldn't give up: and, strangely enough, his concern broke through in a different place, and one which, taken by surprise, we had scarcely thought of.

"If they can't be stopped," he remarked, "it's going to be a blow for Uncle Martin, isn't it?"

There had always been sympathy between Martin and Charles, and in some ways their temperaments were similar, given that Charles's was the more highly charged. Charles knew a good deal about Martin's relation with his son, even though it was one that he wouldn't have accepted for himself and would, in Pat's place, have shrugged off. But now he was thinking of what Martin hoped for. Incidentally, where would Pat propose to live? The studio, where he had conscientiously worked at his painting, would be lost along with the Chelsea flat. But there Charles showed a spark of the irony which had for the past half-hour deserted him. He admitted that even he couldn't pretend that Pat was not a born survivor.

TEN

POSSIBLE HEAVENS

Through the following days and weeks, right into the early summer, there was plenty of to-ing and fro-ing—the bread-and-butter of a family trouble, trivial to anyone outside—of which I heard only at second or third hand. I knew that Pat had been to see Margaret two or three times, begging her to intercede, or, in his own phrase, "tell her I'm not so bad." Margaret had, I guessed, been kind and taken the edge off her tongue: but certainly she had told him there was nothing she could do.

Charles spent several evenings with both Muriel and Pat, but kept the secrets to himself, or at least from his mother and me. All I learned was that at one stage he invoked Maurice, at home for a weekend from the hospital. The two of them, and Pat's sister Nina, now studying music in London, met in Charles's room at our flat, and I believed that Maurice, who had an influence over his contemporaries, went out to make a plea, though to which of them I didn't know. One day Martin telephoned me, saying that he was in London and was having a conference with the Schiffs: he made an excuse for not coming to see me afterwards. That was a matter of pride, and it was just as I might have behaved myself.

On an afternoon early in June, I took Charles with me on one of my routine visits to his grandfather. In the taxi, I was warning Charles that he wasn't going to enjoy it: this wouldn't be like his last sight of my own father, comic in his own eyes, happy in his stuffy little room. He had been stoical because he didn't know any other way to be: while Austin Davidson was putting on the face of stoicism, but—without confessing it to anyone round him—was dying bitterly. I was warning Charles: in secret I was preparing myself for the next hour. For, though those visits might have seemed a drill by now, I couldn't get used to them. The cool words I had trained myself to, in reply to Davidson's, like rallies in a game of ping-pong: but there hadn't been one single visit when, as soon as I got out of the clinic into the undemanding air, I didn't feel liberated; as though solitariness and an inadmissible boredom, by the side of someone I admired, had been lifted from me. That was as true or truer, nearly a year later, as when I first saw him after his attempt at death.

In the sunny green-reflecting bedroom, Austin Davidson was in the familiar posture, head and shoulders on high pillows, looking straight in front of him, feet and ankles bare. He didn't turn his eyes, as the door opened. I said:

"I've brought Carlo to see you."

"Oh, have you?"

He looked round, and slowly from under the sheet drew out a thin hand, on which stood out the veins and freckles of old age. As Charles took it, he said:

"How are you, grandpa?"

Davidson produced a good imitation—perhaps it was more than that—of his old Mephistophelian smile.

"Well, Carlo, you wouldn't want me to tell you a lie, would you?"

Their eyes met. They each had the same kind of cheekbones. Even now, it was easy to see what Davidson had looked like as a young man. But, though I might be imagining it, I thought his face had become puffier these last few weeks; some of the bone structure, handsome until he was old, was being smeared out now.

Charles gave a smile, a smile of recognition, in return.

"Also," said Davidson, "you wouldn't like me to give you an honest answer either, don't you know?"

Charles gave the same firm smile again, and sat down by the bed, on the side opposite to me. For a while Austin Davidson seemed pleased with his own repartee, or, perhaps more exactly, with the performance he was putting up. Then he began to show signs, which I hadn't expected, of something like disappointment, as though he were a child who, out of good manners, couldn't protest at not being given a treat. That was a surprise, for he had, even in illness, displayed a liking for Charles, and had occasionally asked for his company. Not that Davidson had much family sense, few men less: but of his descendants and relatives, Charles, I fancied, appeared most like the young men Davidson had grown up with. Yet now he wished that Charles was out of the way.

Then, when Davidson couldn't resist a complaint: "I suppose it's too much to expect Carlo to take an intelligent interest—" I had it. Charles couldn't pick up the reference: but by now Davidson, always obsessive, had become addicted to our afternoon ritual, first what he called 'intelligent conversation' (that is, about the stock market), and then his reflections on dying. His interests had narrowed to that. It still seemed to me harrowing, that in that clinical room, afternoon following afternoon, we talked about stock exchange prices. I had to tell him what he had gained or lost by his last investment. It was purely symbolic: money had not mattered much to him, except as an intellectual game, and nothing could matter less now. Yet there was something triumphant about his interest, as though he had proved that one could be pertinacious to the end.

However, that afternoon, with Charles present, he was deprived. For a time he fell into silence, indrawn. Whether he was wondering if he ought to talk about death in front of Charles, I didn't know. Probably he didn't trouble himself. Austin Davidson used to feel, as only a delicate man could feel, that it was invariably wrong to be over-delicate. At any rate, after a while he produced a question.

"Carlo. If you believed in an afterlife, which by definition is impossible, which of the various alternatives so far proposed for the afterlife would you prefer?"

Davidson's sepia eyes were shining, as though gratified to be talking again.

"Meaning what in the way of alternatives?" Charles was good at catching the tone.

"Any that you've ever heard of."

Charles considered.

"They're all pretty dim," he said.

"Granted. There's not much to be said for the human imagination."

"I suppose there may be something outside this world—"

I thought, Charles wasn't used to the Edwardian brand of unbelief.

"That hasn't any meaning. No, people have always been inventing heavens. All ridiculous. Now you're asked to name the one you fancy."

Gazing at the old man, Charles realised that he had to play this game according to the rules.

"Well then," he said. "Valhalla."

Davidson gave a genuine smile.

"Not so good, Carlo. Just like a regimental mess."

"Good stories," said Charles.

"My God. Listening to rather stupid hearties talking about battles for all eternity."

"That would be better than listening to harps, wouldn't it?"

"I put it about equal. But all that boozing—"

Like nearly all his circle, Davidson had never gone in much for drink. I recalled, years before I met Margaret, being taken by a Cambridge friend to a party in Gordon Square. The hosts—we now knew from the biographies—intimates of Davidson's and brother Apostles. The thinking might have been high, but the entertainment was austere.

"One would get used to it after the first thousand years, I think."

They kept up the exchange, Charles doing his share as though this were a natural piece of chit-chat. Whether it cost him an effort, I couldn't be sure. His face was grave, but so it had to be to match Davidson's fancy, while Davidson's spirits, so long as they could go on talking, were lighter than I had felt them for weeks past. After the two of them had exhausted the topic of putative heavens, Davidson didn't relapse into the dark silence, when it seemed his eyes turned inward, that I had sat through so often in that room. Instead, and this was very rare, for even Margaret he scarcely mentioned when I visited him, he brought a new person into the conversation.

"Oh that young man, what's he called, your nephew—" he said to me, and I supplied the name. "Yes. He came in here the other day. He's been to see me once or twice, don't you know."

Yes, I knew.

"I gather he's having some sort of trouble with his wife."

It was an extraordinary place to come and confide, but Pat, I thought, wasn't above searching for comfort or allies anywhere.

I said that his wife had turned him out.

"Can't someone make her be sensible? It's all remarkably uncivilised."

His tone was stern and complaining. That was a word of

condemnation, one of the very few he ever used. He began to talk about his own friends. They tried to get the maximum of pleasure out of their personal relations. If this meant triangles or more complicated geometrical figures, well then, one accepted that too. Of course jealousy sometimes intruded: but jealousy had to be kept in its place. They believed in pleasure, said Davidson. If you didn't believe in pleasure, you couldn't be civilised.

Davidson wasn't wandering, I hadn't heard him do so since the first morning in the clinic. Lucidly he returned to his starting point. Muriel was being uncivilised. Of course, Pat might have gone in for a certain amount of old-fashioned adultery. What of it? He wanted to preserve the marriage.

"I should have thought," said Davidson, "that he was a man of fundamentally decent feeling."

I should have liked to discover what Charles made of that judgment. He had been listening with absorption to Davidson speaking of his friends: at Charles's age, though this was his grandfather talking, that period, that coterie, must already have passed into history and have seemed as remote, as preserved in time, as the pre-Raphaelites. Would they have a glamour for Charles? Or would he detest their kind of enlightenment, what Davidson had just called being 'civilised,' as much as his mother did?

We had stayed in the bedroom—I was used to looking at my watch below Davidson's eye-level in that room—half an hour longer than I set myself. But when I began to move, muttering the "Well—" which begins to set one free, he said he would like us to stay a little longer. He realised we were unlikely to share his opinion, he remarked with a flicker of the old devil, but he was having a mildly diverting afternoon.

ELEVEN

REPLICA OF A GROUP

It was getting on for a month later, on an afternoon when Margaret was taking her turn to visit Austin Davidson, that Azik Schiff rang up: would I call round at his house, he wanted (using an idiom known only to Azik) to include me in the picture.

High summer in Eaton Square, trees dense with foliage, leaves dark under the bright sun, car bonnets flashing. The major rooms in Azik's house were on the second floor, a kind of piano nobile, and there in the long drawing room, standing in front of his Renoir, Azik greeted me. He gave his face-splitting froglike smile, called me 'my friend,' put his arm round my shoulders, and conducted me to a sofa where Rosalind was sitting. Then there was conferring about whether it was too late for tea, or too early for a drink. Both of them, Azik in particular, were making more than their normal fuss of me, trying to wrap me round with warmth.

When we were settled down, welcomes insisted on, Azik put his hands on his thick thighs, and said, like one at home with negotiations:

"Lewis, my friend, you are not a principal in this matter. But we thought you ought to be informed."

"After all, you're his uncle, aren't you?" Rosalind said appeasingly, but as though raising an unnecessary doubt.

I said, I had heard so many rumours, I should be grateful for some facts.

"Ah, it is the young who have been talking."

"Not to me," I said.

"Your son is a fine young man."

I explained, I hadn't a clear idea what he had been doing.

"It makes no difference," said Azik. "It is all settled. Like that—" he swept his arm.

"She's as obstinate as a pig, she always was," said Rosalind.

Azik gave a brisk businesslike account. Nothing had affected Muriel. Not that that was different from what I had expected: I imagined that she had stayed polite and temperate all through. While others had been arguing with her, giving advice, making appeals, she had been quietly working with her solicitor. The Chelsea flat had been sold ("at a fair price," said Azik): she had bought a house in Belgravia, and moved into it, along with child and nurse, the day before. The transaction had gone through so fast that Azik assumed that it must have been started months ago.

"Remember, my friend, she is well provided for. She is independent with her money. We have no sanctions to use against her. Even if we were sure of our own ground."

All of a sudden, Rosalind went into a tirade, her face forgetting the gentility of years and her voice its dying fall. She began by being furious with her daughter. After all her, Rosalind's care. Not to be able to keep a man. To get into a mess like this. No gratitude. No consideration. Making her look like an idiot. But really she was being as protective, or as outraged at not being able to be so, as when her daughter was a child. Rosalind's sophistication had dropped clean away—her marriages, her remarkable talent for being able to love where it was advantageous to love, her climb from the suburbs of our native town to Eaton Square, her adventures on the way, all gone.

She had forgotten how she had campaigned to capture Muriel's father, who, when one came down to earth, had not been much more stable with women than Pat himself. As for Pat, Rosalind felt simple hate. Twister. Gigolo. Expecting to be paid for his precious—Rosalind's language, when she was calm, could be slightly suggestive, but now there was no suggestion about it. One comfort, he had got what was coming to him. Then he went whining round. Rosalind began to use words that Azik perhaps had never heard, and that I hadn't since I was young. Mardy. Mardyarse. How any child of hers, Rosalind shouted, could have been taken in by a drip like that—

"She has to make her own mistakes, perhaps," said Azik, in a tone soothing but not quite assured, as though this violence in his wife was a novelty with which he hadn't had much practice.

Rosalind: Who was she going to pick up next.
Azik: We have to try and put her in the way of some nice young men.
Rosalind: We've done that, since she was seventeen. And look what happens.
Azik: We have to go on trying. These young people don't like being managed. But perhaps there will be a piece of luck.
Rosalind: She'll pick another bit of rubbish.
Azik: We must try. As long as she doesn't know we're trying.

The dialogue went on across me, like an argument in the marriage bed, Rosalind accusing, Azik consolatory. It wasn't the first of these arguments, one felt: perhaps the others, like this, faded away into doldrums, when Azik, still anxious to placate his wife, had time to turn to me.

"There is something I have already said to Martin," he told me. "Now I shall say it to you, Lewis, my friend."

I looked at him.

"I should be sorry if this business of these young people made any break between your family and ours. I must say, I should be sorry. It will not happen from our side."

He spoke with great dignity. Uxorious as he was, he spoke as though that was his decision, and Rosalind had to obey. Loyally, making herself simmer down, she said that she and I had known each other for thirty years. On the other hand, I was thinking, I should be surprised if she went out of her way to meet Martin in the future.

Just after I had replied, telling him that I felt the same— I should have had to return politeness for politeness, but it happened to be true—young David ran into the room. He was a handsome boy, thin and active, one of those genetic sports who seemed to have no resemblance to either of his parents, olive-skinned. His father looked at him with doting love, and the boy spoke to both of them as though he expected total affection, and gave it back. He was just at the age when the confidence between all three was still complete, with nothing precarious in it, as though the first adolescent storm or secret would never happen. At his school his record was as good as Charles's had been at the same age, six years before. In some ways, I thought, this boy was the cleverer. It was a triumph for Rosalind, much disapproved of by persons who regarded her as a kind of Becky Sharp, to produce for Azik when she was well over forty a son like this.

As for me, watching (the bonds between the three of them were so strong there wasn't really room for an outsider there) the happiness of that not specially Holy Family, I couldn't have found it in me to begrudge it them. But I was thinking of something else. When they had been talking of Muriel, Rosalind had behaved in what Austin Davidson would have called an uncivilised fashion: in fact he would have thought her strident and coarse, and had no use for her. While Azik had been showing all the compassionate virtues.

Well, it was fine to be virtuous, but the truth was, Rosalind minded about her daughter and Azik didn't. To everyone round them, probably to his wife, possibly even to himself, he seemed a good stepfather, affectionate, sympathetic, kind. I had even heard him call himself a Jewish papa, not only in his relation to his son but to his stepdaughter. One had only to see him with that boy, though, to know what he was like as a father—and what he wasn't to Muriel. Of course he was kind to her, because there weren't many kinder men. He would do anything practical for her: if she had needed money, he would have been lavish. But as for thinking of her when she was out of his sight, or being troubled about her life, you had just to watch his oneness—animal oneness, spiritual oneness—with his son.

If that had not been so, if his imagination had been working, working fatherlike, on her behalf, it was unthinkable that he wouldn't have been more cautious about Pat. At the time (it had happened so quickly, we had all been puzzled that Pat came to know Muriel) I had thought he was taking Pat very easily. Yet Azik was no fool about people. He just wasn't truly interested, neither in Pat nor in the girl herself. If it had been a business deal, or even more anything concerned with Azik's son, Pat would never have slid inside the house. As it was, he got away with it: until he discovered, what no one had imagined, that the young woman was more ruthless than he was.

Which began to have other consequences we hadn't expected. As soon as they knew of Muriel's resolve, Charles, Maurice, and other friends of theirs had been working to bring about a reconciliation. There was a feeling, a kind of age-group solidarity, that Pat had to be helped. He was living in his father's house in Cambridge; occasionally he came to London, and we heard that he was lent money by some of the young people. Nevertheless, as the summer went on, he was—as it were insensibly—pushed to the edge of their group. One didn't hear any of them say a harsh word about him: but one ceased to hear him much talked about at all. Whereas Muriel one always saw, when, as occasionally they did, they invited older people to their parties.

Muriel's own house was modest but smart, the house of a prosperous young married couple, except for the somewhat anomalous absence of a husband. But, instead of entertaining there, she went to the bedsitting rooms in which most of that group lived, such as Nina's in Notting Hill. There seemed to be about a couple of dozen of them drifting round London that summer. Charles, waiting to go up to Cambridge, was the youngest, though some of the others had been at school with him. Young men and girls sometimes called in at our flat for a drink. They were friendly, both with an older generation and each other. They didn't drink as much as my friends used to, at their age: there were all the signs that they took sex much more easily. Certainly there didn't appear to be many tormented love affairs about. A couple of the girls were daughters of my own friends. I sometimes wondered, how much different was the way they lived their lives from their parents' way: was the gap bigger than other such gaps had been?

Often I was irritated with them, as though I were the wrong distance away, half involved, half remote: and it was Charles's self-control, not mine, which prevented us from quarrelling. He was utterly loyal to his friends and when I criticised them didn't like it: but he set himself to answer on the plane of reason.

All right, their manners are different from yours: but they think yours are as obsolete as Jane Austen's. If they don't write bread and butter letters, what of it? It is an absurd convention. If (as once happened) one of them writes on an envelope the unadorned address Lewis Eliot, again what of it?

He wouldn't get ruffled, and that irked me more. Take your friend Guy Grenfell, I said. They had been at school together. Guy was rich, a member of a squirearchical family established for centuries. He might grow his hair down to his shoulders, but once, when he came to an elderly dinner-party, he behaved like the rest of us, and more so. Yet when he was in the middle of their crowd, he appeared to be giv-ing a bad imitation of a barrow boy. Was this to show how progressive he was?

Charles would not let his temper show. Guy was quite en-lightened. Some of them were progressive—

I jeered, and threw back at him the record of Lester Ince and his *galère*. They were just as rude as your friends. Look where they finished. I brought out the old aphorism that when young men rebel against social manners, they end up by not rebelling against anything else.

We shall see, said Charles. Angry that I couldn't move him, I had let my advocacy go too far: but still, there were times when, unprovoked, I thought—are these really our successors? Will they ever be able to take over?

Those questions went through my mind when, one day in July, I received the news of George Passant's death. It had happened weeks before, I was told, very near the time that I had been having that family conference with Azik in Eaton Square. In fact, so far as I could make out the dates, George had had a cerebral hemorrhage the night before, and had died within twenty-four hours. This had taken place in a lit-tle Jutland town, where he had exiled himself and was being visited by one of his old disciples. Two or three more of his disciples, faithful to the last, had gone over for the funeral, and they had buried him in a Lutheran cemetery.

It might have seemed strange that it took so long for the news to reach me. After all, he had been my first benefactor and oldest friend. Yet by now he was separated from everyone but his own secret circle in the provincial town: while I, since my father's death, had no connections in the town any more. There was nothing to take me there, after I resigned from the University Court. It wasn't my father's death that cut me off, that was as acceptable as a death could be: but after the trial there were parts of my youth there that weren't acceptable at all, and this was true for Martin as well as for me. Some of those old scenes—without willing it, by something like a self-protecting instinct—we took care not to see. I still carried out my duty, George's last legacy, of visiting his niece in Holloway Prison. Occasionally I still had telephone calls, charges reversed, from Mr. Pateman, but even his obsessional passion seemed, not to have been spent, but at least after a year to be a shade eroded.

So far as I could tell, there had been no announcement of George's death, certainly not in a London paper. He had been a leader in a strange and private sense, his disciples must be mourning him more than most men are mourned, and yet, except for them, no one knew or cared where he was living, nor whether he was alive or dead.

I heard the news by telephone—a call from the town, would I accept it and reverse the charges? I assumed that it was Mr. Pateman, and with my usual worn-down irritation said yes. But it was a different voice, soft, flexible, excited, the voice of Jack Cotery. I had seen him only twice in the past ten years, but I knew that, though he had a job in Burnley, he still visited the town to see his mother, who was living in the same house, the same back street, whose existence, when we were young and he was spinning romantic lies about his social grandeur, he had ingeniously—and for some time with success—concealed. Had anyone told me about George, came the eager voice. He, Jack, had just met one of the set. The poor old thing was dead. Jack repeated the dates and such details as he had learned. Until George died, there was someone with him all the time: he knew what was happening, but couldn't speak.

"I don't know what he had to look forward to," Jack was saying. "But he loved life, in his own way, didn't he? I don't suppose he wanted to go."

To do Jack credit, he would have hurried to tell me the news, even if he hadn't had an ulterior motive. But that he had. The last time he visited me, he had been trying to convert me to organised religion. Now, over the telephone, he couldn't explain, it was very complicated, but he had another problem, very important, nothing bad, but something that mattered a very great deal—and it was very important, so, just to come out with it, could I lend him a hundred pounds? I said that I would send a cheque that evening, and did so. After what I had been listening to, it seemed like paying a last debt to the past.

Guy Grenfell and other companions of Charles were in the flat, and as I joined them for a drink, I mentioned that I had just heard of the death of an old friend. Who, said Charles, and I told him the name. It meant nothing to the others, but Charles had met George year after year, on his ritual expeditions to London. Charles's eyes searched into my expression. "I'm sorry," he said. But, though he had never told me so, he was too considerate for that, I was certain that in secret he had found George nothing but grotesque. Diffidence. Formality. Heartiness. Repetitive questions ("Are you looking after your health?"). Flashes of mental precision. Slow-walking, hard-breathing figure, often falling asleep in an armchair, mouth open. Once, coming in drunk, he had fallen off a chair. That was what Charles had seen, and not many at his age would have seen more. He could not begin to comprehend the effect that George had once had on me and my first friends.·

The irony was, that the 'freedoms' George—and all the other Georges of his time—had clamoured for, had more or less come true. The life that Charles's own friends were leading was not that much different from what George had foreshadowed all those years ago. A lot of the young men and girls in the Earl's Court bedsitters would have fitted, breathing native air, into George's group. Gentle. Taking their pleasures as they came. Not liking their society any more than George had done. Making their own enclaves. The passive virtues, not the fighting ones. Not much superego (if one didn't use older words). The same belief, deep down, that most people were good.

That would not suit Charles for long, any more than it had suited me. And yet it had its charm. It seemed at times like an Adamic invention, as though no one had discovered a private clan-life before. That was true even with the more strenuous natures among them, like his own. It might have been true, I thought, of Muriel.

So much so that when some weeks after the news about George, to whom I didn't refer again—I told Charles that his friends went in for enclave-making, just as much as the bourgeois they despised, he didn't like it. Once more he felt curiously protective about his whole circle, more so than I remembered being. But he was still not prepared to quarrel; and he suspected there might be something in what I said. He had also seen more subsistence poverty than any of us. All over the advanced world, people seemed to be making enclaves. I thought that wasn't just a fantasy of my own. The rich, like Azik and some of our American friends: the professionals everywhere: the apparently rebellious young: they were all drawing the curtains, looking inwards into their own rooms, to an extent that hadn't happened in my time.

The demonstrations (that was the summer when the English young, including Charles's friends, started protesting about Vietnam), the acts of violence, were deceptive. They too came from a kind of enclave. They were part of a world which, though it could be made less comfortable, or more foreboding, no one could find a way to shake.

Charles listened carefully. This wasn't an argument, though I had touched on the rift of difference between us. Since he had left school and gone on his new-style grand tour, he had been released, happy, and expectant. Inside the family, we had no more cares, possibly less, than most of our own kind. It had been an easy summer, with time to meet his friends and our own. Except that we had to be ready for the death of Margaret's father, we had nothing that seemed likely to disturb us, not even an examination or a book coming out.

"How many of your prophesies have gone wrong?" said Charles, without edge, with detachment.

"Quite a few."

"How right were you in the Thirties?"

"Most of the time we (I was thinking of Francis Getliffe and others) weren't far off. Anyway, a lot of it is on the record."

"In the war? What did you think would be happening now?"

I paused.

"There I should have been wrong. I thought that, if Hitler could be beaten, then things would go much better than in fact they have."

"I hope," said Charles, "that you turn out wrong again. After all, some of us might see the end of the century, mightn't we?"

He gave a smile, meaning that he and his friends by that time would only be middle-aged.

TWELVE

RESULT OF AN OFFER

The Lords were having a late-night sitting, Francis told me over the telephone (it was the last week in October), a committee stage left over from the summer. He would be grateful if Margaret and I would go along and have supper with him there, just to help him through the hours. Yes, we were free: and it was conceivable that Francis wanted more than sheer company, for one of the political correspondents (not our enemy of the spring) had that morning reported that Lord Getliffe had been called to Downing Street the day before. The same correspondent added with total confidence that S————, the old commons loyalist who had been given the job when Francis previously refused it, would be going within days. He was being looked after—a nice little pension on one of the nationalised boards.

It sounded like inside information. Just as Hector Rose and my old colleagues used to ask in Whitehall, often with rage, I wondered how ever it got out. Possibly from S———— himself. Politicians, old Bevill used to say, were the worst keepers of secrets. They will talk to their wives, he added with Polonian wisdom. He might have said, just as accurately, they will talk to journalists: and the habit seemed to be hooking them more every year, like the addiction to a moderately harmless drug.

As we came out of Westminster underground, the light

was shining over Big Ben, there was a smell—foggy? a tinge, or was one imagining it, of burning wood?—in the smoky autumn air. Francis, waiting for us in the peers' entrance, kissed Margaret and led us up the stairs, over the Jonah's whale carpets, straight to the restaurant; we were rescuing him, he said, the parliamentary process could be remarkably boring unless you were brought up to it, man and boy. In fact, he was already occupying a table, one of the first to establish himself, though some men, without guests, were walking through to the inner room. Under the portraits, under the tapestries, taste following the Prince Consort, I noticed one or two faces I vaguely knew, part of a new batch of life peers. Not then, but a little later, when we were settling down to our wine and cold roast beef, there came a face that I more than vaguely knew—Walter Luke, grizzled and jaunty, saying, "I didn't expect to see you here, Lew," as he passed on. It would have been a fair reply that, a short time before, no one would have expected to see *him* there. But here he was, as though in honour of science—and, because there already existed a Lord Luke, here he was as Lord Luke of Salcombe.

Francis, who had always been fond of Walter Luke, was saying, once he had got out of hearing, that no one we knew had been unluckier, no one of great gifts, that was. If things had gone right, he would have done major scientific work. But all the chances, including the war, had gone against him. After which, said Francis, he got this curious consolation prize.

Yet Walter had seemed in highish spirits. As the room filled up, no more divisions till half-past eight, most people seemed in highish spirits. Greetings, warm room, food, a certain amount of activity ahead, the kind of activity which soothed men like a tranquiliser. For an instant, I recollected my conversation with Charles in the summer. Enclaves. Perhaps it was right, it was certainly natural, for any of us to hack out what refuges we could, some of the time: none of us was tough enough to live every minute in the pitiless air. This was an enclave in excelsis.

As the noise level rose, and no one could overhear, I asked Francis if he had seen the paragraph about him that morning.

"I was going to tell you about that," he said.

"How true is it?"

"Not far off."

I asked: "So S———— is really going?"

"To be more accurate, he's actually gone."

"And you?"

"Of course, I had to say what I did before. I had to tell him I'd made up my mind."

That was what I expected.

The Prime Minister had been good, said Francis. He hadn't pressed too much. But after S————, he needed someone with a reputation abroad. Francis added:

"I think you'd better make up your own mind, pretty quickly."

After our talk the previous autumn, that also wasn't entirely unexpected, either to Margaret or me. Despite the attempt to forestall it. There weren't many of us who had this sort of special knowledge: and even fewer who had used it in public. One could make a list, not more than three or four, of men likely to be asked. It might have sounded arrogant, or even insensitive, for Francis to assume that he was No. 1 on the list, and the rest of us reserves. But it didn't sound so to Margaret or me. This wasn't a matter of feeling, about which Francis had been delicate all our lives: it was as objective as a batting order. He was a scientist of international reputation, and the only one in the field. His name carried its own authority with the American and Soviet scientists.

That was true of no one else. He would have been a major catch for the government, which was, of course, why they had come back to him. Now, as he said, they had to fill the job quickly. It would do them some harm if they seemed to be hawking it round.

"Well, that's that," he said, dismissing the subject. He was so final that I was puzzled, and to an extent put out. After those hints, it seemed bleak that he should turn quite unforthcoming. I glanced at Margaret and didn't understand.

Within a short time, however, we were talking intimately again, the three of us. Getting us out of the dining-room early, Francis, with tactical foresight, was able to secure window seats in the bar: there we sat, as the debate continued, the bar became more populated, the division bell rang, and Francis left us for five minutes and returned. That went on —the division bell interrupted us twice more—until after midnight, and in the casual hubbub Francis was telling us some family information we hadn't heard, and asking whether there was any advice he could give his eldest son.

It was one of the oldest of stories. A good many young women might have wondered why Leonard Getliffe hadn't come their way. He was the most brilliant of the whole Getliffe family, he had as much character as his father, to everyone but one girl he was fun. And that one girl was pleasant, decent but not, to most of us, exciting. He had been in love with her for years. He was in his thirties, but he loved her obsessively, he couldn't think of other women, in a fashion which seemed to have disappeared from Charles's circle once they had left school. Whereas she could give him nothing: because she was as completely wrapped up in, of all people, my nephew Pat.

When Pat had deserted her and married Muriel, the girl Vicky (she wasn't all that young, she must now be twenty-six) had—so Francis now told us—at least not discouraged

Leonard from getting in touch with her again. Since I hadn't
visited Vicky and her father since my own father's death,
that was some sort of news, but it was commonplace and natural enough.

"I must say, of course I'm prejudiced," Francis broke out,
"but I must say that she's treated him pretty badly."

Margaret, who knew Vicky and liked her, said yes, but it
wasn't very easy for her—

"I mean," said Francis, "she never ought to have done
that. Unless she was trying to make a go of it."

Margaret said, she mightn't know which way to turn.
There were plenty of good women who behaved badly when
they were faced with a passion with which they didn't know
how to cope.

"If I thought she was really trying—" Then Francis let
out something quite new. In the last couple of months, perhaps earlier than that, Pat had been seen with her.

None of the young people had got on to that. Yet, the moment we heard it, it seemed that we ought to have predicted
it. Vicky was a doctor, she could earn a living, she would
keep him if he needed it. Further, perhaps even Pat wasn't
just calculating on his bed and food: perhaps even he wasn't
infinitely resilient, and after Muriel wanted someone who set
him up in his self-esteem again; after all that, he might just
want to be loved.

But at that time I wasn't feeling compassionate about my
nephew. Like other persons as quicksilver sympathetic as he
could be, as ready to expend himself enhancing life, he had
been showing an enthusiasm for revenge just as lively as his
enthusiasm for making others cheerful: and he had been
searching for revenge against Margaret, feeling, I supposed,
that she had done him harm. Anyway he had spread a story
which was meant to give Margaret pain. Whether he believed
it, or half-believed it, I couldn't decide. He had one of those

imaginations, high-coloured, melodramatic, and malicious, that made it easy to believe many things. The story was that, hearing Austin Davidson talk of his "sources of supply," the people who had provided him with drugs to kill himself, Pat had found out their names. They were Maurice and Charles.

To most of us, this bit of gossip wouldn't matter very much: probably not to the young men themselves. But I knew, it was no use being rational where reason didn't enter, that it would matter to Margaret. To her it would be something like a betrayal, both by her father and her sons. She would feel that she had lost them all. Maybe Pat also knew what she would feel.

For the time being, I stopped the story from reaching Margaret, which didn't make me think more kindly of Pat, for it meant both some tiresome staffwork, and also my being less than open with her. So I had to get the truth from Davidson himself before she found out. That, in itself, meant a harsh half-hour. By this time he seemed to be failing from week to week: unless he led the conversation, it was hard to get him to attend. I had to force upon him that this was a family trouble, and might bring suffering for Margaret. He was silent, a long distance from family troubles or his daughter's pain. For the first time in all those visits, I broke into his silence. He must trust me. He must make an effort. Who had given him the drugs?

At last Davidson said, without interest, that he had made a promise not to tell. That threw me back. I had never known him break a confidence: he wouldn't change his habit now. After a time, I asked, would he answer two questions in the negative. He gazed at me without expression. Had it been Maurice? With irritation, with something like boredom, Davidson shook his head. Had it been Charles? The same expression, the same shake of the head. (On a later visit, when he was less collected, I was led to infer that the

truth was what we might have expected: the "source of supply" had nothing to do with any of the family, but was an
old friend and near-contemporary of his called Hardisty.)

So that had been settled. Nevertheless, when Francis
brought in the name of my nephew, it took some effort to be
dispassionate. There were few things I should have liked
more that night than to say we could all forget him. There
was one thing I should have liked more, and that was to believe that Vicky and Leonard would get married out of
hand.

Francis asked us point-blank:

"Does he stand a chance?"

Margaret and I glanced at each other, and I was obliged to
reply, in the angry ungracious tone with which one kills a
hope:

"I doubt it."

Apparently Leonard, the least expansive of Francis's children and the one he loved the most, had come to his father
with a kind of oblique appeal—ought he to take a job at the
Princeton Institute? That wasn't a professional question:
Leonard could name his own job anywhere: he was mutely
asking—it made him seem much younger than he was—
whether it was all hopeless and he ought at last to get away.

"You really think that she'll go back—to that other one?"

"I'm afraid so." She would not only go back, she would
run to him, the first time he cricked a finger. Knowing (but
also not-knowing, as one does in an obsessive love) everything
about him. On any terms. She was worth a hundred of Pat,
Margaret was saying. On any terms. Nothing would stop her.
Would we try to stop her, if we could? It was not for me to
talk. I had taken Sheila, my first wife, on terms worse than
any this girl would get. I had done wrong to Sheila when I
did so: that I had known at the time, and knew now without
concealment, after half a lifetime. But if I could have

stopped myself, granted absolute free will, should I have done so?

Even now, after half a lifetime, I wasn't certain. If I had made the other choice, despite the suffering, despite the years of something like maiming, I might have been less reconciled. And that, I thought, could very well prove true for this young woman. If she married Pat (which I regarded as certain, since he wasn't exactly a spiritual athlete and wouldn't give up his one patch of safe ground) she would go through all the torments of a marriage without trust. If she didn't, she would go through another torment, missing—whoever else she married—what she couldn't help wanting most of all. No, I wouldn't have stopped her. She might even come out of it better than he did. Sometimes there were ironies on the positive side, one of them being that the faithful were often the more strongly sexed and in the end got the more fun.

It wasn't often that Francis, who had gone to extreme trouble about our children or Martin's (in his cheerful patriarchal home he loved to entertain, and it was there, as a bad joke, that Vicky, staying as a guest of Leonard's, had first met and fallen for Pat), had come for any sort of comfort about his own. But sometimes the kind liked to receive kindness, and he didn't want us to leave until the house was up.

In the taxi, as it purred up the midnight-smooth tarmac, under the trees to Hyde Park Corner, Margaret was saying, what a bloody mess. That triangle, Vicky, Leonard, Pat. People anything like Pat—even if they were more decent than he was—always did more destruction than anyone else. She broke off: "Was Francis sounding you out? Early on. Was he really making you the offer? Had they asked him to?"

No, I said, I didn't think it would be done like that.

"Anyway, I hope it doesn't happen; you know that, don't you?"

That was all she said, before returning to brisk comments upon Pat.

It did happen, and it happened very fast. Late the following night, just as we were thinking it was time for bed, the telephone rang. Private secretary at Downing Street. Apologies, the sharp civil servant's apologies that I used to hear, from someone whom I used to meet. Could I come along at once? Logistic instructions. I was to be careful not to use the main entrance. Instead, I was to go in through the old Cabinet Offices in Whitehall. There would be an attendant waiting at the door.

It all sounded strangely, and untypically, conspiratorial. Later I recalled what Francis had said about "hawking the job round": they were taking precautions against another visitor being spotted: hence, presumably, this Muscovite hour, hence the eccentric route. The secretary had asked whether I knew the old office door, next to the Horseguards. Better than he did, it occurred to me, as I went through the labyrinth to the Cabinet room: for it was in the room adjoining the outside door, shabby, coal-fire smoking, that I used to work with old Bevill at the beginning of the war.

I was back again, going past the old offices into Whitehall, within twenty minutes. Time, relaxed time, for the offer and one drink. I had asked, and obtained, forty-eight hours to think it over. Outside, Whitehall was free and empty, as it had been in wartime darkness, when the old minister and I had been staying late and walked out into the street, sometimes exhilarated because we had won a struggle or perhaps because of good news on the scrambled line.

When I opened the door of our drawing-room, Margaret, who was sitting with a book thrown aside, cried out:

"You haven't been long!"

Then she asked me, face intent:

"Well?"

I said, cheerful, buoyed up by the night's action:

"It's exactly what we expected."

Margaret knew as well as I did the appointment which Francis had turned down: and that this was it.

She said:

"Yes. I was afraid of that."

For once, and at once, there was strain between us. She was speaking from a feeling too strong to cover up, which she had to let loose however I was going to take it. She had been preparing herself for the way in which I should take it: if you didn't quarrel often, quarrels were more dreaded. But even then she couldn't—and in the end didn't wish—to hold back.

"What's the matter?" I was put out, more than put out, angry.

"I don't want you to make a mistake—"

"Do you think I've decided to take the job?" I had raised my voice, but hers was quiet, as she replied:

"Haven't you?"

It had never been pleasant when we clashed. I didn't like meeting a will as strong as my own, though hers was formed differently from mine, hers hard and mine tenacious: just as her temper was hot and mine was smouldering. Also I didn't like being judged—some of my secret vanity had gone by now, but not quite all, the residual and final vanity of not liking to be judged by the one who knew me best.

Just to add an edge to it, I thought that she was misjudging me that night. Not dramatically, only slightly—but still enough. It was true—she had heard me amuse myself at others' expense as they solemnly professed to wonder whether they should accept a job they had been working towards for years—that most decisions were taken on the spot. When one asked for time to 'sleep on it,' old Arthur Brown's imme-

morial phrase, when one asked for the forty-eight hours
grace of which I was bad-temperedly telling Margaret—one
was, nine times out of ten, ninety-nine times out of a
hundred, merely enjoying the situation or alternatively
searching for rationalisations and glosses to prettify a decision which was already made.

That wasn't quite the case with me that night. I had in
my mind all the reasons why I should say no. So far Margaret was wrong. But only a little wrong. What I wanted was
for her to join in dismissing those reasons, take it all lightly,
and push me, just a fraction, into saying yes.

Reasons against—they were the same for me as for Francis, and perhaps by this time a shade stronger. He had said
that he couldn't do much—or any—good. I was as convinced of that as he was, whoever did the job: more so because I had lived inside the government apparatus, as he had
never done. That hadn't made me cynical, exactly (for cyni-
cism came only to those who were certain they were superior
to less splendid mortals): but it had made me Tolstoyan, or
at least sceptical of the effect that any man could have, not
just a junior minister, but anyone who really seemed to possess the power, by contrast to the tidal flow in which he
lived. Some sort of sense about nuclear armaments might
one day arise: what Francis and David Rubin and the rest of
us had said, and within our limits done, might not have
been entirely useless: but the decisions—the apparent decisions, the voices in cabinets, the signatures on paper—would
be taken by people who couldn't avoid taking them, because
they were swept along, unresisting, on the tide. The tide
which we had failed to catch.

That wasn't a reason for not acting. In fact, Francis and
his colleagues believed—and so did I—that, in the times
through which we had lived, you had to do what little you
could in action, if you were to face yourself at all. But it was

a reason, this knowledge we had acquired, for not fooling ourselves: for not pretending to take action, when we were one hundred percent certain that it was just make-believe. If you were only ninety percent certain, then sometimes you hadn't to be too proud to do the donkey work. But, if you were utterly certain, then pretending to take action could do harm. It could even drug you into feeling satisfied with yourself.

By this time, our certainties had hardened, that nothing useful could be done in this job. The year before, when Francis was offered it, we thought we had known all about the limits of government. We had flattered ourselves. The limits were tighter than self-styled realistic men had guessed. Azik Schiff couldn't resist saying that he had warned us about social democracies. Vietnam was hag-riding us. Bitterly Francis said that a country couldn't be independent in foreign policy if it wasn't independent in earning its living. That remark had been made in the presence of some of Charles's friends, and had scandalised them. To many of us, the window of public hope, which had seemed clearer for a few years past, was being blacked out now.

All this was objective, and I didn't need so much as mention it to Margaret. Nor the other reason against, which was more compelling than with Francis. He had his research to do, and I had my writing. He had the assurance that any good scientist possessed, that some of what he had done was right (it was no use quibbling about epistemological terms; in the here-and-now, in Francis's own existence that was so). No writer had that assurance: but, exactly as his work was a private comfort, no, more than comfort, justification, so was mine. And—this was a difference between us—I had more to finish than he had, perhaps because I had started later. I had never liked talking about my books, and should never have considered writing anything about my literary life. I had had my joys and sorrows, like any other writer. In fact, most writing lives were more alike than different, which made one's own not specially interesting, except to oneself. After all, the books were there.

However, quite as much as ever in my life, as much as in the middle of the war, this preoccupation remained with me. It had been steady all through, it hadn't lost any of its strength. In the middle of the war, I had been a youngish man, I hadn't the sense of losing against time. I had been too busy to write anything sustained, but I could, last thing at night, read over my notebooks and add an item or two. It had been like going into a safe and quiet room. If I took this job, I could do the same, but I wasn't youngish now. I should have liked to count on ten years more to work in.

Ten years with good luck. Margaret knew that was what I was hoping for. She couldn't bring herself to talk about my life span. She did say that this would mean time away from writing. Francis, she forced herself to say, had talked about a year or two in office: and he had said that he couldn't afford a year or two. She didn't ask a question, she made the statement in a flat, anxious tone, the lines deep across her forehead.

Yes, in every aspect but one, Francis and I were in the same situation, or near enough not to matter. So that the answer should also be the same. There was just one difference. I should like to do the job. I should enjoy it. It was that, precisely that, which Margaret hated.

She had been utterly loyal throughout our married life. She had tried not to constrict me, even when I was doing things, or showing a vein within myself, which she would have liked to wipe away. It wasn't that she thought that I was an addict of power. If that had been so, she felt that I should have acquired it. And she had learned enough by now to realize that this job I had been offered carried no power at all: and that the more you penetrated that world, the more you wondered who had the power, or whether anyone had, or whether we weren't giving to offices a free will that those who held them could never conceivably possess.

Nevertheless, she would have liked me to be nowhere near it. Her own principles, her own scrupulousness, couldn't have lived in that world, any more than her father's could. She despised, as much as he did, or his friends, the people who got the jobs, who were ready to scramble, compromise, muck in. She couldn't accept, she resented my accepting, that any society under heaven would need such people. She was put off by my interest, part brotherly, part voyeuristic, in them—in the Lufkins, the Roger Quaifes, even my old civil service colleagues, who were nearer in sympathy to her. When I told her that they had virtues not given to her father's friends, or to her, or to me, she didn't wish to hear.

"It's all second rate," she had said before, and said again that night.

Here was I, out of spontaneity (for, though I had trained myself into some sort of prudence, I was still a spontaneous man), or just for the fun or hell of it, ready to plunge in. I should even have enjoyed fighting a by-election: but that wasn't on, no government with a majority of three could risk it. Anyway, if I said yes, I should enjoy making speeches from the dispatch-box in the Lords.

To her, who loved me and in many ways admired me—and wanted to admire me totally—it seemed commonplace and vulgar. As our tempers got higher, she used those words.

"That's no news to you," I said.

"Yes, it is."

"In your sense, I am vulgar."

"I won't have that."

"You've got to have it. If you mean that I'm not superior to the people round us, then of course I'm vulgar."

"I don't want you to behave like them, that's all."

The quarrel went on, and I, because I was not only angry

but raw with chagrin (on the way home, I had been expecting a bit of applause, ironic applause maybe: she spoke
about temptation, but she might, so I felt, have granted me
that this particular temptation didn't come to all that many
men), was having the worst of it. I betrayed myself by bringing up an argument which in my own mind I had already
negated: the necessity for action, for any halfway decent man
in our own time. I even quoted Hammarskjöld at her,
though none of us would have used his words. She looked at
me with sad lucidity.

"You've been sincere in that, I know," she said. "But
you're not being sincere now, are you?"

"Why not?"

"Because this isn't real, as you know perfectly well. It isn't
going to be any use, and if it were anyone else you'd be the
first to say so."

Since that was precisely what in detachment I had
thought, I was the more angry with her.

"Well," she said at last, without expression, "I take it that
you are going to accept."

I sat sullen, keeping back the words. Then I crossed over
to the sideboard and poured myself a drink, the first either
of us had had since I returned. Once more I sat opposite to
her, and spoke slowly and bitterly (it was a conflict that neither of us had the language for, after twenty years).

I said, that if anything could have made me decide to accept that night, it was her argument against. But she might
do me one minor credit: I hadn't lost all my capacities. It
would be better to decide as though she had said nothing
whatever. There were serious arguments against, though not
hers. I should want some sensible advice, from people who
weren't emotionally committed either way. There I was
going to leave it, for that night.

It was already early morning, and we lay in bed, unrecon-
ciled.

THIRTEEN

ADVICE

As we were being polite to each other at breakfast, I repeated to Margaret that I should have to take some advice. She glanced at me with a glint which, even after a quarrel, wasn't entirely unsarcastic. One trouble was, I had made too many cracks about others: how many times had she listened to me saying that persons in search of advisers had a singular gift for choosing the right ones? That is, those who would produce the advice they wanted to hear.

No, I said, as though brushing off a comment, I thought of calling on old Hector Rose. He knew this entire field of government backwards: he was a friendly acquaintance, not even specially well disposed: he would keep the confidence, and was as cool as a man could reasonably be.

Margaret hadn't expected that name. She gave a faint grin against herself. All she could say was that he would be so perfectly balanced that I might as well toss up for it.

When I telephoned Hector at the Pimlico flat, his greetings were ornate. Pleasure at hearing my voice! Surprise that I should think of him! Cutting through the ceremonial, I asked if he were free that morning: there was a matter on which I should like his opinion. Of course, came the beautiful articulation, he was at my disposal: not that any opinion of his could be of the slightest value—

He continued in that strain, as soon as I arrived in their

sitting-room. He was apologising for his wife and himself, because she wasn't there to receive me, to her great disappointment, but in fact she had to go out to do the morning's shopping. As so often in the past, facing him in the office, I felt like an ambassador to a country whose protocol I had never been properly taught or where some customs had just been specially invented in order to baffle me. I said: "What I've come about—it's very private."

He bowed from the waist: "My dear Lewis."

"I want a bit of guidance."

Protestations of being at my service, of total incompetence and humility. At the first pause I said that it was a pleasant morning (the porticos opposite were glowing in the autumn sunshine): what about walking down to the garden by the river? What a splendid idea, replied Hector Rose with inordinate enthusiasm—but first he must write a note in case his wife returned and became anxious. Standing by my side, he set to work in that legible italic calligraphy. I could not help seeing, I was meant to see.

Darling, I have gone out for a short stroll with Sir L. Eliot (the old Whitehall usage which he had inscribed on his minutes, often, when we were disagreeing, with irritation). *I shall, needless to say, be back with you in good time for luncheon. Abiding love. Your H.*

It was so mellow out-of-doors, leaves spiralling placidly down in calm air, that Hector did not take an overcoat. He was wearing a sports coat and grey flannel trousers, as he might have done as an undergraduate at Oxford in the Twenties. Now that we were walking together, it occurred to me that he was shorter than he had seemed in his days of eminence: his stocky shoulders were two or three inches below mine. He was making conversation, as though it were not yet suitable to get down to business: his wife and he had been to a concert the night before: they had an agreement, he found it delectable to expatiate on their domestic ritual, to get out of the flat two evenings a week. The danger was, they had both realised when they married—Hector reported this ominous fact with earnestness—that they might tend to live too much in each other's pockets.

It was like waiting for a negotiation to begin.

When we turned down by the church, along the side of the square towards the river, I jerked my finger towards one of the houses. "I lived there during the war," I said. "When I was working for you."

"How very remarkable! That really is most interesting!" Hector, looking back, asked exactly where my flat had been, giving a display of excitement that might have been appropriate if I had shown him the birthplace of Einstein.

We arrived at the river-wall. The water was oily smooth in the sun, the tide high. There was the sweet and rotting smell that I used to know, when Margaret and I stood there in the evenings, not long after we first met.

On one of the garden benches an elderly man in a straw hat was busy transcribing some figures from a book. Another bench was empty, and Hector Rose said: "I'm inclined to think it's almost warm enough to sit down, or am I wrong, Lewis?"

Yes, it was just like one of his negotiations. You didn't press for time and in due course the right time came. The official life was a marathon, not a sprint, and one stood it better if one took it at that tempo. People who were impatient, like me, either didn't fit in or had to discipline themselves.

Now it was time, as Hector punctiliously brushed yellow leaves from off the seat, and turned towards me. I told him of the job—there was no need to mention secrecy again, or give any sort of explanation—and said, as usual curt because he wasn't, what about it?

"I should be obliged if you'd give me one or two details,"
said Hector. "Not that they are likely to affect the issue. But
of course I am quite remarkably out of things. Which department would this 'supernumerary minister' be attached
to?" The same as S————, I said. Attentively Hector inclined his head. "As you know, I always found the arrangements that the last lot (the previous government) made
somewhat difficult to justify in terms of reason. And I can't
help thinking that, with great respect, your friends are even
worse, if it is possible, in that respect."

'This minister' would have a small private office, and otherwise would have to rely on the department? A floating,
personal appointment? "Not that that is really relevant, of
course."

He was frowning with concentration, there was scarcely a
hesitation. He looked at me, eyes unblinking, arms folded on
his chest. He said:

"It's very simple. You're not to touch it."

When he came to the point, Hector, who used so many
words, liked to use few. But he didn't often use so few as
this.

Jolted, disappointed (more than I had allowed for), I said,
that was pretty definite, what was he thinking of?

"You're not immortal," said Hector, in the same bleak,
ungiving tone. "You ought to remember that."

We gazed at each other in silence.

He added:

"Granted that no doubt unfortunate fact, you have better
things to do."

He couldn't, or wouldn't, say anything more emollient.
He would neither expand his case, nor withdraw. We had
never been friendly, and yet perhaps that morning he would
have liked to be. Instead, he broke off and remarked, with
excessive pleasure, what a beautiful morning it was. Had I

ever seen London look so peaceful? And what a kind thought it was for me to visit a broken-down civil servant! As usual with Hector's flights of rhapsody and politeness, this was turning into a curious exercise of jeering at himself and me.

There was nothing for it. Very soon I rose from the bench —the old man in the straw hat was still engrossed in esoteric scholarship—and said that I would walk back with Hector to his flat. He continued with mellifluous thanks, apologies, compliments, and hopes for our future meetings. The functional part of the conversation had occupied about five minutes, the preamble half an hour, the coda not quite so long.

When I returned home, Margaret, who was sitting by the open window, looking over the glimmering trees, said:

"Well, you saw him, did you?"

Yes, I replied.

"He wouldn't commit himself, would he?"

No, I said, she hadn't been quite right. He hadn't been specially noncommittal.

"What did he think?"

"He was against it."

I didn't tell her quite how inflexibly so, though I was trying to be honest. Then the next person I turned to for advice didn't surprise her. This was what she had anticipated earlier in the morning. It was my brother Martin, and I knew, and she knew that I knew, on which side he was likely to come down. That proved to be true, as soon as I got on the line to Cambridge. Why not have a go? I needn't do it for long. It would be a mildly picturesque end to my official career. Martin, the one of us who had made a clearcut worldly sacrifice, kept—despite or because of that—a relish for the world. He also kept an eye on practical things. Had I reckoned out how much money I should lose if I went in? The drop in income would be dramatic: no doubt I could stand it for a finite time. Further—Martin's voice sounded thoughtful, sympathetic—couldn't I bargain for a slightly better job? They could upgrade this one, it was a joker appointment anyway, ministers of state were a fairly lowly form of life, that wasn't quite good enough, he was surprised they hadn't wanted Francis or me at a higher level. Still—

Margaret, who had been listening, asked, not innocently, whether those two, Hector Rose and Martin, cancelled each other out. I was as noncommittal as she expected Rose to be, but to myself I thought that my mind was making itself up. Then, not long afterwards, we were disturbed again. A telephone call. A government back-bencher called Whitman. Not precisely a friend, but someone we met at parties.

"What's all this I hear?"

"I don't know what you mean," I replied.

"Come on. You're being played for, you know you are."

"I don't understand—"

"Now, now, of course you do."

In fact, I didn't. Or at least I didn't understand where his information came from. Was it an intelligent bluff? The only people who should have known about this offer were the private office, Margaret, Hector Rose, Martin. They were all as discreet as security officers. I had the feeling, at the same time euphoric and mildly paranoid, of living at the centre of a plot, microphones in the sitting-room, telephones tapped.

More leading questions, more passive denials and stonewalling at my end.

"You haven't given your answer already, have you?"

"What is there to give an answer to?"

"Before you do, I wish you'd have dinner with me. Tonight, can you make it?"

He was badgering me like an intimate, and he had no claim to.

I said that I had nothing to tell him. He persisted: "Anyway, do have dinner with me." Out of nothing better than curiosity, and a kind of excitement, I said that I would come.

I duly arrived at his club, a military club, at half-past seven, and Whitman was waiting in the hall. He was a spectacularly handsome man, black-haired, lustrous-eyed, built like an American quarterback. He had won a Labour seat in 1955, and held it since, something of a sport on those back benches. A Philippe Egalité radical, his enemies called him. He had inherited money and had never had a career outside politics, though in the war he had done well in a smart regiment.

"The first thing," he said, welcoming me with arms spread open, "is to give you a drink."

He did give me a drink, a very large whisky, in the club bar. Loosening my tongue, perhaps—but he was convivial, expansive, and not over-abstinent himself. Nevertheless, expansive as he was, he didn't make any reference to his telephonic attack: this evening had been mapped out, and, like other evenings with a purpose, the temperature was a little above normal. More drinks for us both. He was calling me by my Christian name, but that was as common in Westminster as in the theatre. I had to use his own, which was, not very appropriately, Dolfie.

Gossip. His colleagues. The latest story about a senior minister. A question about Francis Getliffe. The first lead-in? Dolfie in the Commons had, as one of his specialities, military affairs. We moved in to dinner, which he had chosen in advance. Pheasant, a decanter of claret already on the table. An evening with a purpose, all right, but he was also a man who enjoyed entertaining. More chat. We had finished the soup, we were eating away at the pheasant, the decanter was getting low, when he said:

"By the way, are you going into the government, Lewis?"

"Look," I said, "you do seem to be better informed than I am."

"I have my spies." He was easy, undeterred, eyes shining, like a man's forcing a comrade to disclose good news.

"You don't always trust what they tell you, do you?"

"A lot of people are sure that you're hesitating, you know—"

"I really should like to know how they get that curious impression. And I should like to know who these people are."

His smile had become sharper.

"I don't want to embarrass you, Lewis. Of course I don't—"

"Never mind about that. But this isn't very profitable, is it?"

"Still, you could tell me one thing, couldn't you? If you've accepted today, it will be in the papers tomorrow. So you won't be giving anything away."

I was on the edge of saying, this discussion would get nowhere, it might as well stop. But I could keep up my end as long as he could, one didn't mind (not to be hypocritical, it was warming) being the object of such attention. Further, I was getting interested in his motives.

"I don't mind telling you," I said, "that there will be nothing in the papers tomorrow. But that means nothing at all."

"Doesn't it mean you have had an offer?"

"Of course not."

"Anyway, you haven't accepted today?"

"I've accepted nothing. That's very easy, unless you've got something to accept."

Whether he had listened to the qualification, I was doubtful. His face was lit up, as though he were obscurely triumphant. With an effort, an effort that suddenly made him seem nervous and over-eager, he interrupted the conversation as we took our cheese. More chat, all political. When would the next election be? The government couldn't go on long with this majority. With any luck, they'd come back safe for five years. Probably ten, he said, with vocational optimism. His own seat was dead secure, he didn't need to worry about that.

It was not until we had gone away from the dining-room, and had drunk our first glasses of port in the library, that he began again, persuasive, fluent, with the air of extreme relief of one getting back to the job.

"If it isn't boring about what we were saying at dinner—"

"I don't think we shall get any further, you know." I was still cheerful, still curious.

"Assuming that an offer—well, I don't want to make things difficult—" (he gave a flashing, vigilant smile) "assuming that an offer may come your way—"

"I don't see much point, you know, in assuming that."

"Just for the sake of argument. Because there's something I want to tell you. Very seriously. I hope you realise that I admire you. Of course, you're an older man than I am. You know a great deal more. But I happen to be on my own home ground over this. You see, you've never been in parliament and I have. So I don't believe I'm being impertinent in telling you what I think. You see, I know what would be thought if anyone like you—you, Lewis—went into the government."

He was speaking now with intensity.

"It wouldn't do you any good. Anyone who admired you would have to tell you to think twice. If they were worried about your own best interests."

He said:

"It's a mistake for anyone to go into politics from the out-

side. It's a mistake for anyone to take a job in the government unless he's in politics already. A job that people in the
Commons would like to have themselves. I beg you to think
of that."

Yes, I was thinking about that, with a certain well-being,
as I left him for a moment in order to go to the lavatory. As
usual, as with a good many warnings, even when they were
least disinterested, there was truth in what he said. And yet,
in a comfortable mood, enhanced by Whitman's excitement
and the alcohol, I felt it would be agreeable—if only I were
dithering on the edge—not to be frightened off. There was a
pleasure, singularly unlofty, in being passionately advised
not to take a job which one's adviser wanted for himself. As,
of course, Whitman wanted this. Not that I had heard him
mentioned. On the contrary, the gossip was that he was too
rich, and too fond of the smart life, to be acceptable to his
own party.

On the way back from the lavatory, those thoughts still
drifting amiably through my mind, I saw the back of someone I believed I recognised, moving very slowly, erect, but
with an interval between each step, towards the lift. I caught
him up, and found that, as I had thought, it was Sammikins.
But his face was so gaunt, his eyes so sunk and glittering,
that I was horrified. Horrified out of control, so that I burst
out:

"What is the matter?"

He let out a kind of diminuendo of his old brazen laugh.
His voice was weak but unyielding, as he said:

"Inoperable cancer, dear boy."

I couldn't have disentangled my feelings, it was all so
brusque, they fought with each other. Affronted admiration
for that special form of courage: sheer visceral concern which
one would have felt for anyone, sharpened because it was
someone of whom I was fond: yes (it wouldn't hide itself,

any more than a stab of envy could), something like reproach that this apparition should break into the evening.
Up to now I had been enjoying myself, I had been walking
back with content, with streaks of exhilaration: and then I
saw Sammikins, and heard his reply.

Could I do anything, I said unavailingly. "You might give
me an arm to the lift," he said. "It seems a long way, you
know." As I helped him, I asked why I hadn't been told before. "Oh, it's not of great interest," said Sammikins. The irritating thing was, he added, that all his life he had drunk
too much: now the doctors were encouraging him to drink,
and he couldn't manage it.

I was glad to see the lift-door shut, and a vestigial wave of
the hand. When I returned to the library, Whitman, who
was not insensitive, looked at me and asked if something had
gone wrong.

An old friend was mortally ill, I said. I had only heard in
the last few minutes.

"I'm very sorry about that," said Whitman. "Anyone close?

"No, not very close."

"Ah well, it will happen to us all," said Whitman, taking
with resignation, as we had all done, the sufferings of another.

He ordered more drinks, and, his ego reasserting itself, got
back to his plea, his warning, his purpose. Politics (he
meant, the profession of politics) was a closed shop, he insisted, his full vigour and eloquence flowing back. Perhaps it
was more of a closed shop than anything in the country. You
had to be in it all your life, if you were going to get a square
deal. Any outsider was bound to be unpopular. I shouldn't
be being fair to myself unless I realised that. That was why
he had felt obliged to warn me, in my own best interests.

I found myself sinking back into comfort again, my own
ego asserting itself in turn. There were instants when I was

reminded of Sammikins, alone in a club bedroom upstairs. Once I thought that he too, not so long ago, had been hypnotised by the 'charm of politics,' just as much as this man Whitman was. The charm, the say-so, the flah-flah, the trappings. It made life shine for them, simply by being in what they felt was the centre of things.

Yet soon I was enjoying the present moment. It began to seem necessary to go on to the attack: Whitman ought to be given something to puzzle him. So I expressed gratitude for his action. This was an exceptionally friendly and unselfish act, I told him. But—weren't there two ways of looking at it? In the event, the unlikely event, of my ever having to make this choice, then of course I should have to take account of all these warnings. I was certain, I assured him, that he was right. But mightn't it be cowardly to be put off? In that way, I didn't think I was specially cowardly. Unpopularity, one learned to live with it. I had had some in my time. One also had to think of (it was time Whitman was properly mystified) duty.

No, Whitman was inclined to persuade me that this was not my duty. He would have liked me to stay longer: there were several points he hadn't thoroughly explained. He gazed at me with impressive sincerity, but as though wondering whether he could have misjudged me. As he saw me into a taxi, he might have been, so it seemed, less certain of my intentions than when the evening began.

FOURTEEN

END OF A LINE

On the Friday morning I said to Margaret that the forty-eight hours would be up that night, and I should have to give my answer.

"Do you know what it's going to be?"

"Yes," I said, in a bad and brooding temper.

She was not sure. She had seen these moods of vacillation before now. Perhaps she had perceived that I was in the kind of temper that came when one was faced by a temptation: saw that it had to be resisted: and saw, at the same time, that if one fell for it, one would feel both guilty and liberated. But we were not in a state for that kind of confidence. I was still resentful because she had been so positive, still wishing that I could act in what the existentialists called my freedom. The only comment that I could take clinically had been Hector Rose's: Hector had his share of corrupt humanity, but not in his judgment: and this was a time when corrupt humanity got in the way. He was, of course—as in lucid flashes I knew as well as he did—dead right.

Yet still, though I had made up my mind, I acted as though I hadn't. Or as though I were waiting for some excuse or change of fortune to blow my way. I took it for granted that Margaret couldn't alter her view, much as she might have liked to, for the sake of happiness.

The only time when we were at one came as I told her about Sammikins. She too had an affection for him, like mine mixed up—this was long before his illness—of respect, pity, mystification. He had virtue in the oldest sense of all: in any conceivable fashion, he was one of the bravest of men. And his gallantry, from the time we had first met him, in former days at Basset, had been infectious. Since then we had learned more, through some of our police acquaintances, about his underground existence. Pick-ups in public lavatories, quite promiscuous, as reckless in escalating risks as he was in war. He had been lucky, so they said, to keep out of the courts. Sometimes, without his knowing it, his friends, plus money and influence, had protected him. When he came into the title, he hadn't become more cautious but had —like George Passant chasing another kind of sensation— doubled his bets.

"What a waste," said Margaret. Strangely enough, before he was ill, he might in his strident voice have said that of himself, but not so warmly.

When we had ceased to talk of Sammikins, I became more restless. I went into the study and started to write the letter of refusal which I could as well have drafted on the Wednesday night. But I left it unfinished, staring out over the park, making a telephone call that didn't matter. Then I went and found Margaret: it might be a good idea if I went to Cambridge for the night, I said.

Temper still not steady, I asked her to call Francis at his laboratory. I was showing her that it was all innocent. While she was close by, I was already talking to Francis—I should like to stay in college that night, no, I didn't want to bother him or Martin, in fact I should rather like to stay in college by myself. Perhaps he would book the guest-room? Francis offered to dine in hall—yes, if it wasn't a nuisance. No, don't trouble to send word round to Martin, I shall see him soon anyway. Nor old Arthur Brown, this wasn't a special occasion. But young Charles—if he would drop in my room soon after hall? Francis would get a message round to Trinity. "There," I said to Margaret. "That ought to be peaceful enough."

Autumn afternoon. The stations paced by: the level fields, the sun setting in cocoons of mist. From the taxi, the jangled Friday traffic, more shops, brighter windows, than there used to be. When I entered the college, the porter on duty produced my name with a question mark, ready with the key, but not recognising me by sight.

As I crossed the court, I recalled that, when I was first there, at this time of year there would have been leaves of Virginia creeper, wide red leaves, squelching on the cobbles and clinging like oriflammes to the walls. Since then the college had been cleaned, and these first court walls were bare, no longer grey but ochre-bright, looking as they might have done, not when the court was built (there had been two façades since then), but in the eighteenth century.

That was a change. But it made no difference to the curious tang that the court gave one in October, quite independent of one's deeper moods, springy, pungent, a shade wistful. Was that climatic, or was it because the academic year had the perverse habit of beginning in the autumn? Anyhow, it had been pleasurable when I lived there, and was so visiting the place that night.

The guest-room lay immediately under my old sitting-room, and it was up the stairs outside that callers used to climb, as light-footed as Roy Calvert, or ponderous as Arthur Brown, during various bits of college drama. Not that I thought twice, or even once, about that. It was fairly early in the evening, but I had some letter-writing to do. It was already too late to get a written answer to the private office by the time I had promised: but all day I had been half muddling through, half planning that I could telephone the secretary (that is, the principal private secretary) in time enough, and have the letter reach him tomorrow.

I waited till seven o'clock before I called on Francis. The first hall-sitting was noisy, rattle of plates, young men's voices, the heavy smell of food, as I pushed through the screens. In the second court, the seventeenth century building stood out clean lined under a fine specimen of a hunter's moon, rising over the old acacia. Francis's lights were shining, from rooms which in my time had been the Dean's. But, now Francis had stripped off the hearty decorations, they were handsome to look at as soon as one stepped inside, moulded panelling, Dutch tiles round the fireplace. Francis gave me a friendly cheek-creased smile, and then, absent-mindedly, as though I were an undergraduate, offered me a glass of sherry. When I said that, except in Cambridge, I didn't touch that dispiriting drink once a year, Francis's smile got deeper; but he wasn't surprised, he was waiting for it, to hear me continue without any break at all.

"I've got the offer of your job, you know," I said.

"Yes," said Francis. "I was given a pretty firm hint about that. Otherwise I wouldn't have said anything on Tuesday night."

We were sitting on the opposite sides of the fireplace. Francis looked at me, eyes lit-up over the umber pouches (misleading, perhaps, that anyone now so content should carry indelibly all those records of strain), and asked:

"Well, what about it?"

I hesitated before I replied. Then I said:

"I'm inclined to think that I ought to give the same answer as you did."

"I don't want to persuade you either way. I just don't know which is better for you."

He was speaking with affectionate, oddly gentle, concern.

Maybe I had expected, or hoped, even with the letter written, that he would say something different. But I should have known. When he had seemed curt or uninterested in the Lords bar, that was nothing like the truth. He cared a good deal for what happened to me. On the other hand, or really on the same hand, he was too fine-nerved to intrude —unless he was sure that he was discriminating right. Only once or twice in the whole of our lives had he intervened into my private choices. On politics, of course he had. On pieces of external behaviour, yes. But almost never when it would affect my future. The only time I could bring back to mind that night was when he told me, diffidently but exerting all his strength, that whatever the cost and guilt I ought, after Margaret and I had parted and she had married someone else, to get her back and marry her myself.

None of my friends, certainly no one I had known intimately, was as free from personal imperialism as Francis. He didn't wish to dominate others' lives, nor even to insinuate himself into them. Sometimes, when we were younger, it had made him seem—side by side with the personal imperialists —to lack their warmth. As they occupied themselves with others, the imperialists were warm for their own benefit. In the same kind of relation, Francis, within the human limits, wasn't concerned with his own benefit. That was a reason why, after knowing him for a lifetime, one found he wore so well.

"I think I probably ought to turn it down." I still said it as something like a question.

"I just don't know for you." Francis shook his head. "I dare say you're being sensible."

A little later, he observed, with amiable malice:

"Whatever you do, you'll be extremely cross with yourself for not doing the opposite, won't you?"

Soon we left it. We could have retraced the arguments,

but there was nothing more to say. The quarter chimed from one of the churches beyond the Fellows' Garden. Francis, opening a cupboard to pick up his gown, said:

"By the by, the Master's dining tonight. You can't say I don't sacrifice myself for you."

This was the third Master since Francis was an undergraduate, a man called G.S. Clark. Francis detested him, and even Martin took his name off the dining list when he found the Master's on it. Clark was a man of the ultra-right (the present gibe was that he monitored all B.B.C. programmes, marking down the names of left-wing speakers, including the Archbishop of Canterbury), and he and his supporters had taken over the college government, so that Martin, as Senior Tutor, was left without power and on his own.

The college bell began to ring, undergraduates were running along the paths, Francis and I walked to the combination-room. It was already full, men, most of them young, pushing round the table, panel-lights glowing over their heads. When I was a fellow, there had been fourteen of us: now, in 1965, the number was over forty: more often than not, they told me, the high table overflowed. Before the butler summoned us into hall, the Master welcomed Francis and me with simple cordiality. "We don't often have the pleasure," he said. He had been a cripple since infancy, and had a fresh pink-skinned juvenile face as though affliction, instead of ageing him, had preserved his youth. His smile gave an impression both of sweet nature and obstinacy. Martin and Francis had certain comments to make about the sweet nature. Everyone agreed that he was a strong character, so much so that, although he dragged his useless leg about, no one thought of him as a cripple, or ever pitied him.

By his side stood his chief confidant, an old enemy of mine, the ex-bursar, Nightingale. To my surprise, he insisted on shaking me strongly by the hand.

The forms were being preserved. As soon as grace was ended and we settled down at high table, at our end, the senior end, conversation proceeded rather as though at an international conference with someone shouting 'restricted' when a controversial point emerged. The immemorial college topics took over, bird-watching, putative new buildings, topics in which my interest had always been minimal and was now nil. I turned to my left and talked to a young fellow, whose subject turned out to be molecular biology. He seemed very clever: I suspected that, when he heard the name of one bird trumping another, when he listened to that beautiful display of non-hostility, he was amused. With him and his contemporaries, so Francis and others told me, there was a change. A change for the better, said Francis. These young men were much more genuine academics than their predecessors: most of them were doing good research. They mightn't be such picturesque examples of free personality as those I used to sit with: but a college, Francis baited me, didn't exist to be a hothouse of personality. These young men were high-class professionals. I should have liked to know what they thought of relics of less exacting days.

When we arrived back in the combination-room, Francis asked me if I wanted to stay for wine. No, I said, the young men were hurrying off; and anyway Charles would presumably be calling at the guest-room soon. With a nod, not devoid of relief, Francis led me out into the first court. He said:

"What was all that in aid of?"

He meant, why had I wanted to dine in hall. I couldn't have given a coherent answer, it wasn't sentiment, it had something to do with the confusion of that day.

Francis asked me to let him know when the decision was made.

"Oh, it is made," I said.

"Good," said Francis, and added that he had better leave me alone with Charles. "He won't give you any false comfort." Francis broke into an experienced paternal grin before he said good night.

A hard rap at the guest-room, Charles punctual but interrogatory. "Hallo?"

I thought that he felt he was being inspected: it was his first term, and though he had made himself a free agent so early, he was cagey about being visited or disturbed.

"This is nothing to do with you, Carlo," I said.

"Oh?"

"It's entirely about me. I wanted to tell you the news myself."

"What have you been doing now?"

"Nothing very sensational. But I've just sent off a letter."

He was watching me, half smiling.

"Refusing a job," I went on, "in the government."

"Have you, by God?" Charles broke out.

I explained, I should have to make a telephone call later that evening. They wanted to receive an answer that night, and the letter would confirm it. But Charles was not preoccupied with administrative machinery. Of course—he was brooding in an affectionate, reflective manner—it had always been on the cards, hadn't it? Yes, it could have been different if I had been an American or a Russian, then perhaps I might have been able to do something.

"Still," he said, "it isn't every day that one declines even this sort of job, I suppose."

He said it protectively, with a trace of mockery, a touch of admiration. He was still protective about my affairs, bitter if he saw me criticised. And he also felt a little envy, such as entered between a father and son like us. But when I envied him, it was a make-believe and a pleasure: when he envied me, there was an edge to it. I had, for better or worse, done certain things, and he had them all to do.

"I'm rather surprised you did decline, you know," said Charles. "You've chanced your arm so many times, haven't you?"

There was the flash of envy, but his spirits were high, his eyes glinting with empathetic glee.

"I've always thought that was because you didn't have the inestimable privilege of attending one of our famous boarding schools," he said. "There's precisely one quality you can't help acquiring if you're going to survive in those institutions. I should call it a kind of hard cautiousness. Well, you didn't have to acquire that when you were young, now did you? And I don't believe it's ever come natural to you."

"Yes, you're right."

So he was, though very few people would have thought so.

I was thinking, when he was looking after his friends, or even me, he could show much sympathy. When he was chasing one of his own desires, he was so intense that he could be cruel. That wasn't simply one of the contradictions of his age. I expected that he would have to live with it. That evening, though, he was at his kindest.

"So I should have guessed that you'd plunge in this time," he said, with a cheerful sarcastic flick. "And you didn't. Still capable of surprising us, aren't you?"

"That wasn't really the chief reason." I played the sarcasm back.

"For Christ's sake!" he cried, by way of applause. "Anyway, not many people ever have the chance to say no. I'm going to stand you a drink on it."

We went out of the college and slipped up Petty Cury towards the Red Lion, just as before the war—especially in that autumn when the election of the Master was coming

close and we didn't want to be traceable in our rooms—Roy
Calvert and I used to do. Neither Charles, nor undergraduates whom he called to in the street, were wearing gowns, as
once they would have been obliged to after dusk: but they
were wearing a uniform of their own, corduroy jackets and
jeans, the lineal descendants of Hector Rose's morning at-
tire, that reminder of his youth.

While I sat in the long hall of the pub, Charles rejoined
me, carrying two tankards of beer. He stretched out his legs
on one side of our table, and said:

"Well, here's to your abdication."

I was feeling celebratory, expansive, and at the same time
(which didn't often happen in Cambridge) not unpleasantly
nostalgic. It was a long time since I had had a drink inside
that place. It seemed strange to be there with this other
young man, not so elegant as Roy Calvert, nothing like so
manic, and yet with wits which weren't so unlike: with this
young man, who, by a curious fluke, had that year become
some kind of intimate—in a relation, as well as a circle, mysterious to me—of Roy Calvert's daughter.

After a swallow of beer, Charles, also expansive, though he
had nothing to be nostalgic about, said:

"Daddy," (when had he last called me that?) "I take it this
is the end of one line for you, it must be."

"Yes, of course it must."

"It never was a very central line, though, was it?"

I was trying to be detached. Living in our time, I said,
you couldn't help being concerned with politics—unless you
were less sentient than a human being could reasonably be.
In the Thirties people such as Francis Getliffe and I had
been involved as one might have been in one's own illness:
and from then on we had picked up bits of knowledge, bits
of responsibility, which we couldn't easily shrug off.

But that wasn't quite the whole story, at least for me. It

wasn't as free from self. I had always had something more
than an interest, less than a passion, in politics. I had been
less addicted than Charles himself, I said straight to the attentive face. And yet, one's life isn't all a chance, there's
often a secret-planner putting one where one has, even without admitting it, a slightly shamefaced inclination to be. So I
had found myself, as it were absentmindedly, somewhere
near—sometimes on the fringe, sometimes closer in—a
good deal of politics.

When had it all started? This was the end of a line all
right. Perhaps one could name a beginning, the night I
clinched a gamble, totally unjustified, and decided to read
for the Bar. That gave me my chance to live among various
kinds of political men—industrial politicians, from my observer's position beside Paul Lufkin, academic politicians in
the college (as in that election year 1937, fresh in my mind
tonight), and finally the administrators and the national politicians, those who seemed to others, and sometimes to themselves, to possess what men thought of as power.

Charles knew all that. He thought, if he had had the same
experience, he would have gone through it with as much interest. But he didn't want to discuss that theme in my
biography, now being dismissed for good and all. He was occupied, as I went to fetch two more pints, with what lessons
he could learn. We had talked about it often, just as on the
night he returned home in the summer. Not as father and
son, but as colleagues, fellow students, or perhaps people
who shared a taste in common. Many of our tastes were different, but here we were, and had been since he grew up,
very near together.

Closed politics. Open politics. That was a distinction we
had spoken of before, and, stretched out in gawky relaxation,
Charles came back to it that night. Closed politics. The politics of small groups, where person acted upon person. You

saw it in any place where people were in action, committees of sports clubs, cabinets, colleges, the White House, boards of companies, dramatic societies. You saw it perhaps at something like its purest (just because the society answered to no one but itself, lived like an island) in the college in my time. But it must be much the same in somewhat more prepotent groups, such as the Vatican or the Politburo.

"I fancy," said Charles, "you've known as much about it as anyone will need to know."

That was said very simply, as a compliment. He was right, I thought, in judging that the subject wasn't infinite: the permutations of people acting in closed societies were quite limited, and there wasn't all that much to discover. But I also thought that he might be wrong, if he guessed that closed politics were becoming less significant. I might have guessed the same thing at his age—that wasn't patronising, some of his insights were sharper than mine—but it would have been flat wrong. For some reason about which none of us was clear, partly perhaps because all social processes had become, not only larger, but much more articulated, closed politics in my lifetime had become, not less influential, but much more so. And this had passed into the climate of the day. Many more people had become half-interested in, half-apprehensive about, power groups, secret decisions. There were more attempts to understand them than in my youth. It was only by a quirk of temperament, and a lot of chance, that I had spent some time upon them, I told Charles: but, just for once, he could take me as a kind of weather vane.

Yes, he granted me that: and where did we go from there?

As we left the Lion, and walked through the market-place, he began to speak freely, the words not edged or chosen, but coming out with passion. The real hope was open politics. It must be. If any of his generation—anywhere—could make open politics real again.

Yes, the machinery mattered, of course it mattered, only a fool ignored it—but there was everything to do. It just wasn't enough to ward off nuclear war or even to feed the hungry world. That was necessary but not sufficient. People in the West were crying out for something more.

Although it was after ten when we reached Trinity, the gate stood open (Charles, unlike me, had not seen it closed at that time of night), and two girls were entering in front of us. The Great Court spread out splendid in the high moonlight: as we passed the sundial, its shadow was black-etched on the turf: Charles was oblivious to the brilliant night or to any other vista. Hadn't one of my old friends, he was asking, once said that literature, to be any good, had to give some intimation of a desirable life? Well, so had politics. Far more imperatively. That was what the advanced world, the industrialised world, the whole of the west was waiting for. Someone had to try. Someone who understood the industrialised world: that was there for keeps. Someone who started there. A Lenin of the affluent society. Someone who could make its life seem worthwhile.

"It may not be possible," said Charles, after we climbed the stairs to his room, his fervour leaving him. "Perhaps it never will be possible. But someone has to try."

I glanced out of his window, which looked over the old bowling green, neatly bisected, light and dark, by a shadow under the moon. Not wanting to break the current (I hadn't often heard him so emotional, in the old non-Marxist sense so idealistic), I asked if this was what, when some of his contemporaries were protesting, they were hoping to say or bring about.

"Oh that. Some of them know what they're doing. Some are about as relevant as the Children's Crusade."

If they had been listening to his tone, which was no longer emotional, I couldn't help thinking that certain contemporaries referred to would not have been too pleased.

"Mind you, I shall go out on the streets again myself over Vietnam."

He gazed at me with dark searching eyes. "First, because on that they're right. Second, because we may need some of those characters. And if you're going to work with people, you can't afford to be too different."

That was a good political maxim, such as old Bevill might have approved of. Charles had not for a long while spoken straight out about the career he hoped for: in fact, I thought that he was still unsure, except in negatives. It would have been easy for him to become an academic, but he had ruled that out. He would work like a professional for a good degree—but that was all he had volunteered. As we were in sympathy, unusually close, that night, I said:

"Is this what you're planning for yourself?"

I didn't have to be explicit. The kind of leader he had been eloquent about, the next impulse in politics.

He gave a disarming, untypically boyish smile.

"Oh, I've had my megalomaniac dreams, naturally I have. The times I used to walk round the fields at school— But no. That's not for me."

For an instant, I was surprised that he was so positive. "Why not?"

"Look, you heard me say, a minute ago, that it may not be possible. The whole idea. Well, anyone who's going to bring it off would never have said that. He's got to be convinced every instant of his waking life. He's got to think of nothing else, he's got to eat and breathe it. That's how the magic comes. But that's what I couldn't do. I'm not made for absolute faith. I'm probably too selfish, or anyway I can't forget myself enough."

He had more self-knowledge, or at least more knowledge of his limits, I realised, than I had at his age and older. But he was young enough to add with a jaunty optimistic air:

"On the other hand, I wouldn't say that I mightn't make a pretty adequate number two. If someone with the real quality came along. I could do a reasonable job as a tactical adviser."

A little later, still comfortably intimate (it was one of the bonuses of that singular day), Charles and I walked back through the old streets to the gate of my own college. I had told him that I should have to hurry to put through the telephone call; and so he left me there, saying, with a friendly smile, "Good luck." We each had our superstitions and he would never have wished me that if I had been waiting for news, any more than I should have done to him before an examination. It was just a parting gift.

I had brought with me the private secretary's home number, but I had to wait a good many minutes before I heard his voice.

"Hallo, Lewis, are you all right?" I had known him when I was in Whitehall and he one of the brightest young principals. I apologised for disturbing him so late.

"I should have been worried if you hadn't. Well, what do you want me to report?"

I gave all the ritual regrets, but still I had to say no. A letter was on its way. Very slight pause, then the clear Treasury voice. "I was rather hoping you'd come down the other way." Like most aides-de-camp, he tended to speak as though it was he I had to answer to. I could have a few more hours to think it over, he said, there might be other means of persuasion. At my end, another slight pause. Then, quickly, brusquely: "No, this is final, Larry." One or two more attempts to put it off—but Larry was used to judging answers, and, though he was duplicating Hector Rose's career, he didn't duplicate Hector Rose's ceremonial. "Right," came the brisk tone. "I'll pass it on. I am very sorry about this, Lewis. I am very sorry personally."

All over. No, not quite all over. There was something else to do. I went into my bedroom, and there, shining white on the chest of drawers, was the letter I had not yet sent. I had told a lie to my son. Not a major lie—but still, quite pointlessly, for underneath the resolve was made, I hadn't brought myself to send the letter off. Had I really hoped that Francis Getliffe would dissuade me, or even Charles, or that there would be some miraculous intervention which would give me the chance to change my mind, pressure from a source unknown?

Probably not. It was just because the wavering was so pointless that I felt a wince of shame. It wasn't the crimes or vices that made one stand stock still and shut one's eyes, it was the sheer sillinesses that one couldn't stop. Vacillations, silly bits of pretence—those were things one didn't like to face in oneself: even though one knew that in the end they would make no difference. I wondered whether young Charles, who seemed so strong, went through them too.

It wasn't that night but later, when I recalled that I behaved in the same manner, ludicrously the same manner, once before. At the time that I was sending my letter of admission to the Bar and a cheque for two hundred pounds (to me, at nineteen, most of the money that I possessed). Then, just as today, the resolve was formed. Everyone I knew was advising me against, but nevertheless, as with Charles, my will was strong and I went through with the risk. But only after nights of hesitations, anxieties, withdrawals: only after a night when I had boasted of the gamble, talking to my friends rather in the vein of Hotspur having a few stiff words with reluctant troops. I explained how the letter— which committed me—had been sent off that day. Then, at midnight, after the celebration, I had returned to my bed-sitting room and found the letter waiting there, the sight of it reproaching me, telling me there was still time to back out.

Then I had been nineteen. Now I was sixty. That had been, in Charles's phrase, the beginning of one of my lines (the first letter went off at last, and I duly read for the Bar). Tonight was the end of that line. Delaying a little less than I had done at nineteen, a few hours less, I went out into the empty moonlit street to post the letter.

FIFTEEN

WAKING UP
TO WELL-BEING

Margaret, glad about the outcome, more glad because the quarrel had dissolved, believed with Francis Getliffe that I should be cross with myself. I might have believed that also: certainly I was incredulous, as though I were observing astonishing reactions in some Amazonian Indian when I found how equable I was. True, I had my jags of resentment. As I opened the paper one morning and saw the job had been filled—it had gone to Lord Luke of Salcombe, which added a touch of irony—I pointed to the announcement and said to Margaret:

"Now look what you've done." On the moment, I was blaming her, it was the kind of gibe which wasn't all a gibe: but I shouldn't have made it if I hadn't been serene underneath.

It would be a singular apotheosis for Walter Luke, making speeches from the despatch box in the Lords. Only a few years before he had been denouncing politicians and administrators with fervent impartiality. Stuffed shirts! Those blasted uncles! Out of inquisitiveness and perhaps fellow-feeling, I went along to hear his first ministerial speech. Walter's cubical head looming over the box: the rich west country intonation that he had never lost. As for the speech itself, it was competent, neither good nor bad. His civil servants had put in all the safeguards and qualifications which used to evoke his considerable powers of abuse. Walter uttered them now with every appearance of solidarity, as though they were great truths. But then, so should I have had to utter them.

That afternoon, walking past Palace Yard in one of the first autumn fogs, I was again mystified that I should be so serene. Work was going well, but there I wasn't at the mercy of my moods, it would have gone as well if I had been cursing myself. Margaret and I were entertaining more than we usually did, catching up with friends and acquaintances, the Marches, the Roses, the Getliffes, Muriel, Vicky Shaw and her father. That was agreeable: but it wasn't the origin of my present state.

The secret lay—though I should never have predicted it —in the sheer fact of saying no, in what Charles called my abdication. I had seen others, among them my brother Martin, gain a gratification out of giving up 'the world': in Martin's case, when he was very much in it and with the prizes dangling in front of him: he had become content, or even euphoric, out of great expectations denied. But that wasn't so with me. This job of Walter Luke's—orating in the fog-touched chamber—hadn't been part of my own expectations. No, the satisfaction came, if I understood it at all, from one's own will. In most of the events of a lifetime, the will didn't play a part. We were tossed about in the stream, corks bobbing manfully, shouting confidently that they could go upstream if they felt inclined. Somehow, though, the corks, explaining that it would be foolish to go upstream, went on being carried the opposite way.

Very rarely one was able to exercise one's will. Even then it might be an illusion, but it was an illusion that brought something like joy. It could happen when one was taking a risk or re-making a life. Sometimes I speculated whether people at the point of suicide felt this kind of triumph of the will. I should have liked to think that Sheila went out like that. What did Austin Davidson feel as he swallowed his pills and took what he believed to be his last drink?

Earlier, it would have been easy to ask him. No one would have been less embarrassed than Davidson, and he would have given an account of classical lucidity. During one of my visits that November, I began telling him of my experience, in the hope that I might lead on to his own. But I hadn't realised, nor had Margaret, seeing him so often, how much further away he had slipped. When I told him that I had been offered the job, he said, eyes vacantly staring:

"Did they give you a book?"

I wanted to leave it, but he insisted. I said, no, since I had refused, I didn't get anything: and then, slowly, sickeningly slowly to one who had been so clever, I tried to explain. Government. Ministers. Politics.

He strained to comprehend, cheeks flushed. He managed to say:

"No serious man has anything to do with politics."

With relief at getting a little communication, I said that was a good Apostolic pre-1914 sentiment. Then I hurried on, abandoning any attempt to try a new question. I went back to the familiar conversational forms. Those he could still understand, and, for some of the time (it was the longest of hours), take part in.

As soon as I returned home, I asked Margaret—what had been her impression of him earlier that week? Much as he usually was, she replied: not taking much interest, but he hadn't done for months. I told her that I thought I saw—I might be imagining it—a difference. If I'd seen him for the first time that afternoon, I shouldn't have given him long to go.

"Of course it may just be a bad day," I said. "But I think you ought to be prepared."

She nodded. "Yes, I am."

Prepared, perhaps, both for loss and for relief. The strain of the long illness told on her more than on me, because it was she who loved him. If you loved—instead of being fond of—someone taking a long time to die, there were times when you wanted the release. What had been my mother's phrase for it? A happy release. One of those hypocritical labels which half revealed a truth. Then, when the release came, you felt the loss more, because it was mixed with guilt. As with so many consequences of love, what you lost on the swings you lost also on the roundabouts.

Meanwhile, I believed that I knew a way to give him pleasure. I had tried it once before—any more often, and he would have been suspicious. He was physically capable of reading, so the doctors said, and yet he refused even to glance at a newspaper. Still, one had to allow for remote chances. It meant a certain amount of contrivance, and a visit to my stockbroker.

Late the following week—I had seen him in the interval —I entered the familiar, the too familiar, hospital room, catching the smell of chrysanthemums and chemicals, with underneath the last echo of cigarette smoke and feces. From the bed Davidson muttered, but it was not until I was facing him that he looked at me. Instead of sitting at the end of the bed, I carried a chair round to his left-hand side. It was becoming forlorn to expect that he would begin a conversation. I had to start straight off:

"You've not lost your touch, you know."

"What are you talking about?" he said in a dull tone.

"I was telling you, you haven't lost your touch. You've made me quite a bit of money."

The bird-brown eyes flickered. "I don't understand."

"You did some listening to financial pundits in your time, didn't you? Well, you're not the only one."

He gave the sketch of a smile.

"Do you remember telling me about a year ago (actually it was slightly longer, soon after he was taken into the clinic) that you guessed that it was time to go into metals? Particularly nickel. And you produced some rules about the right kind of share. I tell you, I did some listening. And took some action."

"Unwise. You forgot the first rule of investment. Never act on tips from an enthusiastic amateur." He was shaking his head, but there was colour in his voice.

"You're about as much an amateur as the late lamented Dr. W.G. Grace."

This esoteric remark, to begin to understand which one had to be born (a) in England (b) not later than 1920, made him laugh. Not for long, but audibly, sharply.

"So I took some action. I thought you might as well know the exact score—here's a letter from my broker. Would you like to read it—?"

"No, you read."

The letter said—"The purchase of Claymor Nickel has turned out very profitable for you. We bought on Oct. 14, 1964, 3,000 shares, which then stood at 21/6. The price this morning is 47/9. This shows a gross gain of just under £4,000. If you wish to sell, there will as you know be a capital gains tax of 30 percent, but the net profit will still be £2,600 approximately. However, in our opinion the price is likely to rise still higher."

I broke off: "I said, you haven't lost your touch, have you?"

"One can't help being right occasionally, don't you know." But he was very pleased, so pleased that he went on talking, though he had to stop for breath. "Anyway, I've not made you poorer, which is more than one can say of most advice. That is, unless you've taken some other tips from me which have probably been disastrous—"

"Not one."

"I must admit, it's agreeable to be some trivial use to you. Even when one's finishing up in this damned bedroom."

"I don't call it trivial—"

Davidson lifted his head a few inches from the pillows. His expression was lively and contented. In a tone in which one could hear some of his old authority, which in fact was curiously minatory, he said: "Now you ought to get out of that holding. Tomorrow. They may go higher. But remember, tops and bottoms are made for fools. That was the old Rothschild maxim, and they didn't do too badly out of it."

"Right," I said obediently.

"There's another point. I should consider that your unit of investment was too large. Three thousand pounds—that was it, wasn't it—is far too much for this kind of risk. It came off this time, but it won't always, you follow. You've heard the units that I use myself—"

"I had more faith in you."

"You oughtn't to have that much faith in anyone—"

I had not heard him take so much part in the duologue for many months. His manner, despite the heavy breathing, stayed minatory and on the attack: but that meant he was enjoying himself or at least self-forgetful. He even asked me to pour him a small whisky, although it was not yet four in the afternoon. It might have been a device to make me stay, for he insisted—suddenly reminding me of Charles as a child, importuning me to talk to him before he went to sleep—that I pour another for myself.

When at last I was outside the clinic, standing in the Marylebone Road looking for a taxi, I felt a little more than the usual emancipation. The afternoon had been easy: of course it was good to be out: slivers of rain shone, as though they were frozen, past the nearest street-lamp, and then bounced from the glistening pavement. I felt some of that zest—disgraceful and yet not to be denied—which came from being well in the presence of someone who couldn't be well again. The lift in one's step, which ought for decency's sake to be a reproach, just wasn't: it was good to breathe the dank autumnal air. It was not unpleasant, even, to stand in the rain waiting for a taxi. For an instant, a surreptitious thought occurred to me: it was rather a pity that I hadn't, in cold fact, bought shares on the old man's judgment. Either those or any others. The trouble was, I believed too much in his maxim about enthusiastic amateurs. If I hadn't, if I had trusted him, I should have been a good deal better off.

That visit took place on a Monday. It was not on the following morning, but on the Wednesday that I woke up early, so early that the window was quite dark. I lay there, comfortable, not sure whether I should go to sleep again or not. It was pleasant to think of the day ahead, lying relaxed and well. Perhaps I dozed off. Light was coming through the curtains. As in a sleep-start, I jerked into consciousness. There was a black-out over the far corner of my left eye.

I knew what that meant, too well. I went to the windows, pulled a curtain, looked out over the Tyburn garden to a clear early morning sky. Trying to cheat the truth, I blinked the eye and opened it again. Yes, for an instant the black-out seemed dissolved. Comfort. Then it surged back again. A clear black edge. Against the lightening sky, a little smoky film beyond the edge.

I couldn't cheat myself any longer. I knew what that meant, too well. The retina had come loose once more. Perhaps the veil didn't spread so far as the other time. But I was complaining, Good God, this is rough, could I face going through all that again?

Margaret was still quiet in her morning sleep. There was no point in waking her. Minutes didn't matter, and I could tell her soon enough.

SIXTEEN

INTO OBLIVION

Before breakfast, Margaret rang up Mansel, the ophthalmologist who had operated on me before. We had learned his timetable by now, since he had been inspecting my eyes each month or so. He would call in, Margaret told me, about eleven, on his way from the hospital to Harley Street.

As we sat waiting, I said to Margaret:

"He'll want to have another shot."

"Let's see what he says."

"I'm quite sure he'll want to." I added: "But I'm not so sure that I can bear it."

I wasn't thinking of the operation, in itself that didn't matter, but of the days afterwards, lying still, blinded, helpless in the dark. Though I had managed to control it, I had always had more than my share of claustrophobia: as I grew older, it got more oppressive, not less: and lying blinded for days brought on something like claustrophobia squared. The previous time had been pretty near my limit: or so it seemed looking back, even more than when I was going through it.

Margaret wanted to distract me. She said, how this would have been more than a nuisance, if I had been in government.

"It's a good thing you didn't take that job," she said.

"If I had taken it, this mightn't have happened," I replied.

Oh come, Margaret said, glad to have found an argument, that was taking psychosomatic thinking altogether too far. But I didn't respond for long.

When Mansel arrived, he was as usual brisk and elegant, busy and unhurried.

"I'm sorry to hear about this, sir," he said to me.

We had come to know each other well, but it was a curious intimacy, in which he, almost young enough to be my son, insisted on calling me sir, while I insisted on calling him by his Christian name. I admired him as a superb professional, and he listened to my observations as possibly useful to his clinical stock-in-trade.

While making conversation to Margaret, he was without fuss disconnecting a reading-lamp, fixing a bulb of his own. The drawing-room was just as good as anywhere else, he said to her with impersonal cheerfulness. He had brought a case with him, packed with White Knight equipment invented by himself: but, searching into the back of my eyes, he had never used anything more subtle than an ordinary lens. As he did now, lamp shining on the eye, Mansel asking me to look behind my head, to the left, down, all the drill which I knew by heart.

He didn't waste time. Within half a minute he was saying:

"There's no doubt, I'm afraid. Bad luck."

Not quite in the same place as before, he remarked. Then, with some irritation, he said that there hadn't been any indication or warning, the last time he examined me, only a month before. If we were cleverer at spotting these things in advance, he went into a short professional soliloquy, it would have been easy enough to use photolysis: why couldn't we get a better warning system?

"No use jobbing back," he said, as though reproaching me. "Well, we shall have to try and make a better go of it this time."

I glanced at Margaret: that was according to plan.

"Look, Christopher," I said, "is it really worthwhile?"

His antennae were quick.

"I know it's an awful bore, sir, I wish we could have saved you that—"

"What do I get in return? It's only vestigial sight at the best. After all that."

Mansel gazed at each of us in turn, collected, strong-willed.

"All I can give you is medical advice. But anyone in my place would have to tell you the same. I'm afraid you ought to have another operation."

"It can't give him much sight, though, can it?" Margaret wanted to be on my side.

"This sounds callous, but you both know it as well as I do," said Mansel. "A little sight is better than no sight. There is a finite chance that the other eye might go. We're taking every precaution, but it might. Myopic eyes are slightly more liable to this condition than normal eyes. Any medical advice is bound to tell you, you ought to insure against the worst. If the worst did come to the worst, and you'd only got left what you had yesterday in the bad eye— well, you could get around, you wouldn't be cut off."

"I couldn't read."

"I'm not pretending it would be pleasant. But you could see people, you could even look at TV. I assure you, sir, that if you'd seen patients who would give a lot even for that amount of sight—"

Margaret came and sat by me. "I'm afraid he's right," she said quietly.

"Would you like to discuss it together?" Mansel asked with firm politeness.

"No," I said. "Intellectually I suppose you are right. Let's get it over with."

I said it in bad grace and a bad temper, but Mansel didn't mind about that. He had, as usual, got his way.

He and Margaret were talking about the timetable.

"If it's all right with you, sir," Mansel turned to me, "there's everything to be said for going into hospital this morning."

"It's all one to me."

"Well done," said Mansel, as though I were an industrious but not specially bright pupil. "Last time, you remember, you had an engagement you said you couldn't break. That delayed us for three or four days. I thought it was rather over-conscientious, you know."

I wasn't prepared to bring those episodes back to mind: any more than to recall a visit to my old father, purely superstitious, just to placate the fates before an operation. Which my father, with his remarkable gift for reducing any situation to bathos, somewhat spoiled by apparently believing that I was suffering from a rupture, the only physical calamity which he seemed to consider possible for a grown-up man.

I was too impatient to recall any of that. I was thinking of nothing but the days laid out in the post-operational dark. I had no time for my own superstitions or anyone else's chit-chat: I was in a hurry to get back into the light.

Within an hour I was already lying on my back, with the blindfolds on. Margaret had driven with me to the hospital, while I gazed out at people walking busily along the dingy stretch of the City Road: not a glamorous sight unless anything visible was better than none. To me, those figures in the pallid November sunshine looked as though they were part of a mescalin dream.

In the hospital, I was given the private room I had occupied before. Someone—through a mysterious performance of the bush telegraph which I didn't understand—had already sent flowers. As she said goodbye, Margaret remarked that last time (operations took place in the morning) I had been quite lucid by the early evening. She would come and talk to me just before or after dinner tomorrow.

After she had left, I assisted in the French sense in the hospital drill. In bed: eyes blacked out: I even assisted in the receipt of explanations which I had heard before. Some nurse, whom I could recognise only by voice, told me that both eyes had to be blinded in order to give the retina a chance to settle under gravity: if the good eye was working, the other couldn't rest.

Helpless. Legs stretched like a knight's on a tomb: not a crusader knight's because I wasn't supposed to cross them. Just as Sheila's father's used to stretch, when he was taking care of himself.

"Mr. Mansel is very liberal," said another nurse's voice. With some surgeons, a few years before, I should have had sandbags on both sides of my head. So that it stayed dead still. For a fortnight.

Tests. Blood pressure—that I could recognise. Blood samples. Voices across me, as though I were a cadaver. Passive subject, lying there. How easy to lose one's ego. Persons wondered why victims were passive in the concentration camps. Anyone who wondered that ought to be put into hospital, immobilised, blinded. Nothing more dramatic than that.

Once or twice I found my ego, or at least asserted it. The anaesthetist was in the room, and a couple of nurses. "I've been here before, you know," I said. "The other time, when I came round, I was as thirsty as hell."

"That's a nuisance, isn't it?" said the anaesthetist.

"I suppose you dehydrate one pretty thoroughly."

"As a matter of fact, we do." A genial chuckle.

"Can anything be done about it? Tomorrow afternoon?"

"I'm afraid you will be thirsty."

"Is it absolutely necessary to be intolerably thirsty for hours? They gave me drops of soda water. That's about as useful as a couple of anchovies."

"I'll see what can be done."

"That's too vague," I said. "Look here, I don't complain much—"

I wrung some sort of promise that I might have small quantities of lime juice instead of soda water. That gave me disproportionate satisfaction, as though it were a major victory.

In the evening, though when I didn't know, for already I was losing count of time, Mansel called in. "All bright and cheerful, sir?" came the light, clear, upper-class voice.

"That would be going rather far, Christopher," I said. Mansel chortled as though I had touched the heights of repartee. He wanted to have one more look at my eye. So, for a couple of minutes, I could survey the lighted bedroom. As with the figures in the City Road, the chairs, the dressing table, the commode stood out, preternaturally clear-edged.

"Thank you, sir," said Mansel, replacing the pads with fingers accurate as a billiards-player's. "All correct. See you early tomorrow morning."

How early, again I didn't know, for they had given me sleeping pills, and I was only half awake when people were talking in the bedroom. "No breakfast, Sir Lewis," said the nurse, in a firm and scolding tone. "Nothing to drink."

Someone pricked my arm. That was the first instalment of the anaesthetics, and I wanted to ask what they used. I said something, not clearly, still wanting to be sentient with the rest of them. In time (it might have been any time) a voice was saying: "He's nearly out." With the last residue of will, I wanted to say no. But, as through smoke whirling in a tunnel, I was carried, the darkness soughing round me, into oblivion.

II
ARREST OF LIFE, LAST BUT ONE

SEVENTEEN

NOTHING

In the dark, a hand was pressing on mine. A voice. The dark was close, closer than consciousness. What was that hand?

A voice. "Darling."

The sound came from far away, then suddenly, like a face in a dream, dived on me. How much did I understand?

"All's well." It might have been a long time after.

Perhaps the words were being repeated. Until—consciousness lapping in like a tide, coming in, sucking back, leaving a patch still aware—I spoke as though recognizing Margaret's voice.

"Why are you here?"

"I just dropped in."

"Is it evening?"

"No, no. It isn't teatime yet."

That was her voice. That was all I knew.

Was there a memory, something else to hold on to?

"Didn't you say you'd come in the evening?"

"Never mind. I thought I'd like to see you earlier."

Utterly soothed, like a jealous man getting total reassurance or a drunk hearing a grievance argued away. That was her hand, pressing down on mine. I began to say that I was thirsty. Other voices. Coolness of glass against my lips. A sip. No taste.

"You were going to give me lime juice." I held on to another memory.

"I'm sorry," that must be a nurse, "it isn't here."

"Why isn't it here?"

Unsoothed again, a tongue of consciousness lapping further in. Darkness. Suspicion.

I was aware—not gradually, it happened in an instant—of pain, or heavy discomfort, in my left side, as though they had put a plaster there.

"What's happening?" I said to Margaret. I could hear my voice like someone else's, thick, alarmed, angry.

Voices in the room. Too many voices in the room. My right ankle was hurting, with my other foot I could feel a bandage on it. Margaret was saying "Everything's all right," but other voices were sounding all round, and I cried out:

"This isn't my room."

"The operation's over." That was Mansel, cool and light. "It's gone perfectly well."

"Where am I?"

Mansel again: "We're just going to take you back."

Once more I was soothed: it seemed reasonable, like the logic of a dream. I didn't notice motion, ramps, lifts, corridors didn't exist, I must have returned to somewhere near the conscious threshold. It might have been one of those drunken nights when one steps out of a party and finds oneself, without surprise, in one's own bed miles away.

I had been in a big room: I was back in one where the voices were close to me, which soothed me because, with what senses I had left, it was familiar: I didn't ask, I knew I had slept there the night before.

I was awake enough, tranquil enough, to recognise that I was parched with thirst. I asked for a drink, finding it necessary to explain to Margaret (was she still on my right?) that I was intolerably dry. The feel of liquid on a furred clumsy tongue. Then the taste came through. This was lime juice. Delectable. As though I were tasting for the first time. All in order: lime juice present according to plan: reassurance: back where I ought to be.

Someone was lifting my left arm, cloth tightening against the muscle.

"What are you doing?" I shouted, reassurance destroyed at a touch, suspicion flaring up.

"Only a little test." A nurse's voice.

"What are you testing for?"

Whispers near me. Was one of them Margaret's?

Mansel: "I want to know your blood pressure. Standard form."

"Why do you want to know?"

"Routine."

In the darkness, one suspicion soothed, faded out, left a nothingness, another suspicion filled it. Did they expect me to have a stroke? What were they doing? Ignorant suspicions, mind not coping, more like a qualm of the body, the helpless body.

"Everything is all right," Margaret was saying quietly.

"Everything is not all right."

A patch of silence. They were leaving me alone. Neither Margaret nor Mansel was talking. For an instant, feeling safer, I asked for another drink.

Time was playing tricks, my attention had its lulls, it might have been minutes before a hand was pulling my jacket aside, something cold, glass, metal against the skin.

"What are you doing now?" I broke out again.

"Another test, that's all." Mansel's voice didn't alter.

"I've got to know. I'm not going on like this."

Fingers were fixing apparatus on my chest.

"What's gone wrong?" Again, that didn't sound like my own voice. "I've got to know what's wrong."

Clicks and whirrs from some machine. My hearing had become preternaturally acute and I could hear Mansel and Margaret whispering together.

"Shall I tell him?" Mansel was asking.

"You'd better. He's noticed everything—"

There was movement by the side of my bed, and Mansel, instead of Margaret, was speaking clearly into my ear.

"There's nothing to worry about now. But your heart stopped."

The words were spaced out, distinct. They didn't carry much meaning. I said dully, "Oh."

I gathered, whether Mansel told me then or not I was never sure, that it had happened in the middle of the operation.

I asked: "How long for?"

"Between three-and-a-half and three-and-three-quarter minutes." I thought later, not then, that when Mansel told one the truth, he told the truth.

"We got it going again," Mansel's voice was cheerful. "There's a bit of a cut under your ribs. You're fine now."

He was at pains to assure me that the eye operation had been completed. It was time, he said, for him to let my wife talk to me.

Replacing Mansel's voice was Margaret's, steady and warm.

"Now you know."

I said "Yes, I know." I added:

"I bring you back no news from the other world."

Margaret went on talking, making plans for a fortnight ahead ("You'll be out of here by then, you understand, don't you?"), saying there would be plenty of time to argue about theology. She sounded calm, ready to laugh: she was concealing from me that she was in a state of shock.

Just as my remark might have concealed my state from

her. In fact, it had been quite automatic. It could have
seemed—perhaps it did to Margaret—as carefully debonair,
as much prepared for, as her father's greeting to me after his
messed-up attempt at suicide. You see God's own fool. I
might have been imitating him. Yet I hadn't enough control
for that. Anything I said, slipped out at random, as though
Margaret had put sixpence in a jukebox and we both had to
listen with surprise to what came out.

Later, when I thought about it in something like detachment, it occurred to me how histronic we all could be. Perhaps we had to be far enough gone. Then, though it might
be right outside our ordinary style, we put on an act. For
Austin Davidson, who had always enjoyed his own refined
brand of histrionics, it came natural to rehearse, to bring off
his opening speech. I was about as much unlike Davidson as
a man could reasonably be: but I too, though as involuntarily as a ventriloquist's dummy, had put on an act. Probably
we should all have been capable of making gallows jokes, in
the strictest sense; we should all, if we were about to be executed in public, have managed to make a show of it. It
might have been different if one was being killed in a cellar,
with no audience there to watch.

It might have been different. It was different for me,
when I had to get through that night. Margaret left me: so
did Mansel, and another doctor, one with a strong deep
voice. Not that I was left alone: there were nurses in the
room, busy and quiet, as I lay there in the hallucinatory
darkness, in full surrender to the state which perhaps I had
concealed from Margaret. It was one of the simplest of states,
just terror.

I had learnt enough about anxiety all through my life.
Worse, I had been frightened plenty of times—in London
during the war, on air journeys, visits to doctors, or during
my illness as a young man. But up to that night I hadn't

known what it was like to be terrified. There was no allevia-
tion, no complexity, nor, what had helped in bad times before, no observer just behind my mind, injecting into unhappiness and fear a kind of taunting irony, mixed up with
hope. No, nothing of that. This was a pure state and apart
from it I had, all through that night, no existence. All
through that night? That wasn't how I lived it. The night
went from moment to moment. There mightn't be another.

Soon after Mansel's good night, fingers were cool against
my arm again, a susurration, a whisper, the rustle of paper.

"All right?" I muttered, trying to ask a casual question,
craving for some news.

"You go to sleep," said a nurse's voice, calm and muted.

Within minutes—I was drugged but not asleep, I couldn't
count the time—fingers on my arm, the same sounds in the
dark.

"What is it?" I cried.

"Try to sleep."

I dozed. But there was something of me left—the will or
deeper—which was frightened to give way. Sleep would be a
blessing. But sleep was also oblivion. Fingers on my arm
once more. Once more I tried to ask. To them I made no
sense. To myself I wanted to talk rationally, as though I
were interested, not terrified. I couldn't. Time after time,
between sleep and consciousness, the fingers at my arm.

It became like one of those interrogations in which the
prisoner is not allowed to rest. I couldn't understand that
they were taking my blood pressure three times an hour.

Once, between the tests, I was aware of my left eye. Staring into the darkness, which wasn't the darkness of a black
night, but, as I recalled from the operation two years before,
was reddened, patterned, embossed, I saw a miniature light,
like a weak bulb, very near to me, as though it were burning
in the eye itself. I was aware of that without giving it a

thought: I might have been a man desperately busy, preoccupied with a major and obsessive task, not able or willing
to divert himself with something as trivial as the condition
of his eye.

It was abject to have no interest—or even, so it seemed,
no time, as though every second of the night was precious—
for anything but fright. I made an effort to address myself
rationally, as I had tried to speak to the nurses. Perhaps I
was trying to put on an act to myself as I did to others.
Under trial, we all wished to behave differently from how
we felt, there was a complementarity which made us less
ashamed. Waiting for the nurse's fingers, I wanted to reason
away the terror, exorcising it by words, thinking to myself, as
I rarely did, in words, using words to stiffen (or blandish or
deceive) myself as one might use them on another.

What was I frightened of?

Death? Death is nothing. Literally nothing. I ought to
know that by now.

Dying? Nothing was easier than dying. Not always maybe.
But if it happened as it had that morning, nothing was easier. If I went out now, it would be as easy.

What was I frightened of?

Not that night but afterwards when I was remembering
dread, not existing in it, I might have given an answer. At
least I knew what didn't matter, what hadn't drifted for an
instant through my mind. Listening by the side of Austin
Davidson's bed, I had heard him say that what chilled him
was to realise that he would never hear the end of any story
that had interested him: nor even be present as a spectator,
or the most tenuous shadow of a ghost. Yes, he was being
honest. But one could feel that at any time in one's life,
thinking about death. Davidson knew he would die soon,
but still he wasn't in the presence of annihilation. If he had
been, he would have been lonelier, less lofty, than that. I

could answer only for myself: yet there I would have answered for him too. One had no interest left, except in the absolute loneliness. Questions that had once been fascinating —they had no meaning. Politics, the world, what would men think about one's work: that was a blank. Friends, wife, son, all the future: that was as dead a blank.

Sometimes, in health, as I couldn't help recalling after a visit to Austin Davidson, I had imagined what dying would be like. You die alone. I thought that I had imagined it as real. Nonsense, I had fooled and flattered myself. It was so much less takeable, near to, identical with, the fright of the flesh itself. Had it been like this for my old father? He had asked for his lodger's company: his lodger held his hand: he must have been quite alone.

What was I frightened of? When I was remembering it, not living it, I might have said, of nothing. Of being nothing. On the one side, there was what I called 'I.' On the other, there was nothing. That was all. That was what it reduced to. In the abyss between the two was dread.

Yet maybe, when I was remembering, I, like Austin Davidson, made it more delicate than the truth.

Beside the bed, a voice I hadn't heard before. Without noticing, I had been the other side of the sleep threshold. This was a different nurse, a different voice, they were coming in shifts. Whispered figures, but louder whispers, almost enough to catch. Out of the dark, I recalled the other figures, Mansel's figures, the only ones that anyone had told me. Three-and-a-half minutes, three-and-three-quarters. Trying to think. Another of the night's cold sweats. The grue down the spine. I could have read or heard—or had my memory gone—that three minutes was enough to damage the brain. The sweat formed at the temples, dripped down. I had to try. What did I remember? My telephone number. Births and deaths of Russian writers—Turgenev 1815–83

Dostoevsky 1821–81. Tolstoy 1828–1910. They came click-
ing to mind, just as they always did. Poetry. I began the first
lines of *Paradise Lost,* then stuck. That was nothing new, I
was calming myself. It was young Charles who had the photographic memory. Characters in *Little Dorrit*—Clennam,
Mrs. Finching, Merdle, Casby, Tite Barnacle—they came out
quick enough. What about problems? The old proof of the
prime number theorem, that once made me wish I had gone
on with mathematics. Yes, I could work through that. There
didn't seem (it was the only reassurance through the night)
any damage yet awhile.

The small light in my left eye had gone out. I was in the
red-dark. Sometimes, nearer sleep, the tapestries took themselves away and the darkness deepened. The previous time
that I had been in that condition, I had thought that blindness would be like this, and I wasn't sure that I could endure it. Now I wasn't thinking of blindness. That was a spec-
ulation one made when one could afford to, like Davidson's
regret about what he was going to miss. Thoughts became
simpler as they narrowed: there wasn't room for luxury,
even the luxury of being anxious. Only one dread was left,
the final one.

Fingers at my arm, jolts into half-waking: like a night in
the prison cellars it went on. Once I asked the time. Someone told me, half-past two.

EIGHTEEN

"YOU'VE GOT TO FORGET IT"

A nurse was giving me a sponge, waking me, asking if I would like to freshen myself. Mr. Mansel was on his way, she said. Then his crisp, light-toned voice.

"Good morning, sir. I hope you've had a good night."

"Not exactly, Christopher. Rather like being in a sleeper on the old Lehigh Valley—"

During the night I had had reveries about blaming him, about letting all the fright and anger loose. Yet I found myself replying in his own aseptic fashion.

He said, professionally cheerful:

"Sorry about that. We thought you might sleep through it."

"If they'd have let me alone for one single damned hour, perhaps I could—"

"That was just a precaution." Mansel told me what they had been doing. "We wanted to see that everything was working. Which it is."

"I suppose that's some consolation." Nevertheless, while he was talking I felt safe.

"I think it should be, sir. Now let's have a look at the eye."

The clever fingers took off the pads, and I blinked into the bright, solid, consoling room. Outside the window, the sky was black, before dawn on a winter morning. If I could stay in the light, perhaps the night would be behind me.

Mansel's face, smelling of shaving soap, was only inches away. His eye, magnified by the lens, was searching into mine. After a minute or so, he said:

"It's early days yet, of course. I don't want to raise false hopes, but it may have gone better than last time."

"That's a somewhat minor bonus in the circumstances, don't you think?"

"Not at all," Mansel answered. "We've had a bit of unexpected trouble, of course we have. That's all the more reason why we want to get the eye right at the end of it."

Quickly, carefully, he put me back into the dark. I wished to say that his professional concern was not shared by me. I had meant to tell him—I had composed the speeches at one stage of the night—that, if I could get out of this hospital alive, it didn't matter a curse what happened to the eye. We never ought to have risked the operation. A tiny gain if all went well. If all didn't go well—that I could tell them about as I lay there that night, side strapped up under my heart, nurses keeping watch. I had been against this operation from the first, and he had overruled me. Anger got mixed up with fright, was better than fright, I had meant to project the anger on to Mansel. Yet I did nothing of the sort. The principal of complementarity seemed to work whenever I had an audience, and I behaved like a decent patient. Though once again in the dark, respite over, the night's thoughts came flooding back.

Mansel's voice was amiably exhorting me to have a cup of tea and some breakfast. I said, making the most of a minuscule complaint, that it was nearly impossible to eat lying rigid. Mansel was attentive: I was blinded, but perhaps my face still told him something. "We may be able to make things easier for you soon," he said. Meanwhile people would be coming in shortly to perform another test. In a couple of hours Mansel himself would return, together with a colleague.

What did that mean? I was as suspicious as in the afternoon before. If only they would tell me all the facts—that was what all sophisticated people cried out in their medical crises. Later, I wondered how much one could really take. How much should I have been encouraged if they had let me know each blood pressure reading all through the night?

Once again apparatus was being fixed to my chest, the chill of glass, the whirr of a machine. Then, for some time, I could hear no one in the room. Out of a kind of bravado, I called out.

"Yes, sir," came a chirping, quiet voice, a nurse's that I hadn't heard before. "Do you want anything?"

"No, as a matter of fact, I don't," I had to say.

I couldn't talk to her: I remained with suspiciousness keeping me just one side of the edge of sleep. It took Mansel's greeting to startle me full awake.

"Here we are again, sir!"

I could distinguish other footsteps besides his.

"I want to introduce a friend of mine—" Mansel again —"Dr. Bradbury. Actually he was here last night, but you were slightly too full of dope to talk to him. He's a heart specialist, as a matter of fact. That's because it's easier than coping with eyes, isn't it, Maxim?"

As soon as I heard Maxim reply, I recognised the voice. It had been present among the commotion—all mixed up by the shock, disentangleable now—of the night before. It was very deep (they were exchanging gibes about which line brought in the easy money), as deep as my brother's or Charles's, but without the bite that lurked at the back of theirs. This was just deep and warm.

A hand gripped mine, and a chair scraped on the floor beside the bed.

"The news is good." Slow, gentle, warm, emphatic. "The first thing is, I want you to believe me. The news is good."

I felt excessively grateful, so grateful that my reply was gruff.

"Well, what is it?"

"Your heart is as sound today as it was yesterday morning. We've looked at it as thoroughly as we know how, and we shouldn't be able to detect that anything had happened. I couldn't tell you this unless I was sure."

Mansel (quietly): "I can guarantee that."

"I need hardly say," I remarked, "that I hope you're right."

"We are right, you know." Deep, gentle voice. "I expect you want to ask, then why did it happen. The honest answer is, we haven't the slightest idea. It was simply a freak."

"A freak which might have been mildly conclusive," I said.

"Yes, it might. I have to tell you again, we haven't the slightest idea why it happened. All we know is that it did. After you'd been on the operating table for an hour and a half. I'm not sure whether Christopher has told you—"

Mansel: "No, not much."

"Well, I think you ought to know. Christopher tried to start the heart again by external massage. That didn't work. Then he decided—and he was perfectly right—that he hadn't much time to spare, so he did it from inside. Fortunately, although he's an eye-man, he's quite a competent surgeon."

Undergraduate teasing, in the midst of all the energy he was spending upon me.

"I've got a certain amount of faith in him," I caught the same tone.

Mansel cachinnated.

"So you should have." This was Maxim. "Now I want you to listen to something else. This has been an unusual experience, and that's rather an understatement, isn't it? It's an experience which could do harm to a good many people. You have to be pretty robust to take it in your stride. Robust psychologically—we can look after you physically, you're absolutely all right there. I should guess you're a tough specimen all the way round, and Christopher gives you an excellent report. But this is going to call for as much toughness as you can find. You've got to put it behind you. Straightaway. Today."

It was a long time since anyone had spoken to me as paternally as this. I hadn't yet seen his face, and, as it happened, I never did see it. He might very well be young enough, as Mansel was, to be my son. Yet I felt, not only gratitude so strong as to be uncomfortable, but also acquiescence, or even something like obedience.

"You've got to forget it." The voice was even warmer, even more urgent. "That's what I'm really telling you. The only danger is that you'll let it stay with you. You've got to forget it."

Curiously enough, that was what another strong-natured patient man had told us, at the end of the murder trial eighteen months before. But, after we had listened, my brother had said that that meant living in illusion: it might have been more comfortable, but it would have been wrong. You've got to forget it. This time, if I could obey, it presumably would do no harm to anyone, it wouldn't mean false hope. And yet, as I thanked Maxim, I added that I wasn't much good at forgetting things.

"Well, you've got to train yourself. This was just an incident. Don't let it make life dark for you. I'm going to tell you again, you've got to forget it."

I heard him get up from the bedside, and then he and Mansel, at the far end of the room, engaged themselves in a professional argument mixed with backchat. I couldn't follow much, the two voices, phone and antiphone, light and clear against deep bass, were kept low. But they each seemed to have a taste for facetiousness which wasn't mine. Somehow I gathered that Maxim was not Bradbury's baptismal name but had been invented by Mansel, who took great credit for it. As for the argument, that was about me.

"Nothing secret," Bradbury called out, considerate and kind. "We're just wondering when to get you up."

Though I didn't appreciate it, they were meeting a dilemma. What was good for the heart was a counter-indication for the eye, and vice versa. For the heart, they would like me sitting up that day: to give the eye the best chance, the longer I lay immobilised, the better.

"Well, I'll see how it looks tomorrow," I heard Mansel tell him, and Bradbury came nearer the bed to say goodbye.

"I probably shan't have to see you again," he said. "I'm very pleased with you. Do remember what I've told you."

The door clicked shut behind them. With that voice still comforting me, I needn't fight against sleep any more. In a moment, seconds rather than minutes, as though I were going under the anaesthetic again, I was flat out.

When I woke, I first had the sense of well-being that came after deep sleep. Then suddenly, eyes pressed by the darkness, I remembered what had happened. That wasn't the first time I had wakened happy and then been sickened by the thought of what lay ahead; there had been a good many such times since I was young: but this was the darkest.

My side hurt a little, so little that I should scarcely have noticed. That brought it all back. It had happened once. It could happen again. I was as frightened as I had been in the night. Perhaps more than that.

I tried to steady myself by recalling Bradbury's words. This was cowardly; it was unrealistic; he said that all was well. If he had been back in the room, I should have been reassured. Totally reassured, effusively grateful once more. But now he had left me, I could see through all the lies: either I had been deceiving myself, he hadn't said those words, or else I could see through his reasons for saying them. They knew that it would happen again. Perhaps that day or the next. He thought I might as well have the rest of my time in peace.

NINETEEN

PRIVATE LANGUAGE

Margaret was speaking to me and holding my hand. It couldn't have been many minutes since I awoke, but I had lost all sense of time. In fact, she had arrived about eleven o'clock; Mansel and Bradbury had made their call quite early, not long after eight.

I muttered her name. She kissed me and asked:

"How is it now?"

"It's too much for me."

Her fingers stiffened in mine, gripped hard. After the other operation, or even after Mansel broke the news the previous evening, she had heard me make some sort of pretence at sarcasm; she had come in expecting it now. She had come in, waiting to break down and confide what she had gone through: the telephone call as she sat in the flat at mid-day: just—would she come round to the hospital at once. The taxi-ride through the miles of streets. Kept waiting at the hospital. No explanation. Twenty minutes—so she told me later. (She remembered as little of them afterwards as if she had been drunk.) At last Mansel at the door, looking pallid. Then he said it was all right. Sharp clinical words to hearten her. After that, the operating theatre, where she sat waiting for me to come round.

Now she had come, needing release from all that: to be met by a tone which brought back all her misery, and, instead of giving her comfort, took it away. She had known me harsh and selfish enough in petty sufferings: but that was different from this flatness, this solitude.

At once she was talking protectively, with love.

"Of course it's not. Nothing ever is—"

"I shan't get over this."

I wasn't trying to hurt her, I was alone, I might as well have been talking to myself.

"You will, you've had a bad time, but of course you will. Look, my love, I've been talking to them—"

"I don't trust them."

"You've got to. Anyway, you do trust me—"

Silence.

She said urgently:

"You do trust me?"

At last I answered:

"No one knows what it's like."

"Don't you think I do?"

Getting no reply, she broke out, and then subdued herself.

"Let's try to be sensible, won't you? I have talked to those two. I'm telling you the absolute truth, you believe that?"

"Yes, I believe that."

"They're completely certain that there's nothing wrong. You're perfectly healthy. There won't be any after-effects. I made sure that they weren't hiding anything. I had to know for my own sake, you understand, don't you? They're completely certain."

"That must be pleasant for them."

"You ought to give them credit, they're very good doctors."

"I'm not much moved by that."

"You're not willing to be moved by anything, are you?"

"I haven't time to be."

She drew in her breath, but didn't speak. Then, after we

had each been quiet, my temper seethed out—with the
anger that I had fantasised about discharging on Mansel, but
which I couldn't show to him or anyone else, except to her.
For it was only to her—who knew all about the pride, the
vanity, the ironies, even the discipline with which I covered
up what I didn't choose for others to see—that I could speak
from the pitiful, the abject depth.

"Why do you expect me to listen to them?" I shouted.
"Do you really think they've been so clever? They even
admit that they haven't any idea why they nearly put me out
yesterday. Why should anyone believe what they say about
tomorrow? They won't have any more idea when I've had it
for good. You expect me to believe them. Remember it was
they who let me in for this."

"It's no use blaming them—"

"Why isn't it? It was an absurd risk to take. Just for a
minor bit of sight which is about as good as yours when
you're seeing through a fog. Just for that, they're ready to
take the chance of finishing me off."

"No, dear." After the harsh cries I had made, her voice
was low. "That isn't right. Christopher Mansel wasn't taking
a chance. It would all have gone normally—except for once
in ten thousand times."

"That's what they've told you, is it? How have they got
the impertinence to say it? I tell you, they don't know anything. It was an absurd risk to take. We never ought to have
allowed it. I blame myself. You might think back. I didn't
like it at the time. Mansel persuaded me. We ought to have
stopped it."

"That wouldn't have been reasonable."

"Do you think that what they've achieved is specially reasonable? We ought to have stopped it."

I went on:

"You ought to have helped me to stop it."

"That's not fair," she cried.

"It's the fact."

"No, it's not fair. Are you blaming me?"

"I'm blaming myself more."

Reproaching me for other times when I had thrown guilt on to her, she was angry as well as wounded. For a time it became a quarrel: until she said, tone not steady:

"Look here, I didn't come for this. Whatever are we doing?"

"Exchanging views."

She laughed, with what sounded like relief. I had spoken in something near the manner she was used to, when I was ironing an argument away. It came as a surprise to her—and so much so to me that it passed me by. To me, it seemed that we had moved into the doldrums of a quarrel (like Azik and Rosalind that afternoon in Eaton Square), when we had temporarily ceased lashing out, but were waiting for the animus to blow up again. But Margaret, listening to me raging, accepted the anger and the cruelty; sometimes she had seen that in me before; she had not seen me as frightened as this morning, but that too she accepted. And so, she was ready to notice the first change of inner weather, long before I recognised it myself. She was sure that I was, at least for the time being, through the worst. Casually she chatted, mentioning one or two letters that had arrived at home, pouring herself a drink: in fact, she was watchful, prepared to talk me to sleep or alternatively to take the initiative.

She did take the initiative, in a language that no one on earth but she and I could understand:

"I've got a lunch date on Saturday," she said. "I expect I shall forget it."

If I didn't or couldn't respond, she would drop it. This was an exploration, a tentative.

"You'd better not," I said.

"It hasn't been imprinted on my memory."

At that, I laughed out loud. She knew she was home. For this was a secret code, one of our versions of the exchange about the cattleya, more complicated than that but just as cherished. It went back to a time in the middle of the war, before we were married. On Saturday afternoons I used to go to her bed-sitting room: there was a particular Saturday afternoon about which we had made a myth. The coal fire. The looking glass. Lying in bed afterwards, watching the sky darken and firelight on the ceiling. The curious thing was, that apparently historical Saturday afternoon didn't really exist. There were plenty of others. Once or twice, in the wartime rush, she had forgotten the place for lunch and I had had to follow her to her room. Many times we had enjoyed ourselves there. Yes, there had been a coal fire and a looking glass. Nevertheless, we each remembered the detail of different Saturdays, and somehow had fused them into one. One that became a symbol for all the pleasure we had had together, and a signal to each other. Often the mood was formalised. "What did I tell you about the fire?" To that there was a ritual reply, also part of the myth. In the hospital that morning, she made the ritual speeches, and I followed suit. Soon she was crying:

"You're *much* better." That also was part of the drill, but for that special moment it was true.

Resurrection, she was saying, not touching wood at all. Until the middle of the afternoon, she remained by my bedside. When she left me it was I who began to touch wood. She had gone, the reassurance had gone, it seemed strange, almost unnatural, that the vacuum hadn't filled. Should I soon be terrified again? I threw my thoughts back, not to Margaret, but to last night, as though I wanted to learn whether it would return. No, my moods were unstable, I hadn't any confidence in them, but I wasn't frightened. Perversely, I wanted to ask why I wasn't. Anything I felt or told myself now, I thought, would be part of a mood that wouldn't last.

Still, the evening—occasionally I enquired about the time —lagged on between sleep and waking. They were taking my blood pressure every three hours, but one nurse told me that would finish next day. During the night I slept heavily, and woke only once, when they took another reading.

I didn't know where I was, until I understood the darkness in front of my eyes. Then the night before returned, but rather as though I was reading words off a screen, without either fright or relief: with a curious indifference, as though I hadn't energy to waste.

TWENTY

OBITUARY

Sponge in my hands, warm water on my face, Mansel's voice, the flurry of early morning.

"They tell me you've slept, sir."

"Better, anyway," I said, as though it were bad luck to admit it.

Eye uncovered, the lights of the room, three dimensions of the commode, standing out like a piece of hardware by Chardin. Mansel's face close to mine. In a short time, he said:

"Good. Qualified optimism still permitted."

After he had blindfolded me once more, his voice sounded as in a prepared speech.

"Now we have to make a decision, sir."

My nerves sharpened. "What's the matter?"

"Nothing. It's a choice of two courses, that's all. You heard me and Maxim discuss it yesterday, didn't you?"

"I heard something."

"You're getting on well, you know. The point is, if we're going to get you generally fit as soon as may be, you probably ought to sit up most of today. Now that may, just possibly, disturb the eye. I'm beginning to think, I may as well tell you, that we're very likely too finicky about keeping eye patients still. I suspect in a few years it will seem very old-fashioned. But I have to say that some of my colleagues wouldn't agree. So, if we let you up, one has to warn you, there is—so far as the retina goes—a finite risk."

I was beginning to speak, but Mansel stopped me.

"I'm not going to let you make the choice. Though I fancy I know which it would be. No, I don't think there is any reasonable doubt. Your general health is much more important than a margin of risk to the retina. Which I don't want you to get depressed about. With a little good fortune, we ought to keep that in order too."

He could see my face.

"And it will be distinctly good for your morale, won't it?"

Mansel gave an amiable, clinical chuckle. "Though it's stood up pretty well, I give you that." He didn't know it all, but he knew something. I was thinking, perhaps not even Margaret knew it all.

After he had given instructions that the nurses were to get me up during the morning, he was saying goodbye. Then he had another thought.

"I wanted to ask you. Which is the hardest to put up with? Having to lie still. Or having to live in the dark."

"You needn't have asked," I said. "Having to live in the dark is about a hundred times worse."

"I thought so. I have had patients who got frantic at being fixed in one position. But you manage to put up with that, don't you? Good morning, sir."

When Charles March arrived, I was already sitting up in an armchair. They had told me that he had visited the hospital twice in the last twenty-four hours, being not only an old friend but also my doctor. Each time he came, I had been asleep. Now I apologised, saying that I hadn't been entirely responsible for my actions. Charles replied that he had dimly realised that that was the case.

I suspected that he was gazing straight into my face. How much did it tell him? There weren't many more ⌐bservant

men. He said, in a matter-of-fact doctorlike fashion, that he
was glad they had got me up. Mansel, in the middle of his
professional circuit, had found time to telephone Charles
twice about my condition, and had also written him a long-
ish letter.

"If either of us were as efficient as that young man," I
said, "we might have got somewhere."

It was not long after, and we were still chatting, not yet
intimately, that I heard Margaret's footsteps on the floor outside. As she came in, she exclaimed in surprise, and ap-
proaching my chair, asked how I was, said in the same
breath that they must be satisfied with me to let me out of
bed. Then she went on:

"How is he, Charles?"

"I think he looks pretty good, don't you agree?"

For some time neither of them enquired, even by implica-
tion, about my state of mind: in fact, I soon believed that
they were shying off it. Margaret had seen enough the day
before: and Charles, who had once known me as well as any
of my friends, was being cautious. We talked about our children and relatives: it was casually, in the midst of the conversation, that she remarked;

"What are you going to do with yourself all day, sitting
there?"

"Exactly what I should do lying there." Blindly I moved a
hand in what I thought to be the direction of the bed. "It's
even a slight improvement, you know."

"Of course it is." Margaret sounded quick, affirmative,
like one correcting a piece of her own tactlessness.

Then I said: "No. There's going to be a difference."

"What do you mean?"

"I'm not going to sit here all day doing nothing. I'd like
you to get some people in. If I can't see them, I might as
well hear them."

"So you shall." But Margaret, busy with practical arrangements, saying that she would pass the word round by tomorrow, promising that she would send in some bottles of Scotch, was nevertheless puzzled as well as pleased. So was Charles: for they both knew that this was quite unlike me, that in illness—as in my first operation—I wanted to hide like a sick animal, seeing no one except my family, and them only out of duty. I couldn't have enlightened them. It was one of the occasions when one seemed to be performing like a sleepwalker. If I had been forced to give an explanation, I should probably have said—very lamely—that I realised, as on the day before, that this mood, or any other mood, wouldn't last, but that I wished to commit myself to it. Perhaps I could fight off regressions, the return to that night, the sense of—nothing, once I had announced that I intended to have people round me.

Later Charles told me that that was very near his own interpretation. He thought that I was trying to hold on to something concrete, so as to ward off the depressive swing. With Margaret it was different. Of the three of us, she alone thought that I was stabler than I myself believed, and that she could see—unperceived, or even denied, by me—not only a new resolve, but underneath it a singular, sharp but indefinable change.

If she had been beside me in a waking spell that night, she mightn't have been astonished at what I felt. First I spoke out loud, to see if there were a nurse in the room. Then I realised that the blood pressure watch had been called off, they were leaving me alone. That didn't frighten me or even remind me. On the contrary, I was immediately taken over by a benign and strangely innocent happiness. I didn't for an instant understand it. It was different in kind from any happiness that I had known, utterly different from the serenity, the half-complaisant satisfaction, in which I had gone about after refusing the government job. Perhaps the nearest approach would be nights when I had wakened and recalled a piece of work that had gone well. But that wasn't very near —this didn't have an element of memory or self-concern. It was as innocent as nights when I woke up as a child and enjoyed the sound of a lashing storm outside. It was so benign that I did not want to go to sleep again.

After Mansel had examined me next morning, he was ruminating on what he called 'morale.' Mine was still keeping up, he thought, with his usual inspectorial honesty. A doctor never really knew how a patient would react to extreme situations.

"You're very modest, Christopher," I said.

"No, sir. Just open-minded, I hope."

Both of us ought to be interested in my morale, he said. I spent some time at it, I remarked, but Mansel was not amused. Tomorrow, he said, there might be another minor decision for us to take.

Taking me at my word, Margaret had telephoned the previous afternoon to say that I could expect some visitors. The first, in the middle of the morning, was Francis Getliffe. His tread sounded heavy, as it used to sound up my staircase in college, for so spare a man. I greeted him by name before he reached me, and he responded as though I had performed a conjuring trick.

"One's ears get rather sharp," I said.

"You're putting up with it better than I could."

"Nonsense. Little you know."

"Yes, you are. You can cope with it, can't you?" His tone was affectionate but hesitant. Perhaps, I thought (for I hadn't seen him with anyone incapacitated before), he was one of those inhibited when they had to speak to the blind or deaf. I said that it was tiresome not being able to see him.

"I bet it must be." But that was an absentminded reply; he

was thinking of something else. As he talked, still hesitantly, I realised that Margaret must have told him the whole case history. Not that he referred to it straight out: he was skirting round it, trying not to touch a nerve, wanting to take care of me. He felt safer when he was on neutral ground, such as politics. The world was looking blacker. We agreed, in all the time we had known each other, there had been only three periods of hope—outside our own private lives, that is. The Twenties: curiously enough, wartime: and then the five or six years just past. But that last had been a false hope, we admitted it now.

"If anyone," said Francis, "can show me one single encouraging sign anywhere in the world this year, I'd be very grateful."

"Yes," I said. Things had gone worse than expectations, even realistic or minimum expectations. As Einstein in old age had said, there seemed a weird inevitability about it all. Very little that Francis and I had done together had been useful.

"This country is steadier than most. But I can't imagine what will have happened before we're ten years older. I'm not sure that I want to."

It was all sensible: yet was he just talking to play out time? I broke out:

"Forty-eight hours ago, I should have been quite sure that I didn't want to."

He said something, embarrassed, kind, but I went on:

"It would have seemed quite remarkably irrelevant. It rather restricts one's interests, you know, when you're told you might have been dead."

"Do you mind talking about it?"

"Not in the slightest."

"I couldn't if I were you."

Strangely—as I had been realising while the earlier con-

versation went on, impersonal and strained—that was the
fact. What I had said, which wouldn't have troubled Charles
March or my brother, risked making him more awkward still.
It was a deliberate risk. Francis, who was a brave man,
physically as well as morally, was less hardened than most of
us.

While he had been talking, so diffidently, I had recalled
an incident of the fairly recent past. At that time it was not
unusual, if one moved in the official world, to be asked to
prepare an advance obituary notice of an acquaintance—all
ready for the *Times*. I had done several. One day, it must
have been three or four years before, someone announced
himself on the telephone as a member of the paper's staff.
Agitation. He had found that by some oversight, on which
he elaborated with distress, there was no obituary of Francis
Getliffe. How could this be? "It would be terrible," said the
anxious voice, "I shouldn't like to be caught short about a
man like Getliffe."

While I was reflecting on that peculiar expression, I was
being pressed to produce an obituary—in forty-eight hours?
at latest by the end of the week? Francis was in robust health
when last seen, I said, but the voice said, "We can't take any
risks." So I agreed and set to work. Most of it was easy, since
I knew Francis's career as well as my own, but I wasn't familiar with his early childhood. His father had married twice,
and I had heard almost nothing about his second wife, Francis's mother. So I had to ring up Cambridge. Francis was out,
but his wife Katherine answered the phone. When I told her
the object of the exercise, she broke into a cheerful scream,
and then, no more worried than I was myself, gave businesslike answers. She would pass the good news on to Francis,
she said. She had listened to some of his colleagues fretting,
in case their obituary should be written by an enemy.

I had met Francis in London shortly afterwards. Without

a second thought, I told him the piece was written and pre-sumably safe in the *Times* files. I asked him if he would like to read a copy. Without a second thought—taking it for granted that he would like what I had written, and also tak-ing it for granted that he would behave like an old-style ra-tionalist. For in that respect Francis often behaved like a doctrinaire unbeliever of an earlier century than ours; like, for example, old Winslow, who refused to set foot in college chapel except for magisterial elections, and then only after making written protests. Francis likewise did not go into chapel even for memorial services; his children had not been baptised and, when he was introduced into the Lords, in-stead of taking the oath he affirmed. Whereas men like my brother Martin, who believed as little as Francis, would go through the forms without fuss, saying, as Martin did, that if he had been a Roman he would have put a pinch of salt on the altar and not felt that he was straining his conscience.

So innocently I asked Francis if he would care to read his obituary. "Certainly not," Francis had said, outraged. Or perhaps hag-ridden, like a Russian seeing one trying to shake his hand across the threshold, or my mother turning up the ace of spades.

When, as Francis was taking care to avoid any subject which might disquiet me, I recalled that incident, it oc-curred to me that someone must have written my own obitu-ary. I expected to feel a chill, but none came. It was curious to be waiting for that kind of dread, and then be untouched.

After I had been brusque, cutting out the delicateness, Francis became easier. He said:

"This mustn't happen again, you know."

"It's bound to happen again once, isn't it?"

"Not like that. I was horrified when Margaret told me. I must say, she was very good."

She had had the worst of it, Francis was saying. Almost as

though I had done it on purpose, it crossed my mind. No, that was quite unfair. Francis, whom acquaintances thought buttoned-up and bleak, was speaking with emotion. He had been horrified. I was too careless. Did I give a thought to how much I should be missed?

Though I was to most appearances more spontaneous than Francis I shouldn't, if our positions were reversed, have told him so simply how much I'd miss him.

I nearly gave another grim answer such as even that seemed a somewhat secondary consideration, but it would have been denying affection. Of the people we had grown up with, we had scarcely, except ourselves, any intimates left. Some had died: other the chances of life had driven away, just as Francis had been parted from his brother-in-law Charles March.

And I, who felt the old affinity with Charles March each time we met, nevertheless had ceased to be close to him, simply because there was no routine of living to bring us together. While Francis and I, during much of our lives, had seen each other every day at meetings. It sounded mechanical, but as you grew older that kind of habit and alliance was a part of intimacy without which it peacefully declined.

Francis's tone altered, he began to sound at his most practical. He proposed to talk to some of his medical friends in the Royal. This never ought to have happened, he said. It was no use passing it off as a fluke or an accident. There must be a cause. What sort of anaesthetic had they used? This all had to be cleared up in case I was forced some day into another operation. There had to be a bit of decent scientific thinking, he said, with impatience as well as clarity— just as he used to speak, cutting through cotton wool, at committee tables during the war.

That could be coped with. And also, he went on, half-sternly, half-persuasively, it was time I took myself in hand.

I had worked hard all my life: it was time I made more of my leisure. "I'm damned well going to enjoy my sixties, and so ought you," he said. He was leading up to a project that he had mentioned before. The house in Cambridge, full of children, happy-go-lucky, called by young Charles and his friends the Getliffe steading, he couldn't bear to leave, he would stay there in termtime always. But he and Katherine were hankering after another house, more likely to get some sun in winter, maybe somewhere like Provence. Why shouldn't we find a place together? They would occupy it perhaps four months a year, and Margaret and I in spring and autumn?

We couldn't travel far while Margaret's father was alive, I replied, as I had done previously. No, but that couldn't be forever. Francis was set on the plan, more set than when he first introduced it. It would be good for his married children and their families. It would be good for ours—Charles, Francis said, would be mysteriously asking to have the house to himself, and leaving us to guess whom he was bringing there.

He was so active, so determined to get me into the sunshine, that I was almost persuaded. It might be pleasant as we all became old. But I held on enough not to make the final promise. I wasn't as hospitable as Francis, nor anything like as fond of movement. Anyway, now the plan had crystallised, I didn't doubt that he would carry it through, whether I joined in or not. It had started as a scheme largely for my sake: but also Francis, decisive and executive as ever, was carving out a pattern for his old age.

TWENTY-ONE

SILENCE OF A SON

Before evening, the room was smelling of flowers and whisky. The flowers were due, in the main, to Azik Schiff, who hadn't come to visit me himself but whose response to physical ailments was to provide a lavish display of horticulture. More flowers than they'd ever seen sent, said the nurses, and my credit rose in consequence. Though I could have done without the hyacinths which, since my nose was sensitive to begin with and had been made more so by blindness, gave me a headache, the only malaise of the day.

As for the whisky, that had been drunk before lunch by Hector Rose and his wife and after tea by Margaret and a visitor who hadn't been invited, my nephew Pat. When Margaret was sitting beside my chair and she was reading me the morning's letters, there were footsteps, male footsteps, that I didn't recognise. But I did recognise a stiffening in Margaret's voice as she said good afternoon.

"Hello, Aunt Meg. Hello, Uncle Lew. Good to see you up. That's better, isn't it, that really is better."

It was a situation in which, given enough nerve, he was bound to win. Whatever he didn't have, he had enough nerve. Though he might have been slandering Margaret and her children, she couldn't raise a quarrel in a hospital bedroom. And he was reckoning that I was quite incapacitated. There he might have been wrong: but, as usual in Pat's presence, I didn't want to say what a juster man might have said. Margaret stayed silent: and I was reduced to asking Pat how he had heard about me.

"Well-known invalid, of course."

"No," I said, "we've kept it very quiet. On purpose."

"Not quiet enough, Uncle Lew." Pat's voice was ebullient and full of cheek.

Margaret had still said nothing, but I listened to the splash of liquid. Presumably he was helping himself to a drink. He said, irrepressible, that he couldn't reveal his sources—and then gave an account, almost completely accurate, of what had happened since I entered the hospital. Massage of the heart. Margaret being sent for.

"It must have been terrible for you, Aunt Meg."

Margaret had to reply.

"I shouldn't like to go through it again," she said. The curious thing was, his sympathy was genuine.

"Terrible," he said again. Then he couldn't resist showing that he knew the name of the heart specialist, and even how he had telephoned Margaret on the first night.

That was something I hadn't been told myself. As before with Pat, just as in the past with Gilbert Cooke, I felt uncomfortably hemmed in, as though I was being watched by a flashy but fairly successful private detective. Actually, I realised later that there was no mystery about Pat's source of information. There was only one person whom it could have come from. My brother Martin had been asking Margaret for news several times a day. And Martin, who was as discreet as Hector Rose in his least forthcoming moments, who had, when working on the atomic bomb, never let slip a secret even to his wife, on this occasion as on others could, and must, have told everything to his son.

Pat might be said to have outstayed his welcome, if there

had been any welcome. Talking cheerfully, the bounce and sparkle not diminishing, he stayed until Margaret herself had to leave. But there had been, aided by alcohol, some truce of amicability in the room. Margaret had taken another drink, and Pat several more. It was I who was left out: for to me, who wasn't yet drinking, there might be amicability in the room, but there was also an increasing smell of whisky.

Later that night, when I had been put back to bed, the telephone rang on the bedside table. Gropingly, my hand got hold of the recceiver. It was Margaret.

"I don't want to worry you, but I think you'd better know. It's not serious, but it's rather irritating."

Normally, I should have demanded the news at once. But in the calm in which I was existing, as yet inexplicable to me but nevertheless very happy, I wasn't in a hurry. I asked if it were anything to do with Charles, and Margaret said no. I said: "You needn't mind about worrying me, you know."

"Well," came her voice, "there's an item in one of the later editions. I think I'd better read it, hadn't I?"

"Go ahead."

The item, Margaret told me, occurred in a new-style gossip column, copied from New York. It read something to the effect that I had been undergoing optical surgery, and that there had been complications which had caused "grave concern."

When she rang up to break the news, Margaret assumed that this would enrage and worry me. She had seen me and others close to me secretive about their health. One of the first lessons you learned in any sort of professional life was that you should never be ill. It reduced your *mana*. When I was a young man, and just attracting some work at the Bar, I had been told that I was seriously ill: I had gone to extreme lengths to conceal it: if I had died, it wouldn't have mattered anyway—and if, as it turned out, I didn't, well then I had been right.

Nowadays I was removed from the official life: but even to a writer, it did harm—an impalpable superstitious discreditable harm—if people heard that your death was near. You were already on the way to being dispensed with. The way they talked about you—'did you know, poor old X seems to be finished'—was dismissive rather than cruel, though there was a twist of gloating there, showing through their self-congratulation that they were still right in the middle of the mortal scene.

So Margaret anticipated that this bit of news would harass me—and, before I went into hospital, she would have been right. Now it didn't. I said:

"Oh, that doesn't matter."

"We'd better do something, hadn't we?"

I was reflecting. The lessons I had learned seemed very distant; but still they had been learned, and one might as well not throw them away.

"Yes," I said. "I suppose we'd better be prudent. I'll make Christopher Mansel send out a bulletin."

"Shall I talk to him tonight?"

"It can wait until he comes in tomorrow morning."

When Margaret had rung off, I lay in bed, not thinking of Mansel's bulletin, but contentedly preoccupied with a problem that gave me a certain pleasure. Whoever had leaked that news? It couldn't be the doctors. It couldn't be my family. Someone in the hospital? Just possibly. Someone whom Margaret had talked to, trying to enlist visitors for me? Possibly.

No, the answer was too easy. There was one person who stood out, beautifully probable. Motive, opportunity, the lot. I would bet heavily on my nephew Pat. He had his contacts with the young journalists. Once or twice before, our doings had been speculated about knowledgeably in the gossip columns. Pat was not above receiving a pound or two as a link-man. There was not much which Pat was above.

The next morning, as Mansel said good morning, I told him about the rumor and said that I wanted him to correct it.

"Right, sir. There are one or two things first, though."

After he had examined the left eye, he said:

"Promising." He paused, like a minister answering a supplementary question, wanting to give satisfaction, so long as it wasn't the final commitment: "I think I can say, we shall be unlucky if anything goes wrong this time."

Quick fingers, and the eye was shut into darkness again.

"That'll do, I think." Mansel was gazing at me as though he had made an excellent joke.

"What about the other eye?" I said.

"You can have that, if you like." He gave a short allocution. What I had said the day before was what he expected most patients to say. He had already decided to leave the good eye unblinded. It was more convenient to have me in hospital for a few more days: I should stand it better if I had an eye to see with. The advantages of blinding both eyes probably wasn't worth the psychological wear-and-tear. "I'm pretty well convinced," said Mansel, "that we've got to learn to do these operations and leave you one working eye right from the start."

I said that I should like to stand him a drink, but in his profession, at 6:45 in the morning, that didn't seem quite appropriate. I said also that, if he would leave me one eye, he could go through the entire eye operation again. Without any frills or additions, however.

Mansel was scrutinising me.

"You could face it again, could you?"

"If it's not going to happen, one can face anything."

He seemed to make another entry in his mental notebook —*behaviour of patient, after being allowed vision.*

"Well, sir, what about this statement? That's really your department, not mine, you know." It was true, he was not so brisk, masterful and masterly when he sat down and started to compose.

Ballpoint pen tapping his teeth, he stayed motionless, like Henry James in search of the exact, the perfect, the unique word. After a substantial interval, at least fifteen minutes, he said, with unhabitual diffidence, with a touch of pride:

"How will this do?"

He read out the name of the hospital, and then—

Sir Lewis Eliot entered this hospital on November 27, and next day an operation was performed for a retinal detachment in the left eye. As a result there are good prospects that the eye will be restored to useful vision. During the course of the operation, Sir Lewis underwent a cardiac arrest. This was treated in a routine manner. In all respects, Sir Lewis's progress and condition are excellent.

"Well, Christopher," I said, "no one could call you a sensational writer."

"I think that says all that's necessary."

"Cardiac arrest, that's what you call it, is it?"

I hadn't heard the phrase before. Though, by a coincidence, when my eye first went wrong, two years earlier, I had been reminded of an older phrase, 'arrest of life.' Perhaps that was too melodramatic for a black veil over half an eye. This time, it didn't seem so.

"After all," I remarked absently to Mansel, "one doesn't have too many."

"Too many what?"

"Arrests of life."

"Cardiac arrests is what we say. No, of course not, most people only have one."

Unfussed, he went off to telephone the bulletin to the Press Association, while I got up, self-propelled again, and, being able to see, was also able to eat. It was a luxury to sit, free from the solipsistic darkness, and just gaze out of the window—though, even as the sky lightened, it was still a leaden morning, and bedroom lamps were being switched on, high up in the houses opposite.

Mansel had told the nurses not to let me move, except from bed to chair. But the telephone was fixed close by, and I rang Margaret up, telling her to bring reading matter. That wasn't specially urgent, it was good enough to enjoy looking at things. But this presumably soon ceased to be a treat. Thirty years ago, I was remembering, an eminent writer had given me some unsolicited advice. Just look at an orange, she said. Go on looking at it. For hours. Then put down what you see. In the hospital room there was, as it happened, an orange. I looked at it. I thought that I should soon have enough of—what had she called it? the physiognomic charm of phenomena.

It was a relief when the telephone rang. The porter in the entrance hall, announcing that Mr. Eliot was down below. "We've been told to send up the names of visitors from now on, sir." Mr. Eliot? It could be one of three. When I heard quick steps far down the corridor, my ear was still attuned. That was Charles.

He came across the room and, in silence, shook my hand. Then he sat down, still without speaking. It was unlike him, or both of us together, to be so silent. There was a constraint between us right from the beginning.

With my unobscured eye, I was gazing at him. He gazed back at me. He said:

"I didn't expect—"

"What?"

"Tnat they'd let you see."

"New technique," I said, glad to have a topic to start us talking. I explained why Mansel had unblinded me.

"It must be an improvement."

"Enormous."

We were talking like strangers, impersonally impressed by a medical advance: no, more concentrated upon eye surgery, more eager not to deviate from it, than if we had been strangers.

Another pause, as though we had forgotten the trick of talking, at which people thought we were both so easy.

At last I said:

"This has been a curious experience."

"I suppose so." Then quickly: "You're looking pretty well."

"I think I'm probably very well. Never better in my life, I dare say. It seems an odd way of achieving it."

Charles gave a tight smile, but he wasn't responding to the kind of sarcasm, or grim facetiousness, with which he and I, and Martin also, liked to greet our various fatalities. Was I making claims on him that he couldn't meet? The last time my eye had gone wrong, and it seemed that I was going to lose its sight, he had been fierce with concern. Then he had been two years younger. Now, in so many ways a man, he spoke, or didn't speak, as though his concern was knotted up, inexpressible, or so tangled that he couldn't let it out.

It was strange, it was more than strange, it was disappointing and painful, that he should be self-conscious as I had scarcely seen him. At this time of all times. I thought later that perhaps we knew too much: too much to be easy, that is, not enough to come out on the other side. He had plenty of insight, but he wasn't trusting it, as the constraint got hold of us, nor was I mine.

A father's death. What did one feel? What was one supposed to feel? Sheer loss, pious and organic, a part of oneself cut away—that would have been the proper answer in my childhood: but a lot of sons knew that it wasn't so clean and comfortable as that. When I was growing up, the answer would have changed. Now it meant oneself at last established, final freedom, the Oedipal load removed: and a lot of sons still knew that it wasn't so clean and unambiguous as that. As Charles was growing up, all the Oedipal inheritance had passed into the conventional wisdom, at least for those educated like him: and, like most conventional wisdom, it was half believed and half thrown away.

Probably Charles and his friends weren't so impressed by it as by the introspective masters: Dostoevsky meant more to them than the psychoanalysts did. Not surprisingly to me, for at twenty, older than they were and having lived rougher, I also had been overwhelmed. I had met, as they had, the difficult questions. *Who has not wished his father dead?*

That hadn't meant much to me since, from a very early age, I could scarcely be said to have a relation with my father. From fourteen or so onwards, I was the senior partner, so far as we had a partnership, and he regarded me with mild and bantering stupefaction. Perhaps I had suffered more than I knew because he was unavailing. His bankruptcy in my childhood left some sort of wound. It was also possible that as a child I knew more than I realised about his furtive chases after women. I had a memory, which might not have been genuine but was very sharp, of standing at the age of seven or eight outside a rubber shop—with my father blinking across the counter, which mysteriously gave me gooseflesh as though it were a threat or warning. Still, all that was searching back with hindsight. During the short part of our lives which we had lived together, we impinged on each other as little as father and son, or even two members of the same family, ever could.

It was not like that with me and Charles. Partly because our temperaments were too much the same weight, and though we were in many respects different, in the end we wanted the same things. And there was a complication, simply because I had lived some of my life in public. That meant that Charles couldn't escape me and that, without special guilt on either side, I got in his way.

That night when he returned home from his travels, I had said in effect that I was leaving him an awkward legacy. He had replied, more harshly than seemed called for, that he wouldn't be worried over. In fact, on the specific point I had been wrong. He didn't mind in the least that, when I died, some of the conflicts and enmities would live on and he would sometimes pay for them. That he not only didn't mind but welcomed. For, though he couldn't endure my protecting him, he was cheerful and fighting-happy at the chance of his protecting me. And if he had to do it posthumously, well, he was at least as tenacious as I was.

It was not the penalties that he wanted to escape, but the advantages. He had seen and heard my name too often. There were times when I seemed omnipresent. Anyone of strong nature—from my end, it was a somewhat bitter irony —would have preferred to be born obscure.

Yet perhaps I was making it too easy for myself. Perhaps —if he had never heard my name outside the family—we should still have faced each other in the hospital bedroom with the same silences. Perhaps it was ourselves that we couldn't escape. He might still have expected me to claim more than I did. I should have still felt ill-used, for I be-

lieved that I had been unpossessive, had claimed little or
nothing, and wanted us to exist side by side.

Was that true? Was that all? My relation with Charles was
utterly unlike mine with my own father. That was certain.
But, as we sat in that room, the familiar sardonic exchanges
not there to bring us together or smooth the minutes away,
I felt a shiver—more than that, a menace and a remorse—
from the past. For Charles was behaving now very much,
nerve of the same nerve, as I had behaved when I sat by my
mother at her deathbed.

It was more than forty years before. Instead of a smell
evoking the past, the past evoked a smell: in my hygienic
flower-lined room, I smelt brandy, eau-de-cologne, the warm
redolence of the invalid's bedroom. Then I had sat with the
tight constrained feeling, full of dread, which overcame me
when she called out for my love. For I couldn't give it her,
at least in the terms she claimed.

"I wanted to go along with you," she had cried, demanding more for me than I did for myself. "That's all I wanted."

I did my best (I was about the same age as Charles was
now) to console her. Yet, whenever I felt remorse, I had to
recall one thing—whatever I did, I hadn't brought her comfort. She was the proudest of women, she was vain, but she
had an eye for truth. She knew as well as I that if one's heart
is invaded by another (that was how I used to think, when
my taste was more florid, and I didn't mind the sound of
rhetoric), then one will either assist the invasion or repel it.
I repelled it, longing that I might do otherwise. And she
knew.

I had been as proud as my mother, and in some ways as
vain. Some of that pride and vanity was exorcised by now:
for I had lived much longer than she did, and age, though it
didn't kill vanity, took the edge of it away. Like her, I sometimes couldn't deceive myself about the truth. Charles was

behaving as I had done. Was it also true that, against my will and anything that I desired, without knowing it I was affecting him as she had me? Had the remorse come back, through all those years, and made me learn what it had been like for her, and what it was now like for me?

Charles's tone changed, as he said:

"There is something I wanted to tell you."

"What's that?"

"Maurice and Godfrey" (Maurice's parson friend) "will be coming in later today."

"That's all right."

"Yes, but you mustn't put your foot in it, you know." His eyes had taken on a piercing glint: there was a joke at my expense. Suddenly he had switched—and I with him, seeing that expression—to our most companionable.

"What are you accusing me of now?"

"You might forget that old Godfrey has a professional interest in you, don't you think?"

"Aren't I usually fairly polite?"

"Fairly."

"Well then. I don't propose to stop being polite, just because the man is an Anglo-Catholic priest."

"So long," Charles's smile was matey and taunting, "as you don't forget that he *is* an Anglo-Catholic priest."

I taunted him back:

"My memory is in excellent order, you'll be glad to know."

"That's not the point."

"Come on, what do you want me to say to the man?"

"It's what I don't want you to say that counts."

"And that is?"

"Look here, it isn't everyone who's done a Lazarus, is it?"

"Granted," I said.

"It's therefore reasonable to suppose that a priest will have a special interest in you, don't you realise? After all, we expect him to have some concern about life after death, don't we?"

"Granted again."

"Well then, you'd better not say much about first-hand knowledge, had you? I should have thought this wasn't precisely the occasion."

We had each known what this duologue meant, all along. About his friends' susceptibilities, or his acquaintances' as well, Charles could be sensitive and farsighted. But also he had constructed a legend about me as a blunt unrestrained Johnsonian figure, in contrast to his own subtlety. It was the kind of legend that grows up in various kinds of intimacy. In almost exactly the same way, Roy Calvert used to pretend to be on tenterhooks waiting for some gigantesque piece of tactlessness from me: on the basis that, just as William the Silent got his nickname through being silent on one occasion, so I had been shatteringly tactless once. With both of them—often Charles acted towards me as Roy Calvert used to—they liked rubbing the legend in. And Charles in particular used this device to make amends. It took the heat out of either affection or constraint or the complex of the two, and gave us the comfort we both liked.

TWENTY-TWO

THE FOUR THINGS

As Charles had prepared me, Maurice and Father Ailwyn duly arrived later that day, round half-past four, when I had finished drinking tea. The quixotic pair came through the door, Maurice so thin that he looked taller than he was, Father Ailwyn the reverse. Since all my family called Ailwyn by his Christian name, I had to do the same, although I knew him only slightly. He gave a shy, fat-cheeked smile, small eyes sharp and uncertain behind his glasses, cassock billowing round thick-soled boots. While they were settling down in their chairs, he was abnormally diffident, not able to make any kind of chat, or even to reply to ours. Maurice had told me that he was quite as inept when he visited the old and lonely: a stuttering awkward hulk of a fat man, grateful when Maurice, who might be self-effacing but was never shy, acted as a lubricant. Yet, they said, Godfrey Ailwyn was the most devoted of parish priests, and the desolate liked him, even if he couldn't talk much, just because he never missed a visit and patiently sat with them.

With the excessive heartiness that the diffident induced, I asked if he would have some tea.

"No, thank you. I'm not much good at tea."

His tone was hesitating, but upper class—not professional, not high bourgeois. Even my old acquaintance, Lord Boscastle, arbiter of origins, might have performed the extraordinary feat of 'knowing who he was'—which meant that his family could be found in reference books.

"I'm pretty sure," said Maurice, "that Godfrey would like a drink. Wouldn't you now, Godfrey?"

The doleful plump countenance lightened.

"If it isn't any trouble—"

"Of course it isn't." Maurice, used to looking after the other man, was already standing by the bottles, pouring out a formidable whisky. "That's all right, isn't it?"

Maurice, taking the glass round, explained to me, as though he were an interpreter, that Godfrey had had a busy day, mass in the morning, parish calls, a couple of young delinquents at the vicarage—

"It must be a tough life," I said.

Godfrey smiled tentatively, took a swig at his drink, and then, all of a sudden asked me, with such abruptness that it sounded rough:

"You don't remember anything about it, do you?"

For an instant I was taken by surprise, as though I hadn't heard the question right, or didn't understand it. I hadn't expected him to take the initiative.

"Maurice says you didn't remember anything about it. When you came to."

"I wasn't exactly at my most lucid, of course."

"But you didn't remember anything?"

"I was more concerned with what was happening there and then."

"You still don't remember anything?"

I was ready to persevere with evasion, but he was not giving me much room to manoeuvre.

"Would you expect me to?" I asked.

"It was like waking from a very deep sleep, was it?"

"I think one might say that."

Father Ailwyn gave a sharp-eyed glance in Maurice's direc-

tion, as though they were sharing a joke, and then turned to
me with an open, slumbrous smile, the kind of smile which
transformed depressive faces such as his.

"Please don't be afraid of worrying me," he said, and
added: "Lewis, I am interested, you know."

"Godfrey said on the way here that he wished he wasn't a
clergyman." Maurice was also smiling. "He didn't want to
put you off."

I should have something to report to young Charles when
next I saw him, I was thinking.

"I'm not going to be prissy with you," said Godfrey. "All
I'm asking you is to return the compliment."

I had come off worst and gave an apologetic smile.

"Eschatology is rather a concern of ours, you see. But most
believers wouldn't think that you were interfering with their
eschatology. They'd be pretty certain to say, and here I don't
mind admitting that they sometimes take an easy way out,
that you hadn't really been dead."

Instead of being inarticulate, or so shy as to be embarrassing to others, he had begun to talk as though he were in
practice.

"I don't think I've ever claimed that, have I?" I said.

"I should have thought that, by inference, you had. And
most believers would tell you that it's very difficult to define
the threshold of death, and that you hadn't crossed it."

"I can accept that—"

"They would tell you that the brain has to die as well as
the heart stopping before the body is truly dead. And until
the body is truly dead, then the soul can't leave it."

I still didn't want to argue, but I respected him now and
had to be straightforward.

"That I can't accept. Those are just words—"

"They don't mean much more to me than they do to you."
Again Godfrey's face was one moonlike smile. "It's a very

primitive model, of course it is. At the time of the early church, a man's spirit was supposed to hover over the body for three days, and didn't depart until the decomposition set in."

Yes, I said, I'd read that once, in a commentary on the Gospel according to Saint John. It was the priest's turn to look surprised. He had expected me to be entirely ignorant about the Christian faith, just as I had expected him to be unsophisticated about everything else. In fact, he was at least as far from unsophisticated as Laurence Knight, my first wife's father, another clergyman, in one of his more convoluted phases.

Godfrey Ailwyn had also one of those minds which were naturally rococo and which moved from flourish to invention and back again, with spiralling whirls and envelopes of thought—quite different from the clear straight cutting-edge mentalities of, say, Francis Getliffe or Austin Davidson in his prime. Quite different, but neither better or worse, just different: one of the most creative minds I ever met was similar in kind to Father Ailwyn's, and belonged to a scientist called Constantine.

What did Ailwyn believe about death, the spirit, or eternal life? I pressed him, for he had brushed away the surface civilities, and I was genuinely curious to know. Though he was willing to spin beautiful metaphysical structures, I wasn't sure that I understood him. Certainly he believed, so far as he believed at all, in something very different from what he called the 'metaphors' in which he spoke to his parishioners. The body, the memory, this our mortal life—if I didn't misinterpret him—existed in space and time, and all came to an end with death. The spirit existed outside space and time, and so to talk of a beginning, or an end, or an afterlife—they were only 'metaphors,' which we had to use because our minds were primitive.

It was about memory alone that I could engage with him. He would have liked to believe (for once, he wasn't intellectually cool) that some part of memory—"some subliminal part, if you like"—was attached to the spirit and so didn't have to perish. That was why, with more hope than expectation, he had wanted to crossquestion me.

On the terms we had now reached (they weren't those of affection, and though I was interested in him, he wasn't in me, except as an imparter of information: but still, we had come to terms of trust) it would have been false of me to give him any agreement. No, I said, I was sure that memory was a function of the body: damage the brain, and there was no memory left. When the brain came to its end, so did memory. It was inconceivable that any part of it could outlive the body. If the spirit existed outside space and time (though I couldn't fix any meaning to his phrase), memory couldn't. And what possible kind of spiritual existence could that be?

"By definition," said Godfrey Ailwyn, "we can't imagine it. Because we're limited by our own categories. Sometimes we seem to have intuitions. Perhaps that does suggest that some kind of remembrance isn't as limited as we are."

No, whatever it suggested, it couldn't be that, I said. He was a very honest man, but he wouldn't give up that toehold of hope. Did I deny the mystical experience, he asked me. No, of course I didn't deny the experience, I said. But that was different from accepting the interpretation that he might put upon it.

As we went on talking, Maurice, unassuming, bright-faced, poured Godfrey another drink. In time, I came to wonder whether, though Godfrey's mind was elaborate, his temperament wasn't quite simple. So that in a sense, detached from his intellect, he wasn't so far after all from the people he preached to or tried to console, stumbling with his tongue at a sickbed, in a fashion that seemed preposterous when one heard him talk his own language as he had done that afternoon.

Soon they would have to leave, he said, his expression once more owlish and sad. He had to take an evening service. Would he get many people, I asked. Five or six, old ladies, old friends of his.

"Old ladies," Maurice put in, "who, if they hadn't got Godfrey, wouldn't have anything to live for."

"I don't know about that," said Godfrey, awkward as an adolescent.

I couldn't resist one final question. We had spoken only of one of the eschatological last things, I said. Death. How did he get on with the other three? Judgment, heaven, hell.

Again he looked as though I weren't playing according to the rules, or hadn't any justification to recognise a theological term.

Did he place heaven and hell, like the spirit, outside of space and time? And judgment too? Wasn't that utterly unlike anything that believers had ever conceived up to his day?

His sharp eyes gazed at me with melancholy. Then suddenly the pastiness, the heaviness, the depression did their disappearing trick again, and he smiled.

"Lewis. I expect you'd prefer me to place them all in your own world, wouldn't you? I'm not sure that that would be an improvement, you know. But if you like I'll say that you've made your own heaven and hell in your own life. And as for judgment, well, you're capable of delivering that upon yourself. I hope you show as much mercy as we shall all need in the end."

When they had departed, I thought that last remark didn't really fit under his metaphysical arch, but that nevertheless, if he allowed himself an instant's pride in the midst of his chronic modesty, he had a good sound right to do so.

TWENTY-THREE

LYING AWAKE

When Charles March called in for ten minutes, later that same evening, I asked him to do a little staff work. Would he, either on his own account or by invoking Mansel, make an arrangement with the nurses? Up to now, they had forced sleeping pills upon me each night. I wanted that stopped. Partly because I had an aversion, curiously puritanical, from any routine drug-taking: I would much rather have a broken night or two than get into the habit of dosing myself to sleep. But also I wasn't in the least tired, I was serene and content, I didn't mind lying awake: which in fact I did, luxuriously, looking out one-eyed into the dark bedroom.

Not that it was quite dark, or continuously so. There was a kind of background twilight, contributed perhaps by the street lamps or those in the houses opposite, which defined the shape of the window and chest-of-drawers close by. Occasionally, a beam from a car's headlights down below swept across the far wall, and I watched with pleasure, as though I were being reminded of lying in an unfamiliar bedroom long ago, at my Uncle Will's in Market Harborough, when as a boy I didn't wish to go to sleep, so long as I could see the walls rosy, then darker, rosy again, as the coal fire flickered and fell.

I was being reminded of something else, what was it, another room, another pattern of light, almost another life. At last I had it. A hotel room in Mentone, regular as a metro-nome the lighthouse beam, moving from wall to wall: in the dark intervals, the sea slithering and slapping on the rocks beneath. Yes, I had been ill and wretched, wondering if I should recover, maddened that I might die quite unfulfilled, longing for the woman whom I later married and did harm to. Yet the recollection, in the hospital bedroom, was happy, pain long since drained out, as though all that persisted was the smell of the flowers and the sharp-edged lighthouse beam.

Other unfamiliar rooms. The hotel bedrooms of a life-time. Why did I feel, not only serene, but triumphant? The half-memories, the flashes, seemed like a conquest. Alone. Not alone. Dense curtained darkness: the sound of breathing from the other bed. Smell of beeswax, pot pourri, wood-smoke. That might have been Palermo. Sound of a sentry's stamp outside. Travelling as an official. Then unofficial, utter quiet, lights across the canal.

Switch of association. Godfrey Ailwyn had talked of the threshold of death. He hadn't been inhibited, he hadn't wor-ried about delicacy or restraint, and that had pleased me. He had set out to argue that I hadn't been dead. Curious to argue whether, at a point of time, one was or was not dead. That hadn't seemed ominous, became the opposite of omi-nous now. As, after the recall of nights abroad, I thought (as-sociations, daydreams, drifting in and out) of some of God-frey's words, I didn't feel less serene but more so. I hadn't minded him crossquestioning me like a coroner: no, I wel-comed it. It was only five nights since I had lain in this room, frozen with dread. Frightened to think back a few hours, to the time they were standing round me and Mansel got to work.

Now—with a change which I hadn't recognized, as it was happening, but which had come to feel delectable and com-

plete—I wasn't frightened to think back, there was nothing which gave me a greater sense of calm or of something
more liberating than calm. November 28, 1965. That morning, round about half-past eleven, I might have died. I liked
telling myself that. Nothing had ever been so steadying, not
at all bizarre or nerve-racking, just steadying: nothing had
set me so free.

I did not have to reason this out to myself, certainly not
on that contented night, or make it any subtler than it was.
It was just a fact of life, an unpredicted but remarkably satis-
fying fact, one of the best. When, however, I tried to explain
it to others (which I didn't want to for a long time afterwards) I didn't even satisfy myself. It all sounded either too
mysteriously lumbering or else altogether too casual. One
difficulty was that, to me as the sole recipient, the emotional
tone of the whole thing was very light. I tried to spell it out
—it made one's concerns, even those which before the relevant morning would have weighed one down, appear not so
much silly as non-existent.

After all, one might not have had them any more.

Just as in the dread which I had experienced only once, in
the hours of November 28–29, everything disappeared, long-
ings, hopes, fears, ego, everything but the dread itself: so
they disappeared in this anti-dread.

Most of us looked upon our lives—not continuously but
now and then—as a kind of journey, progress, or history. A
history, as the cosmogonists might say, from Time $T=0$ at
birth to $T_1 =$ the final date, which it wasn't given us to know
in advance. (Who, at any age, younger than Charles, older
than me, would dare to look in the mirror of his future?)

Somehow that progress, journey, history had for me become disconnected or dismissed. As though what fashionable
persons were beginning to call the diachronic existence had
lost its grip on me.

Yet what I really felt was as simple as a joy. As though I
had smelt the lilac, and time-travelled back to the age of
eleven, reading under the tree at home: as though troubles
past or to come had been dissolved, and become one with
the moment in which I was watching the cars' lights move
across the bedroom wall.

So, when the priest told me to show myself as much mercy
as we should all need in the end, that affected me, but not as
it might have done six days before. They were kind words:
they were good words: once, though I didn't share his theology, they would have made me heavy-spirited as I thought
about my past. But now I was freer from myself. Yes, I could
still think with displeasure about what I had done, and wish
that whole episodes or stretches of years might be wiped
away. But I wished that, and still felt a kind of joy, with no
angst there.

Judgment? Well, thinking with displeasure on what I had
done was a kind of judgment. It wasn't either merciful or
the reverse. I didn't feel obliged to reckon up an account, as
though one ought to tick off the plus and minus scores.
Once I had told a friend (perhaps the least moral friend I
had ever had) that, if I had never lived, nobody would have
been a penny the worse. That was altogether too cut-and-
dried for me now. Too historical, in fact: and actually, in
terms of history, microscopic history, it was not even true.
But on the other hand, when I was recovering from the first
operation, and Charles March had said that it was impossible to
regret one's own experience, I had on the moment been
doubtful, and later to myself (in this same bedroom) utterly
denied it. I did regret, sometimes passionately, sometimes
with remorse, but more often with impatience, a good deal
of my youth. Right up to the time—I was thirty-four—when
Sheila killed herself.

I didn't take more of the blame than I had to. It wouldn't

have been true, it would have been over-dramatic and, curiously enough, over-vain, to imagine that I could have altered all or many of my actions. I had struggled too hard, and with too much self-concentration: but it would have been impossible not to struggle hard. Nevertheless, in a sense, in a sense which was real although one could explicate it half away, I had been a bad son, a bad friend, a bad husband. To my mother I could, without being a different person, have given more. Yes, I had been very young: but I was already old enough to distrust one's own withdrawals, and to know that one's own needs—including self-protection, and the assertion of one's loneliness—could be cruel. And, what took more recognition, could be disciplined.

I had been a bad friend to George Passant—not in later years, when there was nothing to be done except be there, when all he wanted was to spend a night or two in what he thought of as a normal world—not then, but almost as soon as I ceased to be an intimate and left the town for London. It was then that I had blinkered myself. I ought to have known how the great dreams were being acted out, how all the hopes of the son of the morning were driving him where such hopes had driven other leaders before him. I ought to have used my own realism to break up the group or his inner paradise. Perhaps no one could have done that, for George was a powerful character and had, of course, the additional power of his own desires. But I was tougher-minded than he was, and there was a chance, perhaps one chance in ten, that I could have shifted him.

As for being a bad husband to Sheila, it was simply that I shouldn't have been her husband at all. There I had committed the opposite wrong to what I had done (or rather not done) to George Passant. Instead of absenting myself, as from him—or earlier from my mother—I had summoned up every particle of intensity, energy, and will. She, lost and splintered as she was, had to take me in the end. After that, I couldn't find a way, there was no way, to make up for it. Now I had seen in my son Charles the same capacity for intense focussing of the whole self, regardless of anyone and anything, regardless in his case of his normal sense or detached kindness. Regardless in mine of the tenderness that I felt for Sheila, independent of love, and lasting longer.

That I couldn't forget. When Austin Davidson played with speculations about the afterlife, I had a reason, stronger than all others, for wishing that I could, even in the most ghostly fashion, believe in it: a reason so mawkish and sentimental that I couldn't admit it, and yet so demanding that once, when Davidson and young Charles were bantering away, I couldn't listen. Instead, I wanted to hear—it was as mawkish as that—a voice from the shades saying (clipped and gnomic as so much that Sheila had said in life): "Never mind. It's all right. You should know, it's all right."

If I had been given the option, I should have chosen to eliminate the first half of my life, and try again. No one could judge that but myself. Francis Getliffe, who had known me continuously for longer than anyone else, would have been—in the priest's terms—too merciful. He had seen me do bad things, but he hadn't seen those hidden things: and, even if he had, he would still have been too merciful.

For the second half of my life, Margaret had known me as no one else had. At times she had seen me at my worst. But there I should—compared with the remoter past—have given myself the benefit of the doubt. And I thought that she would too. She would have said—so I believed—that I had made an effort to reshape a life. It wasn't easy or specially successful, she might have added to herself: for Margaret was not often taken in, either about herself or me, not so willing to be satisfied as Francis. But she would have given me the benefit of the doubt, even if she had known me from the beginning. She had a higher sense of what life ought to be than I had: but also she could accept more when it went wrong.

Yet, as I lay in bed, it wasn't the remorse—the tainted patches, the days, the years—that became mixed with this present moment. Instead, other moments, dredged up from the past, flickered into this one. Moments which might originally have been miserable or joyous—they were all content-giving by now. Lying awake as a child, hearing my father and some choral friends singing down below: walking with Sheila on a freezing winter night: sitting tired and ill by the sea, wondering how I could cope with the next term at the Bar: triumph after an examination result, drinking, chucking glasses into the fireplace.

I was vulnerable to memories, I wanted to be, some I was forcing back to mind. They were what remained, not the judgments or the regrets. Again I thought of Charles March in that same conversation two years before, saying, as I listened with eyes blacked-out: "You've had an interesting life, Lewis, haven't you?"

An interesting life. Did anyone think—to himself—of his own life like that? That was the kind of summing-up that a biographer or historian might make: but it didn't have any meaning to oneself, to one's own life as lived. Zest, action growing out of flatness, boredom growing out of zest, achievement growing out of boredom, reverie—joy—anxiety—action. Could anyone sum that up for himself, or make an integral as an onlooker might? True, I have once heard an old clergyman, in his rooms in college, tell me that he had had "a disappointing life." He had said it angrily, in a whis-ky-thickened voice. It had been impressive, though not precisely moving, when he said it: on the spot, he was sincere, he meant what he said. But he had a reason for bursting out: he was explaining to himself (and incidentally to me) why he proposed not to do a good turn to another man. I did not believe that even he thought continuously of his life in terms like that. He enjoyed his bits of power in the college: he enjoyed moving from his sessions with the whisky bottle to his prophesies of catastrophe. Certainly a biographer—in the unlikely event of his ever having one—could have summarised his existence in his own phrase. It was objectively true. I doubted if it seemed so to himself for hours together. Even as he was speaking to me, his vitality was still active and hostile, he still was capable of dreaming that, by a miracle, his deserts might even now be given him.

Like most of us, he occasionally thought of his life as a progress or a history. Then he could dispose of it by his ferocious summing-up. That was on the cosmogonists' model which had occurred to me before: from $T = 0$, the big bang, the birth of Despard-Smith, to $T = 79$, the end of things, the death of Despard-Smith. A history. A disappointing history. But that wasn't the way in which he, or the rest of us, thought most frequently to himself about his life. There was another cosmogonists' model which, it seemed to me, was much closer to one's own life as lived. Continuous creation. A slice disappeared, was replaced again. Something was lost, something new came in. All the time it looked to oneself as though there was not much change, nor deterioration, nor journey towards an end. Didn't each of our lives, to ourselves as we lived them, seem, much more often than not, like a process of continuous creation?

So, when Austin Davidson in his last illness dismissed the themes which had preoccupied him for a lifetime (except for his game of gambling: "If I knew I was going to die tomorrow," he once said, "I should still want to hear the latest stock exchange quotations"), he found others which filled their place: and the days of solitariness, though they might be, and often were, bitter, had their own kind of creation.

Even studying his ankles, watching in detail the changes in his physical state, was a fresh awakening of interest, petty if you like, but in its fashion a revival. That was as true for him as it was for my mother, also talking of her ankles in her last illness. Yes, that was a singular outburst of the process of continuous creation. Themes of a lifetime wore themselves out: but we weren't left empty, the resolution wasn't as tidy as that, somehow the psychic heart went on pumping, giving one a new or transformed lease of existence—perhaps restricted, but more concentrated because of that.

Before the operational experience of mine, and in the bedroom since, I had been discovering this for myself. In fact, it was something each of us had to discover for himself: you couldn't reach it by empathy, it was too unfamiliar, and perhaps too disconcerting, for that. Not long ago, in full health, I dismissed the third and slightest of the themes—different from Davidson's—which had preoccupied me, the concern, partly voyeuristic, partly conscientious, for political things. That dismissal was final, I didn't doubt it: but now I could imagine, not playing the chess game of politics in any shape or form, but—if a cause or even a whim impelled me—raising my voice with a freedom which I hadn't known before.

Something similar was true of the second theme, which was the kinds of love. Sexual love, parental love—(so different that we confused ourselves by giving them the same name), they had never let me go: and often my public behaviour had seemed to me like the performance of a stranger. A pretty good performance, since on the level of action I had some of my temperament under control. Well, those kinds of love—I thought of the last talks with Margaret and my son —were creating within themselves something new, in part unforeseeable by me. Not in marriage, perhaps defying fate we should both think that: but certainly in my relation with my son. I hadn't any foreknowledge of what we should be saying to each other in ten years' time, if I lived so long. That wasn't distressing, but curiously exciting, the more so since that date of November 28. It was as though I were quite young again, having to learn, with the sense, on the whole a pleasurable sense, of surprise ahead, what a human relation was like.

Third and last, myself alone. My own solitude, different from Austin Davidson's or anyone else's. In so much we are all alike: but in one's solitude one is unique. I had been confronted by mine, since the operation, more than in all my life before. In a fashion that had astonished me. And given me a sense of change, and also a kind of perplexed delight, for which I had been totally unprepared. Somehow that was a delight too, as though I had suddenly seen a horizon wide open in front of my eyes.

A clock was striking somewhere outside the hospital. I didn't count the strokes, but there might have been twelve. I was sleepy by now, and turned on to my side. As often immediately before sleep, faces came, as if from a vague distance, into the field of vision under the closed lids: one came very clear and actual, nearly a dream, not yet a dream. It was a face which hadn't any waking significance for me, the matey comedian's face of a barrister acquaintance, Ted Benskin.

TWENTY-FOUR

AN UNDEFEATED
VISITOR

Next day (for by this time the press had done its work and so, I guessed, had gossip) I was dividing potential visitors into sheep and goats, those I wanted to see and those I didn't. Among the goats, to be kept out with firmness, were those whose motives for inspecting me didn't need much examination—such as Whitman, my back-bencher acquaintance, who was presumably anxious to see that I was safely incapacitated, or Edgar Hankins, looking for a last personal anecdote to put into one of his elegiac post mortems.

On the other hand, Rosalind was to be welcomed and, a somewhat more surprising enquirer, Lester Ince. Rosalind entered during the morning, bearing more flowers from her husband and, after she had kissed me and sat down, spreading her own aura of Chanel.

"Well, old thing. You don't look too bad." She had never given up either the slang of her youth or the indomitable flatness of our native town.

How was she? She couldn't grumble. And Azik? He was on one of his business trips. Still, there were compensations. What did she mean? She usually got a present when he went abroad. With lids modestly downcast, with a smile that might have been either furtive or salacious, she held out the second finger of her right hand. On it gleamed a splendid emerald.

"What do you think that cost?" she said, and explained, again modestly: "I had to know for the sake of the insurance."

"A good many thousand."

"Fifteen," said Rosalind, with simple triumph.

What about her daughter? No, Rosalind didn't see much of her. The divorce would soon be through. Was Muriel intending to marry again? "She never tells me anything," Rosalind replied, hurt, aggrieved. She recaptured some of her spirit when she switched to young David. "He's a different kettle of fish. He tells me everything."

"He won't always, you know." Rosalind might be as hard as they came, a child of this world, or, in her own language, as tough as old boots: but there (as she had done already with her daughter) she could suffer as much as the rest of us.

"Perhaps he won't. But he's lovely now."

Rosalind continued, as usual not frightened of the obvious. We were all getting older. It would be nice when she was an old lady to have a handsome young man to take her out. David would be twenty-one in nine years' time. "And you know as well as I do," said Rosalind, "what that will make me."

There were few square inches of Rosalind, except for her hair, which had been left to nature unassisted. Couturiers, jewellers, cosmetic makers, had worked for their money, and Azik had duly paid: yet she minded less than many people about growing old.

She also didn't appear to mind overmuch about my misadventures. She had known me so long, she took my continued existence for granted. So far as she showed an interest, she was inclined to blame Margaret, whom she had never liked, for neglecting me.

"You'll have to look after yourself, that's all," she said. If I wanted any advice, there was always the 'old boy' (one of her appellations for Azik). After which, she said a brisk goodbye and departed like a small and elegant warship, succeeded by a wash of scent.

That was still lingering on the air when, a couple of hours later, Lester Ince came in.

"Who's your girl friend?" he said, sniffing, a leer on his cheerful pasty face. "That's not Margaret's."

Lester was one of those men who, solidly masculine, nevertheless were knowledgeable about all the appurtenances of femininity. It made other men more irritated with him, particularly as he seemed—incomprehensibly to them—to have his successes, including his present wife. I had been mildly surprised when I heard that he wanted to visit me. I was a good deal more surprised when he said that he had been thinking about me and had something to propose. He wasn't really a friend: he didn't object to me as vigorously as he did to Francis or my brother, but that wasn't specially high praise. Perhaps he would have been just as concerned if any acquaintance had run into physical trouble. Anyway, his proposal was down-to-earth. He was offering me Basset for my convalescence.

Although I hadn't the most fugitive intention of accepting (all I wanted was to be left undisturbed at home), I was touched, as one was by a bit of practical good nature: touched enough to pretend that I couldn't make up my mind. Of course, one had to be more apolaustic than I was to be fit for Basset— That was a view which Lester sternly repudiated. Compared with many others, he reproved me, it wasn't a *big house:* as the owner of Chatsworth might point out that his establishment was diminutive by the side of Blenheim.

My second line of defence was that we couldn't help getting in their way. Lester bluffly answered that they would be leaving after Christmas anyway: they weren't prepared to endure another English winter. I was reflecting, when I first met Lester he was living with his first wife and family in a dilapidated house in Bateman Street: if I knew anything about Cambridge temperatures, the conjugal bedroom wouldn't get about 50° most of the year, and Lester had found it satisfactory for his purposes. Now, however, he behaved like a frailer plant. He had recently acquired a place in the Bahamas. It would be very good for them, he assured me earnestly. Not only to escape the winter rigours, but because there was a danger in living in a house like Basset. They didn't want to become like *birds in a gilded cage*. And they proposed to avoid that danger, I tried to ask without expression, by having their own beach in the Bahamas? Lester gazed at me, also without expression.

After I had promised to give my answer about Basset when I got out of hospital, he explained that there was another great advantage about the new regime. He could rely on getting each winter free for work, he could sit there in the sun and wouldn't be disturbed. It was time he made a start on another book. It was going to be a long-term project. Several years, he didn't believe in premature publication. Subject? Nathaniel Hawthorne and the New England moral climate.

When at teatime I told Margaret about that conversation, we looked at each other dead pan. He was the kind of visitor who ought to be encouraged, she said. No strain. Off-handed benevolence. But he used to be a humourist. Was all this a piece of misguided humour? If it were, I said, he deserved his fun. No, Margaret decided, she couldn't remember, even in his unregenerate days, Lester being humourous about himself.

About six o'clock she left, and I was feeling peaceful. No more visitors that day, except my brother Martin after dinner. I went back to a novel I had been reading, a Simenon, and I put Lester's moral discrimination out of my thoughts.

In a few minutes, a knock on the door. A peremptory double knock. Before I had said "come in," Ronald Porson lurched into the room.

"How in God's name did you get in?" I cried, with something less than grace. I didn't want to be disturbed: I was irritated, I had given instructions that only those whose names were cleared should be sent up.

Porson gave one of his involuntary winks, right eyelid dropping down towards his cheek: the left side of his face twitched in sympathy. As a result, just as when first I met him, back in the early Thirties, he produced an effect which was conspiratorial, friendly, and remarkably louche. As usual, he was smelling of liquor and his speech was slurred.

"I suppose I can help myself, can't I?" He had already caught sight of the bottle on the chest-of-drawers.

"Yes, do," I said without enthusiasm, and repeated: "How did you get in?"

Porson turned back with his glass, winked again, this time perhaps less involuntarily, and sat down in the other chair. He was wearing his Old Etonian tie, which he—unlike my former colleague Gilbert Cooke—used only on special occasions. The rest of his appearance was more dilapidated than his normal, and in that respect the standard was very high. Cuffs frayed, buttons off waistcoat, shoes dirty, hair straggling, face puffed out with broken veins. Yet, though he was now seventy-two or three, he did not look his age, as though the battered ruleless life had acted—as it had done also with George Passant, in both cases much to the disapproval of more proper persons—as a kind of preservative and given them an air, among the ruins of their physique, of something like happiness and youth.

Actually, Porson had, ever since I first knew him, moved from one catastrophe to another, with a seemingly inevitable and unrelieved decline such as didn't happen to many men. To begin with, he was making a living at the Bar. That soon dropped away, owing to drink, his˙ tendency to patronise everyone he met becoming more aggressive and overpowering the more he failed, and perhaps—for those were less tolerant days—to rumours about his sexual habits. Then he ran through his money and you could trace his progress as his address in London changed. The first I remembered was that of a modestly opulent flat off Portland Place. After that Pimlico, Fulham Road, Earl's Court, Notting Hill Gate, stations of descent. At the present time, so far as I knew, he was living in a bed-sitting room in Godfrey Ailwyn's parish, and the priest and I both guessed he kept alive on national assistance. How he paid for his drink I didn't understand, although it was a long time since I had seen him quite sober. As he grew older, his picking-up became more rampant, and he had spent one term in gaol for importuning. Ailwyn reported that there had been other narrow squeaks.

None of this, none of it at all, prevented him from looking to the future with the expectation of a child wondering what would turn up on his birthday. The last time I had met him, he had been saying, using exactly the same phrase as my mother might have used, very strange for one like Porson brought up in embassies, that there was still time for his ship to come home.

"How did you get in?"

"I've got one or two chums downstairs." He winked again, and put a finger to the side of his nose, rather like Asik Schiff parodying himself. Then, suddenly angry, he burst out:

"Good chaps. Better than the crowd you waste your time with."

"I dare say." I was used to his temper. It was like handling a more than usually unpredictable bathroom geyser.

"Good chums. I've always said, you can get anywhere if you've got good chums."

Now he was swinging between the maudlin and the accusatory.

"You can't deny, I've always got anywhere I wanted, haven't I?"

In a sense it was true. He had been seen in places where none of the rest of us could ever have had the entrée. Some people could explain it only by assuming a kind of homosexual trade union or information network. Ailwyn had once suggested that he had escaped worse trouble because of a contact in the local C.I.D. Not that that had prevented Ronald Porson, when he found himself in more conventional circles, from denouncing 'Jews and Pansies' as the source of national degeneration. With those he trusted, though, he tended to concentrate on the racial element.

"Well, I'm here, aren't I?" he accosted me, hands on knees. "Do you know why?"

After I had failed to reply, he said, accusatory again:

"My boy, I'm here to give you a bit of advice."

"Are you?"

"You haven't always taken my advice. You might have done better for yourself if you had."

"It's a bit late now," I began, but firmly he interrupted me.

"It'll be too late unless you listen to me for once. I'm going to give you a bit of advice. You'd better take it. *You're not to enter this hospital again.*"

"It's a perfectly good hospital."

"It's the best hospital in London," he shouted, getting angrier as he agreed with me. "But damn your soul, it's not the best for you."

"I've got no grumbles—"

"I tell you, damn you, it's not the best for you. I know."

"How can you know?"

"It's no use talking to people who only believe in what they can blasted well touch and see." For an instant he was raging about E.S.P. Then he said, calming himself down, with a look of patient condescension:

"Well, let's try something that you understand. I suppose you admit that you nearly passed out last Friday. As near as damn it. Or a bloody sight nearer. You admit that, don't you?"

"Of course I do."

"You haven't got any option." He spoke indulgently, contemptuously. "And what would have been the use of your blasted reputation then?"

I wanted to stop listening, but his face came nearer, bullying, insistent. The left side was convulsed by a seismic twitch.

"It's no use making any bones about it. You know as well as I do. You did pass out last Friday. You've taken that in, haven't you?"

I nodded.

"You're the luckiest man I know. You won't have the same luck next time."

Again I was trying to put him off, but he overbore me:

"You mustn't come into this hospital again, you understand?"

He added: "I know you mustn't. I *know*."

"I'll try not to."

He stared full-eyed at me, triumphant. He was certain he had made an impression.

"Of course, my boy, *I'm* thinking of you. *You* ought to think of some of the chaps here. In the hospital. What the hell do you fancy they were doing last Friday?"

He paused, and went on.

"I'll tell you. They were peeing their pants. They were

afraid it would get into the papers. If I'd been in your place, the papers mightn't have got hold of it. Somehow they know your name."

(I thought later that that had been a minor mystery to Porson for thirty years. But at the time this was a reflection I hadn't the nerve to make. He had frightened me. To begin with, it had been a frisson, the kind of shiver which my mother called 'someone walking across her grave.' Now it was worse than that.)

"It wouldn't have been good for the place," Porson said, "if you'd gone out feet first."

"Well, I didn't."

"They weren't to know that, were they? I'll tell you something else. They didn't breathe easy until a long time after you'd been brought back. They've told me that themselves. You were all settled down and comfortable and having a good night's rest before they felt sure there wasn't going to be a funeral after all."

"I hope they stood themselves a drink."

"I've done that, my boy. They know you're an old friend."

Later on, I had another reflection, that I had never discovered who 'they' were. Certainly males. Certainly not doctors. I guessed, but never knew for sure, that they must have been porters or medical orderlies. At the time, feeling the sweat prickling at my temples, I had just one concern, which was to get him out of the room.

"Good," I said. "You go and stand them another one for me." I told him where to find my wallet, and soon he was duly pocketing a five pound note. But even then, enjoying the conversation, he wasn't eager to go. Pressed, I had to invent and whisper another pretext, of the kind that Ronald Porson couldn't resist. A visitor was coming soon—no one knew, my wife didn't know—I couldn't tell even him the name, he'd understand. With a look, both confidential and jeering, of ultimate complicity, Porson weaved towards the door, saying at the threshold:

"So long, my boy. I hope you've been listening to what I said."

Yes, I had. I wiped sweat away, but I might have come out of a hot bath. I was ashamed, that I couldn't be steadier: why should my nerves let me down, just because old Porson blustered away? For days past, ever since the first fright left me free, I had listened to everyone without even a superstitious qualm. I hadn't been putting on a front: I hadn't needed to. Definitions of death, theological death, the different degrees of uneasiness with which people, my wife, my son, approached me. I had become something of an expert on relative uneasiness. Nothing had plucked a nerve. Then, after all that, after the visits of those closest to me, came Porson. Drunk, of course. Officious, as he had been ever since I first met him. Nothing new. I had been through it all before. But he had frightened me.

There was no denying, I had felt the chill. If I could have understood why, I might have thrown it off. I had no clue at all. The thought of Porson's cronies, down in the hospital basement, counting my chances—what was so bad about that? (In cold blood afterwards, I doubted if they had been all that wrought up. Porson enjoyed his overheated fancy. They must have had a little excitement, no more.) There was nothing bad, or even remotely unnatural, about that. Yet, when Porson told me, it brought back the dread.

Listening to him, I felt it as on the first night. Now he had gone, I was searching inward, testing how strong it was. It was exactly like the days after the first eye operation, when I was worried by each speck or floater in the field of vision, wondering whether the black edge was coming back. The dread. It would be hard to have that as a regular visitation. No, perhaps it was not quite like the first night. Per-

haps there was already a spectator behind my mind. It wasn't
only the fright and nothingness.

Still, as I tried to eat the hospital supper, I was waiting, I
didn't know what for, perhaps for the chill again, or some
sign that I wasn't in the clear. I was glad that Martin was
due to visit me that night.

When he arrived, though, I was for an instant disappointed. For he had brought his daughter Nina with him,
enquiring about me in her whisper as she kissed me, her face
hiding behind her hair. As a rule, I should have welcomed
her. More and more she seemed the most agreeable girl in
Charles's circle, the one who was most likely to make a man
happy and enjoy her marriage. Nevertheless in her presence
I couldn't talk directly to my brother. Which was probably,
I imagined, why he had brought her. It was a typical quiet
tactic of his, meaning that there was nothing good to say
about Pat and that Martin wished to evade any discussion.
Also, now that Martin at last was compelled to show traces
of realism about his son, he was turning to the daughter
whom he had so long neglected. He even induced her to tell
me about her music: her teachers were certain that she
(quite unlike her brother, Martin might have been thinking) would become a good professional.

Martin had seen me once since the operation, enough to
satisfy himself, but not alone. Now he was watching me.

"How are you?" he said.

"All right."

"Only all right?"

"A little tired of death-watch beetles."

"You've given them a first-class opportunity, you know."
Martin was speaking with a tucked-in smile, but he and I
were signalling to each other, and probably Nina didn't
recognise the code. "Anyone special?"

"Old Ronald Porson's been improving the occasion."

"When?"

"Oh, not long ago."

Martin nodded. "That must have been pleasant for you."

"He was telling me about the preparations downstairs for my demise."

A slight pause. In his misleadingly soft voice, Martin said: "It's high time we began to make modest preparations for his."

"He's inclined to think that he'll outlast me."

"Thoughtful of him."

"After all," I said, "he'd be the first to point out that he very nearly did."

"I'm sure he would."

"Nothing that rejuvenates an old man more, my father-in-law used to say, than to contemplate the death of someone younger."

"Naturally," said Martin. Then casually, as though in an afterthought of no interest, he said: "By the by, did you want to see that old sod?" He didn't explain to his daughter that he meant Porson.

"No. He gate-crashed."

"I imagined so. Well, I'll see that that doesn't happen again."

I looked at my brother, face controlled, eyes dark and hard. I speculated as to whether Nina knew that he was smouldering with anger.

"Never mind," I said. "I can take him."

"I can't see any reason why you should. I can see several reasons why you shouldn't."

That was all. Affectionate goodbyes. I expected that it would be some time before Martin left the hospital. For myself, I didn't abstain from my sleeping pills that night, and wasn't long awake. Then I woke in the middle of the night, feeling calm. Immediately I waited for the fright to grip me.

But it didn't: at least, not enough to be more than a reminder, the kind of reminder of mortality that came at any age, from youth upwards, and wasn't the real thing. Testing the black edge, I forced back thoughts of Porson. No, his voice bullied me in a vacuum, I recalled occasions long ago when he had lost a case and still took the offensive against everyone round him, not to himself defeated. I wondered if Martin had discovered who it was that let him in.

TWENTY-FIVE

OUTSIDE THE HOSPITAL

The morning that Margaret came to fetch me home, I had been in that bedroom for eleven days. On the afternoon before, she, who knew how institutions gave me more than my normal claustrophobia, and that I didn't make fine distinctions between prisons and hospitals, they were just places which shut one in, asked how long it felt. I said that often it had seemed no time at all. She wasn't sure whether I was being perverse. But I had already told her of my relapse during Porson's visit. Perhaps also perversely, that had given her confidence in my state of mind. She hadn't quite trusted the complete serenity, the looking back to November 28 as though that eliminated disquiets past present and to come: now she knew that the serenity could be broken, she trusted it more.

Dressed, wearing my one club tie, the MCC, as though in retrospective homage to Ronald Porson, I said goodbye to the matron, the ward sister, a posse of nurses. I caught sight of myself in the looking glass, grinning cordially like an ageing public man.

Walking downstairs, out to the steps in front of the hospital, I was still wearing a blindfold over the left eye, and hadn't stereoscopic vision when I looked down at the steps: so that Margaret, taking my arm, had to guide me, and as I probed with my feet I looked infirm. Infirm enough for a photographer, on the hospital steps, to ask if I wanted help:

which didn't prevent him snapping a picture of the descent. When we came into the open air, there were a dozen photographers waiting, shouting like a new estate of the realm, telling us to stand still, move, smile. There was the whirr of a television camera. "Look as if you're happy," someone ordered Margaret. "Talk to each other!" Worn down by this contemporary discipline, we muttered away. What we were actually saying, beneath the smiles, was what fiend out of hell had leaked the time. Someone had tipped off the press. Pat? One of Porson's 'chums'?

As we climbed into the car, I looked back at the hospital façade. Nostalgia for a place where I had been through that special night? No, not in the least. It was different from occasions when I was young, and said goodbye to stretches of unhappiness. When I left the local government office, after my last morning as a clerk, I felt, although or because I had been miserable and humiliated there for years, something like an ache, as though regret for a bond that had been snapped. A little later, when I was a young man, and had been sent to the Mediterranean to recover from an illness, I had, driving to the station for the journey home, looked back at the sea (I could remember now the smell of the arbutus after rain). I had been desolate there, afraid that I might not get better: going away, I felt a distress much more painful than that outside the old office, a yearning, as though all I wanted in this life was to remain by the seashore and never be torn away.

None of that now, though this had been the worst time of the three. I regarded the hospital with neutrality; it might have been any other red-brick nineteenth century building. As one grew older, perhaps the nervous rackings of one's youth died down. Or perhaps, and with good reason, one wasn't so frightened of the future. After all one had had some practice contemplating futures and then living them.

It was pleasant, anxiety-free, to be going home.

III
ENDS AND BEGINNINGS

TWENTY-SIX

DISPENSATION

Lying in bed in the hospital, set free by the talisman of November 28, I hadn't so much as wondered how long this state would last. If I had even wanted to wonder so, it would have been a false freedom. And whatever it was (it might make nonsense of a good deal that I expected or imagined), it was not false. Fortuitous, if you like, but not false.

It transferred itself easily enough into my everyday life, as soon as I got back. In a fashion which would have seemed curiously unfair, if they had known about it, to those who thought that all along I had been luckier than I deserved. For the bad times got dulled, shrugged off as though, if November 28 had gone the other way, they wouldn't have existed. But, by a paradoxical kind of grace, the reverse didn't apply, the dispensation wasn't symmetrical: on the contrary, the good times became sharper. Shortly after I left hospital, I published a book which I liked and which fell, not exactly flat, but jaggedly. If that had happened in early November, it would have cost me some bad days. As it was, though I didn't pretend to be indifferent (changes in mood are not so complete as that), I had put it behind me almost as soon as it occurred. Shortly afterwards—and this was just as surprising—I found myself revelling, without any barricade of sarcasm or touching wood, in a bit of praise.

There had been a time when I used to declare, with a

kind of defiance: you had to enjoy your joys, and suffer your sufferings. As I knew well enough, I had more talent for the latter. I had managed to subjugate the depressive streak in action, and conceal it from others and sometimes myself, but it was there half-hidden: it wasn't entirely an accident that I could guess when Roy Calvert was going to swing from the manic into its other phase. With me, what for Roy was manic showed itself only as a kind of high spirits or an excessive sense of expectation: most of the time, I had to watch, as better and robuster characters had to watch, for the alternate phase. Now the balance had been tilted, and I felt myself closer than I had ever been before to people whom I had once in secret thought thick-skinned and prosaic: people who weren't menaced by melancholy and who were better than I was at enjoying themselves.

It was a singular dispensation to overtake one at sixty, faintly comic, humbling, and yet comforting.

When Margaret's father had died, which he did in his sleep in the January of 1966, two months after my operation, she and I were alone together as in the first days of marriage. More alone, for then she had been looking after Maurice in his infancy. Just as when we returned to the flat the previous autumn, it was both a treat and strange to be there by ourselves. We spun time out, lengthening the moments, making the most of them. Work was over for me now by the early afternoon: after that, we were alone and free. I had got rid of any duties outside the home. We had time to ourselves, as we had not had when we were first married. We were able to look at each other, not as though it were the first time (when we saw nothing but our own excitement), but as though we were on holiday, waking up fresh in a hotel.

In another sense, it was as fresh when I walked with my son on spring evenings in the park. I was listening to him, not as though he had changed, but as though something had changed between us. Not that I was less interested in him, or in his friends. Actually, I had become more so, but in a different fashion. I was less engaged in competing with them, or proving to Charles that they were wrong.

My brother Martin had once said, after his renunciation: "People matter: relations between them don't matter much."

Whether he ever thought of that, in his troubles with his own son, I didn't know: if so it must have seemed a black joke against himself. But it was somewhere near the way (so I thought, and didn't have a superstitious tremor) in which I was now taking pleasure in Charles's company. I was interested in him and the rest of them, stimulated by their energies and hopes: it was like being given a slice of life to watch and to draw refreshment from, so long as one could keep from taking part oneself.

It didn't seem like an ageing man's interest in the flow of life, or Francis Getliffe's patriarchal delight in his children and grandchildren and those of his friends, the delight of life going on. It didn't even seem so much like a bit of continuous creation, in which through being engrossed in other lives one was making a new start for oneself. It might, I thought casually, have been all of those things: but if it were I didn't care. I felt closer than that, through being given a privileged position, having those energies under my eyes: it was much more like being engaged with my own friends at the same age, except that I—with my anxieties, perturbations, desires, and will—had been satisfactorily (and for my own liberation) removed.

It was at the end of the Easter vacation, when Charles had returned from another of his trips, that he got into the habit of asking me out for an evening walk. He was home only for a week; each day about half-past five, active, springy on his feet, he looked at me with eyebrows raised, and we went into the park for what became our ritual promenade. Out by the

Albion Gate: across the grass, under the thickening trees, along the path to the Serpentine, by the side of the Row to the Achilles statue, back along the eastern verge towards Marble Arch. It might have been two old clubmen going through their evening routine, I told him after the second trip: Charles grinned companionably, and next day started precisely the same course.

His conversation, however, was not much like an old club-man's. He was relaxed, because I was the right distance from him: the right distance, that is, for him to talk and me to lis-ten. I took in more about his friends than I had done before, and believed more, now that I wasn't conducting a dialectic with him. Yes, they were more serious than I had let myself admit. Their politics (his less than the others) might be uto-pian, but they were their own. They were probably no bet-ter or no worse thought out than ours had been, but they came from a different ground.

The results could be curiously different. Charles and his circle were more genuinely international than any of us had been. The minor nationalisms seemed to have vanished quite. They were not even involved in Europe, though most of them had travelled all over it. It was the poor world that captured their imagination: the Grand Tour had to be un-comfortable and also squalid nowadays, said Charles with a sarcastic smile. That was what he had been conducting in Asia before he was seventeen, and this present vacation he had been rounding it off in Africa.

They weren't specially illusioned. They didn't imagine an elysium existing here-and-now upon this earth, as young men and women of their kind in the 1930's sometimes imag-ined Russia or less often the United States. It was true, dark world-views didn't touch them much. They might hear—in that year 1966 and later—people like Francis Getliffe and me saying that objectively the world looked grimmer than at

any time in our lives. They might analyse and understand
the reasons which made us say so. But they didn't in the end
believe it. They were alive for anything that was going to
happen. That was bound to be so: you live in your own
time.

Listening to Charles those evenings, I thought that, not
only did his friends' opinions have more to them than I had
been willing to grant, but so had he. He seemed more of a
sport—that is, less like me or Martin, less like anyone on
Margaret's side—than I had believed. The family patterns
didn't fit. He wasn't so easy to domesticate. There were contradictions in him that I hadn't seen before.

This was striking home all through that week: on one of
the last evenings, I could not help but see it clear. We had
just crossed the bridge over the water: it was a dense and
humid April night, but with no clouds in the darkening sky;
Charles suddenly began to press me about, of all subjects,
the works of Tolkien. I turned towards him, ready to say
something sharp, such as that he ought to know that I had
no taste for fancy. His eyes left mine, looked straight ahead.

I met his profile, dolichocephalic, straight-nosed, hair curl-
ing close to his head. On the moment he looked unfamiliar,
not at all how I imagined him to look. Curious: feature by
feature, of course, the genes had played their part, the hair
was Martin's, the profile Austin Davidson's: but the result
was strange. So strange that I might have been gazing at a
young man I didn't recognise, much less understand. The
sharp repartee dropped away, I said that naturally I would
give this favourite of his a try.

Curious, I was thinking again. He was in many respects
more concentrated and practical than I had been at his age,
or maybe was now: almost certainly, when he wanted something, he was more ruthless. Yet, if I had no taste for fancy,
he had enough for two: whimsies, fantasies, they hadn't been

left behind in childhood. With him they coexisted, and would continue to coexist with adult desires and adult fulfilments: he was one of those, or would become one, who had the gift of being able to feel guilty with Dostoevsky, innocent with hobbits, passionately insistent with a new girl friend, all on the same day.

Good, he was saying affectionately, as I promised to read the book.

As we walked on, other contradictions of his became as clear. He had proved his own kind of courage. Whether he had set out to prove it to himself, no one knew: but the fact was, none of my contemporaries, not even those as adventurous as the young Francis Getliffe, would at sixteen have contemplated setting out on solitary expeditions such as his. As for me, it would have seemed about as plausible—for reasons of pennilessness in addition to physical timidity—as trying to round the Horn. Of course, most of Charles's friends travelled further than we did: but he was the one who had made it into a trial of nerve. Not nerve, just patience, he explained with a straight face. All calculated and singularly deliberate, as though he had reverted to one of those nineteenth century Englishmen with private means, scholarly tastes, and inordinate self-will.

And yet, he was nervous, more so than most of us, in another old-fashioned, even a primitive, sense. When he had arrived back safe after his second trip and had produced some understatements which were not so modest as they sounded, I asked him how much I should have to pay him to sleep (a) in a haunted house (b) in a graveyard. Again straight-faced, he said: "As for (a), more than you could afford. For (b), no offers accepted. And I suppose you'd do either for half a bottle of Scotch. Or less. Wouldn't you?"

He was being, as usual, truthful about himself. He was capable of getting frightened by ghost stories. There were still occasions, after he had been reading, when he carefully forgot to turn off his bedroom lamp.

Walking by his side—lights were coming on in St. George's Hospital—I mentioned, as though by free association, the name of Gordon Bestwick. This was a friend of his, whom I had met, but only casually, at Christmas-time. Charles, protective about any of his circle, wasn't easy about Gordon's health, and had been suggesting that I should go to Cambridge next term, and meet him again, to see what my opinion was.

"Why did you think of him?" said Charles, clear-voiced.

"Oh, it just occurred to me that he might be more rational than you are."

Charles chuckled.

"I've told you, he's a bit like you. He's *our* Bazarov, you know."

That was a complicated private reference. Charles must have picked up from Francis Getliffe, or more probably his wife, the impression that I made on the Marches when they first befriended me. A poor young man: positive: impatient with the anxieties of the rich. Making them feel over-delicate, over-nurtured, frail by the side of a new force. In fact, their impression was in most respects fallacious. My character seemed to them more all-of-a-piece and stronger just because I was poor and driven on: in the long run, much of the frailty was not on their side but mine. Still, they called me after Turgenev's hero and for a while made a similar legend about me. And that was what Charles and his circle were duplicating in their reception of Gordon Bestwick.

Charles had met him at Trinity, both of them scholars in their first year. He came from a lorry driver family in Smethwick. He was extremely clever; according to Charles, brought up in one of the English academic hothouses, at least as clever as anyone he had known at school. Bestwick was reading economics and had much contempt for the soft subjects, which sounded Bazarov-like enough. I had talked to him only for a few minutes, but no one could have missed noticing his talent. Otherwise he had some presence without being specially prepossessing, and if Charles hadn't forced his name upon me, I doubted whether I should have gone out of my way to see him again.

That evening, as we were turning parallel to Park Lane, Charles reiterated his praise.

"He may easily be the ablest of us," he said. He was pertinacious, prepared to be boring, about someone he believed in. "He's certain to be a very valuable character."

He added, with an oblique smile:

"He's even a very valuable member of the cell."

They thought of themselves—it didn't need saying—as student revolutionaries: Charles knew that I knew: though he, on that October night when I told him of what he called my abdication, had defined with political accuracy where he stood.

He was gazing to our left, where, in the West, over the London smoke, one of the first stars had come out. Charles regarded it with simple pleasure, just as my father might have done. I recalled night walks when I was in trouble, getting some peace from looking at the stars.

"Old Gordon," Charles remarked with amusement, "says that we're fooling ourselves about space travel. We shall never get anywhere worthwhile. He says that science fiction is the modern opium of the people."

He added:

"Sensible enough for you, isn't he?"

During that conversation, and the others we had that week, Charles did not leave out the name of Muriel. He brought it in along with a dozen more, without either obtruding it or playing it down. He spoke of her as though she were one of the inner group (which included not only school and Cambridge friends, but also one or two studying in London, such as his cousin Nina), but he didn't single her out or ask a question about her.

TWENTY-SEVEN

DISCUSSION OF
SOMEONE ABSENT

When Muriel herself invited me to her house one evening, shortly after Charles had gone back to Cambridge, she began in very much the same tone as he had used of her: but there came a time when she was not quite so cautious.

She had asked me round for a drink before dinner, on the first Monday of the month, which happened to be a day when Margaret was regularly occupied with her one and only charity. I had been to Chester Row once before, to a party the preceding summer: I had forgotten that Muriel's house was a long way up the road, near the church, not far from where Matthew Arnold used to repose himself, all seventeen stone of him.

The door was smelling of fresh paint, there was a tub of wallflowers outside, a flower box under the ground-floor windows, everything burnished and neat. The housekeeper told me, in a decorous whisper, as though she had been infected by the house's hush, that Mrs. Calvert was waiting for me in the drawing room upstairs (Muriel had reverted to her maiden name the day that the divorce came through).

In fact, she was standing at the end of the first-floor corridor.

"How very good of you to come, Uncle Lewis," she called out, light and clear. "It's such a long way to drag you, isn't it?"

It was not much more than a mile. As usual, following her into the drawing-room, I was put off by her politeness, which seemed like a piece of private fun.

She led me to an armchair beside the window, inquired what she should give me to drink and precisely how I liked it, fitted me with coffee table, glass, and cigarettes, and then sat down opposite me in a hard-back upright chair. She was dressed with Quakerish simplicity, white blouse, dark skirt: and the skirt, though it showed an inch or two of thigh, looked long that year on a woman of twenty-three.

"I'm so sorry that Aunt Meg couldn't come too," she said. "It's one of her trust days, isn't it? I ought to have remembered that, it's very bad of me. One oughtn't to be careless like that, ought one?"

It was only then that I suspected she hadn't been so careless. It hadn't occurred to me that she wanted me by myself, or could have any motive for it.

"Do please tell Aunt Meg that I am dreadfully sorry. I want to see her so much."

Muriel fixed me with an intense, undeviating gaze. I had admired her acute green eyes (which others called hazel, or even yellow) before, but I hadn't met them full on until now. They had a slight squint, such as was required from prize Siamese cats before the trait was bred out. It might have been a disfigurement or even comic, but on the spot it made her eyes harder to escape: more than that, it made one more aware of her presence.

Self-consciously (I was more self-conscious with this girl than I was used to being), I looked round the room.

"How fine this is," I said.

That was a distraction, but also the truth. It was an L-shaped room, running the whole length of the house, the front windows giving on the street, back window onto her strip of garden, from which an ash tree extended itself, three storeys high. Edging through the same back window came the last of the sunlight, falling on two pictures, by painters once thought promising, that I remembered in her father's college rooms.

"I'm so glad you like it," said Muriel. "I do think it's rather good."

"We all envy you, you know."

She gave a slight shrug. "The Victorian middle classes did themselves pretty well, didn't they?"

"So do you," I replied.

She didn't like that. For an instant, she was frowning, her face looked less controlled, less young. Her self-possession for once seemed shaken. Then, springing up, graceful, she cried:

"Look! You've never seen the house properly, have you, Uncle Lewis? Please let me show you, now."

Show me she did, like a house agent taking round a possible though unknowledgeable buyer. It was one of those tall narrow-fronted houses common in that part of London, built (said Muriel precisely) between 1840 and 1845. Built for what kind of family? She wouldn't guess. Professional? A doctor's, who had his practice in the grand houses close by?

Anyway, it must have been more immaculate now than ever in the past. Basement flat at garden level, three rooms for the housekeeper, as spotless-fresh, as uninhabited-looking, as Muriel's drawing-room. Dining-room on the ground floor, table laid for one, silver shining on the rosewood. Second floor, Muriel's bedroom, scent-smelling, cover smooth in the evening light: as she stood beside me, she said there was another room adjacent, which we would come back to—"that is, if you can bear any more."

She led the way up to the top storey, light-footed as an athlete. The main room was the nursery and I could hear infantile chortles. She hesitated outside the door. I said that I liked very small children. "No, forgive me, he'll be having a feed." Instead she showed me two bedrooms on the same floor. That's where she could put people up, she said. What people, I was wondering. Quick-eyed, she seemed to read my thoughts. American students who were forced out of Berkeley, she said. Those were the last two. They had something to teach us.

She climbed up some iron steps to a balcony garden: she was slim-waisted, she looked slight, but she was nothing like as fragile as she seemed. She gazed across the roofs and gardens before she descended, and took me downstairs again to the second floor. Then she opened the door next to her bedroom: "Would you really mind sitting here just for a little while?"

It was something between a boudoir and a study. There were plenty of bookshelves: there was a cupboard from which she brought another tray of drinks, though as before she didn't take one herself. But also there were what appeared to be other cupboards for her dresses, a long mirror, a smaller looking glass in front of a dressing table. I had noticed another, more sumptuous dressing table in her bedroom: but I guessed that it was here she spent most of her time. It smelt of her scent, which was astringent, not heady: no doubt Lester Ince would have known the name. On the desk stood a large photograph of Azik Schiff and another which later I should have recognised as of Che Guevara, though at the time I had scarcely seen the face. That night I was wondering if this might be a lover: it wasn't the only time that she sent me on a false direction. There was no picture of her mother, and none of her father, nor any reminder of him at all, except, very oddly, for a copy of the seventeenth century engraving of our college's first court, hanging in obscurity on the far wall.

"I do hope I haven't tired you," she said.

I said that it was a beautiful house. I went on: "You're a lucky girl."

"Do you really think I am, Uncle Lewis?" The question was deferential, but her eyes were once more staring me out.

"By most people's standards, yes, I think you are."

"Some people's standards would be different, wouldn't they? They might think it was wrong for anyone like me to have all this." Her eyes didn't move, but there was a twitch, unapologetic, sardonic, to her mouth. "You couldn't tell me it wasn't wrong. Could you? It is, you know it, don't you?"

"I wasn't talking about justice," I said. "I was talking about you."

"Isn't that rather old-fashioned of you, though?"

To say I wasn't provoked wouldn't be true. I heard my words get rougher.

"I don't know whether you're unhappy. But if you are, I do know that it's more tolerable to be unhappy in comfort. You try working behind a counter when you're miserable, and you'll see."

"Aren't you being rather feminine, Uncle Lewis? You're reducing it all to personal things, you know. You can't believe they matter all that much—"

"They matter to most of us."

"Not if one has anything serious to do." Her manner was entirely cool. "Perhaps you don't think I am serious, though. That would be rather old-fashioned of you again. I'm very very sorry, but it would. Because I've got plenty of money. Because I'm living a plushy bourgeois life—not so very different from yours, if I may say so. Then it's artificial if I don't accept this nice cosy world I'm living in. You don't trust me if I want to have a hand in getting rid of it and starting something better. You think I'm playing at being discontented, don't you? Isn't that it?"

I thought, she was no fool, she was suspicious about me, her suspicions were shrewd. As I watched her face, disciplined except for the eye-flash, I had been reflecting on people like Dolfie Whitman, that invigilator of others' promotion. Philippe Egalité radical, his enemies had called him. Rich malcontents. I had known a good many. Some had seemed dilettantes, or else too obviously getting compensation for a private wound. Often they weren't the first allies you would choose to have on your side in a crisis. A few, though, were as unbending and committed as one could be. Such as the scientist Constantine or Charles March's wife. What about this young woman? I was mystified, I couldn't make any sort of judgment. I still had no idea why she wanted me in her house. Surely not to sit alone with her in her study, having an academic discussion on student protest, or any variety of New Left, or the place of women with large unearned incomes in radical movements?

It was time, I felt, to stop the fencing.

"I don't know you well enough to say." I went on: "You're cleverer than I thought."

"Thank you," she said, gravely, politely, imperturbably, as unruffled as if I had congratulated her on a new dress. It was the manner which I couldn't break through, and which had made me, not patronising as it might have sounded, but harsh and rude.

"For all I know," I said, "you may be absolutely in earnest."

"It would be rather upsetting for you, wouldn't it," she replied, "if you found I was."

"What do you hope for?"

She wasn't at all put off. Her reply was articulate, much of what I had heard from friends of Charles's, less qualified and political than from Charles himself. This country, America, the world she knew, weren't good enough: there must be a

chance of something better. The institutions (they sometimes called them structures) of our world had frozen everyone in their grip: they were dead rigid by now, universities,
civil service, parliaments, the established order, the lot. One
had to break them up. It might be destructive: you couldn't
write a blueprint for the future: but it would be a new start,
it would be better than now.

All that I was used to; the only difference was one thing
she didn't say, which I was used to hearing. She didn't talk
about 'your generation,' and blame us for the existing structures and the present state of things. Whether that was out
of consideration, or whether she was keeping her claws
sheathed, I couldn't tell.

"What can you do about it? You yourself?"

The question was another attempt to break through. She
didn't mind. Her reply was just as calm as before, and this
time businesslike. Money was always useful. So was this
house. She could help with the supply work. (I had a flicker-
ing thought of young women like her doing the same for the
Spanish war and the 'Party' thirty years before.) Of course
she couldn't do much. In any sort of action, though, one had
to do what came to hand: wasn't that true?

Yes, it was quite true. In fact, I fancied uneasily that I
might have said it myself: and that she was impassively quot-
ing it back at me.

"Why are you in it at all?"

The first flash of anger. "You won't admit I believe in it,
will you?"

It was my turn to be calm. "I said before, you may be absolutely in earnest."

"But you really think it's a good way to keep some men
round me, don't you? It's a good way to keep in circulation,
isn't it?"

The words were still precise, the face demure with a kind of false and taunting innocence. But underneath the smooth skin there was a storm of temper only just held back.

"I might even collect another husband, mightn't I? If I was lucky. Now that would be a reason for being in it, you'd accept that, wouldn't you?"

I said (she was suspicious of me again, this time the suspicion had gone wrong):

"It hadn't even occurred to me. I should have thought, if you did want another husband, you wouldn't have to go to those lengths, would you?"

She gave what for her was an open smile, like a woman, utterly confident with men, suddenly enjoying an off-hand, not over-flattering remark.

"But now you're talking about it," I went on, "I suppose you will get married again, some time?"

"I don't know," she said. "I just don't know." Then she added, as though she had spoken too simply: "It's the only thing I was brought up for, you see. And that isn't a point in its favour, particularly."

In the same quiet, judicious tone she was blaming her mother for her education, being prepared for nothing but that, protected, watched over. In the quiet judicious tone she wasn't concealing that she disliked her mother—with not just a daughter's ambivalence or rebellion, but with plain dislike. If she hadn't been trained for the marriage stakes, she might have done somehing. Anyway she had made her own marriage. That hadn't been a recommendation for trying it again. She didn't refer to Pat with dislike, as she did her mother, but with detachment, not mentioning his name. She spoke of her marriage as though it had been an interesting historical event or an example of mating habits which she had happened to observe.

"I don't intend to make a mess of it again," she said. "But you needn't worry about me. I shan't die of frustration. I can look after myself."

It seemed as though she was being blunt: but even when she seemed to be, and maybe was, trying to be direct, she could sound disingenuous at the same time. Was she suggesting, or stating, that she wasn't going to risk another marriage, but took men when she wanted them? Was that true in fact?

There had been a time when I thought the opposite. As I watched her getting rid of Pat, or as the centre of attraction at one of the previous summer's parties, it seemed to me that she might have had bad luck: the bad luck that goes with beauty. Not that her face was beautiful: people looked at her long nose, wide mouth, didn't know how to describe her. Pretty? Alluring? But she behaved like others whom everyone called beautiful. It wasn't good to be so. Those I had met— there were only two or three—had been unable to give love or else were frigid. It wasn't simply the shape of a face that made others decide that a woman had the gift of beauty. They had to feel some quality which set her apart and came from inside. There was nothing supernatural about it: it might very well be a kind of remoteness, a sensual isolation, or a narcissism.

Whatever it came from, the gift of beauty—as the old Yeats knew too well—was about the last one would wish for a daughter.

When I had seen Muriel surrounded by Charles and his friends, attention brushing off her, she was behaving as though she need not look at them, but only at herself. As I said, I thought then that she had had that specific bad luck, or, if you like, that fairy's gift.

Now I had changed my mind. I didn't know much about

her, there were things which I couldn't know: but I was
fairly sure that she was less narcissistic than I had believed
and, underneath the smooth, the sometimes glacial front, a
good deal more restless. She didn't radiate the hearty kind of
sexuality that anyone could find in the presence of, for example, Hector Rose's new wife. But she had—I wasn't certain but I guessed—a kind of sexuality of her own. It might
be hidden, conspiratorial, insinuating. Some man would discover it (I couldn't tell whether Pat had or not), and then
would find the two of them in a sensual complicity. It
wouldn't be hearty: it might even seem corrupt. But some
man, not put off by whispers or secrets, enjoying the complicity, would find it. He might be fortunate or unfortunate,
I couldn't guess that far.

I didn't like her. I never had: and, now that I had seen a
little more, I didn't like her any better. She might be easier
to love than to like: but, if that was what she induced, it was
a bad prospect for her and anyone who did love her so. If I
had been younger, I should have shied away.

Yet, in a curious sense, I respected her. Of course, her attraction had its effect on me as on others. But though that
sharpened my attention, it didn't surround her with any
haze or aura. She was there, visible and clear enough, not
specially amiable, certainly not negligible. She was not much
like anyone I had known. The links one could make with
the past didn't connect with her. She was there in her own
right.

Earlier on, as we climbed up and down the house, and
again when she talked about the programme of action, she
had mentioned Charles. Almost precisely as he had mentioned her, when it would have been artificial, or even note-
worthy, not to do so.

Now, shortly after she had switched on the reading lamp,

which, throwing a pool of light upon the desk, also lit up both our faces, she asked a question. It was casual and matter of fact.

"By the way, do please tell me, what is Charles going to do?"

"What ever do you mean?"

She was smiling. "Please tell me. I'm fairly good at keeping quiet."

I said: "I'm sure you are. But I've no idea what you mean."

"Haven't you really?"

I shook my head.

She was still smiling, not believing me. To an extent, she was right not to believe.

"Well then, do forgive me. What is he going to do about his career?"

"I haven't the slightest idea."

"But you must have."

"I'm not certain that he has himself. If so, he hasn't told me."

"But you have your own plans for him, haven't you?"

"None at all."

She gazed at me, showing her scepticism, using her charm. "You must have."

"I'm not sure how well you know him—"

Her expression didn't alter, she was still intent on softening me.

"—it would be about as much use my making plans for him as it would have been for your father. But I haven't the faintest desire to, I haven't had since he was quite young."

I told her, when he was a child, I watched his progress obsessively from hour to hour. Then I dropped it, determined that I wouldn't live my life again in him. Fortunately, now

that I could see what he was really like. I didn't tell her, but
now for me he existed, just as she did, in his own right. Embossed, just as persons external to oneself stood out. Like
that, except perhaps for the organic bonds, the asymmetry
that had emerged for moments in the hospital bedroom.

"That's very splendid," said Muriel, "but still you're not
quite so simple as all that, are you?"

"I've learned a bit," I said.

"But you haven't forgotten other things you've learned, I
can't believe it. I've heard my father say (by that she meant
Azik Schiff, whereas a few minutes before I had been thinking of Roy Calvert) that you know as much about careers as
any man in England."

She went on:

"You won't pretend, I'm sure you won't, that you haven't
thought what Charles ought to do. And whatever it is, you
know the right steps, you can't get rid of what you've done
yourself, can you?"

"I might be some use to one or two of his friends," I said.
"Such as Gordon Bestwick. But not to him."

"You're being so modest—"

"No, I know some things about him. And what I can do
for him. After all, he's my son."

She said: "You love him, don't you?"

"Yes, I love him."

She was totally still. Sitting there, body erect in the chair,
she seemed not to have moved an involuntary muscle, except
for the play of smiles upon her face.

I wanted to say something emollient. I remarked:

"I've told him, I shall make him financially independent
at twenty-one. That's the only thing I can do."

Suddenly she laughed. Not subtly, nor with the curious,
and not pleasing, sense of secret intention which she often
gave: but full-throatedly, like a happy girl.

"It really is extraordinary that that's still possible today, isn't it? Talk about justice!"

"My dear girl, it would have seemed even more extraordinary forty-odd years ago, when I was Charles's age, if someone had done the same for me."

I explained that, until my first wife died, I had received exactly £300 which I hadn't earned. And even that made a difference. Muriel was not in a position to talk, I told her, waving my hand to indicate the house in which we happened to be sitting. But now she didn't resent being reminded about being an heiress. Somehow that exchange, singularly mundane, about riches, poverty, inherited wealth, had made us more friendly to each other.

Not at the instant when I heard her question about Charles, but soon after, I had realised that this was the point of the meeting. For some reason which she was hiding or dissimulating, it was to ask about his career that she had taken pains to get me to her house alone. Not for the sake of information, but to face me and what I wanted. Why she needed that so much, was still a mystery to me.

There was lack of trust on both sides, or something like a conflict or a competition, as though we were struggling over his future. I suspected that she intended to keep him close to their group, cell, movement, whatever they cared to call it: she had power over a good many young men, maybe she had power over him. I didn't know whether she felt anything for him. Did she assume that I was playing a chess game with her, thinking some moves ahead to counter hers? If so, I thought, she was overrating herself.

Yet Muriel had faced me. Though there was nothing to struggle about, we had been struggling. Underneath the words, precise on her side, deliberately off-hand on mine, there had been tempers, or feelings sharper than tempers, not hidden very deep. Now we were quieter.

"He is very unusual," she said without explanation.

"In some ways, yes." I had heard that opinion from his friends, as well as from her: it struck them more than it did me.

"So it matters what he does."

"It will probably matter to him."

We weren't crossing wills: this was all simple and direct.

"He is very unusual," she repeated. "So it might matter to others."

"Yes, if he's lucky, so it might."

TWENTY-EIGHT

TWO PARTIES

Cambridge in May. Margaret and I walked through the old streets, then along Peas Hill, where in winter the gas flares used to hiss over the bookstalls. The gas flares would have looked distinctly appropriate that afternoon, for a north-west wind was funnelling itself through the streets, so cold that we were bending our heads, like the others walking in our direction: except for one imperturbable Indian, who strolled slow and upright, as though this was weather that any reasonable man would much enjoy. The clouds scurried over, leaden, a few hundred feet high. It was like being at Fenners long ago, two or three of us huddled in overcoats, waiting for ten minutes play before the rain.

Soon Margaret and I had had enough of it, and turned back. Cambridge in May. It was so cold that the early summer scents were all chilled down: even the lilac one could scarcely smell. We were staying with Martin (I had come up, as I promised Charles, to have a look at his friend Best-wick), and we hurried back to the Tutorial house. There in his drawing-room we stood with our backs to the blazing coal fire, getting a disproportionate pleasure from the wintry comfort and the spectacle of undergraduates haring about in the wind and rain below.

We were not so comfortable in the early evening, when Charles, in order to produce Gordon Bestwick without making him suspicious, had arranged something like a party in

Guy Grenfell's rooms. It was the least lavish of parties. As I had noticed before, the young men and women drank very little, much less than their predecessors. Some of their friends smoked pot, and they didn't condemn it, any more than they condemned anything in the way of sex. But they condemned racism, which had become, even to contemporaries of theirs who weren't militant at all, the primal sin: which meant that when Grenfell, as a concession to the past, gave Margaret and me small glasses of otherwise unidentifiable sherry, one knew that it was not South African. Most of the group (it might have been because they intended to have a meeting that night, or even because Grenfell, who was well off, was also mean) contented themselves with beer or even the liquid emblem of capitalism, Coca-Cola.

The room was on the ground floor, and very handsome: but it was also very cold. Before the war, there would have been a coal fire, as in Martin's sitting-room: but now Grenfell's college had installed central heating, and turned it off for the Easter term. I remarked to Bestwick, soon after I met him, that privileged living had become increasingly unprivileged, ever since I was a young man. Just in time to do him completely in the eye, he said, which pleased me, being less stark than I expected. Young men came in and out, sometimes meeting Margaret or me, usually not introduced. There were some good faces, one or two (as in any company of the political young that I had ever seen) with idealists' eyes. There was plenty of character and intelligence moving through the room. A young woman, voice strained with distress, blamed me for Vietnam. One or two asked questions about Russia, which I knew, and China, which I didn't: but were more interested in the second than the first. Charles March's younger daughter passed by, and my niece Nina, who must have made a special trip from London. Someone spoke angrily about students' rights.

It was no use speaking to the young as though you were young yourself. If you did, they distrusted you. Often they suspected you of a sexual motive: and they were sometimes right.

Students. They all called themselves students. Yet the term was scarcely heard in Cambridge when I first arrived there. They wouldn't have been interested in that reflection. They were singularly uninterested in history. Not that that differentiated them much from other generations. We had all believed that we were unique: and these, as much as any.

Did anything differentiate them? On the surface, looks and manners. When one couldn't see, or didn't notice, their faces, some did look unlike anything this century. Guy Grenfell, for instance, grew his hair as long as a Caroline young man. Which seemed odd, since his face had the port wine euphoria, the feminine (but not effeminate) smoothness, of one of his eighteenth century ancestors. And his manners once more struck me as strangely managed, as though he were determined to forget any he had ever known and was hoping to invent some for Year One, and to find the equivalants of citoyen and tovarishch. The result was not, as he presumably hoped, that he sounded like my forebears or Gordon Bestwick's, but like his own at their most aggressive, on a foreign railway station in brazen voices hailing a porter.

But all that brushed off (if they were different, and they might be, it was because of their time and place) when I had a word with him alone, or later with Gordon Bestwick. Talking to Grenfell I felt obliged to bolster up his confidence. He was a nice and humble man, inconveniently torn between an embarrassing pride in his antecedents and the necessity of feeling more passionately modern than anyone around him. He wouldn't have felt like that if he hadn't been quite humble: he liked tagging on to people whom he believed with simplicity to be cleverer and better than he was. This led him to displays of exaggerated sensibility. His school had been "beastly and brutalising." The mere thought of the army, his family profession, was beastly and brutalising too. He was very much preoccupied with the number of examination suicides at Cambridge, almost as though, frail plant that he was, he couldn't expect both to pass his first year Mays and to survive. In fact, he was a tough and hardy character, who didn't need so much sympathy as he felt entitled to and modestly induced.

Whereas, in some respects, Gordon Bestwick needed more. With him, not long before Margaret and I were due to leave, I sat down on a window seat. Charles had had the intuition to guess that Bestwick and I would have something in common, and I had been told what to look for. Physically, he was gawky and tall, taller than Charles or Guy Grenfell, themselves over six feet, but he had not been as peach-fed as Grenfell; as he stretched out his legs, the thighs were thin, and there were deficiency lines from nostril to mouth. There were also other lines, premature furrows, on his forehead: his face was not exactly ugly, but plain, with wavy hair already thinning, hard intelligent eyes, square jowls. It was a physical makeup not uncommon in those whose temperament wasn't easy to handle, what with natural force, ability, and a component of anxiety. It was the anxiety that Charles had asked me to watch; for Bestwick had been complaining, to Charles alone, of physical symptoms, and Charles had heard something of similar troubles of mine as a young man.

At that time I had been too proud to say a word. My first impression was that Bestwick was at least as proud. All I could risk was to let fall reminiscences about what it was like in my youth to be born poor. Charles had probably told him that I wasn't stupid. It didn't matter if he thought I was a bore. Reading for the Bar. Gambling on nothing going wrong. Strain. Lying awake at night. Sleep-starts. Pavement giving way under foot. When the game looked in my hands, sent away ill.

If none of that applied to him (his expression was lively, but gave nothing away) he must have thought me a remarkably tedious conversationalist. Before we sat alone, he had been analysing the economic thinking of the old Left. Informal, confident, not rude but dismissive. I thought I would test him. Sometimes the brightest demolition men weren't so easy with the biological facts of life. "Anyway," I said, "there wasn't anything much wrong with me. I recovered well enough to have my heart stop last November."

He gave a grim friendly smile. "I heard about that," he said. "You look as though you're hanging on all right, though. Aren't you?"

He was treating me as an equal, that was good. It was just possible that psychosomatic recollections hadn't been a bad idea. He might have been glad to hear that he wasn't unique. I should have been glad of that, at his age.

We went on talking. An American black had been talking to a knot of admirers earlier on. Now they (American blacks), said Bestwick, were in a genuinely revolutionary situation. While the total of the United States society was nowhere near it, as far away as you could get. So that with Americans of student age, the counterparts of the people in this room, you had a revolutionary climate without a revolutionary situation. Had that ever occurred before?

He was worth listening to, I was thinking. Charles might have over-estimated him, but not excessively. Perhaps his mind was not as precise as Charles's, which, as the mathematical analysts used to say, tended to be deep, sharp, and narrow. Bestwick's mind was certainly broader than Charles's, and possibly more massive. It was a pleasure to meet ability like this: a pleasure I used to feel, then for a time lost, and now had begun to enjoy again.

There was something else about him, quite minor, which interested me. His voice was pleasant, his tone was confident but unaggressive, but he hadn't made any audible attempt to change his accent. If I hadn't known his home town, I should still have guessed that he came from Birmingham or somewhere near. There were the intrusive g's, ring-ging, hang-ging, which I used to hear when I travelled twenty miles west from home. In my time those would have gone. Except for the odd scientist like Walter Luke, people of our origins, making their way into the professional life, tried to take on the sound of the authoritative class. It was a half-unconscious process, independent of politics. Bestwick hadn't made any such attempt. Yet he was a man made for authority. The social passwords had changed. Again it was a half-unconscious process. Perhaps he took it for granted that there wasn't an authoritative class any more, or that it existed only in enclaves, bits, and pieces. Curiously enough, I thought, that might not make things easier for him.

Just then Nina came up, smiled at me through her hair, and whispered to Gordon Bestwick. "When the party's over, we're all going to the Eagle. Is that OK for you?"

"Fine," said Bestwick, and she slipped away. His eyes followed her, and he called out, "Mind you wait for me." It sounded masterful: was it as relaxed as when he talked to me?

I had not been told that those two knew each other. On the other hand, he must have been aware that she was a relative of mine. That might have made me more tolerable, I wasn't sure. Anyway, when I said that Charles must bring him to stay with us at the end of term, he was eager, and less certain of himself than he had been at any time before.

Half an hour later, out at the Getliffes' house, the level of comfort rose again. When we moved into the dining-room, the long table was not set for so many places as it often was:

only for nine, which slightly took away from the normal resemblance to a Viking chieftain's hall, that resemblance
which was responsible for Charles naming it the Getliffe
steading. We were used to the sight of Francis at one end of
his table presiding over a concourse. That night, as it happened, besides Margaret and me, there were only Martin and
Irene, who had followed us out from the college, the Getliffe's second son Peter and his wife, and their elder son,
Leonard. Francis was pushing decanters round, gazing down
the table with an expression of open pleasure, just faintly
tinged with saturnine glee. Everyone there knew each other.
Martin and he had, after a good many years of guarded and
respectful alliance, at last grown intimate. While Martin,
before he and Francis became specially friendly, had long
been fond of the Getliffe sons. And there was, as often in
that house, something to celebrate. Leonard had been offered
a chair in Cambridge, and one that even he, at the top of his
profession, was pleased to get. How far he had recovered
from his unrequited love, I didn't know, and probably
Francis didn't. But he wasn't migrating to Princeton after all,
and Francis and Katherine, who liked their dynasty round
them, were happy. Peter, settled in a University job: Ruth,
the elder daughter, married to another don: now Leonard,
persuaded to come back. That left only their youngest,
Penelope, who was pursuing an erratic matrimonial course
in the United States.

In the warm candlelight—one could hear windows rat-
tling in the wind—Katherine was saying:

"It's funny, your Charles being so high (she put her hand
below the table) and ours grown up."

"He's taller than I am, dear," I replied, "and just about to
take Part I."

"No! No! I meant, when you brought him here and Mar-

garet put her foot in it and that woman from Leeds thought
you were a clergyman."

Katherine was proceeding by free association: that was an
occasion something like sixteen years before, though all the
details were lost, certainly in my memory and Margaret's,
probably in that of the woman from Leeds, and were preserved
only in Katherine's. If you wanted to live outside of history,
to dislocate time, then Katherine was the one to teach you:
but, it happened very rarely, for once that total recall had
slipped. At the time of this incident, Charles would have
been about two. If so, Leonard, their eldest, had barely left
school.

I pointed this out to Katherine, who expostulated,
wouldn't admit it, laughed, was disconcerted like an avant-
garde American confronted by an example of linear thinking. Katherine's thinking, I told her, was far from linear:
then had to apologise, and explain with labyrinthine thor-
oughness (for Katherine didn't easily subside) what the reference meant.

That led, transition by transition, to the party from which
Margaret and I had come. Yes, we had been mixing with the
local avant garde: or the protesters: or the New Left: or the
anarchists: or the post-Marxists: they had all been there, all
they had in common was the *Zeitgeist,* they wanted different
things, they would end up in different places.

"Oh well," said Francis, "that has happened before."

I corrected myself, hearing him take it so facilely. Perhaps
I had spoken like that too. I said that for some purposes, just
at present they were at one.

Up and down the table, the others argued with me. There
was one feature of that family party; on most issues, either of
politics or social manners, we were, with minor temperamen-
tal shades, pretty well agreed. Irene had taken on most of

Martin's attitudes: Katherine had always been ready to believe that her husband was usually right. That wasn't true of
Margaret, certain of her own beliefs, which weren't quite
mine; she would have fitted better in an age when it was natural to be both liberal, or Whiggish, and also religious. Still,
in terms of action she was close to the rest of us.

As for the young Getliffes, there seemed next to nothing
of the fathers-and-sons division. Even that family couldn't invariably have been so harmonious: but certainly on politics
they spoke like their father, or like other radicals from the
upper-middle-class—not so committed as he had been, perhaps, but independent and ready to take the necessary risks.
They were scientists like Francis, and that gave them a posi-
tiveness which sometimes made Margaret, and even me, wish
to dissent. Nevertheless, those shades of temperament didn't
matter, and on the likely future and what ought to be done
—the future of fate and the future of desire—there wouldn't
have been many dinner tables that night where there was
less conflict.

Such conflict as did emerge was on a narrow front. The
young Getliffes, both in their early thirties, were more cut
off from Charles and his society, more impatient with them,
than the rest of us.

"It's all romantic," said Leonard Getliffe at one point.
"I'm not a politician, but they don't know the first thing
about politics."

"That's not entirely true," I said.

"Well, look. They think they're revolutionaries. They also
think that revolution has something to do with complete
sexual freedom. They might be expected to realise that any
revolution that's ever happened has the opposite correlative.
All social revolutions are puritanical. They're bound to be,
by definition. Put these people down in China today.
Haven't they the faintest idea what it's like?"

That was a point I had to concede. I was thinking, yes, I had seen other groups of young people dreaming of both their emancipation and a juster world. That was how George Passant started out. Well, all, and more than all, of the emancipation he prescribed to us had realised itself—in the flesh—before our eyes. And we had learned—here Leonard was right—you can have a major change in sexual customs and still leave the rest of society (who had the property, who was rich, who was poor) almost untouched.

"The one consolation is," said Martin, "human beings are almost infinitely tough. If you did put them down in China, they'd make a go of it. I suppose if we were young today, we shouldn't be any worse off than we actually were. They seem to find it pretty satisfactory."

He might have been speaking of his son or, nowadays more likely, of his daughter.

"Think of the time I should have had!" Irene gave a yelp of laughter. Her husband laughed with her, troubles long dead, and so did the rest of us. One could have remarked that, considering the restrictions, her actual time had not been so uneventful.

Francis brought out a bottle of port, which nowadays we didn't often drink. Sexual freedom apart, I asked them, did they think there was nothing else in this—assertion, unrest, rebellion, alienation, of the young, you could call it what you liked? It was happening all round the world. Yes, it might be helped by commercialism. Yes, it hadn't either an ideology or a mass political base. But they (the Getliffes) were writing it off fairly complacently, they might be in for a surprise. Of course, if people of that age (I returned to something I had been thinking in Grenfell's rooms) were different at all, it was nothing ultramundane, it was because of their time and place. But somehow their time was working on them pretty drastically. I wasn't much moved by his-

torical parallels. This was here and now. There were sometimes discontinuities in history. On a minor scale, we might
be seeing one. I didn't find it necessary to explain that, the
previous summer, I should have been arguing on the Getliffes' side in the opposite sense. Well, I had changed my
mind.

As completely as all this?

Perhaps my experience of the young Pateman and his student following had prejudiced me against Charles's friends,
perhaps I had over-reacted to him. Anyway, of these (Charles's
friends) weren't another crop of Lester Inces, some day I
ought to tell them that there I had been wrong.

Most of the dinner party knew that I wasn't detached, and
that I was so interested because of my son. But Francis and
Katherine had an affection for him, as well as for us. Martin
and Irene too had their reasons for being interested. It was
only the young couple and Leonard who were regarding the
phenomenon as being a pure exercise in sociology. Since it
was a cheerful evening, I didn't suppress a gibe at the expense of Peter and his wife. They already had two children,
five and three. A dozen years or so, and it would be their
turn next. Either like this, or something different. Possibly
stranger still.

That night at the dinner table, it was natural to think of
Francis's grandchildren a dozen years ahead. Francis's life, at
times strained, dissident, dutiful, had nevertheless held more
continuity than most of ours. His father had lived not unlike
this. His sons were already doing so. Though Francis's hospitality was all his own, spontaneous and disconcerting to
those who knew only his public face. That night he was in
cracking spirits, talking of changes he had already seen, prepared to see more, jeering at himself and me for false prophesies, of which there had been plenty, gazing with astringent

fondness at his family and friends. It was natural to think of that family going on.

While we were having our evening at the Getliffes, Bestwick and Charles and the others were at work. They were more active than we, or any of their predecessors, had been: or rather, we had talked a good deal but not acted, while they didn't recognise any gap between the two. They weren't ready to wait, as we had waited, until we had won a little, even the most precarious, authority. At eighteen, nineteen, twenty, they were getting down to business. They were doing so that night. Where in Cambridge they met I didn't know, either then or later: nor what was decided, nor who took part. Charles had learnt discretion very early, and so I found had Bestwick, when I knew him better; neither of them at any stage told me, or even hinted at, anything I shouldn't hear. It was only later, from another source, and a most unlikely one, that I could piece together fragments of the story.

TWENTY-NINE

WALKING SLOWLY
IN THE RAIN

"The only examinations they'd heard of were medical ones. They weren't very good at getting through those."

It was Gordon Bestwick, talking of his family.

"The same would be true of mine," I said. "I doubt if any one of them had ever taken a written examination until I did."

Bestwick nodded his massive head, but he was faintly irked. He didn't want me to be a partner in obscurity. He had been staying with us for a week, the first time, he said, that he had been inside a professional London home. It might have suited his expectations better if this had been more like my own first visits to the Marches, back in the Twenties, butlers, footmen, wealth for generations on both sides. I had a feeling that he was disappointed that we lived so simply.

That evening he was sitting in our drawing room after dinner, alone with Margaret and me. On the other days since Bestwick's arrival, Charles had prompted me into having a series of guests to dinner, but that night he had some engagement of his own and had begged off. It was late in June, somewhere near the longest day, and the sky was like full daylight over the park.

"Carlo didn't suffer from the same disadvantage, though," he said.

274

"If it was a disadvantage," I replied. "In some ways you and I may have had the better luck. He thinks so—"

"And it's like his blasted nerve. I don't mind all that much his having been given ten yards start in a hundred, but when he gets explaining that it made things more difficult for him, that's more than I can take."

Margaret smiled. The two young men were more than allies, they were on comradely terms. Gordon was, so far as I had heard, the only one of Charles's intimates who called him by his family pet name. But there was a mixture of envy and admiration which flowed both ways. Charles would have liked the dominance which he, and other acquaintances of ours older than he, couldn't help feeling in Gordon. One didn't have to be a talent spotter to recognise Gordon's ability, that shone out: but I wondered whether there wasn't something else. One or two chips bristled like iguana scales on his shoulders: but he managed to sink them, when he talked about those who really were deprived. He knew and cared. Privileged men were still vulnerable when they heard that kind of voice.

But those were times when Gordon was on duty. During his week with us, especially when he was talking to Margaret, one saw another aspect. He became attentive and anxious to please. Once or twice, trying to entertain her, he looked not mature, as he did addressing Hector Rose, but younger than his years.

In private Margaret told me that, though she liked him, she didn't find him attractive as a man: and she believed that would have been the same if she had been his own age. After that I asked Charles how Gordon got on with women. Charles reflected. Perhaps Gordon wasn't his first choice for sexual confidences. "Oh," said Charles at length, "he's a bit of a star, you know, he's had one or two offers. Chiefly from very rich girls—" Charles grinned. But Gordon, he went on, was pretty concentrated, he didn't have much time to spare. The only girl in whom he seemed "interested" (the peculiarly anaemic word which they used and which their more inhibited predecessors would have thought genteel) was Nina.

It was thundery, as Gordon sat in the drawing-room with us, and Margaret said she had a headache. I invited Gordon to come out for a drink. He looked hesitant, as though we weren't being solicitous enough or as though there were an etiquette in which he hadn't been instructed. Margaret said go on, It'll do you good, and promised, in case Charles returned, to send him after us.

In the heavy air Gordon and I walked through the back streets, as I had done with my stepson one Christmas Day. The clouds were thickening, but it hadn't yet begun to rain; outside a pub people were sitting round the open-air tables, at one of which Gordon and I settled down with pints of beer. Lightning flashes from the direction of the park. Growls of thunder far away. Close by the pavement curb, cars, headlights shining in the murk, passed as on a conveyor belt on their way from Paddington.

It used to be a quiet pub, I remarked to Gordon, when I first lived in Bayswater Road. Now we might as well be sitting in a café in one of the noisier spots in Athens.

"Never been abroad," he said, big frame relaxed, ingesting bitter.

"Come off it, Gordon. We all know there is no sorrow like unto your sorrow. We also know that you could get large grants to travel any time you chose to ask for them. Which is more than I ever could. You're rather inert physically and rather unadventurous, that's all."

He was used to some of my techniques by now, and gave a matey smile. I went on baiting him. He blamed too much on environment and hoped for too much from environment.

That had always been the mistake of romantic optimists. If he and his friends were going to hammer some sense into progressive thought, they had to dispose of that mistake. Gordon didn't mind a challenge. He didn't believe in any sort of Calvinism, scientific, intuitive, or any other. The only thing you could change was environment. Change the environment of the working class—and he knew what the working class was like, he was born right there, he didn't romanticise them, he didn't want them to stay as they were—and they would become better.

Granted, I said: but what you could do by changing environment for anyone or any group of people had its limits.

We've got to believe that there are no limits, said Gordon.

In that case you're in for another of the progressive disillusions.

If so, he said, we'll take that when we come to it: we've got to act as though we can make a new species.

You've got to act like that; but you mustn't expect it.

It does good to expect the best.

There I wasn't with him, I said. If you expect the best, then you're blinding yourself to the truth.

Truth sometimes has to be put into suspended animation.

I don't believe, I said, that you achieve good action—not for long—if the base is anything but true.

It was an old argument, but new facts were flooding in. He knew them as well as I did. He was an honest controversialist, ready to grope and brood. I had never had a great taste for argument, had lost what little I once had: but it was pleasant arguing with him. In the headaching night we drank more beer, talked on, heard from inside the pub the call of time, and then saw the first half-crowns of rain bombing the pavement.

"We'd better hurry," I said. "We're going to get wet."

Running in bursts, sheltering under porticos, lumbering,

panting, we reached the main road. He was more mobile than I was, but not a track performer. The storm had broken, water was sploshing up to our shins. We made a last run to the block of flats. There, under cover of the doorway, we halted, so that I could get my breath.

"Good God," said Gordon, pointing up the street towards Marble Arch. There was a solitary figure on the pavement, sauntering very slowly. When it passed into a zone illuminated by the arc lamps, one saw it through lances of rain.

"Carlo," said Gordon.

He came towards us, not altering his pace. Watching him, I caught a fresh smell of wet leaves, bringing peace.

When one saw his face, he was wearing a smile, as though satisfaction were brimming over from inside. For an instant I thought that he was drunk.

"Hello," he called, from a couple of yards away.

He was dead sober.

"Christ, man," Gordon greeted him, "you're wet through."

It wouldn't have been possible to be much wetter.

"So I am," said Charles in a mild tone. He looked at us with something like affectionate surprise. He didn't say any more, but his smile was pressing to return, and he didn't restrain it.

About a fortnight after Gordon had returned home, in the middle of July, Charles insisted on treating Margaret and me to a show and taking us out to supper afterwards. The show had to be a film, since to him and his circle the theatre was an obsolete art form, which ought to have gone out with the Greeks or certainly with Shakespeare. The show also had to be a film he had seen before so that he could guarantee it. In the cinema he placed himself punctiliously between Margaret and me, whispering to her during the film, showing her an obsessive, and for him unusual, degree of filial attention.

Nothing was said that night. It was the next day, after tea, sitting with both of us in the drawing-room, when he said, quietly but with no introduction at all:

"As a matter of fact, I'm thinking of moving into Chester Row. I'm sure you don't mind, do you?" He was speaking to Margaret, with whom his surface conflicts had in the past flared up. "Of course you don't mind, I shall be around, of course."

"Chester Row?" she said in a flat surprise.

"Are you, by God?" I said. I had a picture of him walking in the rain, the other night: slow walk, smile of joy, smell of wet leaves. I should never know whether I was right. Had he just come away from her? Was he retracing the history of the race? Did he feel that this was a unique achievement, that it had just been done for the first time?

"When are you aiming to go?" said Margaret, as though she were gripping on to practicalities.

"As a matter of fact, if it doesn't put anyone out, I was thinking of moving tonight."

"How long for?"

"Indefinite." He gave her a smile, reassuring but secretive.

She began to speak and then thought better of it. Charles was giving out happiness, now that he had broken the news, but wasn't willing to say another word about it. By a curious kind of understanding, almost formal, we all behaved as on the most uneventful of evenings. We looked at the television news at 5:50. Afterwards at dinner Charles made a fuss of his mother. The only references he made to his announcement were strictly practical. He didn't want anyone at all, including Guy Grenfell, Gordon, his cousins (there were good reasons for that at least, I thought), to hear where he was living. He would collect letters every two or three days. As for telephone calls, we were to say that he was out but would ring back, and then pass the message on to Chester Row. He apologised for the nuisance, but it was necessary.

I didn't enquire why. It was true that he often carried se-

curity precautions to eccentric lengths. If this had happened
to me in comparable circumstances, I couldn't help thinking, I should have been a good deal less self-denying and
more boastful.

After dinner Margaret went with him to his room and
helped him pack: which reminded me of one of my hyper-
civilised acquaintances doing precisely the same for her
husband, each time he left her for a new girl friend.

In the bright warm evening the three of us stood outside
on the pavement, large suitcase standing beside Charles,
waiting until a taxi came along. He waved to us from inside,
and then we were left gazing as it joined the traffic stream to
Marble Arch.

Back in the drawing-room, Margaret looked at me.

"Well, that's cool enough," she cried. She burst out into
laughter, full, sisterly, sensual.

I hadn't been sure what she was feeling: at that moment,
she was feeling exactly as I was, it wasn't just a fatherly response, she shared it. Nothing subtle, just pleasure, the
warmth of sexual pleasure at second-hand. Mixed with approval that he didn't lack enterprise. But mainly we were
getting what, if you wanted to be reductive, you could think
of as a voyeuristic joy. That was there: but it wasn't quite all:
it wasn't quite so self-centred as that. It wasn't in the least
lofty, though. We were animals happy about another animal.
And to parental animals, the happiness was rich.

In that sense Margaret—and it surprised me a little—felt
as I did. If this had been a daughter? No, there was a dispar-
ity one couldn't escape. I was certain that I should have
been miserable. Perhaps there would have been some sexual
freemasonry underneath, but worry would have overwhelmed it. I supposed that would have been true, and presumably more true, of Margaret also.

After a time, in which we had taken an evening drink,
Margaret became more pensive.

"I don't think this is going to be good for him, you know."

"Oh well. If it hadn't been her, it would have been another."

That sounded platitudinous and non-controversial, but it provoked Margaret.

"But it is her. You can't brush that away."

"He might have done worse, in some ways—"

"I don't like her."

"I've told you before, I don't like her either."

"You like her a lot more than I do," said Margaret. "She's a cold-hearted bitch."

I didn't remind Margaret that once she had been a partisan of Muriel's and had tried to look after her.

"You're not going to pretend, are you," she burst out, "that she's in love with him?"

"Does that matter?"

"Of course it matters. Do you think it's good to have your first affair with someone who doesn't give a damn for you?"

"My impression was, she had some feeling for him. I don't understand what it is."

"She's five years older." Margaret had flushed, her eyes were bright with temper. "You all say she's attractive to men, she could have her pick, unless there's something wrong with her. Why in God's name should she throw herself at him? What has he to offer her? He's too young. I could understand it perhaps if he were her own age, then he might be a good prospect—"

She went on:

"I tell you, I can't understand it. Unless—there are just two reasons why she might be doing it. And neither of them is very pleasant."

"Go on," I said.

"Well, she might be one of those women who like seducing boys. That would be bad for anyone like him—"

"It's possible," I stopped to think. "I shouldn't have thought it was likely, though. I haven't heard her talk about his being young. I doubt if she thinks of him like that."

"Anyway," I added, "I'd guess that he'll soon be able to look after himself in that sort of way."

"If it's not that," she said, "it's something worse. She's determined to get him to herself. Away from us. So that she can fix him right inside that wretched movement of theirs. And she's chosen the one certain way to fix him."

I had already thought something not unlike that myself: this might be the second stage of the struggle. In that case, she had all the advantages.

"Are you happy about that?" Margaret was distressed by now: and, as often happened, her distress turned into anger.

"No."

"Do you want him to waste himself?"

"You might remember, that I'm not responsible for any of this. Just because I've said one word in her favour—"

Margaret broke into a guilty smile, then hardened again.

"But he may be wasting himself, you can't deny it, can you? If she gets control of him, and makes him sink himself in this nonsense, then he could be a casualty, of course he could. To begin with, if that takes up all his time, his work is going to suffer."

"He's pretty tough, you know. And he likes doing well. I really do doubt if that will happen."

"Anyway, it's a waste of anyone like him. He ought to be thinking of something worthwhile. If he spends his energy on something which anyone of his sense ought to see is useless, and worse than useless, then he can do himself harm. Whatever he wants to do later. It'll take him a long time to recover. Just because this woman has got hold of him."

I hadn't any answer which satisfied either of us. She was exaggerating, I said, she was making Charles out to be weaker than he was; she was leaving out all that he would do, if Muriel didn't exist. But none of that was comforting. She had made me apprehensive, as I hadn't been for a long time: in a fashion which I had become released from, the future was throwing its shadows back.

THIRTY

DAUGHTER-IN-LAW

Our housekeeper, getting it both ways, mourned the departure of the last young presence from the flat and simultaneously showed robust Mediterranean enthusiasm for its cause. When Charles, becoming punctilious towards her as to Margaret, telephoned to say that he would call on us for a meal, he was welcomed by his favourite dishes. This happened regularly twice a week throughout the late summer; Charles came in at six, talked cheerfully through dinner without mentioning Muriel or his way of life, and left at ten. He did take care to dispel one of Margaret's qualms. Yes, he was working: he was too much conditioned not to, he said, teasing her over the exploits of her academic grandfather and uncles. Their reading parties! He was prepared to bet that he did more work by himself than they did smoking their pipes, taking marathon walks, cultivating personal relations, and revering G.E. Moore.

All was serene, on the plane of conversation. It was harder for her than for me to accept that most of his existence she couldn't know.

Then, soon after he had returned to Cambridge for the Michaelmas term, she had news of her other son. It was in the middle of an October afternoon when, reading in the study, I heard the doorbell ring. Moments afterwards it rang again, long and irritably. No one was responding. I got up and went to open the door myself.

There, on the landing, stood Father Ailwyn, bulky, white face shimmering over black cassock. He didn't smile: he moved his weight from one foot to the other.

I asked him to come in. His awkwardness infected me. I wasn't fond of uninvited visitors: and also he was one of those of whom I thought kindly when he wasn't there—and uneasily when he was. And yet, I had a regard for him after that talk—or interrogation—in the hospital.

As I led him into the drawing-room, neither of us spoke. When he was sitting down, light falling on the pale plump face, which might have looked lardlike if his growth of beard, clearly visible after the morning shave, hadn't been so dark and strong, he was still mute. Then we managed to exchange words, but his tongue seemed as thick as it usually did, and mine more so.

My first attempt was an enquiry about his parish.

"It doesn't alter much," he replied.

Stop.

I tried to repeat something I had read about an oecumenical conference.

"No, I don't know anything about that," he said.

After that he felt that an effort was up to him. Suddenly he asked, with exaggerated intensity, about my eye. I said, all had gone well.

"Is it really all right?"

"It's got some useful sight. That's the best that they could promise me."

I closed the good eye. "I can see that you're sitting there. I might just be able to recognise you, but I'm not sure."

"Very good. *Very* good." His enthusiasm was inordinate, but that was where it ended. Silence again.

He stared at me, and broke out:

"Actually, I was hoping to see your wife."

That seemed not specially urbane, even by his standards.

Still, it was a diversion, and I went to find her. She was in the bedroom, sitting at her dressing table in front of the mirror, having not long come back from her hairdresser. I told her that Godfrey Ailwyn was asking for her, and that she had better come and take the weight off me.

But, after they had shaken hands, the weight was not removed. His eloquence was not perceptibly increased. There were now two people for him to gape at awkwardly, instead of one. Margaret, who had had some practise at making conversation, found the questions falling dead.

Ignoring her, Father Ailwyn looked straight and soberly at me.

"I think," he said, "I ought to speak to Margaret by herself."

She gave me a baffled glance as I went out. I was more than baffled, as I sat alone in the study. I had no premonition at all about what he had come to tell her.

It was not long, not more than a quarter of an hour, before Margaret opened the study door.

"You'd better come back now," she said. She was looking flushed and strained, her eyes so wide open that the lids seemed retracted.

"What's the matter?"

"It's about Maurice."

"Is he ill?" My thoughts had flashed—not because I had ever imagined it of him, but because of a groove of experience—to suicide.

"Nothing like that."

I was standing by her, and had put my arm round her.

She went on:

"No. He's going to get married."

"Oh well—" I was beginning to laugh it off, when she broke in:

"To someone who is handicapped."

"What does that mean?"

She shook her head, and moved, like someone impelled to hear a verdict, towards the drawing-room.

Rising as she entered, Godfrey Ailwyn was clumsy as ever on his feet, but more comfortable, and more authoritative, now that he had done his duty. From their first remark I gathered that he had delivered a letter from Maurice; I wasn't given this to read until later, but it was full of love for Margaret and explained that, though he knew this would cause difficulties and disappointments for her, he proposed to marry someone whom he "might be some good to." The wedding and all the arrangements would have to be "very simple and private" because she wasn't "used to these things and mustn't be frightened or given too much to cope with." Godfrey Ailwyn knew all the circumstances and would be able to discuss what should be done.

With Godfrey re-settled in his chair, I picked up most of this, and another piece of information, which was that the girl was the sister of a patient in the hospital where Maurice worked.

Margaret was looking at me. There was a question which had to be asked.

"Is she mentally affected?" I said.

"No."

"You're not keeping anything from us?"

"Lewis," he replied, "you needn't have said that."

He was both stern and wounded, and I apologised.

"Well then, what is wrong with her?"

I didn't know how much Margaret had discovered. I had better make certain.

"She has a limp. It looks like the kind of limp that polio leaves them with, but I believe she's always had it."

"Is it very bad?"

"One is aware of it. Perhaps it's more distressing to others than to herself. I think, taken alone, no, it is not very bad."

"Taken alone? You mean there's something else?"

"She is also partially deaf," said Godfrey. "I think that is congenital too, and she has never had normal hearing. Of course, that made her backward as a child. But mentally she has caught up. I mustn't give you the impression that she is brilliant. There is nothing wrong with her there, though. What is more serious is that being deaf kept her out of things. She is very uncertain of herself, I doubt if she has ever made friends. And that is why Maurice has changed everything for her."

"Is that what he means," said Margaret, voice tight, "when he says she's handicapped?"

"That is what he means."

"And that is all he means?" I pressed him.

"That is all he means."

"You're certain? You do know her?"

"I know her. She is staying at the Vicarage now."

"Then I can see her?" Margaret broke out.

"I'm afraid not, Margaret," said Godfrey in a gentle tone, but with cumbrous strength.

"Why not?"

"Maurice thinks we must make everything easy for her. And he knows more about the unlucky, and how to help them, than any of the rest of us will ever know."

"But I must see her. This is his whole future."

"Margaret, your son is trying to lead a good life. I don't believe you could alter that, but I beg you to listen to me, you mustn't let him see that it brings you pain."

Godfrey was speaking to her as though I was not present. After all, Maurice was not my son. Maybe that was why Godfrey, giving the impression of bumbling incivility, first insisted on telling the news to her alone. He was her son, not

mine. And Godfrey—one had to remember—did not approve of divorce.

"I wish," said Margaret, her eyes bright with tears held
back, "that he was leading a life like everyone else."

"If I were you," Godfrey replied, "I should wish the same.
But I don't think it would be right, do you?"

"I can't be sure. For his sake, I can't be sure."

My own feeling might have been different from hers, certainly was different from Godfrey's. But this wasn't a time to
speculate. Godfrey was continuing to tell us more about her.
She was, he thought, a "nice person" (which, at that moment, seemed one of the flatter descriptions). She was twenty-three, the same age as Maurice. It was not until that point
that I learned her name. That may have been true of
Margaret also, for Maurice had not mentioned it in his letter. It was, Godfrey said in passing, Diana Dobson. He believed that in her family she was called Di.

"You must remember," Godfrey told Margaret, "she comes
from the very poor. Her mother is a cleaner in a factory.
The father left them long ago. They are as poor and simple
as they come. I'm afraid that's another difficulty for you—"

Margaret flared up.

"Do you think *that* would make the slightest difference to
me?"

She was angry, seizing a chance to be angry. Godfrey gazed
at her with a sad, doughy smile. He said:

"Without meaning to let it, and feeling bad in the sight of
God, I have to confess that it always makes a difference to
me."

He must have been speaking of his visiting round in the
parish. Maurice once told me that, when he went as companion, he usually enjoyed it, but Godfrey almost never.

Margaret's expression changed. All of a sudden she was

open and naive, as few people saw her. She said, as though it
was the natural reply:

"I am sorry, Godfrey. I know you're a good man."

"No." Heavily he shook his head. "I wish I could be. It's
your son who is a good man."

He added:

"I'd often hoped that he'd become a priest. It would be
the right place for him. But now there's this marriage
instead—"

I was thinking, Godfrey strongly disapproved of divorce:
the only thing he disapproved of more strongly was marriage. At least for himself and his friends. No, that was unfair. But it was the kind of unfairness—or slyness or malice
if you like—that showed that I was becoming fonder of him.

He and Margaret got down to business. Maurice had
given instructions which weren't to be departed from. There
were to be no press announcements of the engagement: and
none of the wedding, except for a single notice in the
Manchester evening paper, for the sake of Diana's relatives.
No announcements. He would write himself to his friends.
(Why all this? However his friends might behave in other
situations, here he could have trusted them: Charles and all
the rest would have set out to welcome her. That was part of
their creed. They would be far kinder than, in the past, my
circle would have been. Yet Maurice was being excessively
cautious, like Charles but unlike himself, or anything that
he had written to his mother or told to Godfrey: acting—it
was hard to believe—as though he were ashamed of it.)

The wedding was to be in Godfrey's church, in a fortnight's time. Here—and this was entirely understandable,
for, as Godfrey said, it was in order not to harass the girl—
there was to be no one invited, except a cousin of Diana's to
give her away.

Very quietly Margaret said:

"Am I not to come?"

"He thought she might be more panicky—"

"No."

Margaret's tone was level, unemphatic. "I shall come. I can sit at the back of the church."

She did go. I offered to go with her, but she refused. When she returned—the wedding had been early in the morning, and it was not yet eleven o'clock—her expression would to others have seemed controlled.

"That's done," she said.

She sat on the sofa, smoking, not looking at me.

"You know, one always imagines what one's children's weddings will be like. Do you do that about Carlo's?

"No, never."

"Perhaps it's a mother's privilege." For an instant, her tone was sharp-edged. Then she went on:

"I've imagined all sorts of weddings for Maurice. I haven't told you, but I have. So many women would have married him, wouldn't they? But I never imagined anything like this."

I asked something pedestrian, but she didn't hear.

"He looked very nice. Very handsome. I think he was happy. No, I'm certain he was happy. I used to tell myself, all I wanted was for him to be happy."

Had she met the girl? Oh yes, Maurice had brought her (Margaret) into the vestry. She and the best man were the witnesses. There had been one other person, a stranger, in the church: not Maurice's father, who had sent flowers and a cheque.

What was the girl like—the question wanted to come out, but I hesitated. Margaret didn't need to hear it. She said:

"She's almost pretty."

She added:

"She wanted to say something to me, but she could hardly get out a word."

After a moment, still not letting go:

"I wanted to say something to her, but I wasn't much better."

Three weeks later, I was able to see Maurice's wife for myself. He brought her to tea one afternoon, and trying to settle her down and to smooth away her shyness (and our own), Margaret and I complained heartily of the misty weather, and made a parade of drawing the curtains and shutting the evening out.

"Oh, never mind," said Maurice, entirely serene. "It'll be worse where we live, won't it, darling?"

His wife didn't reply, but she understood, and gave a dependent, trusting smile. I was thinking, as she sat in the armchair, turning towards him, Margaret's description wouldn't have occurred to me. She hadn't a feature which one noticed much, but she wasn't, either in the English or the American sense, homely. Often she wore the expression, at the same time puzzled, obstinate, and protesting that one saw in the chronically deaf. How deaf she was, I couldn't tell. Maurice spoke to her with the words slowed down, deliberately using the muscles of his lips, and she seemed to follow him easily. Sometimes he had to interpret for Margaret or me.

She was wearing a nondescript brown frock. But, as well as her limp catching the eye, so did her figure. Standing still, she looked shapely and trim.

We should have had to quarry for conversation if it hadn't been for Maurice: but he took charge, like an adoring young husband acting as impresario. Each time he spoke to her, she smiled as though he had once more called her into existence.

Yes, they had a place to live in. They were buying a

three-bedroom house in Salford, so that Di's mother could live with them. I knew about this in principle, for as our wedding present Margaret and I had paid the deposit. Maurice would continue at his job at the mental hospital. Di would earn some money, typing at home.

"We shall manage, shan't we?" he said to her, with his radiant unguarded smile.

"If we can't," she said, "we shall have to draw in our horns." When she spoke to him, her tone was transmuted: it became not only confident and trusting, but also matter of fact.

All that we could learn about her, through the deafness (our voices sounded more hectoring as we tried to get through, the questions more inane), was that she was utterly confident with Maurice, and not in the least surprised that he had married her.

I did manage to have one exchange with her, but it couldn't have been called specially illuminating. I had been casting round, heavy-footed, for gossip about the Manchester district. I happened to mention the United football team. Her eyes suddenly brightened and became sharp, not puzzled: she had heard me, she gave a sky-blue recognising glance. Yes, she liked football. She supported the United. There wasn't a team like them anywhere. She used to go to their matches—"until I met him." It was the first time she had referred to Maurice without directly speaking to him, and they were both laughing. "I'm not much good to you about that, am I?" said Maurice, who had no more interest in competitive games than in competing at anything himself.

In time, it had seemed a long time, Maurice got up and said:

"Darling, we shall have to go. Old Godfrey will miss us at the service. You know, there mightn't be anyone else."

They had a little church backchat to themselves. I had

never been certain whether Maurice was a believer, or just a fellow-traveller. The girl seemed to be devout.

Then they got up, and Margaret went towards her and embraced her. Looking at Maurice, she stood uncertain, not knowing which way to go, while I in turn approached and laid my cheek against hers.

When we heard the lift door close, Margaret sat down again and sighed.

After a while, she said:

"Tell me, Lewis" (actually she used a pet name which meant that she needed me) "is that a real marriage?"

"I haven't the remotest idea."

"No, I want to know, what you think?"

"For what my guess is worth," I said, "I'd say that it probably was."

"It would be a consolation, if I were certain of that."

As she had told Godfrey, she wanted Maurice to be like everyone else: or as near like as he could come. Perhaps she was thinking, as she did later, about the nature of goodness. He was behaving, as he so often did, in a way which would have been impossible for most of us. If behaviour was the test, then he did good, and most of us didn't. Margaret and I had often agreed, behaviour was more important than motive. And yet she, as a rule less suspicious than I was, had her moments of suspicion about this son she loved. Was it too easy for him to be good? Was it just an excuse for getting above, or out of, the battle? Did he really feel joyous and whole only with those who were helpless?

She didn't ask me, because she felt that I was likely to be hard. In fact, I shouldn't have been. There was something, I should have said, in what she suspected. He might even desire a woman only when she was disabled and had him alone to turn to. That was why, incidentally, I was ready to believe that his was a real marriage. But also, not in terms of desire but of well-being, he might be at his best himself only when he was with the unlucky and the injured. But that was true of everyone who had his kind of goodness. Did that make it less valuable? Maybe yes. It depended whether you were going to give any of us the benefit of the doubt.

Nevertheless, I thought, when I was a young man, if I had met Maurice and my nephew Pat, I should have been hypnotised by Pat's quick-change performances and attributed to him depths and mysteries which he didn't in the least possess. Whereas I shouldn't have been more than mildly interested in Maurice and should have said that you couldn't behave like that if you were a man.

After having seen more people, nowadays I should be much more sceptical about my "explanation" of either of them: but I shouldn't be in the least sceptical of one thing, which was which of the two I preferred to have close by. Virtue wore well, after all.

THIRTY-ONE

A PRACTICAL JOKE?

There weren't many dates which Margaret and I celebrated: there was one that November which I couldn't celebrate with her. The twenty-eighth. First anniversary. For her it meant nothing but pain and extreme isolation—the hospital waiting room, the dead blank, no news. She didn't wish to be reminded. So I called in at my club and, avoiding friends and acquaintances, stood myself a drink.

That was the most private of celebrations. After all, it had been the most private of events.

I knew by now, not that it was a surprise, that traumas didn't last in their first efficacy. This trauma didn't keep me immune from hurt, as it had done for a time, when I had only to recall the date and bring back oblivion. One's character and one's nature weren't so easily modified or tamed. Traumas weren't as magical as that. And yet, they weren't, or this one wasn't, quite unavailing, and the effect took some time to fade right away. Not always but often I could ride over disappointments and worries, just as people more harmonious than I was had been able to do, without effort, all their lives.

That autumn (it hadn't always been so) Margaret was worrying more about Maurice than I was about Charles. Walking alone in the park I wasn't thinking of what he used to say when he accompanied me. Which added to my well-being and perhaps, if he had known, to his.

After Maurice's visit with his wife, Margaret heard of them only by letter. And it was not until December, when his term had ended, that we had a sight of Charles. He called on us ostensibly to pick up letters, but really to invite us to dinner the following week at Chester Row.

As we got ready to go, we hadn't an inkling of what to expect. Margaret said it was like going out when she was a young woman, not on terms with social occasions. She was trying to dissemble that she was more than a little tense. When we arrived, we might not have known what to expect: but, whatever we had expected, it wouldn't have borne any resemblance to this.

The housekeeper, beaming, took our coats from us in the bright hall. "Mrs. Calvert wonders if you would mind going straight up to the drawing-room, Lady Eliot." Inside which, the first thing we saw was Azik Schiff, sitting on the sofa, looking unusually subdued. Muriel came towards us. "I'm so very pleased you could come, Aunt Meg," she said, giving us formal kisses. She was wearing a long frock, so that Margaret appeared distinctly under-dressed: and, I noticed by a sideways glance, so did Rosalind, who was installed in an armchair. I wondered how long it was since Rosalind had gone out to dinner and found herself under-dressed.

"You'll both probably have Scotch, won't you?" said Charles, standing beside Muriel, polite and decorous in a dark suit. Though he and Muriel drank so little, they had provided for all our tastes: both Azik and Rosalind had been given Campari, presumably from domestic knowledge acquired by Muriel. As though to make us feel at home, which was the last thing any of their guests were feeling, Charles joined us in taking a whisky, which must have been another display of courtesy.

Two sofas, three armchairs, made an enclave at the street end of the long room. Muriel disposed us and then sat in one of the armchairs, utterly composed, like one presiding over a salon. Charles took his place near to the shelf of drinks: just once I thought or fancied I caught a flashing dark-eyed glance.

They each asked hostlike questions, but the conversation didn't flow. Margaret, trying to sound easy, remarked that the room was nice and warm. Yes, said Muriel, the heating system was efficient. "Actually," she went on, "we both like it a little cooler. But it was a case of majority opinion, we thought. So we stepped it up five degrees. I do hope that was right?"

Her eyes fixed themselves earnestly on her mother, then came back to Margaret. Nothing could have been more thoughtful or made them more uncomfortable. "Don't mind about me," said Rosalind, out of countenance. "*Of course* we mind about you," said Muriel in a clear voice. An instant of silence. Up in the square, the church clock struck once: it must have been a quarter to eight.

"How quiet it is here," I remarked, thinking it was not the most brilliant of conversational openings. Charles said: "At the weekends" (this was a Saturday night) "we might as well be living in a small country town."

I didn't have the presence of mind to enquire when he had ever lived in a country town, small or otherwise. Azik made a contribution, standard Mittel Europa, not Azik's own uninhibited self, about the charms, the variety, the changes every quarter-mile, the village shopping streets, of London.

It went on like that, after we moved downstairs to the dining-room. I sat on Muriel's right, Azik on her left, Rosalind next to me, Margaret next to Azik, Charles at the head of the table.

"Six is the easiest number, isn't it?" Muriel said with demure pleasure.

The food was excellent, soup, grouse, a savoury. They had

acquired some good claret, such as Azik and I might have provided. It was all as formal as any small dinner party we were likely to go to. In fact, it was appreciably more formal, since not many of our friends had the domestic help for this kind of entertaining, nor the peculiar deadpan style which Muriel found natural and which, that night at least, it amused Charles to adopt. It all seemed—would they have done this for anyone else's benefit?—like an elaborate, long-drawn-out practical joke: the kind of joke in which Muriel's father used to involve himself, so that sometimes it looked as though he had forgotten that it was a joke at all.

The conversation round the dinner table was stylised also. Azik and Charles had an exchange about Asian politics, on which Azik was knowledgeable because of his business. They might have been meeting for the first time. Neither gave much away about his own political opinions, or whether he had any opinions whatever. Enquiries about Muriel's child, not fended off, politely replied to: yes, he was bright and flourishing. Enquiries from me about Charles's friends: those were fended off, though Charles gave an amiable smile as he did so. The only direct talk, propriety for once relaxed, came when Azik produced the precious, the inevitable topic of his son. Next October, 1967, David would be going to his public school. They had finally decided on Westminster: despite all their resolves, they couldn't let him go away from home: he might win a scholarship ("certain to," said Charles with professional competence), but even so he would enter as a day boy. For a while Azik's parental passion dominated the table and the family relations spread among us all. At the end of the meal, however, we had returned to a discussion of jewellery.

Then Muriel gazed along the table towards Charles.

"Darling," she called out, "will you bring the others up when you're ready?"

"Of course," said Charles.

Margaret gave me a stupefied glance before she went with the other two women out of the dining-room. Now I felt sure that this evening must have been prepared for, though it seemed due more to Muriel's sense of—humour? mischief, even impudence? than to Charles's. He might have thought up a charade, but he wouldn't have carried it so far. He might have considered that last touch inartistic. He knew as well as anyone there that Margaret and I had never separated men from women after dinner since we set up house. Nevertheless, still grave and decorous, he apologised to Azik and me for not being able to offer us port; could we make do with brandy?

Until we left, I didn't hear an intimate word spoken. Chat when the party re-formed in the drawing-room, Charles having kept us below for a precise fifteen minutes. Chat admirably tailored for a dinner party in a remote diplomatic mission, third secretary and wife doing their duty by elderly compatriots. Once Rosalind asked her daughter: "What are you doing for Christmas?" where the 'you' was intended to be in the singular.

"Oh?," said Muriel, "we shall have a quiet time, I expect, we shan't be going away." She contrived to make their ménage sound remarkably like the end of *Little Dorrit*. Occasionally their eyes met. Otherwise they behaved, not only as though they were safely married, but as though they had been so for a long time.

Glances at watches. Goodbyes. Margaret unusually effusive with thanks for a delightful evening. Ritual of gratitude. Ritual of kisses. Margaret and I back home by eleven o'clock.

The departure of their guests so early might have suggested to Muriel and Charles that the party had not been an uproarious success. Presumably that wasn't weighing on their spirits. And yet, as with so many of Muriel's father's exploits,

there was a faint, an almost imperceptible doubt. It was a
thousand to one against—but what if they had been serious?
What if they had been to obsessive trouble and given their
first dinner party?

In that case, said Margaret, tender to the embarrassments
of the young, it would have been a major disappointment.
She didn't believe it: but she didn't utterly and absolutely
disbelieve it. I laughed at her, and wasn't unaffected myself.
Muriel had a gift for disquiet, I thought: that is, she stayed
still and here were we, more mystified about them both than
we had been before.

We were not the only people who were mystified that
night. Two days later, on the Monday afternoon, Azik's secretary telephoned me. Mr. Schiff would be very grateful if I
could spare him a few minutes. When? Straight away, if I
could manage it: otherwise— Yes, I was doing nothing, I
said, I would come round. Mr. Schiff will send a car for you.
That wasn't necessary. Oh, Mr. Schiff insists—

Mr. Schiff did insist, just as Lord Lufkin used to, and as
in Lord Lufkin's time I was driven in a Daimler to the office. Driven in state for something like eight hundred yards.
For Azik, like other tycoons, had moved his office westwards,
into the Park Lane fringe of Mayfair, and now inhabited a
mansion which in the nineteenth century had been the town
house of a Whig grandee. All, including the car, was as
sumptuous as Lord Lufkin's accoutrements used to be: thick
carpets on the office floors, Regency decorations restored, re-
gilded. There was just one difference. Of these two, Azik was
by far the more outpouring: which wasn't saying much, since
very few men were less outpouring than Lufkin. In fact,
Azik was lavish by any standard, his tastes were exuberant, as
witness his house in Eaton Square. Yet Lufkin's personal office had reminded one of the Palazzo Venezia in one of the
Duce's more expansionist phases: whereas Azik's office in

Hertford Street, which I had not visited before that day, must have been something like a closet or at best a dressing room in the old mansion, much smaller, darker, more shut-in than the room of his own secretary, and, apart from a desk and a couple of chairs, almost totally unequipped.

There were no offers of tea, drinks, or even cigarettes. Azik did all his hospitality at home. He shook my hand, and immediately asked:

"I wanted to hear, what do you think of our young friends?"

"I suppose you knew about them?"

I meant, did he know, before Saturday night, that they were living together. Azik laid a finger to the side of his nose.

"My dear Lewis, what do you take me for?"

As a matter of historical fact, it had not required superhuman acumen or any other quality with which I was willing to credit Azik. Muriel had, for some purpose of her own, first raised her mother's suspicions and then, after various misdirections, had gone into a fit of apparent absentmindedness and told her.

"They have presented us with a fait accompli, I should say," Azik put it like a question. "I don't understand why they wish to remind us of it, do you?"

That was only one of the things I didn't understand, I said. Including the whole situation.

Azik nodded.

"The only certain feature of that situation is that it won't stand still." He went on, he'd never known a situation with a woman which did stand still, until he married Rosalind: and not always then. He spoke with a shamefaced smile, not so unquenchably the hypermasculine or the Jewish papa.

Then he said:

"Your son is a lucky young man, shouldn't you say?"

"Is he?"

"He loves her, of course. He'd be very hard to please if he didn't. Believe me, I know more about the girl than you do. He's very lucky to love and find everything teed up. We didn't have so much luck, you and I, my friend."

I said yes. I was thinking—me at Charles's age, walking the town streets, virgin, craving, about to fall in love without return. As for Azik at that age, I knew nothing: it must have been about the end of Weimar, he might perhaps have been wondering whether he would have the chance, not to love, but simply to live.

"Well then," said Azik. "It would be more of a blow to him if she dropped him. And if you'll listen to me, I have to assure you, that might happen."

I had a sudden sense of affront, that he should suggest Charles was going to be ill-treated in love. If he said it about me, well and good—so that I was more off-hand than I need have been, when I replied:

"It has happened to better men than him." I went on: "But I've seen no sign of it. Have you? Have you heard anything?"

Azik slowly shook his great head. There was a long pause, as though he were hesitating whether to speak or alternatively was re-organising his case. With the apologetic air of one putting a probing amendment, he said:

"How would you regard it if they got married?"

I wasn't prepared. I blurted out:

"He's far too young—"

"As far as that goes, he is grown up. He has grown up very fast. But I didn't mean now, my friend. Not yet. Not yet."

"I haven't given it a thought." That wasn't true. It had passed through my mind as a possibility, one that seemed unlikely and that I didn't like.

"Perhaps you might some day." He gave me a cheerful,

watchful, evaluating glance. Another pause. "I should say, there would be no objection from our side. My side." (Was that a correction? Did Rosalind, as I could well believe, disagree with him? Was that why we were meeting in his office?) "There would be no objection. No, I should welcome it."

"Oh well, there's no hurry," I said, playing for time.

"I want her to have a good life. She mustn't make another mistake. That was a disaster, the last one. But this time she has chosen something worthwhile." He broke into a grin.

"I must say, she is making a habit of being covered by members of your family." He had been speaking of his stepdaughter with genuine fondness, something like the affection of the flesh: he was still doing so, though I hadn't expected that last remark.

He went on:

"I couldn't have chosen better for her if she'd asked me, this time. You have a fine boy there."

"So have you with yours." That was tactical. I wanted to break the conversation up.

"We have both been luckier than we deserve. Oh yes, David will give me something to live for when I'm an old man. And your Charles is a blessing too." The mention of his son hadn't distracted him for long. He said:

"You needn't wonder why my girl is in love with him."

"I don't wonder. I doubt it. I don't know."

"I tell you, Lewis, I do know. I know her. She puts on a front, she wears a mask, she drives you mad. But she feels without anyone seeing. I know. I know because she used to feel for me. She is in love with him."

This was the direct opposite of anything that Margaret or I had thought. How much did Azik believe it? He was out to persuade me, he did it with fervour. Of course, he was set on making some sort of bargain—though he must have known that I hadn't any control over Charles. Perhaps he wanted something quite simple, such as that I shouldn't use my influence against the marriage, if I were asked. He was pressing her claims, softening me by insisting (he could have known no more than I did, I thought) that she was in love.

"We'd better leave it to them, hadn't we?" I said.

"Tell me, Lewis. We are good enough friends to say anything, I should think. Why are you against her?"

"Wait a minute. Haven't you something to explain to me? Not very long ago you were warning me that she might drop him. Now you're talking about serious love. You can't have it both ways—"

He didn't blink, he gave his wide-lipped froglike smile.

"Oh yes I can. You see, she has been bitten once. If she feels in danger now, if she's getting in too deep, and doesn't see marriage at the end, then she would pull out and save herself. She won't risk another fiasco. If she thought that was happening she'd be capable of cutting her losses. And breaking both their hearts in the process."

That was altogether too elaborate, I said. When I was young, I invented some labyrinthine explanations for the way I behaved with Sheila. I shouldn't trust them now. I had come to be suspicious, more than suspicious, of second-order emotions and motives.

Azik shrugged.

"If they come apart, you may have to see who did it." He broke off: "But you haven't told me. Why are you against her?"

What I said wasn't all I felt. I was afraid, I was speaking without much emphasis, that if he married young she might confine him.

"What do you mean, confine him?"

"She won't alter. She's set by now—"

"Are you saying her opinions are set? And that young man is going to adopt them? God in Heaven, Lewis, do you know your own son?"

"Not quite that. No, they might confine each other. They both happen to have a passion for politics." (Did he know that about his stepdaughter?) "That might restrict them, they might never get out of the groove—"

"Politics shmolitics," said Azik, who encouraged, irrespective of merit, anything which gentiles accepted as Jewish jokes.

The meeting, which seemed to have been disappointing for him and was disconcerting for me, ebbed towards, not a conclusion, but an end.

THIRTY-TWO

STAFF WORK,
NEW STYLE

"We shall have a quiet time, I expect," Muriel had said in her own drawing-room, when asked about their plans for Christmas. She might have expected it, if she were less shrewd than any of us imagined: what was certain is that she didn't get it.

Otherwise there was not much one could be certain about. What happened to them in the winter of 1966–67, no one knew in detail but themselves. I received a partial account some time afterwards, from, I kept thinking, the one source I shouldn't have contemplated. Much of it seemed honest: but it had the disadvantages of all accounts which were given with hindsight. However, some of it I could check against events which I observed for myself. Like most bits of second-hand history, it left one dissatisfied, possibly both too credulous and too sceptical.

Still, that account was all that I had to work on. Later, I sometimes wondered what I should have said, if I had had information at the time. Certainly, that they were expecting too much, that they had fallen into the occupational disease, for politicians of any age, of over-optimism. So that they sometimes seemed romantic, if not silly. But if I had known it all, I should also have admitted, perhaps only to myself, that some of them were capable. They would sit in my contempories' chairs soon enough, or perhaps in different chairs which they had constructed for themselves.

To begin with, it seemed—and there was nothing surprising here—that during the Christmas period and the New Year, they were preoccupied with, or at least spent much of their time upon, what was now in private jargon called "the movement." But they were preoccupied in a complex and sometimes ambiguous fashion. They were taking part in plans for the movement's operations: the interesting thing was, they and their intimates, including Bestwick, had plans within plans, and these often, for security's sake, had to be concealed.

Not that they were unrealistic or undisciplined. It was their own choice to join, as very much the junior partners, with a core of London students. A London college was to be the point of action. The Cambridge group hadn't much to offer, except as a token of good will, rather like a contingent of New Zealanders being attached to American forces. They found a leader whom they would in any case have had to accept: but who in fact had a quality none of them possessed or had come across before. He was already a national figure and was to become more so. I did not meet him until much later, and then only casually: but like most other people I was soon used to seeing his face on television and hearing him talk. His name was Olorenshaw. The television interviewers and commentators called him by his Christian name of Antony, or, when they knew him less well, Tony. However, that was something like affable ministers strolling through the smoking-room and addressing back-benchers by the wrong first name. All Olorenshaw's friends and comrades called him nothing else but Olly, following a good old lower-class habit, much in use among professional games players. Olly actually was a goodish cricketer, and had played in the Bradford League. His father was a journalist on the *York-*

shire Post, and Olly had been brought up in modest comfort. He was a muscular, shortish, low-slung young man, with
a snub-nosed face that one wouldn't have noticed in a crowd.

Yet there was no doubt that he had, to use the fashionable
word of that period, charisma. Characters as different as
Charles, Gordon Bestwick, Grenfell, Muriel, all recognised it
and succumbed to it; perhaps some envied it. Quite why he
had it, or what it consisted of, none of them could analyse,
even later in cooler blood. He was a fair organiser, though
not as competent as some of his student colleagues: he had
considerable powers of decision. He possessed some knowledge of the theory, Marcusian and so on, which was running
round the student world. His intelligence was better than
average, but Gordon and Charles couldn't have thought him
a flier. He was an impassioned but repetitive speaker.

None of that added up to the effect which he produced.
Perhaps the answer was quite simple. He really did feel exactly as others round him felt, and had the gift of voicing it
an instant before they recognised it for themselves. That
night in Trinity, over a year before, Charles had said—with
self-knowledge, with inhibiting self-knowledge—in politics
you couldn't afford to be too different from everyone else. In
behaviour Charles to some extent acted on that maxim, and
Bestwick more so: but not in feeling. Whereas to Olly it
came as natural as his strong-muscled walk.

He had no irony, such as Charles in private couldn't suppress. Irony would have been a crippling disqualification for
Olly's kind of leadership, and probably for any other. When
he heard a battalion of his followers, mobilised and drilled
according to plan, chanting Dinshaw-out (Dinshaw was the
principal of the college), Johnson-out, Wilson-out, Brezh-
nev-out, any other disyllable-out, Olly was at one with them,
all he wanted was to join in. Charles and others like him
might have forced themselves to join in, but they would

have felt the discomfort of simultaneously watching performing animals and being performing animals themselves.

In a similar manner, Olly didn't suffer from intellectual
reserves. Quite sensibly, he believed that student protests
could, before too long, exact their own demands from universities. Equally sensibly, he believed that student protests
would end where they began, unless they were supported by,
and finally submerged in, the working class. The working
class, with students acting as catalysts, was the only force
which could break the old order— As an article of faith,
Olly believed that that would happen. Gordon Bestwick
argued that it was intellectually untenable. Gordon, still living among the English working class, didn't dramatise them.
Olly, more prosperous, did. His faith was untouched. Once
the working class took over, he was willing not to lead anything or anyone' again.

That Christmas, Olly and his London lieutenants met a
number of times at Chester Row. They weren't trying to has-
ten the revolt—the current word was blast-off—at the college. That wasn't necessary, it was coming anyway, they
judged it good tactics to let it start, as it were, out of the
ruck, with no leaders at all. What they wanted was to be
ready with plans and take control just before the countdown.

It was the kind of preparation and patient waiting which
would have been familiar enough to any politician, public
or private. Their planning of the phases of the revolt, so it
appeared in the event, was excellent. Here Gordon, Charles,
and others who were let into their confidence had nothing to
give. They were beginners, and Olly's staff were experienced
professionals. Some of them were first-class organisers. It was
a mistake to think that young men in their early twenties
(most of the London group were round Muriel's age) had
much to learn about organisation. That didn't require experience, but energy and some clear minds. These did their

job as briskly and unfussily as Hector Rose in middle age
might have done it. Where they could still have learned
something from Hector Rose was, not in primary organisation, but in foreseeing consequences.

Under the cover of those plans, which the Cambridge cell
imbibed lessons from, they were also devising one of their
own. It was not clear (or at least I never knew) who had the
first conception, but Gordon and Charles passed it on to
Olly, and Muriel used persuasion on him too. Not that he
made difficulties about others' ideas; he was ready to give
these bright outsiders a run: that showed one of his
strengths. All the evidence suggested that he was quick and
active in getting their plan worked out. He thought it valuable enough to call it top secret (they had adopted many of
the official forms). A number of followers had to receive logistic instructions, but the only persons Olly informed about
the inner purpose were his number two and three.

The plan was, in essence, quite simple. The revolt, when
under full control, was designed to occupy the main block of
college buildings. Food, drink, bedding, new-style chemical
closets, even books, were already being stored in a warehouse
close by, enough for a stay of one month. As a result of
American experience, the principal's office and the administrative floors were to be seized also, in the first hour—which
was pencilled in as 4:30 A.M. (shortly before dawn on a summer morning). All that would have been arranged, in precisely the same fashion, without a minute's change in timetable, if the Cambridge cell had not existed. The only addition that they and their sub-plan had brought about seemed
innocuous enough. It was that there should be a side foray,
needing perhaps a dozen men, to take possession of two offices in the biochemistry department.

That was not so innocuous as it seemed. Almost everyone
concerned with secrets, particularly military secrets, lived

under the illusion that they were better kept than ever happened. We had learned that in the war. Heads of State rested happily in the conviction that their own ministers were totally ignorant of the manufacture of nuclear bombs. They probably were: but there were thousands, including humble and entirely unexpected people, who weren't.

Through an identical process, which was set going by words slipping out, occasionally in fits of conscience, but more often because of self-importance or even the sheer excitement and ebullience of living, friends of Gordon and Charles had picked up what to officials would have been a horrifying amount of knowledge about government work on biological warfare. Second-year science students such as Guy Grenfell could make a fairly sharp guess about the operations at the Microbiological Research Establishment at Porton: they could have written out a list of the viruses which were being cultivated, and the diseases which were available as weapons of war.

Further, they wouldn't have had to guess, they knew, which pieces of the work had been sub-contracted to university departments. Here their intelligence was often precise. They knew, for instance, that research upon psittacosis was being carried out, under Ministry of Defence subsidy, at this London college. They knew it. The difficulty was to prove it. That was the point of the sub-plan, which someone had christened Asclepius. Two professors were known—one of the best intelligence contacts was an obscure laboratory assistant—to be in charge. It occurred to Gordon and Charles that, if their offices could be ransacked, there might with good luck be some evidence. They didn't expect much. They had consulted some acquaintances in the civil service and had learned how secret contracts were drawn up. Probably not so much through delicacy as through prudence, they didn't come to me, who if I had chosen could have told them more. They had considered employing a professional safe-breaker. They had made up their minds to look for 'indications.' Even a hint about biological war would be enough, Olly had become vociferous in proclaiming, to 'blow the roof off.' They could get their hands on nothing so useful. There was no propaganda equal to this.

That sounded cynical, just as their operations sounded, because they were thought out. It would be a mistake, however, to imagine that any of them, facing the prospect of biological war, were in the remotest degree cynical. Young men like Gordon and Charles—it is worth remembering, that during this period of planning Gordon was not yet twenty, and Charles a year younger—knew a good deal about power politics. Other states might possess both ultimate weapons and the will to use them. Charles was an amateur of military history, and knowledgeable about it. Nevertheless, when it came to the manufacture of disease, they felt exactly like the simplest of the young people around them. They felt a sheer horror, not in the least sophisticated, naive if you like, that this should be done. That it was done in their own country didn't soften the horror, but added anger to it.

THIRTY-THREE

CONVERSATION
IN THE OPEN AIR

Through the spring they were still waiting for their time. While I remained in total ignorance of any of their plans. When I saw Charles, which wasn't often, he was in good spirits, composed and lively, interesting on books he had read. He gave no sign of strain that I perceived. When, months later, I heard something of the story, I wondered how much I had missed or whether he had become a good actor.

One morning in May, Martin rang me up from Cambridge. What about a day at Lord's? I didn't see much inducement, but he pressed me. When I had said yes, I felt cross with him. He must have known that I had given up watching cricket. Even if I hadn't, the match, when I looked it up in the papers, had no attractions either for him or me. It wasn't even good weather. Although the sky was bright, it wasn't warm enough to sit with pleasure in the open air.

Waiting for me in front of the pavilion, Martin gave an impassive smile. Not too exciting to be unbearable, he said. We were almost alone, sitting there in the cold sunlight. Above the spring-fresh grass, the stands shone white and empty. Nothing was happening. A few runs, no wickets. From one end a large man with a long run bowled medium-paced inswingers to a legside field. From the other end an almost identical man did almost identically the same. Curious

314

how the game had developed, Martin commented. It was probably still great fun to play. He couldn't pretend it was great fun to watch.

Yet he continued to watch with absorption. The technique was always interesting, he said. All I admitted was that the fielding looked marvellous, out of comparison better than when I followed the game. The score seeped up to twenty-five after an hour's play. One wicket fell, to a good catch at legslip.

Just before one o'clock Martin said that we had better have a snack before the rush. I was glad to move, but I couldn't understand where the rush was coming from. In the pavilion bar, under layers of team photographs, stood half a dozen men, one of whom Martin knew. To one of the ledges under the photographs, we carried our sandwiches and glasses. Martin continued to talk cricket. I asked how he had had the inspiration for us to spend the day like this. He looked at me with a fraternal recognitory glance, and then exchanged a word with his acquaintance close by.

As we left the bar, he suggested that we might take a walk round the ground. Through gaps in the stands, one saw the players still moving in the middle, not yet come in for lunch. We arrived at the practice nets, the expanse of turf behind the Nursery end. There was no one anywhere near.

"Yes, there is something," he said.

I was at a loss. Then I realised that he was replying to my question in the bar, which had actually been entirely innocent, just a mock-complaint.

"I'm not sure how reliable my information is," he said.

"What is it?"

"Had you heard that Charles and company are trying to crash Porton wide open?"

That was the first intimation I had. Those meetings in Muriel's study, which were later described to me, had not been so much as suspected, and still weren't, either by Martin or me, that morning at Lord's. He had been given—so I discovered—only the slimmest of hints.

It was enough for him. Most people would not have taken so long, wouldn't have eased away time by technical analyses of the game, before they broke the news. But Martin, as he grew older, had developed the habit, not uncommon in men who had seen many things go wrong, of deliberately slowing himself down, of adapting the displeasing to his own pace. It was a habit which I had noticed long before in his predecessor in college office, Arthur Brown.

"I've heard nothing at all," I said.

"Does it make any kind of sense? Is it in their line?"

"It could be."

"How would they get hold of anything? I suppose it mightn't be impossible."

He knew very little more. Martin and I exchanged remarks about biological warfare in our old kind of Whitehall shorthand. We might have been back in wartime, talking about the most recent news of the nuclear bomb. In fact, that was why Martin had led me to the practice ground, where we could speak without being overheard, just as in the war we held some secret conversations in the middle of Hyde Park.

"It could be dangerous," said Martin.

"Who for?" It didn't need asking.

"For anyone who wants to broadcast something he hasn't any right to know."

"Yes. Meaning Charles."

"Charles. One or two others as well, I fancy. I'm thinking of Charles."

We had reached, walking slowly, the rough and piebald grass where, during festive matches, the tents were pitched. Martin said:

"He might get into desperate trouble. If he gives them a chance to use the law against him, they could take it. He wouldn't stand a chance."

"They'll try to keep it quiet—"

"He might have gone too far for that." He was speaking very quietly. "Good God, he's making a nuisance of himself."

"That's the least of it."

"Why in hell does he want to set up as the conscience of the world?"

For an instant, I got away from thoughts of Charles.

"I'm not sure," I said, "that that comes too well from you."

Neither of us could forget that when Martin had been in his thirties, years older than Charles was now, he had behaved in a fashion that was (if one had been feeling like sarcasm) comically similar. From inside the nuclear project, he had attempted to write a letter of outrage when the bombs were dropped on Hiroshima and Nagasaki. I had stopped him, at a cost to our relation which had taken some time to put right. Then later, with the headship of the whole English operation open to him, he had, without flurry and almost without explanation, resigned. All Charles's friends would have thought Martin a hard and worldly man: he could be both those things. Yet, among the middle-aged people whom Charles knew, Martin was one of the few who had made a sacrifice.

Hearing my jibe, he gave a grim smile, lips pulled down.

"I should have thought," he said, "that I was in a privileged position."

He went on talking of the penalties that anyone breaking official secrets might pay. We both knew all about it. Some careers could be closed, or at least impeded: one would find mysterious obstacles if one attempted most kinds of official life. Martin's concern, and mine, became practical, almost as unethereal as though we were trying to watch over Charles's health.

To some, it would have seemed puzzling, or even unnatural, that Martin should be so much affected. True, he had shown a glint of brotherly malice, of obscure satisfaction, that, after all his troubles with his son, I should run into one with mine.

But that glint emerged from feelings which contradicted it. Martin had a family sense much stronger than my own. Charles might have existed for years as an incarnate reproach to Martin's son: but he was also the chief hope of the whole family. With any luck, Martin believed, he was going to make his independent name. And Martin imagined him making a name in the official world where Martin could himself have been successful. It was noticeable, I thought, that people living inside what Charles's friends called a 'structure' couldn't easily picture able men fulfilling themselves outside. That had been true of me when I lived, as Martin did now, in a college, or afterwards in Whitehall and Westminster. Somehow these institutions, which had their own charm to those inside, set limits to one's expectations. Enclaves which made for a comprehensible life. When one left them behind, as I had done, it was a bit of a surprise to find that enclaves weren't necessary, and that comprehensibility wasn't such a comfort as one had thought.

So that some of Martin's hopes for Charles I could get on without, and my concerns, as we walked back and forwards across the Nursery turf, were less sharp-edged. Yet still I was shaken by thoughts of prosecution—or less than that, plain scandal, almost as my mother would have been. One's self-sufficiency dropped away. One cared where one didn't choose to care: often where one ought not to care. Scandal, notoriety, row. He was proposing to act—so far as I could tell—according to his beliefs. To many—what did I think myself?—they were decent beliefs. Scandal, notoriety, row. I wasn't a stranger to them myself, and had survived.

Yet that wasn't a consolation, as I walked with Martin in the chilly afternoon.

"I'm not certain," Martin was saying, after a period in which we had each been brooding, "that what I did" (he meant, his resignation) "was right. If you think of what has happened, it wasn't."

"You couldn't have predicted that."

"There is not much excuse for being wrong."

It was true, we had all been wrong. We had foreseen that if men made nuclear bombs, they would use them. There would be the slaughter of many millions. We shouldn't escape a thermonuclear war. It was because he couldn't accept his share of that responsibility that Martin abdicated. As it turned out, what we expected was the opposite of the truth. We shouldn't have believed it, but an equilibrium had set in. It might be an unstable peace, but it had been peace for over twenty years. By this time, we were afraid of other fates, but not of major war.

So the most quixotic action of Martin's life looked, in retrospect, like a bad guess.

I said:

"Perhaps it helps the rest of us if one or two people show they don't approve of mass annihilation."

"I wonder."

He had been right about Hiroshima, I said. We got hardened to killing with astonishing speed: it was one of the horrifying features of the human animal.

"I dare say," Martin remarked, "that you and I have become hardened too, don't you think?"

"Does that surprise you?"

"You know, this business that Charles is kicking about, there was a time when I couldn't have taken it, could you?"

"Most people can take anything. Not many kick."

"Perhaps that will be a comfort to him some day," Martin said.

"It's the only one he's likely to get."

What was to be done? "You could do more harm than good," said Martin, thinking of his own attempts to guide Pat, who put up no resistance and then found some new manoeuvre. With Charles it would be a mistake to try anything remotely subtle: he wasn't labile as Pat was, but he was hard to take in. The only way was to be direct. We arranged that I should write him a letter, saying that this gossip had reached me, and telling him he ought to be aware of the Official Secrets Act. Then Martin, back in Cambridge, would ask him round. They were on good terms, it would be easier, and conceivably more effective, for Martin to talk to him than for me.

The pavilion bell was clanging, and Martin showed a disposition to return to the game. I delayed him, having something else to ask.

"Your information," I said. "How did you get it? You haven't told me—"

He hesitated.

"Everything is in confidence, you needn't worry," I told him, playing a family joke, that he was so secretive that he didn't like telling one the time.

He returned the jibe.

"Within these four walls," he said, waving a hand towards the bare expanse, mimicking a colleague of ours long since retired.

"Well then," he went on, "it was through Nina."

I exclaimed and recalled some talk about attachments.

"From the young man Bestwick, I suppose?"

"I think not."

Martin's reply, unusually brusque, sounded as though he didn't favour Bestwick.

I said:

"I have a lot of use for him, you oughtn't to write him off
—"

"I'm not writing him off. I rather wish that it did come from him. But it was from someone else."

"Why did she tell you?"

"I fancy she was trying to protect him."

"Not Charles, of course?" She was fond of her cousin, but they had never been close.

"Oh no."

It seemed that Martin was not certain whom she was protecting. That afternoon, I couldn't identify the name.

But I could identify the way secrets leaked. Just as they got hold of news about Porton, so they had let out their own news. There was a certain perverse symmetry about it. Particularly as Nina was the channel, one of the most trustworthy of girls.

"Look," I said, "this mustn't go any further."

"Nina told me that." Martin smiled. "Just to make certain, I told her the same."

I didn't like what I had to say next.

"You'd better impress on her that she mustn't tell her brother."

That was the nearest I could go to impressing on Martin that he mustn't tell his son. It was bitter to have to say anything, but after the disclosures of last year I dared not take a risk.

Martin said, without expression:

"I don't think that's necessary. You needn't worry, he won't be told."

THIRTY-FOUR

COMMUNIQUÉS
FROM HEADQUARTERS

The results of our communication with Charles were not dramatic. To me he wrote a civil and affectionate answer, saying that since he had now studied the Official Secrets Act, there was some danger that he would get mixed up and include it in his papers in the Mays: while Martin reported over the telephone that Charles had in conversation been completely sensible, but neither admitted nor denied that the rumour was correct. "If he is considering anything," Martin said, "then he's got it worked out every step of the way." Which had been true of Martin himself, in his days of action.

With that I could do nothing but leave it. There were some disturbances at London colleges throughout May, but they did not amount to much more than shouting in the streets and in the quadrangle at King's. I paid them very little attention, since I still knew nothing of any link between student risings and this warning about Charles. In the same spirit, when the major rising actually started, in the first week in June—at the end of the Cambridge, but not the London, term—I watched the film shots on television with a detached interest, not much more involved than if these events had been taking place in Stockholm or Warsaw.

Which, in everything but language, they might have been. The students, and especially the students milling in the

streets, looked as international as airports. Hair, dress, ex-
pressions, slogans, pop music—as well as the same hatreds and
the same hopes—had broken across frontiers like nothing
else in the century. Watching these spectacles, I thought the
only local difference was that the police weren't using
shields. This was the most international activity I had ever
seen.

Pictures of the principal, students at each shoulder, being
interviewed on the pavement. Yes, he had been requested
not to enter his office. Requested? No reply. Communiqué
that night from *Students' Headquarters, Principal's Office*.

Messages of support from Essex, Oxford, Sussex, Cambridge . . . That conveyed nothing to me. If I had known,
I might have reflected that the sight of young men and girls
fighting in a porter's lodge, swearing like George Passant in
a rage, some of them being frog-marched by policemen—it
seemed some distance away from quiet conferences in the bou-
doir-study at Chester Row, a dozen heads round the table,
talking in the low unassertive voices that were common
form, refreshed by some maidenly coffee or Coca-Cola. It was
as long a distance as from any staff headquarters to the front
line.

For Margaret, who had taken part in 'demo's' in her
youth, and for me, who had seen the street mobs in Ger-
many, the sight of violence wasn't pretty. Maybe it wasn't to
some of the planners. That I didn't know and, since I was
uninterested, didn't think about. But I did have a passing
thought that there were organising minds behind it.

Anyone who had spent half an hour inside a political
movement would have realised that. There was a fair
amount of chaos. Some allies, including Muslim liberators
and a free drugs party, must have been an embarrassment.
There was some violence which didn't appear premeditated.
But too many contingents arrived at what seemed the right

time. Too many squads (the serious invaders, as opposed to the irregulars, seemed to work in platoons of round about a dozen) knew what to do. College porters, secretaries, staff, were picked up, led out, put gently enough into cars, all too quickly and smoothly to be true. True, that is, in terms of the student manifestoes, or what we heard on the news or on discussion programmes from Olly himself.

Spontaneous. Rising against grievances not attended to for months. Complaints not recognised. Student rights. Participation. He gave us all that, as his face became familiar on the screen. He wasn't smooth. He had what had come to be called a classless accent, meaning one which could belong only to a small but definable class. He had the gift of speaking like a human being, who believed what he said and wanted you to believe it too. He didn't appear clever, and sometimes not coherent. Several of my acquaintances said that, if he joined either of the major parties, he would get office before he was thirty.

"Tell me, Antony," said one of the cordial television interviewers, "do you expect to get most of your demands?"

"We can't help not get them."

"But what, I know you're explaining what the students are insisting on straightaway, what do you really expect to get?"

No smile. "We shall get what we take."

He wasn't hectored on the screen, as the national politicians might have been.

"Yes, I understand, but that isn't your basis for negotiations, is it, Antony?"

Long, disjointed, sincere speech.

"You mean, do you, Tony, that you want to establish rights for all students everywhere?"

"We're not only struggling for students, but for everyone who's not allowed to speak for himself."

"That means, doesn't it, that even if and when you reach a satisfactory settlement at the college, you'll still go on protesting—"

"The struggle will go on."

The principal of the college, interviewed in the same programme two nights later, wasn't so comfortable, nor so respectfully treated. He was a man in his mid-forties, with a neat small-featured face. I hadn't met him, but as he was a physicist and a good one, the Getliffes knew him well. He was said to be fun in private, and to be conscientious and open-minded. Why he had given up science and taken to university administration, none of his admirers could understand. Perhaps he couldn't, as on the box he gave an impression—so unjustified, that he ought to bring a slander action against himself, someone said—of being irresolute and even shifty.

Yes, he was in favour of student participation at all levels. They would be welcome on suitable college committees.

"But aren't you on record as saying, Dr. Dinshaw, that the students' claim to a place on appointments committees—" Dinshaw: That, of course, was a special case: it wasn't considered in the students' interest to take part in appointments of lecturers or professors. (Why the hell, said Margaret, doesn't he say that they'd be totally incompetent to judge.) But didn't Dr. Dinshaw agree that the students felt it was very much in their interest? Dinshaw: There were two views about that, after all, there were students and students. The students with whom Dr. Dinshaw would have to negotiate, however, had only one view? Dinshaw: The real academics among the students, the one who would really understand about academic excellence, and that was the important thing about a place of higher education, didn't take part in this kind of student activity. Of all his remarks, that one sank the principal into most trouble with the press. From then on, the interviewer was needling him. What did the principal understand by the students' wider aims? If they reached a settlement with the college, then Mr. Ollorenshaw had pointed out there were claims on behalf of others? At last, badgered, Dinshaw broke out that it wasn't his function to negotiate for the entire human race.

For us, a few minutes' diversion. Each night for a week, there was something about the students. When Charles came round one morning to fetch some clothes, I mentioned that, to begin with, we didn't like to miss the news. But, as a spectator sport, rioting became monotonous. We were getting tired of it. He smiled. I didn't think of asking him whether he knew any of the participants. Instead, he mentioned that he had seen Francis Getliffe, who was off to spend the summer at the house outside Montpellier, which, with his usual decision, leaving me out of it, he had bought that spring.

It might have been two or three days later when, not on television, but in the *Times,* I saw an item of news. One headline ran: STUDENTS CHARGE COLLEGE WORKING ON GERM WAR.

That was it. I needn't have read any more. Angry that I had seen so little, I still didn't see all the connections, or even most of them: but I saw enough. Enough to be waiting for what was coming next.

Actually, the students' announcement was, like most of their official utterances, discreet. It was issued as one of their communiqués from the principal's office, said simply that documents had been found demonstrating that the college microbiological department was under contract to the Ministry of Defence, through the MRE at Porton. The students would insist that all work on biological warfare should be stopped forthwith.

That was ingeniously drafted, I thought. Unless it were a sheer invention, which seemed unlikely, they had got hold of some papers, and the authorities wouldn't know which or how much they gave away.

The signatures, as with all the previous communiqués, were those of Olly and his two adjutants from the college.

Apart from the headlines, the newspaper wasn't spending much space on the announcement. Nor did any of the others that I read. In one leader it was referred to, in an aside, as another sign of "immature thinking." The leader went on to ponder whether the grants of student protesters should be withdrawn, and rather surprisingly used this example of immature thinking to conclude that they should not.

There was no reference anywhere to collaboration from outside, or to any Cambridge group. For some reason, perhaps technical, they were being kept in the background, and I was asking myself how much respite that would give.

THIRTY-FIVE

A FOG OF SECRETS

Margaret was already going to bed when, late the following night, the front-door bell rang. I had been sitting in the drawing-room, not certain how much longer I could bear to wait: whether it was wise or not, I should have to talk to Charles. For an instant, I thought this caller might be he. Opening the door, I saw—with disappointment, with letdown—that it was Nina. Rain was trickling from her mackintosh cape and hood.

"I'm so sorry, Uncle Lewis, I don't know what the time is —" she said breathlessly.

"Never mind."

"But daddy asked me to give you a message, without fail, he said, tonight."

"Come in." The letdown had vanished. I couldn't delay in getting her coat off, bringing her into the drawing-room, meanwhile answering a call from Margaret about who it was.

"Well?" I asked Nina, pressing a drink on her which she wouldn't take. Just then Margaret, in her dressing gown, joined us, kissed Nina, interposed another wait.

"What did your father say?"

Nina swept dank hair from over her eye. She said:

"I tried to tell him something on the telephone this morning—"

"What was it?"

"Give her a chance," said Margaret. Nina smiled at her,

and then at me. She was shy, but firm and self-possessed.

"I told him I'd heard something about people making enquiries at Chester Row, but he stopped me. He wouldn't let
me speak on the phone. So I had to go to Cambridge. Then
he wouldn't ring you up either, so I had to come back and
see you tonight."

"Yes," I said, restless with impatience, "what was this message?"

"He said to tell you—*it looks as though someone like
Monteith is already on the job. You must advise them
straightaway.*"

I glanced at Margaret. It was all plain. Too plain. Martin's precautions about the telephone had probably been automatic: he had lived with security all through the war and
after. So had I, for longer. I had had dealings with Monteith
myself, when he was number two in one of the security services. I had dropped out of that claustral system, but I remembered hearing that he had been promoted.

"You were told this morning, were you?" said Margaret.
She was quiet but as urgent as I was.

"Yes," said Nina. The previous evening, two visitors had
called at Chester Row. One was a conspicuously fat man
(that must be Gilbert Cooke, I broke out, he had taken
Monteith's place at number two, the investigation was starting at a very high level).

They had asked all sorts of questions. They had been very
friendly and polite—

"They would be," I commented. There was a technique in
interrogation. The next interview, if Gilbert took it himself, wouldn't be quite as friendly.

"Who did they ask?"

"Charles. Muriel. They'd seen Olly already, somewhere
else. Oh, and Gordon Bestwick was at Chester Row last
night too."

"What did they seem to be after?"

"How much they knew about b.w." (Biological warfare.) "Where they'd been for the last week. Had they been inside the college. Had they seen the files from any of the offices. You know."

I knew, and Margaret also, that Nina herself was remarkably well informed. She was as cool as any of them. She reported that, early in the proceedings, before they were interrogated separately, Muriel had enquired whether she could send for her solicitor, if it seemed a good idea. Charles had stopped her, saying that it was a very bad idea. That was, Margaret and I agreed without a word spoken, good judgment on his part.

They had parted with cordiality. The next step, the fat man had said, was—if they wouldn't mind and if it wasn't too inconvenient, for them to have a talk with his superior. That sounded like Monteith himself. I still couldn't understand—and if I did understand, I was more troubled —why they should be working this enquiry from the top. Normally it would be done by agents very much junior, though Cooke might have been shown the papers.

Those 'talks' were beginning tomorrow: that is, since it was now nearly midnight, in a few hours' time. Olly and the signatories to the communiqué had been 'invited' to attend in the morning, Charles, Muriel, and "poor Gordon" in the afternoon. They were to go to the Admiralty—which everyone else took for granted, but which seemed to me like a piece of mystification for mystification's sake. Monteith and Cooke had perfectly good offices of their own, together with a dislike for using them.

"Why 'poor Gordon'?" Margaret was asking.

"He seems to be taking it harder than the others," said Nina, with a sort of clinical kindness. Then she told us, now that she had given us the hard news and could be off duty for a moment: "Do you know, when Daddy heard that all this happened at Chester Row, that was the first time he had realised that Charles and Muriel were living together?"

She gave an innocent smile at the innocence of the elderly.

"What did he think about it?" Margaret said.

"I think he was rather shocked."

As a matter of fact, about a sexual adventure Martin and a none-too-prim citizen of Antonine Rome would have been about equally shockable. If he disliked this one, it was because the woman had been his son's wife, and he was still capable of blaming her.

I had been thinking, it would be better if Nina, not I, rang up Chester Row. If they were at home, I ought to go there at once. As she was obeying, she hesitated and remarked, as though it were an afterthought:

"I don't think anyone mentioned Guy Grenfell last night. I don't think he's having to go tomorrow."

Then she went to the telephone. Those last words seemed inconsequential: but Margaret looked at me with eyes indulgent but sharp. She had no doubt that Guy Grenfell was Nina's channel of communication—and very little more that she had brought him into the conversation, partly because she was anxious about him, partly for the pleasure of uttering his name. Uttering his name with people there to hear: she might be self-possessed, an excellent courier, but she wasn't immune to the softer pleasures. Margaret liked her for it. As for me, in the hurry and tension of the evening, I wondered for a moment whether this also would come as a surprise to Martin, and whether or not he would approve.

In the hall of our block of flats, I waited, Nina beside me, for a taxi. I was feeling the special chagrin of no transport that came upon one in big towns. It was raining as hard as that night the previous summer when Charles had sauntered slowly home, absentminded with joy. If we walked to the tube station, I said to Nina, we should get drenched. Did she mind? Don't be silly, Uncle Lewis, she said, taking my arm, as physically relaxed as she was shy, dark hair falling from under her hood, cheeks flushed, looking already naiadlike in the rain. I had an irrelevant thought, it was absurd, that on this particular night I should arrive at their house, Muriel's and my son's, just as inspissatedly soaked as when I first arrived, long ago, at Sheila's.

We were, however, rescued. A car drew up—"Aren't you getting wet?" came a cheerful but not original question. The driver happened to be the one neighbour with whom, after twenty years living there, I was on social terms. Chester Row? No problem. Humming merrily, rosy after a party but driving with care, he took us through the midnight-empty streaming streets.

At the house, Charles opened the door, with Muriel waiting close by, but there was at once a hiatus. He held my coat, but both of them were looking, with glances that were not unfriendly but steady and purposeful, at Nina.

"How are we going to get you home?" said Charles, quite affectionately, giving a good impersonation of an elder brother. He didn't look it, but he was a month younger.

"I think I'd better order a car. We shan't get a taxi tonight," said Muriel.

They weren't going to talk in front of Nina. They had realised, it didn't take much divining, where my information had come from. They didn't seem to resent my possessing it (in fact they had greeted me with warmth and perhaps relief) but they weren't giving Nina the chance to transmit any more. They had become, and no one could blame them, as security-conscious as the men who had been questioning them.

They were doing less than justice, though, both to themselves and Nina. It wasn't through their laxness that she had learned any single fact: as I discovered later, Guy Grenfell had of necessity to know all the secrets, and they couldn't have foreseen that, apparently all of a sudden, he wanted to share everything with this girl. Whereas Nina, who was really as discreet as her father, had spoken only to him. She couldn't do more, because of her obligations to the others, nor less, because of her duty to do her best for Guy.

Anyway, Muriel did not take her upstairs. We all waited down in the dining-room, Charles pouring me a drink, making a kind of family conversation about Irene's sciatica and Maurice's new wife, whom by this time they had all met. Nina, not at all touchy, showed no sign of resentment at being shut out. She had the talent for acceptance which one sometimes found in the happy. We were all listening, me with impatience, for the car to drive up outside.

At last the three of us were alone in the long drawing-room. Charles and Muriel sat on the sofa facing me, his arm round her and fingers interlaced. It was not often that they were demonstrative in public, if by public one meant anyone else's presence, such as mine.

I said:

"Well, I've heard these people came and questioned you. You'd better tell me what they said."

Their account, though fuller, agreed with what I had been told already once that night. They both had precise memories, and sometimes they reproduced conversations word by word. There was one point of interest, though it was predictable. When they were being interrogated separately, the two agents had left them for a few minutes, obviously to confer, and returned to concentrate on a day, the preceding Wednesday, for which Charles had already given a story of his movements. She had been taken over the same hours, asked where she had been, how much of the time he had been with her, whether she could sketch out her diary of

the day. It was an old trick, and I was surprised that Cooke
had used it so blatantly. It had got nowhere. Their reconstructions coincided, and they had demonstrably been telling
the truth.

"Yes," I said. "That's all right. But it's tomorrow that matters."

"Or rather today," said Charles looking at his watch. It
was now past one o'clock.

"You've been summoned for the afternoon, haven't you?"
They nodded.

"That gives us a bit of time. There are several ways you
ought to prepare yourselves—"

"Look," said Charles, "I can handle this situation for myself. For us both."

It sounded like, it was, a flash of adolescent pride, such as he
might have shown two or three years before but had long out-
grown. It was strange to hear it from him now. For an instant
he seemed sham-arrogant, young, or even pathetic. I was moved
by a once familiar yearning, now forgotten or submerged.

"Don't be a fool," said Muriel, squeezing his fingers, calling
him by a pet name which I had never heard. "He knows
things, we don't. You've got to listen."

Charles's face was close to hers, as he broke into a slight acquiescent smile.

"The first thing is," I said, "don't underestimate them. They
don't work the way we do. They don't believe in intuition
much. They just go on adding one and one. But they tend to
get there in the end."

I went on:

"Which means, whenever they have a fact right, and they
will have a large number of facts right, your best line is to
agree with them. Don't deny anything which they can prove.
That makes it easier, if you want to deny something which they
can't prove."

"I follow," said Charles, who was now gazing at me with concentration.

"Don't say any more than you need. You can tell them you disapprove of biological weapons. They'll be used to that. Don't elaborate. Don't go in for systematic theory. Remember their politics are simpler than yours."

"What do I do?" asked Muriel.

"The same."

"Won't it look as though he's rehearsed me, though?"

"You can't provide for everything. People aren't clever enough to pretend for long. No, you say the same. Same facts, same timetable, same attitude. That's natural. After all, to some extent I presume it happens to be true."

Muriel gave a neutral smile. For the first time I noticed a very small dimple on her right cheek, close to her mouth, which didn't appear to have its replica on the other side.

"I want to ask you something," I said curtly. "For practical reasons I ought to know. It's almost certainly Charles they're after" (I was addressing myself to Muriel) "not you. So I ought to know." Then I spoke straight at him: "What have you done?"

He leant back, the whites of his eyes visible under the irises. "That's not so easy to answer—"

"That's nonsense."

She was coming to his help, saying "No, it's really not," when he sat up and faced me.

"No," he said, in a level tone, "I don't mind telling you, but it isn't so easy. I don't want to fake it either way."

"Well then. Did you extract those letters from the office?"

"No," he replied. "Not with my own hands, that is. But that's the trouble, I don't want to pretend that I'm not involved."

"How much are you involved?"

"I knew about it before and after."

"But you didn't take the letters?"

"I've told you, no."

"You had them in your hands?" As I asked, Muriel was shaking her head, but he wasn't looking at her for confirmation.

"Not that either. But I've seen photostats."

That, though it was clearly true, seemed an odd piece of bureaucratisation.

"Have you been inside those offices?" I meant by that, those of the principal and the professors.

"Not at the relevant times." (That is, when the files were ransacked.) "But I have been inside them, yes."

"So have I. So have the others," Muriel intervened. On the spot, that baffled me. It appeared that each of the Cambridge group had been by himself inside the college. Charles and Muriel, not together but on their own, had been smuggled in at night. Later it occurred to me that Olly might be making certain that they were committed. He had made use of them, very sensibly, as staff officers, and hadn't wasted them as crowd fodder. As for spokesmen, he didn't want too many public faces. But the private faces had to perform some token action: so each of them had made his visit and had, in form, taken part in the occupation. After they had told me of those incidents, so far as I could guess holding nothing back, I said:

"That is all?"

"That is all," said Charles.

"They will know nearly everything you've said, either of you." I was talking of Monteith and his people. I emphasised that they would almost certainly know of meetings in this house and of the nocturnal visits. They would probably know that Charles was one of those who had been shown photostats. It was not impossible that they had had an informer somewhere near: it was not impossible, it was probable that they had one, though how close to the centre I couldn't guess. It was not impossible that they knew of Charles's staff work and of the first idea about the b.w. documents, but that would be very difficult to prove. On that he needn't volunteer anything.

"It comes to this, doesn't it?" Muriel was speaking, having been subdued most of the night, acting only as a support for Charles. "They'll know that he's connected, we couldn't cover that up if we wanted to, could we? But that's really all they'll know. And I suppose something like that applies to me."

"That's the best you can expect," I said.

Neither of them was soft, but they were lost, and to an extent frightened because they were groping, in the security fog. I had been in my mid-thirties when, at the beginning of the war, I had my first taste of that peculiar chilling swirl. They had walked into it very early. When I mentioned that there might have been an informer among their circle, even in this house, they had looked both astonished and, unlike either of them, dismayed. They had felt an intimation of the mosaic of paranoia, the shrinking or freezing of one's own nature, that came to any of us when overwhelmed by secrecy. You had only to feel that paranoia for a short period in your life, to live just temporarily with security, to understand what happened to conspirators once they gripped the power and then realised there might be other conspiracies, this time against themselves.

Quietly, Charles asked:

"What is the worst we can expect?"

"They might know effectively everything that you've said and done."

"What would that mean? For him?" Though, as the night went on, Muriel's eyes were becoming reddened with tiredness, they were brilliant. She had become much more aggressive than he was. She sounded, all the tricks of politeness gone, as though she were defying me.

I replied, doing my best to seem professional, that it was almost unthinkable they would prosecute. It wouldn't be worth the publicity. Incidentally they wouldn't like to give away their sources of information. There would, however, be entries on personal dossiers. There would be communications about Charles and his friends with persons at Cambridge. It was conceivable that one or two promising academic careers would be interrupted.

"Do you think that will happen?" he said.

"Your guess is about as good as mine."

"If it does, you wouldn't like it, would you?"

"No."

He said: "Nor should I."

He had been speaking intimately, equal to equal. He didn't ask if I understood why he had acted. He might have taken that for granted, or thought it irrelevant. He wasn't trying to be considerate. It was knowledge, of himself and me, that he was speaking from, not emollience.

"You know," he said, in genuine, unaffected surprise, "I didn't think I should mind—if it came to trouble. I find that I do."

Muriel broke in fiercely, as though rallying him, though he was much calmer than she was. It couldn't and didn't matter practically: nothing would break his academic career for long: anyway, it didn't matter, he couldn't really be touched. Anything he had ever talked of doing, was quite outside anyone else's power.

I sat silent while she stormed at him, once or twice her gaze flashing towards me.

Charles smoothed back her hair, and said:

"All right. All right. But some of us don't find it quite so easy to escape from the respectable embrace, you know."

He said it teasing her, with affection. Yet, strangely enough, though he had made remarks which sounded arrogant once or twice that night, that was the only one which struck me so.

A little later, as I was getting ready to go, he said to me, in an altogether different tone:

"I'm sorry if all this is a trouble to you. I know it is."

I said, taken by surprise at his naturalness, more bluff than I usually was, that there were worse things.

Muriel, brilliant with courtesy returned, said:

"We've been very grateful for all your help, Uncle Lewis, you're much too kind, aren't you? I'm very sorry if we're a trouble to you. I am so very sorry."

THIRTY-SIX

A SELECTED
MEETING-PLACE

Next evening, Gordon Bestwick called on me. By this time they had become obsessively careful about telephoning or any other means of communication short of physical presence: thus Charles hadn't rung me up to report on his interview with Monteith, but had sent Gordon round instead.

At least, that was the ostensible reason for the visit, but I soon found that he was consumed with worry. Perhaps Charles thought I might give him some relief.

It was hard work, either when Margaret was present or when she had made an excuse to set Gordon and me free for a walk outside. To begin with, he wouldn't talk at all about the interview that afternoon. Whether they had resolved not to speak to unauthorised persons, and whether they had decided that Margaret was such a one, I couldn't tell. It might have been that she still kept an air of something like privilege, whereas I was nearer to the ground he knew.

If that was so, it was a classic case of misjudgment. For Margaret, used all her life to her relatives making exhibitions of themselves for conscience's sake, was the least disturbed of any of us. After all, her father and his friends had received obloquy and worse through being conscientious objectors in the First World War: they had been under inspection twenty years later as premature anti-Fascists, being used as front men by the other side. They were people who had been brought up—and

who had the not negligible encouragement of private means—
not to give a damn.

So, though she hadn't much patience with the students'
cause, she felt in the nature of things that spirited young
men would join it. If they didn't count the risks, well, since
her marriage she had come to know so many of my colleagues who (and she had once felt this of me) counted the
risks too much. Not that she didn't count the risks for
Charles: but she would have said, except when the superstitious flesh was over-ruling her, that she hoped he wouldn't
do so for himself.

She did her best to get Gordon talking, as he sat sprawled
on the sofa, great formidable head back against the cushions,
at times fidgeting upwards as though he were trying to take
part. The head wasn't less formidable, but more grotesque,
on account of a large acne pustule on his nose. He looked so
miserable that we both forgot that he was a man probably
stronger, and with the certainty of more powers to come,
than either of us. We just saw him lolling there, with the
lost-forever misery of youth. And it was a double misery.
Once he roused himself and asked Margaret when she last
saw Nina.

"Last night, actually," said Margaret, speaking the truth,
not knowing whether she should.

"Oh." A hard noise. I felt a kind of pity, sentimental perhaps, for young men who had no confidence with girls.

Soon afterwards Margaret left us, and immediately I asked
him what had happened yesterday. Even then he did not
reply at ease. I had to say, my brother and I felt safer, discussing security affairs in the open air. Would he prefer
that? When we were walking up the street towards Lancaster
Gate, for the first time his voice lost its dullness.

The interrogations, he said, had lasted about an hour
each: there was mention of more to follow. At intervals "the

man" (who had not introduced himself) interjected not as questions but as facts, statements about the examinee—"where I was, what I had been doing," Gordon told me. "Irrelevant, a lot of it. But they had collected stuff about me that they seemed to know better than I did." They had been to his school, and to people who knew his family. That was standard technique, I said. It seemed strange to have it brought up now, he replied. That was standard response, everyone felt that, I said. As for what happened, both in the rising and in the plans, they knew plenty. "They're leaving us guessing in spots. Whether they know or whether they're bluffing. But they know enough to fix us. If we try to fool ourselves about that, we shall make things worse."

Apparently one or two of the principals, though not Charles or Muriel, were still self-buoyant with optimism (the adrenalin-optimism of action, perhaps; Gordon had spent last night upon them, using his bitterest and most competent tongue). As we walked along, he wasn't saying anything that couldn't have been foreseen. Up a side street, people were carrying their tankards outside a pub, standing on the pavement in the warm air. I asked Gordon if he would like a drink. No, he said, he wasn't feeling much like it. He might be one of those—I could sympathise—who in trouble shied away from any sort of solace.

Except perhaps the solace of making resolutions.

"This is a lesson for us, anyway," he said roughly, not looking towards me but as though I were a companion who had to be convinced. "We mustn't make the same mistake again. We tried to do two things at once, and that's because we were too conceited. We made it all too complicated, it was my fault and Carlo's. It seemed a good idea, but it was an infantile mistake. It mustn't be repeated—"

He meant, and it was probably true, that without the inner plan of seizing official correspondence the rest would have been a total success. Which to the external world it had already been. Olly and his committee were getting their demands piecemeal: by the end of the summer their whole charter would have been met. But that was easy, Gordon was reflecting with harsh realism. Whatever students wanted as students would be given them on a plate. It was child's play to make that kind of impact. But when the impact broke through a bit deeper, got right among the things which the society would hold on to like death, then the forces of resistance suddenly crept round you—

"Damn them to hell," said Gordon, "why do they always know when to use their blasted advantages?"

I replied, with the kind of sarcasm that I should have used to Charles, that it didn't seem to me entirely unreasonable. You used your means of offence: established society replied with its own.

"Damn them to hell," said Gordon. "I hate them. I hate them and everything they stand for."

He was not disposed either to dispassion or irony. What was right for him was wicked for the other side. That capacity for anger was a great help to him that day, and might, I thought, be a strength in the future. Nearly all men of action possessed it. You had to believe the other side was a hundred percent wrong, and preferably evil, to be a hundred percent committed to your own. It was one of the more disagreeable facts of life. I much preferred Gordon when he was sad, trying to cope with a heavyweight temperament, mind sharp, senses rebelling: but it was his talent for anger which acted like a blood transfusion that evening, lifted him out of sadness or even fright, made one simultaneously less engaged by his company and more certain that he would survive.

It must have been shortly after that night, possibly in the same week, that he met with the rest of the inner circle on two occasions. Which, according to the accounts I heard later that year, were more eventful, or at least more tense, than any of their planning sessions in Chester Row.

There had been a geographical change. These two meetings didn't take place in Muriel's study. The whole group had now become hypnotised by security, as we all did when it percolated round ourselves, as detestable as the smell of gas. They decided that Chester Row, and they were not necessarily wrong, was not security-proof. So they shifted the venue.

Their choice of a second meeting-place seemed to bear the imprint of ingenious minds familiar with political history, possibly Gordon's or Charles's: for, with what must have been a tinge of satisfaction, they chose a setting not likely to be kept under surveillance. That is, they chose the London house, in Halkin Street, of Guy Grenfell's father, Chairman of his local Conservative Party, Baronet (for political and public services), member of the Carlton, Beefsteak, Pratts, The Turf, and White's.

A disinterested observer might have gained a subdued pleasure from the fact that this house, in period, style, structure, and market value, was remarkably similar to Muriel's, and only just over half a mile away.

Present at both these meetings were Olly, his two deputies, Muriel, Gordon, Charles, and Guy Grenfell. The first of them lasted from nine P.M. till something like one the next morning, the second rather longer. There was little to eat or drink. Before them was a single topic, the security attack on the b.w. disclosure, and how to get out of it with the least damage.

It was possible to think, as some of them did in calmer times, that they exaggerated their danger. Perhaps for the first time they were not behaving like experienced operators. If so, I was partly to blame: for my warnings, which had been overstressed and more darkened by pessimism because I was thinking of Charles, had been taken as a precise, almost official, forecast by Muriel and Gordon, and relayed as such to Olly. So that from the beginning they all assumed that lies or stonewalling weren't going to last them for long: they had, as a minimum, to produce a story which admitted some of the truth. That is, that letters about the sub-contract had been suspected, deliberately searched for, and then, as was public knowledge, used.

The story ought to be kept as simple as possible. It ought to involve as few persons as possible. Security might know or half-know more than they could reveal, and so would conceivably be placated by an account which was less than complete but was self-consistent.

All this was debated, and often repeated, for they were all under strain, at the first session. It seemed that Muriel played more of a leading part than usual. She wasn't as creative as one or two of the others, but she was as acute, particularly for this kind of semi-legal argument, as any of them. She also had influence on Olly, so that in the end she brought him round to a solution. It could be very simple. It could be just one person's private initiative. And that meant one thing. Someone had to take the rap.

That phrase had been used by Olly—who, like other leaders, had no fastidious objections to a cliché—to sum up the first meeting. It would not be difficult to develop a history of how one person became committed to the idea and executed it. Who? It had, in order to agree with the facts which security were known to possess, to be one of the Cambridge cell. In the end, it reduced to one of the three, Charles, Gordon, Guy.

As I had already been told, the real conception had emerged, not only from those three, but from several others, all drawn together in a sort of invisible college or committee

of young men. Who carried it through, that is who was present when the offices were invaded and the files searched, I
never knew, nor (I was nearly certain) did my source of all
this information. Apart from his own denial, I had some reason, circumstantial but strong, to believe that it was not
Charles. I was inclined to think that the balance of evidence
pointed to Gordon. In any case, it was very largely chance
who had been the actual agent. Olly paid no attention to it
when, in the second session, he made them come to a decision. Someone had to take the rap. It had to be the one
whom the movement could most easily spare. Olly might not
be a brilliant young man: possibly he would not be heard of
much again. But in that meeting he showed his quality. Not
brought into contact with him (I was told that I should be
bored) I thought he sounded something like a junior Par-
nell. Not bright: not specially articulate: but somehow he
could stay still and people waited to listen to him.

The one whom the movement could spare. There was no
sentiment about the choice. If it fell on Gordon, he would
suffer most, being poor and depending on his grants and the
prospect of a Fellowship. While Charles was the youngest of
the whole party. So far as anyone could see, Olly didn't give
even a token consideration to either of those claims. He cut
out what old Pilbrow used to call the personalia. He was cordial, and without making a show of it, ruthless.

None of this was done quickly. Leaders of his type didn't
utter laconic orders out of the side of the mouth. It was a
long churning conversation, more like a trade union committee than a meeting of the Stavka. The more astute,
though, didn't take long to see that the result was already determined. Gordon was the last man to sacrifice, Olly led one
of his aides into saying: they needed him for the future, he
was their best economic brain, probably the best brain all
round that they possessed. On a reduced scale there was

some similar opinion in favour of Charles. He wasn't specially popular with Olly: perhaps his ironic tongue, or the fact that some of them thought him unduly lucky, had made enemies. He himself said that he was reasonably dispensable: the consequences, in practical terms, would not be all that important to him. But the majority would not have it. Whether living with Muriel went in his favour or not, it was impossible to make out. All in all, the positives outweighed the negatives, and they said that he was too useful to lose.

So, slowly, talk gradually converging, never pointed, the party came to look towards Guy Grenfell. Just how it was made clear to him that he had to volunteer, remained obscure, even when I was told the story. Almost certainly, there was no direct remark or question. On the other hand, there must have been a number of hints, and not too subtle ones. In his own house, very likely of having thoughts of his parents, Guy for a long time managed to avoid seeing them.

It must have been, I thought later, like a drawing room version of more mortal sacrifices. You couldn't read the diaries of the Scott expedition without realising that it had been hinted, more than once, to Captain Oates that he ought to go. The solemn issue of morphine pills a few days before. No one I knew who had been in any kind of collective danger, doubted the tone in which that was done. The finale was grand. They were brave men. Actions weren't the less grand because those who performed them were recognisably like the rest of us.

It took a long time, but Guy brought out his offer. Not in a gallant manner, but with a touch both of truculence and superciliousness. The others responded with relief, but taking it very much for granted. They all knew he had money of his own. They all knew also that he was not a star academic. Charles, who was fond of him and felt he was a richer character than most of them, first repeated his own offer and then acted as impresario, in producing enthusiasm for Guy's. The others crowded round with comradely applause. Courtesies over, they set to work composing a history— where Guy was a solitary figure—which security would find it hard not to accept. They did not break up until that was tested and done.

Security either did find it hard not to accept, or, more likely, for their own reasons were glad to pretend to do so. All that outsiders—including me, at the time—knew was that, suddenly the fuss about biological warfare disclosures died down. There was an official statement, of a muffled nature, saying that no secrets had been revealed and that precautions about the Official Secrets Act in relation to Government Research Establishments were being enquired into, as a routine precaution. The College issued its own statement saying that, in general principle, contracts from Government departments were not normally undertaken: that the demands of the students for representation had been met: and further that the College and the students had set up a joint committee to examine any further points in dispute.

Some time in July, Charles and Muriel paid us a call, and with meaning but without explanation said that Guy Grenfell would in September be leaving for Harvard and would complete his studies there.

THIRTY-SEVEN

A GARDEN AND
LIGHTED WINDOWS

When Muriel asked over the telephone if I "could possibly call round" for a drink, and I said yes, neither of us pretended the invitation was just a casual thought. As before that year, she had chosen Margaret's evening away from home: arriving at Chester Row, I should have been surprised to find Charles in. At once, as I entered the drawing room, Muriel apologised blank-faced for his absence. Then she kissed me, not in the happy-go-lucky English fashion, but as though it were a deliberate, an hieratic gesture. Our cheeks parted, and she was standing upright, her eyes not far below mine: I noticed, which I hadn't before, the first starry lines at the corners, fine and faint on the smooth healthy skin.

She led me to the window seat, where she had been sitting. At the bottom of the window, a few inches were open.

"Is that too much for you?" she asked.

"Not a bit," I said, amused by the old-fashioned phrase. Actually, the breath of air was warm: outside it was a beautiful night for late September.

Facing me on the seat she said:

"I wanted to tell you, Uncle Lewis."

"Yes?"

"We're fairly certain now that we're in the clear."

349

I nodded. I didn't ask for evidence. On such a matter, I had confidence in her judgment.

"We thought of letting you know before this. But he was keeping his fingers crossed a little."

"So should I have been."

"Would you?" She looked at me with a flash of interest, as though searching my lineaments for the most vestigial resemblance to my son.

There was a momentary silence. She said:

"It really is all right, Uncle Lewis."

"Excellent."

As we sat there on the window seat, there was another, and a longer, silence. I was used to her enough by now to feel that this wasn't the only point of the meeting. Her legs were intertwined, one foot jerking from the ankle. It was rare for her not to have her body, as much as or more than her expression, under complete control.

She said:

"I wonder if you could possibly bear to have your drinks in the garden? It's almost nice enough, perhaps. Of course it's being a terrible nuisance—"

"Let's go," I replied. She was taking refuge in politeness which didn't sound like politeness, which might have been mocking. But when I began to move, she leapt up, crossed the room to the sideboard, agile with physical relief. She arranged the tray, and preceded me down the stairs, through her back sitting-room, out to the patio garden. Carrying the tray, she was as poised as a shipboard steward. Some women, I thought, with a figure like hers would have been conscious of it, but that impression she had never given me.

At the end of the garden, table and chairs were waiting under an overhanging rose bush, a bloom or two gleaming out in the twilight. There was a smell, already autumnal, of

drying leaves, blended with something less wistful, perhaps
—I couldn't place it—a tobacco plant? She poured out a
drink for me, and I sat comfortably sipping. The news was
good. Whatever she was intending to say, I was ready to
wait. It was getting on for seven o'clock in the evening. In
the west, towards the King's Road, the sky was still lumi-
nous. From the houses on each side of Muriel's, lighted windows were already shining.

Looking at one of them, amber curtains drawn with a
chink between them, a standard lamp just visible, for an instant a shape passing across, I felt a curiosity, or something
softer like a yearning, which when I was younger I should
have thought inadmissible, maudlin, and nevertheless undeniable, and which was just as undeniable now. Once, long
before, when I was an outsider, gazing at strangers' windows
from the nocturnal streets, it might have been explicable
that I should have imagined the hearth-glow of homes such
as I didn't have: when I longed for one to return to. Often I
had pretended to myself that it was sheer inquisitiveness
about others' lives, trying to feel proud because I wasn't
tamed and was on my own. That wasn't altogether false. The
inquisitiveness was there also. Walking with Maurice on the
sombre Christmas afternoon, two or three years ago, I had
been oddly gratified—more than the event deserved—as he
pointed to lighted rooms in the derelict squares and told me
some of the stories that lay behind.

Yet that evening in Muriel's garden, when curiosity and
longing ought both to have been satisfied, I felt the same
emotion as I should have felt as a young man. Habits, I had
told myself before this, at a time when I had learned less,
lived longer than freedoms. Sometimes they told one more
about oneself.

We had been sitting quietly. Muriel gazed up the garden
at her own house, so that I could see only her profile, which

was becoming softened as the light grew dimmer. Then she said:

"I'm sorry, but I think you're misunderstanding me." Her tone was clear, but (I thought I heard) not quite composed.

"What about?"

"Charles."

"What about him?"

"You won't see it. But you and I, we're on the same side."

"Are we?" My voice had become rough and unconceding.

"I think we are."

She wasn't to be beaten down. Her eyes were fixed steadily on me now. She said:

"You'd like him to make the best of himself, I think you would. And so should I."

"We might not agree," I replied, "on what that means."

"It means, that we should like him to make the most of his talent. Or wouldn't you?" For an instant, she gave a sharp and attacking smile. There was nothing between us, though. Neither age, nor sex, nor subliminal dislike.

"Of course I should."

"Yes. I'm afraid that he may take one risk too many."

"You mean, what you've just been doing—"

"No, no, no. We've learned something. That's not the correct way, we shall have to find another method. By the way, I'm not apologising for us. I'm sure he'd be angry with me if I did. And I don't feel like doing so on my own account."

"What is this risk that he's going to take?"

She shook her head. "Haven't you noticed that he keeps his secrets?"

"From you?"

"Oh yes. From me."

"What do you know then?"

"I don't know. I may be imagining it. You can guess how one does—" Just then, she lost her crispness.

"Well, what are you afraid of?"

"It's not for tomorrow. It's not until he's finished at Cambridge." (That is, until he graduated in the following June.) "Then—"

"Then what?"

"I think he may be deciding to get away from us all."

"Will he leave you?"

"Men have left women before, haven't they?" She added in a level tone: "He would also be leaving you."

"Men have left their fathers before, haven't they?" I replied, copying her. Then, to make amends, I said: "But that's different. He's bound to do that. In fact, he's done it already."

"When he came to me?"

"Long before."

"Do you think he's quite as free as that?" Eye-glint in the expressionless face. She went on:

"Who do we believe he's escaping from? You think it must be me, don't you? I rather prefer to think that it's really you."

I smiled. Even now, when she was speaking in earnest, her kind of subterranean impudence once or twice broke through. I said that it might not be either of us: I had come, I told her, to distrust the subjective explanations. His motive might have nothing to do with anyone but himself.

"I don't care why he's doing it," she said sharply, "so long as we can keep him safe."

"You still haven't told me, safe from what?"

"I wish I knew."

"No, what are you thinking of?"

She looked away, frowning.

"In some ways, he's cautious, isn't he? He always says he's very timid, but all that means is that he likes working things out in advance. He can be very cool, but he's a gambler too.

I think that's what I'm afraid of. He might decide to do something sensational if he thought it was worth the risk."

She might be right. My nerves were getting tightened in tune with hers. At the same time, I was thinking, it was strange to hear Charles, whom I assumed that I knew well, described by someone who also knew him well.

"I wish," she said, "we could find something for him that kept him away from that—"

"What would you like him to do?"

Eye-glint again.

"Just about the same as you would. Something nice and quiet for a few years. Like Gordon Bestwick—" She told me that Gordon was proposing to get a job in academic life, waiting "in the slips" (which of them had invented that ridiculous idiom?) to see where he might go into action. There wasn't any doubt, she said, that some Cambridge college would soon snap him up. There wasn't any doubt that the same would happen to Charles also, if we could persuade him to stay.

"Well, that's what I should like for him, to begin with. There couldn't be anything more respectable than that, could there?"

She gazed straight at me, and went on:

"You used to think that I wanted to get hold of him, didn't you? Just to be useful in campaigns?"

"Yes, I did."

"You were quite wrong, you know. I doubt if anyone could get hold of him like that. I should never have stood a chance. No, it wasn't that. You can see it wasn't that, can't you?"

I nodded. "What is it, though?"

She replied:

"I want him."

After a pause, she added: "I wanted him before we started. I want him more now."

She was speaking even more quietly, like a reticent neigh-bour at a dinner table asking one to pass the salt. At the same time, there was an undertone of something like blame —no, heavier than that—directed not at him nor me, but at herself. She wasn't convinced, it seemed, that I believed or trusted her. She was playing for me as an ally, she hadn't pretended anything else: now, as though the treaty were not signed and one party had to produce evidence of good faith, she was searching for something to tell me.

It was then that I heard some history. About the meetings in her house, and the undercover plans. She described the sessions in Halkin Street, which were, of course, utterly un-known to me. In fact, there wasn't much of her story I was likely ever to have known: for neither she nor Charles would have spoken without a purpose. Ostensibly her purpose was to persuade me that she hadn't over-influenced Charles, that in their political efforts they had been partners, and that, so far as there was influence, it had been more on his side than hers. That I couldn't judge, though her reporting seemed as precise as his would have been. In any case, the balance of influence didn't interest me so much. I was listening to what she was saying—whether intentionally or not, I didn't know —about herself and Charles.

I remembered hearing Azik Schiff talking about them in his splashy exuberant domestic fashion. His stepdaughter's taste was distinctly more austere. She did not once admit or confess that she was in love. She certainly wasn't rejoicing at the state in which she found herself. She seemed to feel re-sentful, or at least not pleased with fate, at being emotion-ally trapped: just as another woman, starting a casual affair, might curse at another trap, the more primitive one of being pregnant.

The curious thing was, that about her feeling for Charles Azik had been right: right for the wrong reasons perhaps, but still right. She was in love. Myself, long before, even when I had been frustrated and wretched, I drew a kind of elation out of the state itself: other people were dull dogs, here was I, borne up in a special capsule of my own. Nothing like that was true of Muriel. If I had mentioned my own experience to her, she might have regarded it either as a sign of self-deception or alternatively as though it was as irrelevant as some reminiscence from the Languedoc courts of love.

As we gazed up the garden, lights had sprung out from other windows. Muriel's house had the second and third floors left dark. Her voice sounded more than ever clear. None of us had been sure that we knew much about her. Was it possible, I was wondering, that she was one of those who were abnormally free of sexual guilt, and who, on the other hand, weren't easily touched by what I called love and in my youth boasted about? So that, if they were threatened or overcome by that kind of love, they felt it as a dark and frightening force. If you took sex without guilt or any other consequences or ancillaries, were you at risk? That is, did you fear all the menace of emotion that most of us had taken as part of love? That seemed to be true of some of the old Greeks. Or the Japanese. Might it be true of this young woman, so disciplined, trying to persuade me as we sat in her garden?

It was noticeable that, when she spoke of other human relations, she wasn't inhibited at all. Just as she had once asked me whether I loved Charles, so she spoke without any reserve about her love for her own child. As though parental love wasn't a danger, and we could in tranquillity use the word. Well, she hadn't yet known in full what parental love was like. Perhaps she was right though, in talking as though they were different in kind. As I thought one night lying in the hospital bedroom, if love was the proper term for what (as I had that evening accepted) she felt for Charles, then, though parental feeling could be as desperate, and could bring as great a solace, it ought to be called by a different name.

Talking of how much she loved the infant, she mentioned that Charles was very fond of him.

"He loves children, did you know?" she said.

She added:

"I'd be glad to give him all he wants."

It sounded casual, but she hadn't said much that was casual all that evening. When I let her see that, if she was right about Charles's intentions, then obviously I would help her if I could, she wasn't satisfied. She couldn't leave it alone, almost as though she were persuading, not me, but him.

THIRTY-EIGHT

INTERROGATION
BY A STATESMAN

When the rumour spread that someone was intending to speak about the summer's disturbances in the Lords, most of us believed it. If acquaintances eagerly brought a vaguely displeasing rumour, it usually turned out to be true. None of Charles's group—all except Muriel were now back for the university term—appeared to be much perturbed: but Charles decided that it ought to be watched.

That was the reason that he and I, one afternoon at the end of October, were sitting in the gallery of the Lords' Chamber. I had tried to get tickets from Francis Getliffe, but was told that he hadn't returned to Cambridge: so I had fallen back on Walter Luke, who said that he was down to answer a question that afternoon. As soon as I looked at the order paper, I expected that it was the question Charles and I were waiting for. It was fourth and last on the list. *The Lord Catforth To ask Her Majesty's Government whether the defence contracts alleged to be disclosed during the disturbances at ———— College in June had actually been placed with the College.*

It wasn't a masterpiece of legal drafting: but the civil servants who had to write the official answer would have realised at first sight that it wasn't innocent. I could recall similar questions arriving flagged in my in-tray in days past: and Hector Rose's glacial and courteous contempt for all the

trial shots at the answer, including, though for politeness'
sake not mentioned, the most senior, being my own.

The civil servants would have known, it was their business
to know, something about the questioner. He was a back-
bench Labour peer, recently ennobled, who had served a
long time in the Commons: a trade unionist who had made a
speciality of military subjects, on which he was considerably
to the right of the Tory front bench.

It was a Thursday, about five past three. High up in the
gallery (there was, as mountaineering books used to say, an
uncomfortable feeling of space in front of one) we looked
down on a packed house. A house so packed that it might
have been one of the perspectiveless collective portraits of
historical Lords' debates, hung in their own corridors. The
scarlet and gold was swamped. Grey heads gleamed, bald
heads shone: there were some very young heads also, one or
two as hirsute as Guy Grenfell's. This attendance was not,
however, in honour of Catforth's question. A debate on
Southern Rhodesia was to follow later that day, and there
might (or might not) be a vote. For most of those present,
the preliminary questions were merely curtain-raisers or
minute-wasters; to be endured, just as for parliamentarians
anti-climatic business was always having to be endured.

Not so with Charles. He was leaning forward in the gallery, hands clasped round one knee. The fourth question
might—it was not likely but it was possible—have its dan-
gers. He was keyed up, but actively so, as, so I guessed, he
would have been before an examination. If he could have
taken part, he would have been happy.

He was also, I supposed, not put off by flummery. He and
his friends were disrespectful towards English formalities,
but they were used to them. A stately question number two
about salmon fisheries in Scotland made him smile, but not
so incredulously as if he had been a foreigner.

Content changed, forms stayed, I used to think. I was no nearer knowing the answer to an old puzzle of mine, how much of the forms he and his contemporaries would leave intact.

At last the fourth question. "The Lord Catforth." A big man, with large spectacles and a black moustache, rose from the middle of the government benches, opposite to us in the gallery. "I beg leave to ask—" standard formula, but not mumbled, sententiously uttered.

Walter Luke, who had been putting his feet up from the front bench, stood at the dispatch box. His hair was now steel-grey, not pepper and salt, but his face had filled out in his fifties, the lines, instead of being furrows, had become undramatic creases.

In the comfortable west country burr, from his official file he read:

> Her Majesty's Government are aware that certain allegations were made during the June disturbances. As my honourable friend said in another place on June 29th none of these correspond to the facts as known by him. It is true that from time to time defence contracts have been placed with the college, as with many other university institutions. All such contracts are of a research nature which makes them suitable for work in university laboratories. They are placed in accordance with recognised procedures which have been used for many years, in the case of the college in question, since before 1939.

Loyal hear hears from those near Walter. The civil servants must have calculated, I was thinking, that the wider, the better.

Lord Catforth, on his feet again: "While thanking my

noble friend for that answer, it does not appear to answer the question."

Scattered hear hears.

"Will my noble friend tell us whether any contracts of a specifically military nature relating to biological warfare have been placed with the college?"

As soon as I heard that, I was sure that there had been some colloguing with Lord Catforth. Perhaps the whips had got at him. Anyway he was not the man to disapprove of any weapon either already in existence or ever to become so.

And Walter Luke was suspiciously quick in glancing at the answers to possible supplementaries with which he had been briefed.

Lord Luke of Salcombe: *I can assure the house that no contracts of a specifically military nature, either relating to biological warfare or any other kind of weapon, have been or will be placed with the college under the present government.*

Louder hear hears.

Someone gave voice from under the gallery whom I couldn't see.

"Does the noble lord deny that there has been a security leak? Can he estimate how valuable the information about biological warfare will be to the Russians—

Order, order.

Now I thought I recognised the voice. Man of the ultra-right. Probably attending to speak about Rhodesia.

Lord Luke of Salcombe: *As I have said to my noble friend, Lord Catforth, there has been no contract of a military nature relating to biological warfare, and so no information about biological warfare could have been or has been elicited.*

Defence spokesman from the Tory front bench, rising quickly:

Can the noble lord assure us that appropriate security precautions have been taken?

Lord Luke of Salcombe: *I can certainly give that assurance.*

The last question had been intended to be helpful. But it didn't, as it was meant to, silence the interlocutor below.

Can the noble lord tell us how much information reaching the public press during the riots carried security classifications?

Lord Luke of Salcombe: *It would not be in the public interest to answer questions which might bear on security matters.*

Very loud hear hears from both sides of the house.

Voice: *Well then. Was any of the information which reached the public press covered by the Official Secrets Act? I should like a straight answer from the noble lord. Yes or no.*

Lord Luke of Salcombe: *I am not prepared to let the noble lord form my answer for me. My answer is in fact the same as my answer to his last question.*

Voice: *The noble lord seems incapable of giving a straight answer.* (Order, order, and a few hear hears.) *Perhaps, since we shall be bound to hear in due course, he might conceivably answer this one. Is the government intending to prosecute any of the persons concerned under the Official Secrets Act?*

Lord Luke of Salcombe: *No, my lords.*

A few cries of why not, and then a venerable figure spoke, with a disproportionately strong voice, from the government rear.

Lord F.: *Does the government realise that many of us on this side and throughout the country share our young people's detestation of this atrocity called biological warfare?*

Lord Luke of Salcombe: *We fully realize what my noble friend has said.*

Lord F.: *Further does the government realise that anything said about biological warfare by any of the young spokesmen during what I prefer to call the events of last June were said in a spirit of genuine and absolutely spontaneous indignation?*

I looked at Charles, so that his glance met mine. The whites of his eyes were as milk-clear as a child's, the irises almost black. For an instant, blinking not winking, the lids came down and opened again.

Lord F. had spent his life in liberal faiths and never lost them, but Walter Luke could have done without him that afternoon.

Lord Luke of Salcombe: *We all know, at any rate, how genuine my noble friend's spontaneous indignation is.*

The voice under the gallery was raised again, but there were grumbles of order, the leader of the house was half-getting up to intervene, until, among a hubbub, the supplementaries ceased. One of his colleagues was patting Walter on the knee, and—because another was speaking near to a microphone—we heard a bass and presumably confidential "well done."

Walter's cheeks were ruddy and shining. Probably not knowing that he had done an old friend a good turn (for Monteith and his apparatus didn't pass on much to ministers, perhaps in this case the bare results, not names which they regarded as peripheral as Charles's) he had enough reason to be modestly pleased with himself. His permanent secretary was likely to have warned him that 'this might be an awkward one': students by themselves were a delicate subject by now, students plus security were as delicate as you could reasonably get short of espionage. I should have been prepared to bet that the officials had done some conferring with Walter's political boss (the Secretary of State, Walter's 'honourable friend,' who sat in the Commons and for whom Walter, as his number two, answered in the Lords). Any official would have wished that an experienced politician had to cope with that subject, not an amateur such as Walter.

Still, Walter had done well. I hadn't had attention to spare, but now I was thinking, he might have sunk the government into trouble. He had got away with it. If this had been the commons, he would have had a rougher time.

Just then I noticed Azik Schiff entering the chamber and jerking his head in the direction of the throne. I hoped that he wouldn't look up towards the gallery. He had been made a peer that summer and for a few weeks had revelled in it. He had still been at his most exuberant, when in Muriel's garden, I thought of him and two different kinds of love, thought of him as a happy man with emotions spilling over.

Now I didn't dare to meet him. Certainly not with Charles by my side. Perhaps, if I believed that I could have been any use to Azik, I might have found the courage, or shamed myself into it. As it was, all I wanted was to avoid his eyes.

It was easier (and more selfish and self-protecting) to return to thinking of Walter. Just as when, not so long before, I was planning a Christmas party and George Passant told me that he was in horrifying trouble: then as now, one's first impulse was to escape, one needed to get him out of the house.

Yes, Walter might have got the government into trouble. Strange how tactful he had been. Transformed from the brash scientific roughneck of his Barford years. As though he were acting. Sweet reasonable public face. Once upon a time he used to make brisk observations about men with public faces. Stuffed shirts. Then, as though no happier phrase had ever been invented, he would repeat it.

But I recalled that as a very young man, when he was first elected a fellow of the College, he had been as tactful as he was this afternoon. Also self-effacing. Perhaps he had overdone the brashness. It was a part that suited him. Now he seemed to be returning to his youth. I wondered whether he was bland to his officials. Or whether they were treated to the middle-period Walter: unregenerate, behaving like a tycoon in a film, cracking insults out of the corner of his mouth. Strange how a man so rigid in character should act parts in his life. No, not so strange. Just because he was so rigid, the transformations had to be hard-edged. With others they happened in the flux of life, merging into one another, like the colours of an iridescent film, merging continuously and still preserving the same and unique film.

It hadn't been only Walter's tact, though. There had been some operating in private, through 'the usual channels' perhaps, or with Walter and his colleagues conducting some informal little talks themselves. Lord Catforth must have been exposed to blandishments. It was clear that the official opposition had been squared. That was easy to do in a security matter: besides, the official opposition was at least as gently disposed to young rebels as the government, probably more so. Almost certainly, Walter Luke would have had a drink with his opposite number on the Tory side. The opposite number would know, without being told, that Walter proposed to obscure the issue and tell a ministerial fraction of the truth. The opposite number would also know that the students' disclosures were factually true. Walter would wrap up his answer so as to avoid a direct lie. In effect, though not in legalistic words, he might be telling one.

Both front benches, and many experienced persons in the House, would know all those things. It would be a mistake to imagine that they felt qualms of conscience. This was how you had to behave, if you were going to govern at all. Walter had taken it as all in the day's work.

I must have been letting loose a smile, for Charles, sitting at my side in the gallery, returned it, though he could not have guessed anything near the reason. I was thinking about him and one of fate's practical jokes. For it was because of him, who had with strong approval seen me shut the last door on politics and so dismiss the most minor of the three themes of what Margaret's forebears would have called my moral life—it was because of him that I was here, returning to the old subject, interested in the machinery as I used to be. No, as I had confirmed to myself in hospital, it wouldn't capture me again, but there it was.

Just as it was because of Charles that I had been reminded of the other themes, stronger than the first. I had been reminded that they could revive, and had—face to face with Muriel I knew it—already done so.

Walter had instructed me that, when we were tired of sitting in the gallery, we were to make our way to the tea-room. If questions had been followed by the Rhodesia debate, it would have taken more force than mine to tear Charles away: but in fact the next item on the order paper was the second reading of a bill to legalise the use by other denominations of certain redundant Anglican churches. Charles's spirit was not so deeply stirred by that, and so soon we sat close to the tea-room tapestry, waiting for Walter Luke.

When he arrived, I had to introduce Charles to him. He was asking us both, before he sat down, had we heard the bit of fun and games? By which he meant his performance. It was an unnecessary question, since he knew we had come for nothing else. We nodded.

"Was it all right?" said Walter.

"Fine," I said.

"Did you think it was all right?" Walter had turned to Charles.

"Yes, it was excellent, sir."

"I thought it was all right myself," said Walter Luke.

He wasn't being jocular at his own expense, comparing his present incarnation with the not-so-distant past, or recalling his onetime animadversions on persons fulfilling public functions such as he now fulfilled. There was no irony about Walter Luke. There never had been. He was enjoying his existence, and he proceeded to make a hearty tea, eating several cakes and pressing them on Charles, very much as my father had done at their only effective meeting.

Walter was asking Charles about Cambridge, and said— and this surprised me, much more than similar apostrophes from Lester Ince—that he had never liked the place. Why not? Well, as soon as he got really going on his research, the Cavendish was proceeding to break up. As for the College, it got on his nerves. Sometimes men like old Winslow made him feel there ought to be a servants' entrance constructed specially for him, Walter. (Loud, crackling laugh which caused heads to turn from nearby tables.) Then there was Roy Calvert. It got you down, living within touching distance of melancholia.

I hadn't realised that the young Walter—he was speaking of himself at twenty-four or -five—had observed so much.

"You knew Roy Calvert then, did you, sir?" Charles asked, polite and expressionless.

"You've heard of him, have you?"

"Just a little. From my father."

"I was jealous of him sometimes," said Walter with simplicity. "Poor chap."

To him, Charles's question must have seemed pointless. Yet Charles himself he seemed to have taken a fancy to, though he couldn't have found much in common.

After tea, he asked us not to go unless we had to: it was a bit early to start drinking, but we might as well pre-empt a corner in the guest-room.

It was the same tactic that Francis Getliffe had used on my last visit there, and the same window corner. Walter stood for a moment, spine as upright as though he were in surgical splints, gazing over the river through the November drizzle. The necklace of lights on the south bank dimly glimmered. It was not a spectacular vista, but he was gazing at it with proprietorial pleasure, as though he owned it.

When we sat down, the room was nearly empty, though one figure was in solitude drinking gin at the bar. In a comradely, roughly casual but unaggressive tone, Walter said to Charles:

"My lad, what are you going to do with yourself?"

"Do you mean tonight, sir?" Charles, trying to gain time, knew that Walter meant no such thing.

"No. I mean what are you going to do with your life?"

Charles asked, gently:

"What do you think I ought to do?"

"Damn and blast it, old Lewis will be better on that than I am."

Charles looked at me and said:

"He's been very good."

It was a gnomic remark, but it sounded genuine and without edge, and I was touched.

Charles went on:

"I should be grateful for some advice, I mean it, you know."

Charles forgot nothing. He remembered Margaret teasing

me after I had refused Walter's present job. And the family exchanges about asking advice. One's truisms had a knack of coming home.

"Well, you're obviously bright, anyway you've proved that. So that you must be sure of what you can do best—"

"Yes. But how many things are worth doing?"

Suddenly Charles's tone had changed. He was now speaking with intensity and force. So much so that Walter dropped his avuncular manner. His horizon-light eyes, set full in the rugged head, confronted Charles's deep-set ones.

"No, not many. That's why most of us just do the things that come to hand. That's what I've done."

"But is that always good enough?"

"How do I know? Only God would know, if he happened to exist."

"Would you have liked to do anything different, yourself?" If you'd had an absolutely free choice?"

That wasn't disrespectful. There wasn't any offence, umbrage, mock-humility, or presumption on either side. They were talking with a curious mixture of impersonality and friendliness, something like Mansel and a colleague discussing an eye operation.

"I used to think," said Walter, "that I should like to have done some first-class physics. I never did. Not within bloody miles of it. The war came along and I got shunted from one job to another. They said they were useful. I thought they were useful. That was a hundred percent copper-bottomed excuse for not doing real physics. And sometimes I looked at myself in the shaving glass and said Walter my lad you're a fraud. It isn't any blasted excuse at all."

Charles was listening, hand under chin. Just for an instant, perhaps because of Walter's rolling Devonshire, and his Christian name, the tableau brought back the old Victorian picture, the youth hanging on to the sailor's tale: in my early childhood I had it fixed in my mind that the sailor must be Raleigh.

"Then I began to get my head down to its proper size," Walter went on. "All that was just damned silly inflation, I thought. What difference should I have made if I'd stayed in a physics lab every blasted minute of my life? The answer is, damn all. There aren't more than five or six men in the whole history of science who've made a difference that you can call a difference. And that's where you don't belong, Walter Luke.

"Take old Francis Getliffe. He's kept at it year in, year out. He's done some pretty nice work. If I'd stuck at physics as long as he has, I might have done about the same. I should have chanced my arm more than the old boy." (After hearing Francis, not far from that same, express pity for Walter's ill-fortune, there was a certain pleasure in witnessing the same process in reverse. Did Charles know that, of the two, most of their fellow scientists thought that Walter had the bigger talent?) "Well, if old Francis had never existed or had gone in for theology or stamp collecting or something of the sort, someone else would have come along and done exactly the same work within a matter of months. All that happens is that the old boy gets a hell of a lot of satisfaction. I suppose I might have got that too. But damn it to hell, what does that matter? When you know that you could be got rid of and no one would feel the difference?"

Walter finished in a cheerful, ruminative, acceptant tone. "That's the point, isn't it? If your head's the proper size, you see that you're not all that significant. Anywhere. So I finished up here." Walter swept an arm as though to take in the Palace of Westminster. "Hell, it's good enough for me."

"What you're saying," Charles asked him, "would apply to anything creative, wouldn't it?"

"Unless you were old Will Shakespeare, I should think it did."

Charles had gone over this argument with me before; not that I disagreed about the fundamentals, though I should have altered the stress. I knew that he had argued it also with his cleverer friends at school since he was thirteen. He said:

"No one wants to do second-hand things, do they? Scholarship's second-hand, even the best of it. Criticism's second-hand—"

"That comes from having a literary education," Walter burst out in his old-style raucous vein. "You think a bloody sight too much of criticism if you put it as high as second-hand. Our infernal college" (he turned to me) "after we'd cleared out elected some damn fool who'd written a thesis on the Criticism of Criticism. Instead of electing him they ought to have kicked his bottom down the Cury."

Charles smiled, but wasn't to be put off. "Anyway, no one wants the second-hand things. And there's no use doing first-hand things unless one is superb, is that right?"

"That's a bit stronger than I meant," said Walter, who, despite his conversational style, was a moderate man.

"Well, is this nearer? You wouldn't allow the old romantic conception of the artist. That is, an artist is justified whatever he does and it doesn't matter much whether he's any good so long as he thinks he is."

"That's piffling nonsense," said Walter Luke.

"I believe it's disposed of forever. Among my generation anyway," said Charles. "You've never had any time for it, have you?" He turned to me.

"That's putting it mildly," I replied.

"Well, we've wiped off quite a lot of possibilities, haven't we?" Charles had the air of one who, very early in a hand at bridge, could name where the cards lay.

"For God's sake, lad, don't let me discourage you from anything."

Walter was subtler than he seemed, or wanted to appear. He had realised some time before that this discussion was not entirely, or perhaps not at all, academic.

"Please don't worry. You wouldn't discourage me from anything if I didn't discourage myself. Most of those things I'd ruled out long ago."

"I hope you've left something in," said Walter, boisterous and avuncular again.

"A little."

"Well, what's it going to be?"

"I can't tell you anything definite yet."

"Tell me something indefinite, then."

Charles grinned. Not perturbed, he said: "I do think that the things worth doing in my time are going to be a bit different."

"Why? Different to what?" Walter said.

"Different from things that your contemporaries did. I think we ought to do things which will actually affect people's lives. Quite quickly. Here and now. Not in a couple of generations' time. In our own."

"What does all that add up to?"

"Don't I wish I knew?"

"You're thinking of something like the other end of this place?" Walter jerked a thumb in the direction of the commons.

"No, not quite that, perhaps."

"Anyway, you don't know yet, do you?"

"No, not yet."

"Oh, don't rush yourself. There's plenty of time," said Walter.

When Charles was expressing indecision, speaking almost bashfully, I doubted it. I didn't believe that Charles had started the conversation for my benefit, either to challenge or (what might have been more likely, as our relation changed), to prepare me. It was a mistake, growing out of egotism or paranoia, to suspect that all actions were aimed in one's own direction. Even with a person to whom one was close: he could have, and had, his own purposes which were quite independent of one's own. That, I was sure, was true of Charles as they started talking in the guest-room. The mention of Roy Calvert had no reference to me, or to any thought of his that Roy's daughter and I had been dissolving hostilities because of him. He had her on his mind, that was all.

But there had come an opportunity, or a turn in the talk, so that he could say something, not much but something, which he wished me to hear. It might have been easier to do so via Luke, using him as an interpreter, so to speak: quite likely it was: whether out of consideration, or semi-secretiveness, or father-son aphasia, of which we all knew the intermittences, scarcely mattered.

The one certain thing was that he had passed on a message. If I asked for its final meaning, should I be evaded? There had been the best of openings to tell me, if he chose. He knew, it didn't need repeating, it would oppress him if repeated, what I wanted for him. Not his happiness: that was for him to get: to wish that would have been mawkish, and though I could be so about acquaintances, I wasn't about those closest to me. But I did wish, in the most elementary and primal fashion, for his well-being. He knew that well enough. Once when he was nine or ten I had taken him for a walk, and he had rushed in front of a car. Quick-footed he had backed away, with not more than inches to spare. The driver cursed "You won't have a long life, you won't." Charles saw that I was pallid and couldn't speak. Sometimes when still a child he asked me about it, and got brushing-off answers. Then he gave up asking. But when my eye went wrong he took my arm with solicitous and much more than filial care, much more compensatory than filial, whenever I had to cross a road. On our corner table, there was a round of drinks. Walter Luke was giving instruction to Charles about science in the last war, pointing with blunt fingers at the end of a stiff, strong arm. Charles had returned to his absorbent posture, chin in hand.

THIRTY-NINE

UNINVITED GUEST

Although towards the end of November Margaret received news that Maurice's wife was pregnant, it was not until Christmas that we saw her. Meanwhile Margaret, whom I have never known beg for favours except for her elder son, was shamelessly using any influence either of us possessed to get him a job in London. She wasn't searching for anything lofty—just the equivalent of what he was doing in the Manchester hospital or perhaps a clerkship in an almoner's office. "Though I expect he'd think that was too soft an option for him, wouldn't he?" she said. She was smiling, making a decent show of being sarcastic, but underneath the sarcasm melted away.

Still, she was being practical. When the baby was born, she was determined to be within reach. Expecting what? Her moods oscillated as I watched them; some moments she was very happy, almost triumphant, as she had been when she was pregnant herself; at others she was dreading, with a rational dread with which I was touched myself, that the child would be born afflicted. Yes, there was a chance, said some of the medical scientists, told of the mother's family history. Not worse than one in four, perhaps better than one in sixteen. But these were worse odds than one got in any of the ordinary risks of life.

Whatever could be done, Margaret was doing. From the

375

beginning the child was to have the best doctors, whether Maurice and his wife liked it or not. I told her she was behaving like old Mr. March in his heyday (I should have mentioned Azik Schiff too, if this conversation had happened three months earlier). Margaret replied: "You know what I feel about his marriage, you haven't needed telling, have you?" Just for once she was asking for pity or even pitying herself. "Well, if they get a healthy child, that'll make up for everything, I swear I'll be good to it. And to her as well."

"So you will if the child is born—unlucky," I said. "Even more so."

I meant it. There were some, including Margaret, who thought that her son Maurice was naturally good. Margaret had more original sin, maybe, but she made herself good by effort. There was no one who would behave better and more patiently—though she wasn't patient by nature—if the baby was what she often feared. She would cherish it and its mother, so that everyone thought such love came easy to her. She had invited them to stay over Christmas with us, and on Christmas Eve we had what by courtesy one could call a family dinner party—with Margaret and me, Maurice and Diana, Charles and Muriel. Until recently that had been a night when we had often filled the flat with a mass all-comers' party. But, because I was surreptitiously as atavistic or superstitious as my mother, we had killed the custom dead. On December 23rd, 1963, George Passant had called on me and had, not broken, but declared the news which still at times hag-rode me: which had cut off many thoughts about one whole phase of my youth. The following night, I had had to be host to one of those mass parties. Not again. That was four years before, and the memory was still sharp and shrivelling.

And yet, as we sat at dinner, I would almost have welcomed a crowd of people trampling in soon. Diana took her place at my right hand, sidling in with her head down, giving out an air of being ill-treated, injured, self-regarding, and full of conceit. I had suspected it the first time I met her: now I couldn't miss it. Margaret had, half-heartedly to be sure, accused me of being hard on her. That I couldn't take. If I pretended not to see her as I did, who was that a kindness to? I wasn't going to patronise her. In fact, as Margaret had discovered that afternoon, she wasn't at all easy to patronise, even for the most necessary of purposes.

To begin with, she had enjoyed being made such a fuss of, which Margaret was doing, spontaneously and happily, as soon as they arrived. Wonderful about the child. Margaret's sister had no children. Margaret had the two boys. In Margaret's family this would be the first child of the new generation. Diana was frowning to understand, but Maurice did some explaining. When she had gathered in the praise, she tossed her head, just as I remembered girls at a Palais-de-Danse in the provinces when I was a youth, giving the same response when they were asked for a dance. It didn't mean they were going to refuse. It meant that they would graciously accept, saying, in the phrase which I had heard not long since from the lips of Muriel's mother, "I don't mind if I do."

Margaret was not used to north country manners, but she detected that Diana was pleased. On the other hand, she didn't detect that when Diana was pleased she did not become less obstinate but more. So that, immediately the prospect of a move to London was conveyed to her (by this time Margaret had three different offers arranged for), she refused point-blank. "I don't see why we should."

Maurice had to placate her. He might have been over-considerate or even too diffident (for it was he who did the wooing), but it was clear he hadn't mentioned the possibility, though his mother had been writing to him about it, and his replies had been grateful and willing.

"It might be a good idea, sweetie," he said.

"That's as may be. I don't see why we should."

Well, they would be nearer to his family and friends. To which she replied, with truculent accuracy, that they would be further from her family and friends.

Doctors, Margaret was speaking of. She could recommend some of the best—

"We've got doctors where we live. Ours aren't that bad."

By this time Margaret realised that this wasn't shadow-boxing. In a mother-cum-sister fashion she began to speak of the flukes of childbirth, how she was certain that Diana wasn't frightened of anything, but it would take a load off her (Margaret's) mind if they took some precautions. She would feel happier—she didn't approve of herself and she didn't expect them to, but they might humour her—if they didn't have the baby on the national health. There was a good nursing home where she had had Charles—

Diana sat with an internal smile, looking deferred to and unmoved.

As a result, when she came to the dinner table, she was the centre of attention. As usual, she was wearing a dress in dingy chocolate brown, a colour for which she seemed to have a strong predilection. In my eyes, she was plain, not ugly but plain, and the other young people were all persona-ble, her husband much more than that, the most handsome man of his age whom I had seen in that room. Still, by a proc-ess of group hypnosis, it was she whom everyone was mak-ing up to and was anxious to please. I had had a word with Charles on our own before dinner, and told him, for his mother's sake, to do his best. He gave a workmanlike smile, and as he sat by her at the table, I was surprised to see how good his best could be. I had heard from his friends that he took much trouble to help: when he hadn't a purpose of his own, he had, so they suggested, a lot of free energy, which he would dispense on anyone, without much favouritism or horns-and-halo partiality, who seemed to need it.

Certainly he was making more progress with Diana than any of us. I heard him begin on the attractions of London. Well, that might soften her some time, I thought, concerned for Margaret. As for myself, I shouldn't have been sorry for that dinner party to be broken up. I was sitting between Diana with whom I couldn't communicate and who showed no desire to communicate with me—and Muriel, with whom I could communicate, but who had communicated much that we couldn't mention at that table, so that we were shy and abrupt with each other.

After dinner, Diana was sitting on the sofa between her husband and Charles. She was still being courted by Charles, but his conversational energies were flagging. Maurice watched with an affectionate smile, apparently gratified that she was receiving so much attention. The rest of us scattered round the room, Muriel preoccupied, Margaret once or twice glancing at me as though wishing that she and I had been trained to do simple conjuring tricks. It was about a quarter past nine, just about the time when, before the George Passant trauma, the first big wave of the Christmas party came breaking in. I asked round the room whether anyone would like more to drink. No takers. With someone to join me, I should have been ready to drink a good deal, which nowadays I rarely did.

Then there was a ring at the front-door bell. While Margaret and I were speculating—it wouldn't be a visitor, perhaps a Christmas delivery from a shop—Charles went out to answer. A voice from the hall. He returned, looking not self-possessed but clouded, followed by his cousin Pat.

"Hallo, Aunt Meg!" He kissed her cheek. "Hallo, Uncle Lew!" He made a bow, ceremonious and stately, to his former wife. He shook hands with the other two, and stood in the middle of the room, brown eyes bright, vigilant and defiant, rocking springily on his heels.

"What are you doing in London?" I was the first to speak to him.

"Oh, I just thought there might be a party on."

That couldn't be true. He knew, as well as anyone there, that the old parties had been suspended for four years past. He didn't even bother to make the pretext plausible.

Where was his wife, Margaret asked. That was his second wife, Vicky, whom we liked much more than we liked Pat. Oh, she was in Cambridge with his father. He (Pat) would drive down and join them late that night.

"Who else do you think is there?" He darted the question at his cousin with the sparkle of one who held the initiative and intended to keep it.

"How do I know?" Charles was gruff.

"A friend of yours?"

Charles made no response.

"A boy called Grenfell."

"Is he, by God?" Charles couldn't keep back a flash of interest.

"I have a tiny suspicion—of course that may just be me—but a tiny suspicion that my lady mother fancies that he might be rather a good match."

Smiles, reluctant, wintry, but nevertheless smiles from Margaret and Muriel. Maurice, who had often defended Pat, said amiably:

"What does Nina think?"

"My dear sister doesn't give a thought to such mundane things." Pause. "That doesn't mean, though, that she won't snaffle him."

More shamefaced smiles. His deserts might be small, no guest had ever appeared more often uninvited, but there was no denying that he had brightened the evening. But why had he come? Not to indulge in mild malice at the expense of his family. Not even to bring out miscellaneous items of news, regardless of accuracy. Was he there simply out of inquisitiveness? Or mischief-making? (In the midst of his high jinks, his eyes strayed more than once in the direction of Muriel.) More likely, I thought, it was nothing more than one of his whims.

When he had sat down, taking a chair midway between Muriel and Charles, and been given a glass of the Christmas champagne, he began telling me about my native town. For, since he had at last married Vicky, he had been living there, supported, one presumed, by Vicky's earnings as a doctor. It was strange to have those two as my only link with that place. Particularly as Pat's news, though it might be inaccurate, had a knack of being disconcerting. He had been seeing the Patemans, father and son. With glee he told me that they were inclined to think that I had "let them down." Particularly Pateman Senior. He had come to the conclusion that I wasn't a "man you could rely on." "Fine words butter no parsnips" was Mr. Pateman's considered view of my intervention in his affairs. Unless, and this was more sinister, I had my own reasons for not helping him as he patently deserved.

I cursed. When I thought of the time and trouble, and even the money, that I had spent on that man—the hours in that horrible back room of his, listening to the grating voice —Margaret and Charles, who knew the whole story, were laughing out loud at me. They couldn't understand how I had put up with him. I was supposed to be realistic: I had heard him speak with disapproval, rancour and hate of everyone who had helped him: and here I was, upset when I found he was doing the same about me. While they were laughing, I noticed Pat address Muriel directly for the first time. I didn't pick up the question, but across the room came Muriel's clear reply.

"Very well."

By this time, Charles, cutting his laughter short, was attending. We all heard Pat continue:

"How's the new house?"

"Doing very nicely, thank you."

Charles put in:

"It's very comfortable to live in."

If he had been older, he might have left that alone, I thought. He need not have impressed the situation upon Pat —who certainly knew, not only that Charles was living in the house, but also the exact date when he moved in.

"I'm very very glad that's worked, I really am." Pat was still speaking to Muriel, with great earnestness, as though he had been deeply concerned about the practicability of the house. Yet there was a streak of ambiguity, as if he just conceivably might not be referring to the house at all.

Muriel had been answering with unflurried coolness. I doubted whether an outsider, judging from her manner alone, could have imagined that they had ever been married. It sounded as though he might not have been inside Chester Row, though I knew he had been, at least once, to pay a dutiful visit to the baby. When he did so, his manner wouldn't have varied, it would have been precisely as it was now.

Pat turned, like a friend of the family, to Charles.

"How's the work going, Carlo?"

Just as Charles had seen the beauty of Mr. Pateman's behaviour, so I saw the beauty of this. Pat had done no work either at Cambridge or the College of Art, and had been ejected from each: Charles worked like a scholar. Now Pat was enquiring with an expression of faintly worried responsibility, like an elder person concerned about an undergraduate's progress.

"Well enough." Charles sounded oddly gauche, unable to match Muriel's style.

"Never mind, you won't have to stand it much longer."

"You needn't worry about me."

"My dear Carlo, of course we do, we all do, you know that, don't you?"

Charles muttered something. It was a long time since I had seen him at such a disadvantage. The rest of us were embarrassed—or more uneasy than that—at Pat's display. I for one couldn't tell whether it was effrontery for the sake of effrontery or whether there were double meanings.

"Of course you'll soon be going out into the great wide world, won't you?"

"Who knows?" Charles tried to be casual.

"Why shouldn't you?" Pat gave him a knowledgeable nudging smile. "We all know that there's some money coming to you before long. After all you'll be twenty-one in a year and a bit, March, isn't it? Then you can do what you damned well please."

Here I was taken off guard. The only person who should have known about the trust for Charles were Margaret, the trustees, who were lawyers, Muriel, whom I had told, and Charles himself.

"You know, you can get married if you want, can't you?" said Pat.

Charles didn't reply.

"You two can get married soon, there's nothing to stop you, is there?"

This had to stop. But neither Margaret nor I were much more effective than Charles. It was Maurice who said: "Don't bother, Pat, everything will be all right, he'll be fine."

Whether that would have stopped Pat before, one couldn't tell. Perhaps he had gone as far as he intended. He went on with minor semi-affectionate jabs at Charles, but nothing outrageous. Among those who were listening, there was one curious feature. Muriel was not taut; she wasn't even cool or blank-faced: she was smiling, like one who, used to this kind of scene, was ready to laugh it off.

Not so much later, Diana, who could have thought that the attention had faded from her, announced to Maurice that she wanted to go to bed. Seizing on the excuse, I was on my feet. I heard Pat talking to Muriel and Charles. He could drive them to Chester Row. It would be no trouble, he wouldn't get to Cambridge anyway until the early morning. It was clear that he intended to go into the house with them, as though nothing ought to be allowed to separate the trio.

When we were in our bedroom, door shut, safe by ourselves, Margaret sat on the bed and exclaimed: "God, what a night."

I said I'd had more than enough of Christmas Eves.

"I take it," said Margaret, "that nephew of yours is trying to break up their ménage?"

"It looks like it," I said.

"Why?"

"He might be after her again himself. It might be sheer devilry."

"If it wasn't for Martin," she said, "I'd get rid of him for good."

She looked reflective, and went on:

"Once, you know, I'd have been glad for anyone, even if it was that little snake, to get Carlo out of her hands."

She added:

"I don't know, now I sometimes think I'm getting reconciled to her."

Before we went to sleep, after we had talked over Maurice and his wife, soothing ourselves with the inquest, Margaret said: "I wonder if any single one of us got what he wanted tonight?"

FORTY

CALL NO MAN
HAPPY UNTIL—

After Christmas we did not see Maurice again, and Charles only for an hour or two, during the rest of the winter. Letters from Maurice were, however, arriving often, and untypically they were businesslike letters: for, to my surprise if no one else's, Margaret had got her way, and Maurice and his wife were moving to London after Easter, well before the child was due. Whether this was a success for Charles's persuasive powers, none of us could tell: but certainly he not only cajoled Diana on Christmas Eve, but had persisted, spending a weekend with them in Manchester to do so.

There was also another kind of cajolery going on. Pat, so we heard, had been seen with Charles in Cambridge, and Muriel told me, as a matter of fact, without explanation, that he had called on her twice when she was alone. She said nothing more, but it had all the appearance of a deliberate campaign. With labile characters such as Pat, the line was precarious (as I had learned with bitterness much earlier in my life) between being a busy-body and being destructive for destructiveness's sake.

In January, I had heard something which made our family seem lucky. For some reason that went out of mind, I had been dining by myself at the Athenaeum. Towards the end of my meal, I was staring out of the window at the reflection of the table lights, when someone close by uttered my name. It was Leonard Getliffe.

"I've very glad to see you, Lewis. I was going to ring you up."

I asked him to help me finish the wine, which he wouldn't: he sat down on the opposite side of the table.

"I wanted to tell you about my father," he said.

His clever conceptualiser's face looked cheerful, and at the sight of him I felt so myself.

"He's been ill. Oh, it's coming out all right, we're all delighted. But it's important that the news shouldn't get around."

I said that I had had some practice in guarding the news of illnesses, including my own.

"We thought of telling you when it happened. Three or four months ago. But we decided that the possibility of leakage was directly proportional to the number of people who knew."

That might be statistically true, I was thinking. It was also somewhat bleak to tell to a man's oldest friend. But Leonard wasn't really being bleak, he was indulging in what his colleagues called cat-humour.

Francis hadn't been specially well all the summer. "At Viredoux" (that was the house in Provence) "he'd been coughing a lot, but said it was bronchitis. He used to have it in Cambridge, you know, that was one of the reasons for taking a pied-à-terre somewhere else."

Leonard went on.

"Well, he wasn't feeling quite up to coming back at the beginning of last term. So Katherine persuaded him, he'd always hated the idea of doctors of course, to go and let them look him over in Nîmes."

"Yes?"

"They found he had a spot on one lung. They operated at

once, very skilfully, Francis says. He has a lot of use for their experimental technique. It was perfectly successful. He's convalescing down there now. It'll be a bit of time before he's back to optimum form, but he's remarkably well. His morale is very high and he's fretting about not being back at the lab. He's feeling stronger every day. We're all extremely pleased with him. I think we were more worried than he was, but that's gone now. We want to get him back in Cambridge by April. He's very eager to see you, by the by."

I tried to show no sign of disbelief as I gazed into the intelligent innocent face. From the moment he mentioned the operation, I had been horrified. Perhaps, I wanted to think, old anxieties were running away with me, Leonard might be right, Francis was not a self-deceiver.

I could not shift my own mood for an instant. I found Leonard's euphoria dismaying, and anything he said of Francis's. After a few flat questions—I did not want to puncture Leonard's well-being, but I could not, for premonition's sake, not honesty's, give any expression of pleasure or relief— I made an excuse, and went home.

As soon as I arrived there, I telephoned Charles March. Since old Mr. March's death, Charles had been reconciled to his sister and her husband, but it was the kind of reconciliation in which the years of difference were covered up, not eliminated or transformed. Still, he might have heard from them.

When I asked, that turned out to be true. What did he think, as a doctor?

There was a long pause at the other end. "I haven't enough to go on, I haven't even seen him. One's opinion isn't much use—"

Charles was growing more hesitant as he passed into his sixties. The fire and devil of his youth—and the unfairness

—did not often show. He was more inclined to speak like a responsible citizen who didn't want to be quoted.

"No, but what is it? I want to know what you think, that's all."

Another long pause.

"If it were you or me, I doubt if we should be as optimistic as they are."

"No."

"Mind, sometimes these operations really work." Charles mentioned some cases of cancer which he had seen.

"How would you put his chances?"

He refused to make a guess. Then he said: "If what you're afraid of did happen—and you know I'm as afraid of it as you are—then I'm terribly worried for Katherine. She loves her children, but he's been her whole life."

That same night, I wrote to her, carefully casual, saying I had just seen Leonard and was hoping that all continued well. A reply came about a fortnight later, from Francis himself, as euphoric as Leonard's report had been. Of course, he couldn't expect to get all his strength back overnight; it would take months rather than weeks; but they would expect Margaret and me in Cambridge in the summer. With a blend of invalid concentration and scientific interest, he enclosed a sketch of the original X ray of his lungs, and a diagram showing how the surgeons had operated.

That letter arrived at the beginning of February. In April —our own family concerns still, so far as we knew, unchanged—came one from Katherine. In her bold and steady hand, it read: "All the children have had to be told, and I have also written to my brother. I'm sure that Francis would think that you ought to know too. He has not been so well for two or three weeks past, and last weekend went into hospital again. The disease has spread to the other lung and has advanced quickly there. There is nothing to say except that this promises badly. Francis has a desire to return home. The hospital people are trying to resist this, but I cannot see that they have any reason on their side."

At the end of May, just at the time when the examination results were coming out, a telegram from Cambridge:

Francis died peacefully this morning. Katherine Leonard Lionel Mary Penelope

The obituary notices were the longest of those for any of my friends, but they were stiff records of achievement, as though Francis's public persona had warded off the writers from coming anywhere near him. A few personal notes followed, a surprisingly warm one from L of S (Luke of Salcombe), one from me. The funeral was private. That seemed to be the end.

Then in the post arrived the neat little envelope, the printed slip, announcing a memorial service after a Cambridge death. How many services for fellows of the college in my time? Vernon Royce, Roy Calvert, Despard-Smith, Eustice Pilbrow, C.P. Crystal, Winslow, Paul Jago, Crawford, M.H.L. Gay. But this was the one I least expected to hear of. Even after I was anticipating Francis's death. For he was the firmest of unbelievers, who didn't attend memorial services for others and would have repudiated one such for himself. True, he had made a kind of apology for not going to Roy Calvert's, but that had been a gesture of consolation to me, perhaps of regret that he had not liked Roy better. When that had happened, and we were all young men, I had not imagined, in the midst of grief, that one day I should be attending a service for Francis himself. Nor could I have imagined that I should feel such a sense of loss.

Staying in Martin's house, within the college precincts, the night before the service, I confessed, what Margaret already knew, that I was sad in a way I didn't look for. After all, at my age one had seen enough of death. Including one's own, said Martin, with his own brand of nordic irony. Including one's own, I agreed. Oh, be quiet, said Irene, who had become fond of me, now that she was middle aged.

Margaret had spent the afternoon with Katherine, and was silent now.

Through the open window of Martin's drawing-room, we could hear shouts in the court below. Glancing down, I caught sight of a posse of young men jostling along the path, some of them carrying suitcases. Another young man was walking between a middle-aged couple, perhaps his parents. That had been the last of the degree days, one of the less dramatic ritual occasions, graduates kneeling before the Vice-Chancellor and then being congratulated by tutors with meaningless heartiness on a feat which had been public knowledge some weeks before. In my time, the ceremony was becoming obsolescent, the independent young did not bother to attend: yet those below had been participating, somehow it still survived.

Although the sky was clear, turning dense indigo to the east, away from the sunset, it had been raining during the afternoon. The night seemed warmish, which we were not used to in that wet and frigid summer. There blew in wafts of flower scents, strong in the humid air. The smell of syringa, tantalising, aphrodisiac, poignant, prevailed over the rest. It brought back, not a memory, but a kind of vague disquiet: if I could remember an occasion when I had smelt the syringa so— Perhaps in that place? No, I couldn't trace it. Just the scent, unease, the sensual knowledge that there had been other nights like this.

We had already heard from Martin how the memorial service had come about. As soon as Francis was dead, the Master, G.S. Clark, had been pressing condolences upon Katherine. The fact that he had detested Francis, and that

Francis had not been over-indulgent in return, seemed only to have enhanced the Master's compassion. In his ardour, he had insisted there should be a service. Katherine believed as little as Francis and must have known his wishes: so did Leonard and the rest of the Getliffe family. The Master had borne them down.

It wasn't that Katherine was as yet deadened by sorrow: on the contrary, having had to watch her husband through the long illness, she had returned to a kind of activity, an illusory vigour that might not last her long. She had argued about the service, and so had the family, but the truth was, they all wanted to agree.

They were holding on to anything that kept Francis in others' minds: or perhaps, more primitive than that, they had the feeling that while his name was being mentioned he was not quite obliterated, his shadow (they would have liked to say his spirit or his ghost) was still there. Just as Martin himself had returned to a primitive piety when our father died, and had proposed that he should be buried according to religious rites in which Martin was the last person to believe.

Once Clark had won the Getliffes over, there followed one of the traditional college struggles, though for kindness's sake Martin had let none of this reach Leonard, not to speak of Katherine. The question was, who was to give the memorial address. In the past this had been the prerogative of old Despard-Smith, the only fellow then in orders. With the result that he had made the oration over Roy Calvert, for whom he cherished extreme and ominous disapproval. Now, by a grisly coincidence, the pattern was repeating itself. There was at present no fellow in orders. So the Master assumed it was his own prescriptive right to make memorial orations. He had every intention of doing so for Francis Getliffe, for whom in life he had scarcely had one amiable thought.

Martin couldn't explain why Clark was so set on this. It might have been he couldn't resist, Martin suggested, "getting into the act": after all, Francis was an eminent man. Or it might have been Christian charity. Martin, who was no more disposed to give Clark the benefit of the doubt than Francis had been, did not regard that suggestion of his own with favour.

In any case, Clark's address was not to happen. Feeling ran round the college, for Francis had become revered by most of the younger fellows. And Arthur Brown, the elder statesman, seventy-seven years old, was deputed to make representations to the Master. Over Roy Calvert's memorial service, Arthur Brown had tried to displace Despard-Smith, and had failed. This time, in old age, the senior fellow since the death of Gay, Arthur was happy to have another go. He was himself, so Martin said, as moved as the younger men. He had a good deal of affection, and more respect, for Francis, despite his affiliations with a government which Arthur was increasingly prone to describe in terms that a Russian emigré in 1920 might have considered sensible as applied to Lenin's administration, but perhaps a little over-strong. As for Arthur's opinion of the Master, he would not have mentioned that except to one of his old allies, and they had died or left the college, leaving him alone.

The upshot was that Arthur Brown had emerged from the Lodge, looking contented but flushed, and told the protesters that he would deliver the oration himself. "It won't be exactly a rabble-rouser," Martin had said that evening when he told the story, "but it'll be perfectly decent. Which is more than we had a right to expect."

Since we arrived, Martin and Irene had been waiting to

tell us their own news. Irene had known Francis only as an acquaintance, and wasn't pretending to more than a social sorrow. Martin had lost a friend, and more significantly, an ally, but you could lose friends and allies and still enjoy your joys within the next half-hour. Unlike me, Martin had not known Francis for a lifetime. I was absentminded, even when they felt that deference to mourning had been duly paid.

I was absentminded, thinking of that occasion in hospital when Francis had said that if I died he would miss me. At the time it had sounded unusually unrestrained for Francis, and simultaneously a little inadequate and a little sentimental. Now I could test it for myself. He had known better than I had. I was already missing him. No more, no less. It wasn't the fierce and comminatory grief which came like a brainstorm or illness at the death of someone you loved. This was different. Someone you had known for a lifetime. Missing was the right word. To say any more would have been sentimental: but so would to say any less.

Meanwhile, Martin and Irene hadn't been able to suppress their triumph. The day before, Nina had become engaged to Guy Grenfell. All tied up and formal. The announcement would appear in *The Times* later that week. There had been family conferences and negotiations because she was so young.

I had seldom seen my brother look so happy. It seemed that all those disappointments and humiliations over his son had been cancelled. It was a pleasingly sarcastic flick—very much in his own style, though he wouldn't have been grateful for being reminded of it now—that this should happen through the daughter to whom until recently he had given casual affection but not much more.

"Old Grenfell," he said, "isn't a bad old creature. Eton, and the Brigade, and the City. But he's not very good at chairing a meeting. There was him and his wife, the two of us, and the young couple. It was a pretty fatal combination for getting anything done quickly. There was only one thing to settle, ought they to wait a year or not."

"I'd been around more than she was before I was her age," said Irene with a lively lubricious grin.

"You weren't marrying into a respectable family, my girl." Martin's smile was congratulatory, as though addressed not only to his wife but to Nina's mother.

"We haven't any money, of course," Martin went on. "That was made quite clear. It seemed to puzzle Mrs. G. They have quite a lot of money. That was also made quite clear. And that seemed a very reasonable state of things to Mrs. G. Somehow it also seemed a rather strong argument to her for them to wait until she's twenty-one. Old G. didn't quite see the logical connection, but he felt there was some force in it."

He said, face illumined from inside, as it appeared when for once his self-control had slipped:

"But they could have argued till the sun blows up, it wouldn't have made any difference. The girl and boy were fine. I thought Guy was a bit of a wet when she first brought him here, but I couldn't have been more wrong. He was like a rock. Very polite, long hair and all, but like a rock. He was apologetic, but they were going to get married in August. They were absolutely sure. They didn't want to be awkward, but they were absolutely sure. They would make any concessions—they'd even have a smart wedding if that would give any pleasure—they didn't want to disappoint anyone, so long as they were married in August."

Martin was extracting pleasure, more even than Irene, from the last detail of their daughter's engagement. He was fundamentally a healthy man, despite his pessimism—or perhaps it was because he was healthy that he could let his pessimism rip. My thoughts cast back to Francis: he too had rejoiced when each of his children married: it was part of the flow, there was a proper time to become a patriarch. Now Martin, whom occasionally I still regarded as my young brother, was enjoying that same proper time. It wasn't made worse (as he had commented, executing a complex gibe against himself, worldly people in general, and the worldliness of the world) because Guy was, by the standard of Martin's society, a distinctly desirable husband. Martin had had, in all external things and in some closer to him, less luck than most of us. It was good to hear him saying, without any reserve, tight lip all gone, that this was luck he hadn't counted on.

He said something else, which made me feel that I had been facile in thinking about Guy. I had assumed that he was a rich young man who relished talk of world convulsions, so long as they took place in drawing-rooms. I remembered predicting to Charles that he would finish up in a merchant bank. So far, said Martin, there was no sign of that. He was trying to find a job in famine relief. And was being held up, by a beautiful piece of security machinery, because of his part in last year's revolt.

No doubt their elders would go on waiting for Charles's circle to renege. As yet, none had done so. The only half-exception was the leader, Olly, who had recently been chosen as a Labour candidate; but as he was standing in one of the richest constituencies in London, he couldn't be said to have compromised with professional politics yet awhile.

Next morning, from Martin's drawing-room, we heard the chapel bell begin to toll. Charles had joined us there, after spending the previous night in his own college, packing ready to depart: he was wearing a black tie, as Martin and I were. As we walked along the paths through the college, other parties were converging on the chapel, women in black, like Margaret and Irene. It was all as it used to be for other memorial services, all as it was for Roy's. Through the great gate, a group of a dozen people were entering, and the first court's flags were jolted by men moving slowly, as though in time with some inaudible march, clothes and gowns dark in the bright shower-washed sunlight. The grass on the lawn was so green, the eyes dazzled.

The Chapel, its interior Georgian and seemly, was already full. Seats had been reserved for fellows and sometime-fellows and their families, and we took up ours. Opposite sat Katherine, in a grey dress, not in full mourning, the Getliffe sons and daughters, their wives and husbands. Charles and Ann March were close by, and others of Katherine's family. Chairs had been placed in the ante-chapel, under which some early Masters had been buried (and where old Gay had expressed a wish, not honoured, to lie himself). The moulded doors had been left open, and from our seats we could see the ante-chapel also full, with young men standing. Most of the faces, having been so long away from Cambridge, I didn't know. Some of them must have been from Francis's own laboratory, and I recognised one or two senior scientists from the Cavendish. There were several ministers, officers in uniform, civil servants, reminders of the strata of Francis's public life. One pair I saw, inconspicuous in the distance, Roger Quaife and his wife.

(It was, I thought later, a slice of official, or functional, England, but not one that the young were familiar with. Few people there were likely to be mentioned in gossip columns and fewer were rich. Some of the scientists had creative work of the highest order to their credit, but a young man as well informed as Gordon Bestwick would scarcely know their names.)

A hymn. A prayer: the kind of prayer, I thought, that one heard at American ceremonies, designed not to give offence to any religion. Another hymn. Then Arthur Brown, surpliced, hooded, bejowled, high-coloured, mounted the pulpit. He mounted with firm heavy steps. He had always been heavy, but getting towards eighty he was hale and carried his stomach high.

In a strong voice, vowels well rounded, he began. He began much as we expected. Yes, we were thinking, it won't be exciting, but it will be acceptable. About how Francis had been a pillar of the college, the university, the scientific community, the state. About how he was a man so just that some had thought him over-nice. "But no juster man has ever walked the courts of this college." About how he was absolutely upright in all his dealings. "He was the most scrupulous of colleagues. As well as being one of the three or four most eminent members of our society during the present century."

All that was good enough. Orotund, like Arthur Brown in public. More from the outside than he could be, talking with slow cunning about someone he knew well. Perhaps he had never known Francis well. Or not noticed the struggle between the disciplined and the acerb.

Then Arthur Brown clutched the lectern, looked down the chapel, right out through the doors, with a hard, dark, resolute gaze. "Now I have to speak in a way which may be painful for some present. But if I did not, it would be hypocrisy on my part, and hypocrisy of a kind which our colleague would have been one of the first to resent. I have to tell you that he was not a Christian. He did not believe in the religion to which this chapel is dedicated, and which some of us here profess. What is more, he did not believe in religion of any kind. He was an utterly truthful man, and he would not compromise on this matter. So far as I can remember, he entered this chapel only for the purposes of electing a Master, that is only twice in his whole life. I am certain that, if he had honoured us by becoming our Master himself, he would not have felt able to perform any ceremonial duties within the chapel." Anyone who knew Arthur Brown must have been astonished. All his life he had been confining himself to emollient and cautious words. He had much dislike for the brash or those who said "something out of place." Civility meant being careful: one's own convictions and much less one's self-expressions were no excuse for embarrassing others. But now—how much effort had it cost him?—he was letting go. Perhaps with a touch of defiance (that last remark about Francis's not taking the Mastership was not calculated to give pleasure to the present occupant, sitting in the magisterial pew) such as the prudent felt when, just for once, they were not being prudent: but more so out of duty to a dead man.

"And I cannot and will not talk of him in terms of the Christian virtues. It is more appropriate to talk and think of him in terms of a world before Christianity existed.

"He was the absolutely upright man, such as the classical world admired. His life would have been a model to them: it is easy to imagine Lucretius saying that this was how a man should be. I wish to say that to you myself, but I was not prepared to let you hear it on false pretences. He lived a life better than most of us can aspire to, but he did it without the support of any faith.

"I wish to press another thought upon you. He was, in his later years, a very happy man. Earlier he had his struggles— struggles for a better world in which some of us cannot believe, struggles on behalf of his country where we are all grateful to him. He had throughout the blessing of an ideally happy marriage, and he was doubly blessed in a family of exceptional gifts. All our sympathy goes out to his wife and children, but they should have the consolation of being certain how happy they made his life. For years past he lived in an Indian summer. He was not a man easily contented, but he had become totally contented. His scientific work had received full recognition. Only last year he was awarded the Copley medal of the Royal Society, the highest honour that the Society can give. In these past years, he had private happiness and the esteem of his peers to an extent which is not granted to many men.

"It is because of that I am presuming to offer what may be another small consolation to those who loved him. Life is always uncertain, as they have too much reason to know. Even that happiness of his might have been broken. There is a word from the classical world which he would have appreciated: *Call no man happy until he is dead*. It is little comfort to those who have lost him, but sometimes perhaps they will be able to tell themselves that he left them with his felicity unbroken."

I was gazing at Katherine, whose fine features, strong and not congruent with the matronly form, had not stirred. Arthur Brown had been through serious illness: but had he known what it was like to be warned about his death? Or what Francis felt in his last months? Call no man happy . . . what did that sound like to those who had been close by? I had heard very little about the final illness. Either Arthur Brown had forgotten both his realism and his tact, or else he had found out more.

He retired, his tread audible in the silent chapel, from the pulpit to his place. Hymn. Prayer. The fellows began to file out, the Master stopping beside the Getliffes so as to ask them to go first. In the court, knots of people were gathering on the flagstones. The Master nodded to Arthur Brown, but did not speak. Nor did Nightingale, the only other man besides Brown who had remained a fellow from my time to this.

Katherine had, however, shaken Brown's hand, and the Getliffe family were clustering round him. All seemed pleased, and without qualms. In the crowd, Margaret was talking to an old acquaintance, the Getliffes were being joined by colleagues of Francis, and I hung about waiting for a chance to speak with Arthur Brown.

When we were able to move off, the two of us, out of the ruck, I said:

"Well done."

"I hope Francis would have liked it."

"I'm sure he would." Francis wouldn't have been above thinking that, if G.S. Clark and Nightingale were affronted, not only as personal enemies, but also as religious devotees, so much the better. I didn't say that to Arthur, who was a latitudinarian member of the Church of England: disapproving of "enthusiasm", though, very much as his nineteenth century predecessors had done.

"Old friend," said Arthur, "he'll leave a gap here, you know. We're dropping off one by one."

He was speaking with regret, or nostalgia, but not like an old man. He went on:

"I wish you hadn't gone away from us, Lewis. Oh, I know you couldn't have done what you had to do if you'd stayed. But still—this isn't quite the place it was."

I said, with the whole university expanding, it couldn't be—

"I dare say it's better, but it isn't quite the same. It's not very loyal to criticise, because the college has been enormously kind to me, it has given me so much more than I deserved." That was not mock modesty, but the real thing: Arthur had never had much opinion of himself.

"But I can't get used to changes. I've reached the stage when I don't really enjoy a person's company unless I've known him for a long time."

I said: "I've found young Charles's friends a bit refreshing—"

"Ah. That reminds me." Suddenly Arthur had brightened

up. "I did want to have a word with you about that young man. Just for your ear alone. He's done perfectly splendidly, of course. It did occur to me that we might manage to construct a vacancy for him here. Mind you, I can't promise anything. I couldn't think of guaranteeing anything until I'd found out how the land was lying. There are some people who mightn't be entirely favourable. But there might be a chance that we should turn out too strong for them—"

With a touch of his old zest, with more than a touch of his old labyrinthine pertinacity, Arthur proceeded to examine how the College might be induced to elect Charles to a fellowship before "others get in first." The college had to poach nowadays, especially in subjects like Charles's which were becoming short of first-class talent— Someone had mentioned another Trinity man called Bestwick, but Arthur didn't at present feel "so keen about him."

"Of course," Arthur reiterated, "this is entirely between ourselves. I can't possibly promise anything. It might be better if you regarded this conversation as not having happened, at any rate for the time being—"

Then Arthur went up to his rooms, after an affectionate goodbye, still dubious about my discretion and inclined to treat me, as he had always done, as a man of promise not yet old enough or experienced enough to be entirely trustworthy in serious affairs.

Now the court had emptied, Margaret and Martin taking a porter with them to fetch our bags: Charles alone remained, who had earlier transported his own to the porter's lodge. He came and joined me, at the foot of the staircase which I used to climb.

"I expect you're glad that's all over," he said in a quiet and sympathetic tone, indicating the chapel. I nodded.

He hesitated. We had scarcely been alone together since Francis's death.

"I didn't know him well," he said. "But it was a comfort to feel that he was there."

That was an epitaph of which Francis might have been glad. Charles went on to mention the memorial address. Didn't it deserve very high marks for ruffling dovecotes, and putting cats among pigeons? Wouldn't it be mildly fun to be dining at high table that night? Charles didn't need telling that this had been the most uncharacteristic gesture— almost the only gesture—of old Arthur's peaceloving college life.

He did need telling, though, of something which wasn't at all uncharacteristic, Arthur's desire to manipulate the college machine once more, this time on behalf of Charles himself. Charles said:

"He's a sweet old man."

Not always so sweet, when he was in action, I said. Charles was smiling. He gave no indication of whether the offer meant anything to him, yes or no: or even whether he would, in Arthur's own old phrase, sleep on it.

On the other hand, he was disturbed that Arthur seemed to have ruled Gordon Bestwick out.

"What the hell is the matter? If you don't mind me saying it, this isn't a great College. By God, they won't get a chap like Gordon once in ten years—"

Somebody else would take him, I said, but Charles was not appeased.

Couldn't I use my influence with Arthur to get him to think again? I said, neither I nor anyone else had any influence with Arthur. Once his mind was set, he was as obstinate as a mule.

Charles, not satisfied, was wondering about other approaches. It hadn't occurred to him, apparently, that Gordon's reputation as an activist would not be an overpowering inducement to Arthur Brown. Perhaps because Charles did not find his own getting in his way: but then he had been more discreet, and would in any case be forgiven a great deal by Arthur. Anyway, I was relieved that Charles was for once less than acute. I didn't wish to quarrel about politics that day; nor more did he. He was being easy and friendly, ready either to amuse or soothe or just stay at my side.

We walked, very slowly, clockwise round the court. Looking at the Lodge and Hall, lines clear, stone honey-coloured in the sun, I told him what I thought to myself that October evening nearly three years before. When I first saw those buildings, they were grey with the soot of years, and covered with creeper. Now, the theory was, we saw them as when they were built—except that the windows would have been entirely different, the façade of another kind of stone, and the roof of the Hall feet lower. Charles, not specially modernist in visual taste, said:

"I expect it always looked pretty pleasant, though."

He added:

"It's very handsome, in a quiet way, isn't it?"

He might have said that to please me, but it was true. He might have said also—but that wouldn't have come so easy to him—that it was very English. At least, I had never seen anything like it out of England.

In the bedroom of the Lodge, a light had been left on, pale and unavailing in the sunshine.

"You must have walked round here a good few times," he said.

"Yes, quite a few."

He smiled. "In various assorted moods, if I know you."

"Yes, that too."

He couldn't have divined it, but without any justification at all, since Martin was there to be visited, I had had a feeling, hard-cut, dismissive, that I was seeing the place for the last time.

FORTY-ONE

A BEARER
OF BAD NEWS

It was a domestic scene such as we had once been used to,
and were no longer. Our drawing-room: lights already on,
though the time was only nine o'clock, a few days after mid-
summer. Outside, a cool cloudy evening, for, since the day of
Francis's memorial service, the weather had returned to
form. Present, along with me, Margaret and her two sons. It
was a family evening which, a few years before, we should
have taken for granted and thought nothing of.

As it was, Maurice had come to the flat because his wife
had gone into hospital. The baby was a few days overdue,
and both he and Margaret were conscious of the telephone
beside the door. It was the first time I had seen Maurice
show the effects of suspense, or of waiting. In the periods
when he had taken examinations, he had, with maddening
acceptance, not been anxious about the results, assuming
them to be bad: he hadn't ever appeared worried about
someone turning up for an assignation, as the rest of us had
been, watching the clock on the restaurant wall, making excuses for the non-arrival, with pique, anger, and with longing.

Now Maurice, though he made no complaint, seemed no
better at waiting than anyone else.

His only sign of the old self-forgetfulness came soon after
he had met Charles that evening. Maurice had said, gently

405

but unhesitantly, that he hoped Muriel was well and happy. And that he hoped Charles was "looking after her." No one else would have spoken to Charles like that. It might have seemed impertinent, if it hadn't been said with so little self-assertion. Anyway, Charles took it, though he didn't make an explicit reply.

Whether Maurice knew or not, Charles had been sleeping in his old bedroom at the flat since, less than a week before, we returned from Cambridge.

During the daytime he had been nearly always out, possibly with Muriel: one heard him telephoning her each morning. He seemed in high spirits, with patches of contemplativeness. He gave no indication that he also was in a period of waiting.

That evening, as we sat chatting, chatting to induce the telephone to ring, Margaret occasionally gazed at the two of them—her innocent, her strenuous one—and then at me. She might have been thinking of the time we had talked about them in that room. The events of their growing up, commonplace to everyone else as another family's photographs, at times dramatic, searing rather than dramatic, to us. I recalled (I didn't have to bring it back to memory, it was always there) the morning when we sat there, having been told that Charles, then an infant, was recovering from meningitis. In thanksgiving, we didn't speak about him but about Maurice. We repeated, just as we had said in the hospital, *we must save him from everything we can.* Margaret had been as good as her vow: her love for Maurice had deepened, not grown less, deepened with the trouble he had caused her, not through conflict but through ineptitude or lack of self. As for me, I had tried to follow her. Other men, I thought again that evening, would have done better.

Two days later, the child, a girl, was born. The first medical reports were encouraging. As a newborn baby, she

seemed everything she ought to be. Of course, some disabili-
ties they couldn't test for, yet. It would be weeks or months
before they knew. So that one of Margaret's anxieties was
not eliminated, though for the time being assuaged. She
couldn't let herself go, but, trying to suppress it, she was full
of joy.

The baby was born on the second of July. The medical
opinions reached her next day. That same evening, I was entertaining a foreign acquaintance at a club. When I arrived
home, it was quite early, not yet half-past ten, but the drawing-room lights were switched off. Margaret called from our
bedroom.

She was not undressed, but was sitting on the chair in
front of her dressing table.

"Carlo has been talking to me," she said. "I think he's
gone off to tell Muriel."

"What is it?"

"He asked me to tell you. Of course he'll see you tomorrow."

"What is it?"

I knew her face so well, yet it was difficult to read. Her
eyes were bright, her cheeks a little flushed. In a temper she
sometimes looked like that, but at that moment her temper
was cool. "He's come out with his plans. I ought to say that
he was extraordinarily nice. He even waited to talk until he
knew that I wasn't anxious about the baby." (Just as, I had a
recollection, my first wife had once delayed telling me the
most wounding news—until I was in good health.) "Mind
you, I fancy he's been certain himself for quite a time."

"What is it?"

She made me sit down on the bed. She said:

"My love, a part of this you're not going to like. Most of it
seems perfectly sensible. Anyway it may be right for him."

Angrily, I told her that I liked news broken fast. I was already ready to punish her for being the bearer of bad news. Sitting there, she seemed more guilty than Charles could be—

"He has it all worked out."

Then, quite quickly, she told me. He had decided that he must make a name within a few years. The world was going too fast, he wanted to have some sort of say before he was middle aged. He had been studying the careers of the American foreign correspondents in the Thirties. They had done their piece. He didn't see why he shouldn't do as well. Languages weren't a problem to him. Politics he knew as much about as most people his age. He had no racial feeling, he could live anywhere. He was used to hard travelling—

"That's not very dreadful," I said. Yes, it might suit him.

"You haven't heard it all." He was determined to have his say in the minimum possible time. Other people could do what he proposed to do. He had to get his nose in front. Once he was recognised at all, he could rely on—what he was too cautious to call his talent. Though he was right, Margaret said, he had most of the qualities to become a pundit. He wanted to be a sane voice. But, to do that, he had to start with something a bit out of the ordinary—

"What is it?" I cried out again.

"That's where the risk comes in," said Margaret.

"What risk?"

He accepted that he couldn't persuade a paper to use him yet awhile, she said. He had to prove himself. So he was setting off to get near the action: meaning, to begin with, the Middle East. He would have to work himself as near battles as he could. Somehow, within a year or two, he was going to find something to sell: then some paper or other would employ him. It wasn't going to be pleasant. He insisted that he was extremely cowardly. Still, that was part of the exercise. Brave men weren't specially good at becoming international pundits. He had worked out the odds, and meant to take his chance.

"Good God," I said, "how romantic is all this?"

I asked her, still angry with her because she had borne the news, whether she had tried to dissuade him.

"I said that it wasn't what I should have chosen for him," said Margaret.

"What did he say to that?"

"He said that he realised it. And that you wouldn't have chosen it for him either."

He had told her also that he had wished all along that he could settle for something which we should like. But you can live only in your own time, he said.

"And he's determined to go on with this?"

"He didn't tell me in so many words, but I'm sure that the arrangements are already made."

That rang clear as truth, as soon as I heard it. As with my brother Martin, Charles's calculations were performed long before he spoke, perhaps before he knew that his own decision was already final.

"Does he know," I said, "that I shan't have an easy night until this is over?"

"Do you think I shall?"

"That may be for the rest of my life."

"Have you forgotten that he's mine as well as yours?"

For an instant we were blaming each other. She was appealing for me to come close to her: while in pain and rage I was wishing that everyone round us could be torn down, along with me, if this I had to endure. I felt as savage, as possessed, as I had in other miseries, not many of them in my entire life, two deaths perhaps, Charles's own illness. I felt at that moment without relief or softening from age or any consolation that had come to me.

"Is he thinking of anyone else at all?"

Margaret did not reply.

"Does he know what it means to anyone else?"

Margaret said:

"He's pretty perceptive, and I'm certain that he does."

"Is *that* why he's doing it?"

Margaret and I glanced at each other, thinking of how we had protected him in his childhood, knowing that we couldn't have another, telling ourselves that this was a precious life. The first time I saw him in hospital, I had taken him, rolling-eyed, waving-fingered, into my arms, resolved that no harm should come to him.

"No," said Margaret, "you mustn't take more responsibility than you have already."

She meant, what I had said to her often enough, that affections, especially in families, didn't carry the same weight on either side. I ought to have known that, from the way I behaved to my mother. It was a kind of vanity to suspect that another's choices depended on his relations with oneself. Choices, lives, were lonelier than that. Charles was making a choice lonelier than most of ours had been. That was no consolation for me, sitting there in the bedroom. All I could do was think of him not with affection, not even with concern, but with anger mixed with a kind of fellow-feeling, or a brutal sympathy of the flesh.

It took me a long time before I could say to Margaret that I had been cruel, shutting her out when she spoke about Charles as her son, and that without her to tell it, the news would have been worse.

FORTY-TWO

FINGERTIP
TO FINGERTIP

The next morning, Charles did not get up for breakfast, but soon after joined me in the drawing-room. After he had uttered a greeting, bright and neutral, he sat in a chair opposite mine across the disused fireplace.

"I think Mummy has told you, hasn't she?" His tone was easy and intimate: the only sign that he might not be free from strain was that he fell back on that term from childhood.

"Yes, she has. Last night."

He said:

"I'm sorry if I've disappointed you."

I did not reply at once and he went on:

"I'm very sorry. Believe me."

"Of course you haven't disappointed me."

"Well," he said, more freely now, "it isn't exactly what you might have looked for, is it?"

"You've done far more than I had at your age. With any luck you'll go on doing more."

"I shall need a bit of luck—"

"Yes, I know that."

I hadn't been speaking out of self-control, or even out of resignation. I hadn't prepared myself for how to meet him, there were none of the speeches which one made up in one's head and never spoke. In his presence I felt nothing of the anger, or the suspicion, that a few hours before I had projected onto Margaret. To my own astonishment I was buoyed up—by what was it? Maybe his energy or his resolution. Or it might have been his nerve. At no time in my life could I have done what he was committing himself to do. It seemed as though a new force had taken charge.

He must have realised that there were going to be no reproaches. More, he may have seen that a kind of relief, not happiness or content but more like trust, had come into the air between us. Neither of us could have known the reason. Ties, half-memories, the sympathy of those who are close together even where their purposes contradict each other? Later, I wondered whether I was stirred by something of myself which, that morning, had been long forgotten.

When I was younger than Charles, less educated, much less sophisticated, I had once declared my hopes. They had been embarrassing to recall in middle life. Asked by a girl who loved me a little, what I wanted, I had said—not to spend my life unknown: love: a better world. Those hopes might have been embarrassing later, but they were true of me at the time I spoke, a good deal truer than any refinements and complications would have been.

Yes, the first of them died on one, or waned. Yet it drove me on for the first half of my life. As for the second, when I said it in that old-fashioned schoolroom, I didn't have any intimation of where it would lead me, either in the search for sexual love or that other kind, which I felt for my son, sitting there across the fireplace: but it had lasted until now. But the one that I shouldn't have confessed to, even a few years later, because it sounded so priggish or worse still so innocent, that had been true too.

It wasn't as passionate as personal desires—nor as haunting as the sense of the "I" alone, oneself alone—but it was there. It had bound Francis Getliffe and me together all our

working lives. It led us into defeats and sometimes humiliations, led us either through our temperaments or through a
set of chances, into backstairs' work, secrets, all kinds of
closed politics. Of course, it wasn't pure. Our own self-esteem took part, or certainly mine did. Nevertheless, trying to
judge myself as indulgently as Father Ailwyn had instructed
me, I believed that I had wanted some good things. Whether
I had helped to get any, that was another matter. Very little,
I had often thought before, both of Francis and myself. The
only work which I was certain had been useful took place in
the war; and there we were avoiding a worse world, not making a better one.

Yet some of the pleasure—utterly unanticipated by either
of us—which I felt in Charles's presence that morning, was
because he too had the same desire. He too might be rapa-
cious, as much as I had been, and self-absorbed, possibly
more. There was, though, something left. It wasn't the simple and good, such as Maurice, who had vitality to spare for
tasks outside themselves. Charles had plenty. He would use
it differently from the way I had done. He might be more
effective. All might go wrong. He might throw himself away.
Still, even the bare desire was like a touch fingertip to fingertip, conducting a phase of life.

I said: "I can understand that you're in a hurry. But can't
you get a footing in some slightly less dramatic way?"

"You don't believe I haven't thought of that?"

"Well, why not?"

"It isn't on." Charles gave a rationale, clear and patient, of
what he was aiming at. Only in his generation, he said, could
you become a spokesman before the age of thirty. But plenty
of people, at least as competent as he was, would like to be
such a spokesman. To get there, you had to do something
special.

"You're telling me this is the only way?"

"I think it is for me. If I were more of a performer, I might find another way in. But I'm not."

He broke into a friendly smile.

"Look, you realise, that I'm a lot more careful than you are. I have plenty of respect for my valuable life. I don't even like flying in aircraft much. Let alone in an aircraft which is being pooped at. So you needn't worry about me going in for heroics. I'm much too sane. I'm only too damned sane."

Although he was trying to reassure me, he was not pretending. But I knew, and he knew that I knew, that none of that, however much it wasn't invented, would affect his actions. He would brood over a risk for days or weeks or months, just as he had presumably brooded over this choice of his, calculating all the odds: and then, if he thought it worthwhile, take it.

I had never been able to disentangle the nature of his courage. In some ways he had, before this, reminded me of Roy Calvert, Muriel's father. Their minds were similar, precise, concentrated, clear. Their willfulness was similar. But their courage was different in kind. Roy was a brave man, in a sense that Charles would for himself have totally disclaimed. Roy, though, had a suicidal streak. I had heard him, on a night which I should have liked to forget, tell me during the war how he had tried to throw his life away. He had done it out of despair, out of a melancholia he couldn't shift. He had made a choice: it wasn't one which Charles would have considered making. It wasn't a gamble, it was an abdication. Roy had impressed on me that when he made it, he wasn't mad. He wasn't mad, he said, he was lucid. "Perhaps if everyone were as lucid as that, they would throw in their hands too."

I hadn't to cast back for those words. Charles could never have said them. He would have distrusted Roy's protestations of not being mad. But it was with absolute confidence that he had made his own simple statement about being "too damned sane."

I believed him, totally. It was I, not he, who was tempted to read a pattern into events which he didn't even know. If he had known them, he would have repudiated with impatience what I was tempted to see. History wasn't like that, he would have said. Not personal history. He would have been right. The patterns weren't real. Perhaps the weaver of the pattern, however, told one something about himself.

Then Charles asked me for an introduction. It was to a Jewish friend of mine who worked at the Weizmann Institute.

"Of course," I said.

"That's nice of you," said Charles. He was beginning his Levantine journeys on the other side: easier, or at least not impossible, that way round, he said, but despite our connections he might have some explaining to do in Israel.

"You needn't write to————" the Jewish friend. "But I can use your name?"

"Naturally."

"Bless you." He looked at me with what appeared like a filial grin. I was gratified that, even at this stage, he was invoking me.

Suddenly I began to think. Of all my acquaintances who might be of use to him, this one was about the most obscure.

"Carlo," I said, "what are you up to?"

Bland gaze. "I don't understand."

"Why have you just thought of him? What about David Rubin? And——?"

David Rubin, grey eminence in the United States, was also one in Israel: for years he had been an intimate of mine.

The gaze flickered. "As a matter of fact, I wrote to David R. myself, a little while ago——"

"Come on," I said. "What are you up to? Anything this chap can do, Rubin can do a hundred times over. You know that as well as I do."

"Yes, but—"

"But what?"

Another surprise that morning. He blushed. It was a long time ago, when I had last seen him do so. Poise precarious, he broke into a weak smile.

I had it. He had been making an attempt to appease or to soothe me. He wanted to demonstrate that he had finished with his pride; he would use my influence when it was a help; any conflict had gone, he was glad to have me behind him. It was well meant, I thought, as, knowing it all, mocking each other and ourselves, we couldn't keep our eyes from meeting.

It was well meant, but not quite careful enough in execution. Actually he had been meticulously thorough, not neglecting any contact, and taken the best advice open to either of us. This had been happening for months past, possibly before he admitted to himself that the choice was clinched.

Then, and only then, I realised that his timetable was already fixed: and that he had broken the news only a few days before he was due to leave.

FORTY-THREE

"IT MIGHT MATTER
TO OTHERS"

As a result of Margaret's persuasion, I telephoned Muriel. Would she care to see me? One of us ought to make the offer, Margaret had said: and, since she herself had at the best of times been uneasy with the young woman, it had better be me. The voice at the other end of the line was polite but frigid. Yes, she was by herself. She wouldn't think of asking me to go out of my way—I must be extremely busy, but of course if I had nothing else to do—

When I went to her in her drawing-room, where she had once invited me in a different mood from this, she turned to me a desensitised cheek: as desensitised as Sheila's, I had a flash of random but chilling memory, as she said goodbye one night at a railway station and had become shut within herself.

There might be some play in the test match, Muriel observed from a distance. It was mid-day, the rain had stopped earlier in the morning, there was an interval of sunshine. The ground would be pretty wet, I replied, as awkward as a young man not knowing the next move. Perhaps the bowlers would get some help, she said.

I sat silent, rather than go on with spectatorial exchanges. Her hair glistened as though it had been attended to that morning, falling, though not luxuriantly, to her shoulders.

At last she said:

"So he's going, is he?"

"He must have told you?"

"Yes, he's told me."

"I'm sorry—"

"You needn't be sorry. If it hadn't been for you, this would never have happened."

Her tone, light, impersonal, was intended to give pain.

"Do you think I like it?"

"You made it happen. You made him want to outshine you."

Her tone was still impersonal, but unrelenting. I tried to answer without expression.

"That's not all of it."

I added:

"I tell you, it's not even most of it."

"If it hadn't been for you, he'd be happy here today."

She had been sitting with her usual stillness. She broke it just enough to spread out her hands.

I said:

"Are you so sure that you know everything that's moving him?"

"I know that if you'd been different and out of his way, he'd have been content."

She was looking at me, not so much with hatred as with cruelty. She had set out to stop any attempt to console her, or even to share her feelings: up against that, she was opposing a satisfaction of her own.

I was on the point of leaving her. I had had enough of ruthlessness: maybe this was how she had dismissed her husband and was now, in a different situation, dismissing me.

She said:

"Why didn't you stop him?"

"You ought to realise that no one can stop him."

"You could have done—"

"If what you say is right, perhaps me last of all."

"You would have stopped him," she cried, "if you'd liked me more."

That was said with as still a face as her harshest remarks: and yet, it was the nearest she could come to an appeal. So I replied, more gently than I had spoken up to now:

"That's nonsense, and you know it."

"If you'd thought I was right for him."

"That didn't even enter. If I'd thought you were the most perfect woman in the world, I couldn't have done any more." All of a sudden I felt that she might crack unless I came closer. I said:

"As for you, I'm not sure whether I like you or not. I never have been. But I admire you a good deal. Charles has been lucky."

She braced her shoulders, gave something like a smile of recognition. Possibly I had judged right. The silence had become less strained.

After a while she said, quietly, almost placidly:

"Do you remember, the first time we talked about him here. I said that what he chose to do—it might matter to others. Well, I wasn't far wrong, was I?"

She went on:

"And you said something like—if he's lucky, so it might. It's a peculiar way of being lucky, isn't it?"

I wondered if she had used that kind of irony on Charles.

She offered me a drink, but I said no, unless she would join me. She shook her head. She said:

"I suggest we go and sit in the garden. Just for a few minutes. You can have a look at Roy."

For an instant, the name recalled only her own father, about whom we had not once spoken. Then I grasped that she was speaking of the child. As she led me through the

downstairs sitting room, I saw the pram, open to the sunshine, standing by the garden wall. The little boy had a pile
of bricks in front of him. With great Viking shouts, he was
methodically hurling them, one at a time, over the side of
the pram. The curious thing was, he seemed to be register-
ing regular intervals between each throw, something like
thirty seconds, as though he were timing himself by a stop-
watch or engaging in some obscure branch of time and motion study.

I burst out laughing.

"Was is dat de joke?" young Roy enquired, solemn face
ready to grin.

"Difficult to explain."

"Was is dat de joke?" he asked his mother.

"Uncle Lewis thinks I shall have to pick up all the
bricks," she said, like one rational person to another.

Loud laughs. A vigorous hurl. "Dat is de joke."

He looked a bright intelligent child. His head was taking
on the shape of Muriel's, with her forehead and high crown.
The only features that seemed to come from his father were
the dark treacle-colour eyes which Irene had brought into
Martin's family and which were dominant over the blue.

I mentioned this to Muriel.

"Yes. It's rather a pity, don't you think?" she said coolly,
as though Roy ought to have been born by parthenogene-
sis.

"He's fairly good value, though, he really is," she said, still
trying to speak coolly, but without success, as sitting on a
garden seat she gazed devotedly towards the boy. Was she
one of those, I thought, who after the splendours and miseries of sexual love—about which she had her own kind of
knowledge, less ornamented and perhaps clearer than most
of ours—turned for a different, untroubled, idyllic affection
to their children? Just as old Mr. March had presumably

done, when he watched his son in infancy. Just as my brother Martin had done. Just as I had done myself. None of us learning anything from what we had watched, with sympathy and even with pity, in others. Not even learning that this idyll was at its best, and of its nature, one-sided: whereas sexual love gave one at least a chance of full return.

Sexual love could look the more dangerous: some of those who had explored both might bring back a different report. Was Muriel, with all her deliberate composure, going the same way? After what she had seen of her own mother's love for her and what she had been able to give back? After what she had not only seen, but sadistically said, of me and Charles?

"He hasn't taken anything else from his father, as far as I can see," said Muriel possessively, watching another chuck, accompanied by yells of laughter, as though he had found the best of all possible jokes. "That's just as well," she added.

She turned to me, less armoured than she had been in the drawing-room.

"Did you know?" she said, "that his father tried to do me a good turn not long ago?"

I shook my head.

"You'd heard that he was always latching on to Charles and me?"

"Yes."

"You expected that he was after the main chance, didn't you? Can you guess what he was really doing?"

I said, I hadn't the slightest idea.

"As a matter of fact, he was trying to badger Charles into marrying me. It would be a good idea, he kept telling him. You'd have everything between you. All the old patter. I expect you've heard your nephew at it."

"Well, he seems to have been capable of being good-natured for once."

"He always was, if it didn't get in his own way." Her face darkened. "I don't know. He may have worked it out that if he interfered between me and Charles, and bullied Charles about marrying me, that he'd produce the opposite result. I wouldn't put it past him."

"That sounds too subtle."

"He was so subtle sometimes he didn't know what he was aiming at himself. You can't believe what a bore that was to live with. When one didn't have an idea what he was using one for. And when he didn't have an idea either."

She went on:

"He was no good. I was well rid of him. It never ought to have begun. After him, Charles was someone to fasten on to. He can be secretive, you know that. But at any rate he is a man."

To my astonishment, she seemed to be visited by euphoria.

"Mind you," she said with something like sternness, "I don't want to leave you with a false impression. I haven't given him up, you know. There's plenty of time. Touch wood, he'll do what he's setting out to do. He couldn't go back on that, that's not the way he's made. But when he's done it, he won't go an inch further. He'll call it a day. He won't take more chances than he need, he'll settle down very early. It won't be long before he's much older than I am. Isn't that so?"

It was not for me to deny.

To begin with, she had behaved as though she wanted to dismiss me, clear me out of her life. I might be fancying it, but here if nowhere else she appeared like a repetition of Roy Calvert. He was much kinder than she was, but no more hypocritical: I had seen him get rid of emotional lumber, when it was a case of *sauve qui peut,* just as finally as she had dispensed with Pat.

But no, she might desire to, but she was not doing so with me. There was a practical reason why she shouldn't. She was holding on to Charles, with tenacity, with tenacity which exuded its own hope. She wanted me as one of her channels to him, or her card of re-entry, exactly as, during the separation between Margaret and myself before our marriage, I had preserved the acquaintance of Austin Davidson.

That was a practical reason for talking to me and in fact confiding, as she had just done. It was useful that she should have me within calling distance. Yet, though she might not admit it, there was another reason, perhaps a stronger one, why, holding on to Charles, she also needed to hold on to me. Anyone as unpadded as she was, and as contemptuous of nonsense about human relations, thought they were easy to cut off sharp—by a stroke of the will, clean, sharp, and clinical. One could imagine her, much older, thinking that all such relations had been a self-deceit: sexual relations, they turned mechanical and came to an end: friendships in the long run were a habit and no more: love for one's children, of that she had had warnings, and they had come true. With an obscure pleasure, she might, alone, old, reflecting by herself, reduce them all to nothing. The trouble was, that reduction was entirely abstract, no one lived like that. Human relations might be no more than she had come to think: but with them, however old she was, she would have to make do.

There were even some, very much more tenuous than the primary ones, which she would find surprisingly hard to cut. One could over-complicate them, I had often been guilty of that, but still there were some which, not at all imperative, nowhere near the centre of one's life, continued to dog one. To an extent, that was true of her relation with me. It bore a family relation to many others. It was, in a sense, the relation of rivals, that is of two who had a claim on the same thing. On a job, if you like: or, what was more common, on a person. Of all the relations that one saw or entered, these could be the most miragelike, shimmering, hardest to define even in one's own mind. Yet two men struggling for the same post could, for a fluctuating instant, feel closer than any friends. The same was occasionally true between rivals for a woman: and much more often, so far as I had seen, between an old intimacy and a new. Thus Muriel, wanting Charles alone, without any residual link to me, couldn't help attaching some resonance of that link on to herself. I had watched that happen several times: with Mr. March and his son's wife: with *Sammikins,* when his sister married Roger Quaife: even with Margaret and Martin.

Muriel, more emotionally streamlined than most of us, would have had no patience with any of these sideshows. Secondary feelings were nothing but tiresome, and should be thrown away. She was not, however, as independent as she believed, and whether she accepted it or not, she was behaving like a softer character, turning to me with something like trust, assuming, as we sat there beside the pram, that this was not the last time she would confide in me.

FORTY-FOUR

IT MIGHT HAVE
SEEMED AN END

"Be kind to him," Margaret told me, not long before
Charles was leaving. "He's been very kind to me."

She was smiling, but her eyes were bright. She repeated,
that I was to be as kind over the parting as he had been to
her. In fact, it was Charles who was in control, not I. He had
himself, not at all by accident, set the tone of that whole day.
He had arranged it so that, when he left, we were not all to
be together. It was an afternoon when Margaret was visiting
Diana's baby, and so Charles had said goodbye to her before
lunch, and then gone off to visit Muriel.

He did not return until after the time for Margaret's departure: it was about half-past two and I was sitting alone in
the drawing-room.

"Hallo," said Charles, face businesslike, telling nothing of
the parting just completed. "I'd better hump my stuff
along."

Footsteps, as quick as when he was on holiday from
school, up and down the passage. Thump of a rucksack on
the drawing-room carpet. His "stuff" was simple enough,
just that and a hand case for typewriter and papers.

"Got everything?" I said, unable to repress the fatuous
pre-journey questions.

Charles, sitting down on the sofa, grinned. "I shall soon

find out if I haven't." He was experienced in travel, and took it as it came.

He smiled at me. If there had been a clock in the room, I should have begun hearing it ticking time away: but Charles would not let us sit in silence or even endure a hush. One or two practical points, he said, sounding brisk, though they had all been settled days before. Communications: in case of emergencies at home, journalist acquaintances would trace him. Whatever newspapers couldn't do, they could find you. Otherwise he would write when he reached a town. Addresses —not to be relied on, but I had them, hadn't I? All this, which we each knew had been established, as though we were obsessively tearing open our own envelope to make sure it didn't contain the wrong letter, was repeated with the blitheness of a new discovery. The same with money. He wouldn't need more, he didn't wish to take another pound from me; but it was sensible to have an arrangement in reserve. This again Charles spun out, as though there were nothing safer than the sedative of facts.

At last his powers of repetition began to fail. Then he gazed round the drawing-room, which he had known all his life, like one playing a memorising game.

"You've never been on your own abroad, have you?" he asked.

"Not for a long time." Then I had to correct myself. "No, never, in the way you have."

"It's curious, the things you hanker after. Nothing dramatic. Nothing like a handsome dinner at the Connaught. No, a sandwich in front of the old television set is nearer the mark."

With deliberate casualness, he had let his eyes stray to his wristwatch.

"Good Lord," he said, "it's after three o'clock."

Not much longer to play out. Soon he was able to say:

"Well, I really think it's about time we moved."

In front of the house, waiting for a taxi, Charles beside me, I glanced down towards Marble Arch, the way from which he had walked in the rain, oblivious and triumphant, after his first night with Muriel. He looked in the same direction, but it meant nothing to him: he had not seen himself.

Traffic was sparse and travelling fast: no taxis were passing either way, in the mid-afternoon lull. I felt the same chagrin as when I waited there with Nina. I had offered to order a car to drive him to the airport, but he had said, smiling: "No, that's not quite my style." Nowadays, he went on, chaps like him contented themselves by going to the terminal and taking the tumbril (airline bus) "like everyone else."

He was more schooled in travel waiting than I was. Impatient, though there was plenty of time, I searched for taxi lights up and down the road. It was a Wimbledon week, cloud layer very low, weather grey, chilly and in some way protective, such as we had become used to in those Julys. Roses loomed from the bushes in the park opposite; there had been roses standing out in Muriel's garden a few days before, roses all over the London gardens.

At last a taxi, turning left from the Park Lane drive, on the other side of the road. Charles rushed across waving long arms. Blink of light. As we settled inside, he said:

"Here we go."

Passing through the Albion Gate, we could see, without noticing, the grass hillocks and hollows which we knew by heart; that was the way we walked in his holiday two years before, and earlier still, when he was a small child. None of it impinged, it was taken for granted now. Instead, he was recommending a film to which he insisted that I should go.

"Parting injunction," he said, explaining precisely why it

was necessary for me, why his friends admired it, and which aspects he required my views about. The long descent down Exhibition Road: still talk of films. Last lap, stop and go, brakes and lights, among the Cromwell Road snarl. For the first time Charles was quiet, sitting forward, as though willing the taxi on.

Then he thought of another request, for a book which he wanted sent after him.

In the terminal, he disappeared, rucksack lurching and bobbing, among the crowd, which was jostling with the random purposefulness of a Brownian movement, faces of as many different anthropological shapes and colours as on the Day of Judgment or on an American campus at mid-day. It was some time before he returned. All in order. He had made contact with someone else who was flying on the Beirut plane.

On the fringe of the crowd, noise level high, we looked at each other.

"Well," he said.

"Well," I said.

The word of all partings. Davidson's bedside. The old railway station in the town, on my way to London. Liverpool Street. Now the airports. Always, if you were the one staying behind, you were wishing, even though you were saying goodbye to someone you loved, that it was over.

"Don't stay," said Charles. "It's tiresome waiting."

"Well, perhaps—"

We embraced. As Charles went quickly into the crowd, he said:

"I'll be seeing you."

Not quite in his style, as he had said about a private car, but I didn't think of that, as I watched his head above the others, and then turned away, out into the cool air.

It might have seemed an end. But not to me, and not, perhaps to him. He might know already, what had taken me so much longer to learn, that we made ends and shapes and patterns in our minds but that we didn't live our lives like that. We couldn't do so, because the force inherent in our lives was stronger and more untidy than anything we could tell ourselves about it. Just as a young woman like Muriel believed she could discard affections which she thought she had outlived, so I, growing old, believed that my life had constricted, and that, with not much left of what I had once been hungry for, I should find them—those last demands— weakening their hold on me. We were wrong, and wrong in the same fashion. Muriel was bound to discover that her life was going to surprise her: and mine, even now (no, there was no "even now" about it, time and age didn't matter) hadn't finished with me.

Since the nights in the hospital room, when I saw one moment transformed into another, so that one's feelings were astonishing, and often self-ridiculing, as they created themselves afresh, I hadn't been certain when I could say—I shall not feel like that again.

Watching my son, I had revived much that I had thought long dead. And even when one came to the last hard core of feeling—interests worn out, both kinds of love (so far as one could believe it) now slackened—when one came to confront oneself alone, then still there was a flux of energy, of transformation, yes tantalisingly an inadmissible hope, getting in the way. I had thought, in some of the crises of my life, that if all went wrong, I should be finally, and once for all, alone. Now I knew that that was one of the shapes and sounds with which we deceived ourselves, giving our life a statuesqueness, perhaps a certain kind of dignity, that it couldn't in fact possess. In the hospital room I had been as nearly alone as I could get. I had imagined, and spoken of, what it would be like, but what I had imagined was nothing like the here and now, the continuous creation, the thrust of looking for the next moment which belonged to oneself and spread beyond the limits of oneself. When one is as alone as one can get, there's still no end.

The only end, maybe, was in the obituary notices: that might be an end for those who read it, but not for oneself, who didn't know.

Whether one liked it or not, one was propelled by a process of renewal, or hope, or will, that wasn't in the strictest sense one's own. That was as true, so far as I could judge first-hand, for the old as well as the young. It was as true of me as it was for Charles. Whether it was true of extreme old age I couldn't tell: but my guess was, that this particular repository of self, this "I" which felt and spoke for each of us, lived in a dimension of its own.

Whether this was a consolatory thought, I couldn't answer to myself. It was, I thought, more humbling than otherwise. It took the edge off some kinds of suffering. It took the edge also off some kinds of conceit. But yet one had to think it—and this perhaps was a consolation or even a fighting shout—because one was alive.

Through the cloud-shielded afternoon, I began to walk back the way which we had come. It was a familiar way home, the last mile in each air journey, as it had been for Margaret and me, returning from holiday, the week before her father's attempt to kill himself. Bridge over the Serpentine, trees dense beyond: I was walking, not thinking to myself, not acting like a camera, in something like the image-drifting stupor which came before one went to sleep. I wasn't thinking of other homecomings to that house: or to any others (some forgotten, one didn't remember in biographical terms) to which, once known as home, I had returned.

From the park I could see our windows, no lights inside,

no sun to burnish them. There was no one at home. I didn't feel any of the anxiety that had afflicted Margaret and me at other homecomings: and which I had been possessed by, without understanding, as a child running home along the road from the parish church. For that evening, all was peace.

It was certain that, in days soon to come, I should go home, those feelings flooding back, as alive as ever in the past, as I thought of cables or telephone calls. As alive as ever in the past. That was the price of the "I" which would not die.

But I had lived with that so long. I had lived with much else too, and now I could recognise it. This wasn't an end: though, if I had thought so, looking at the house, I should have needed to propitiate Fate, remembering so many others' luck, Francis Getliffe's and the rest, and the comparison with mine. I had lived with much else that I would have had, and begged to have, again. That night would be a happy one. This wasn't an end.

(Who would dare to look in the mirror of his future?)

There would be other nights when I should go to sleep, looking forward to tomorrow.

The End

ANNOUNCEMENTS——1964–68

(From the London *Times*, unless otherwise stated)

DEATHS

ELIOT On June 14, 1964, Herbert Edward Eliot, father of Lewis and Martin, aged 89.*

OSBALDISTON On March 16, 1965, Mary, beloved wife of Douglas Osbaldiston. No flowers, no letters.

Death of English resident. George Passant of England died yesterday, July 26 (1965), at the house of Fröken Jenssen, 15 Bromsagatan, aged 65.†

GEARY On August 7, 1965, Denis Alexander, beloved husband of Alison and dearly loved father of Jeremy and Nicolette, aged 51.*

DAVIDSON On January 20, 1966, Austin Sedgwick Davidson, Litt. D., F.B.A., dearly loved father of Helen and Margaret, aged 77. Cremation private.

EDGEWORTH On June 22, 1966, in University College Hospital, after much suffering gallantly borne, Algernon Frederick Gascoyne St. John Seymour (*Sammikins*), 14th Earl of Edgeworth,

---

* local paper
† translated from Viborg local paper: the only mention of George Passant's death.

DSO, MC, much loved brother of Caroline, aged 45. Funeral St. James's Church, Houghton, 2:00 P.M. June 26. Memorial Service, Guards Chapel, July 10, noon.

ROYCE   On February 7, 1967, at the Crescent Nursing Home, Hove, Lady Muriel Royce, widow of Dr. Vernon Royce, mother of Joan Marshall, aged 86.

SCHIFF   On September 15, 1967, victim of an accident, David, beloved and adored son of his heartbroken parents, Azik and Rosalind, Lord and Lady Schiff, aged 12 years 11 months. Funeral, Central Synagogue, 11:00 A.M. Sept. 18.

COOKE   On May 22, 1968, suddenly, Gilbert Alexander, C.M.G., husband of Elizabeth, aged 59.

GETLIFFE   On May 27, 1968, after a long illness, at his home in Cambridge, Francis Ernest, Lord Getliffe, F.R.S., adored husband of Katherine and dearly loved father of Leonard, Ruth, Peter Lionel, and Penelope, aged 64. Funeral private.

Died *   Lord (Francis) Getliffe, 64, British physicist, who was one of his country's leading figures in radar and operational research in World War II: of lung cancer. U.S. Medal of Merit. Adopted controversial stance over atomic warfare. Temporary difficulty (McCarthy era) over U.S. Passport, roused protests from leading U.S. scientists. Was due to receive honorary degree, Yale commencement, on day of death.

MARRIAGES

ELIOT–CALVERT   On 12 July, 1964, at St. Peter's, Eaton Square, Lewis Gregory (Pat) Eliot, son of Dr. and Mrs. M.F. Eliot, to Muriel, daughter of Mrs. Azik Schiff and the late Roy Clement Edward Calvert.

* *Time* Magazine

ROSE–SIMPSON On November 12, 1964, in London, Sir Hector Rose, GCB, KBE, to Jane Barbara Simpson.

OSBALDISTON–HARDISTY On December 6, 1965, Sir Douglas Osbaldiston, KCB, to Stella Hardisty, daughter of Mr. and Mrs. Ernest Hardisty, 126 Upper Richmond Road, Putney.

MRS. PENELOPE ALTSCHULER to wed DR. HIMMELFARB * Mrs. Penelope Altschuler, daughter of Lord and Lady Getliffe, of Cambridge (England) announces her engagement to Dr. David Ascoli Himmelfarb, son of Dr. Isaac Himmelfarb and the late Rachel Himmelfarb, of Cleveland, Ohio. Both Mrs. Altschaber and Dr. Himmelfarb have had previous marriages.

ELIOT–SHAW On January 4, 1967, quietly, Pat Eliot to Victoria Shaw.

HOLLIS–DOBSON * In London, at St. Mary-the-Virgin, Bayswater, Maurice Austin Hollis, to Diana, daughter of Mr. and Mrs. Thomas Dobson, of 16 Inkerman Road, Salford.

GETLIFFE–MACDONELL On 17 February, 1968, in Trinity College Chapel, Professor the Hon. Leonard Horace Getliffe, FRS, elder son of Professor Lord Getliffe, FRS, and Lady Getliffe, and Pauline, daughter of Professor and Mrs. Macdonald, of 66 Madingly Road, Cambridge.

MR. G.S.F. GRESHAM and MISS N.R. ELIOT † The engagement is announced between Guy Stephen Falconbridge Gresham, only son of Colonel and Mrs. Stephen Gresham, of Whissentdine Hall, Rutland and 29 Halkin Street, and Nina Rosemary Eliot, daughter of Dr. and Mrs. Martin Eliot, The Tutor's House, ───── College, Cambridge.

MANSEL–MARCH On July 7, 1968, at St. Cuthbert's, Philbeach Gardens, Laurence Massinger Mansel, son of Mr. Christopher Mansel, FRCS, and the late Mrs. Mansel, of 16 Poultons Square,

---

* *New York Times,* June 7, 1966
† local paper
‡ *Times* of June 29, 1968

Chelsea, and Vera March, elder daughter of Dr. and Mrs.
Charles March, of 27 Warwick Gardens, Kensington.

BIRTHS

ELIOT   On January 28, 1965, at 81 Eaton Square, to Muriel (née
Calvert) and Lewis Gregory (Pat) Eliot—a son (Roy Joseph).

GAY   On November 17, 1965, at Bury St. Edmunds General Hospital,
to Joyce (née Crawford) and George Harvey Laurence Gay—a
son * (Harold Harvey Laurence).

INCE   On June 20, 1966, at the London Clinic, to Marcena Prescott
(née Johnson) and Percival Lester Ince—twin daughters (Cyn-
thia and Valentine).

OSBALDISTON   On June 26, 1966, at St. Mary Abbots Hospital, to
Stella (née Hardisty) and Douglas Osbaldiston—a son (Edward
Bartholomew Maynard).

HOLLIS   On July 6, 1968, to Diana (née Dobson) and Maurice Austin Hollis—a daughter (Freda Elizabeth).

* the great-grandson of M.H.L. Gay